HARPER H

Copyright © 2024 by Harper Hawthorne.

Cover Art by KD Ritchie at Storywrappers Design.

Interior Design by Harper Hawthorne.

Line & Copy Edits by Cat Knowles.

All rights reserved.

No portion of this book may be reproduced in any form without written permission from the publisher or author, except as permitted by U.S. copyright law.

CONTENTS

Author's Note	IX
Map of Atlas	X
Dedication	XI
Epigraph	XIII
Prologue	1
1. Chapter One	13
2. Chapter Two	21
3. Chapter Three	27
4. Chapter Four	35
5. Chapter Five	40
6. Chapter Six	51
7. Chapter Seven	58
8. Chapter Eight	64
9. Chapter Nine	70
10. Chapter Ten	77

11. Chapter Eleven — 82
12. Chapter Twelve — 92
13. Chapter Thirteen — 95
14. Chapter Fourteen — 107
15. Chapter Fifteen — 118
16. Chapter Sixteen — 125
17. Chapter Seventeen — 138
18. Chapter Eighteen — 145
19. Chapter Nineteen — 152
20. Chapter Twenty — 163
21. Chapter Twenty-One — 172
22. Chapter Twenty-Two — 183
23. Chapter Twenty-Three — 190
24. Chapter Twenty-Four — 202
25. Chapter Twenty-Five — 212
26. Chapter Twenty-Six — 220
27. Chapter Twenty-Seven — 226
28. Chapter Twenty-Eight — 232
29. Chapter Twenty-Nine — 238
30. Chapter Thirty — 245

31.	Chapter Thirty-One	249
32.	Chapter Thirty-Two	255
33.	Chapter Thirty-Three	261
34.	Chapter Thirty-Four	266
35.	Chapter Thirty-Five	271
36.	Chapter Thirty-Six	282
37.	Chapter Thirty-Seven	294
38.	Chapter Thirty-Eight	300
39.	Chapter Thirty-Nine	307
40.	Chapter Forty	314
41.	Chapter Forty-One	321
42.	Chapter Forty-Two	325
43.	Chapter Forty-Three	328
44.	Chapter Forty-Four	337
45.	Chapter Forty-Five	344
46.	Chapter Forty-Six	349
47.	Chapter Forty-Seven	358
48.	Chapter Forty-Eight	365
49.	Chapter Forty-Nine	372
50.	Chapter Fifty	377

51.	Chapter Fifty-One	388
52.	Chapter Fifty-Two	393
53.	Chapter Fifty-Three	399
54.	Chapter Fifty-Four	408
55.	Chapter Fifty-Five	413
56.	Chapter Fifty-Six	423
57.	Chapter Fifty-Seven	431
58.	Chapter Fifty-Eight	439
59.	Chapter Fifty-Nine	451
60.	Chapter Sixty	458
61.	Chapter Sixty-One	463
62.	Chapter Sixty-Two	468
63.	Chapter Sixty-Three	475
64.	Chapter Sixty-Four	481
65.	Chapter Sixty-Five	488
66.	Chapter Sixty-Six	492
67.	Chapter Sixty-Seven	496
68.	Chapter Sixty-Eight	506
69.	Chapter Sixty-Nine	514
70.	Chapter Seventy	521

71. Chapter Seventy-One	527
72. Chapter Seventy-Two	533
73. Chapter Seventy-Three	541
Epilogue	551
To Be Continued...	559
Author's Note	561
Glossary of Terms	563
Acknowledgements	569
About the Author	575

Author's Note

This book is intended for adults only, and contains subject matter that may be difficult or disturbing for some readers. Sensitive material includes, but is not limited to: frequent profanity, violence, torture, murder, child abduction, the tattooing of a child without consent (on-page), emotional abuse, explorations of implied mental illness (depression, anxiety) & neurodivergency (adhd, autism), socio-economic power imbalances, frequent mentions of blood, references to cults and sex work.

Of Blood & Aether also contains explicit, open-door sexual content, as well as explorations of kink and BDSM themes that will escalate over the course of the series.

Reader discretion is advised.

To all of my fellow star-seekers, and the bearers of Light who take comfort in the Shadows.

Harbinger of Hel.

The time had come for this young prince, just barely nine, to be tested as all who had come before him.

It was sheer strength of will that kept the boy from trembling as he approached the massive entryway to the Tower, knocking thrice as he had been instructed. As the old rosewood groaned out the echo of his arrival, his hair stood on end. He toyed anxiously at the silver pendant around his neck, a failed attempt at self-soothing. Every survival instinct that the little prince had told him to run, to somehow escape, but he could not.

He *would* not.

He would honor his duty, and he would honor his Father.

"Greetings, your Grace. Your Majesties," a trio of voices called out in unison. "We welcome your arrival to the Tower of Scáth. You may enter."

Two members of the kingsguard flanked the young prince, pushing open the heavy tower doors so that he could enter. The chance to flee was long gone, and all he could do was step forward into the center of the circular chambers. Dimly lit sconces hung on the stone walls, and there was a dismal looking wrought-iron chandelier which hung several floors overhead.

Three women stood before a large blackstone altar, their bodies and faces unknowable—obscured, somehow. The prince blinked several times, but he still could not ascertain if any of the three were short or tall, young or old, beautiful or haggard, though their presence was distinctly feminine. Darkly feminine, and deeply terrifying.

Before the Crones stood a single basalt pedestal that housed two objects: A simple silver chalice, and an obsidian athame. The boy knew what was to come next.

"In order for the ritual to begin, you must freely offer your blood to the Crones," his mother had explained the night prior.

"One cut against each palm, like this," she'd said as she traced the sacral pattern on his hands with a gentle fingertip. "Can you remember that? Show me, my little raven."

He did remember, because he had practiced them for several hours before bed, repeating the motions alongside the words that he now spoke aloud, gripping the athame with sweating fingers.

"With the hand of my Father, I offer the Crones my blood," he said, refusing to cringe as the black blade bit into the soft flesh of his palm. He was no stranger to pain. "So that they may taste the truth of my bloodline."

As he opened his fist above the chalice, several rivulets of blood trickled inside, and he could only hope it was enough. Wielding the athame now with his non-dominant hand, he continued the ritual.

"With the hand of my Mother, I offer the Crones my aether," he said, carving the next rune. "So that they may taste the truth of my fate."

This time, a quicksilver substance swirled alongside the blood from his palm as it dribbled into the chalice, and it was an effort for the boy not to sigh with relief.

It had worked, he thought. *He had done it right.*

"We welcome your offerings, princeling," the Crones replied as one.

As the trio stepped forward towards the pedestal, the boy could begin to make out their shapes—but just barely. They were still somehow shrouded from clear view, though they were only a few feet away. A silent attendant approached to wrap his hands in gauze before motioning him to step into the center of the room, the space between the altar and pedestal.

It was said that the Tower stood at the intersection of every single leyline across the Shadow Plane, and that it was here where the veil between their realm and the Divine Source of All Life was thinnest. Only the Crones could survive an extended stay in this sacred space, both blessed and cursed to be bound to the leylines.

Guarding them for eternity.

The boy glanced back at his mother briefly, who offered him a reassuring smile and a nod as he stepped forward and took his place.

The Crones joined hands as they encircled the pedestal and chalice. He could see now that one pair of hands was soft and smooth as a young maiden, another more akin to the hands of a matron—delicately aged, not unlike his mother's hands. And then there was the last pair, wrinkled and pockmarked, blue veins bulging as the owner gripped the hands of her sisters. They all began to hum and chant.

"O Blessed Source, we welcome thee," the Crones began, tilting their heads back, casting their eyes towards the heavens. "Through we of three, speak your will. We offer open arms and open minds, to chart the course of Fate. If the prophecy is to continue this night, let us know through the aether, through the blood that has been freely offered."

Though they spoke in unison, it was also discordant, somehow—grating upon the ears of the young prince. His skin prickled with discomfort as they raised the silver chalice to the skies, and then one by one, each of the Crones drank.

When the final Crone had sipped the last of the sanguine liquid, she gasped—the cup slipping from her hands, dropping to the floor with a startling clatter.

"Could it be?"

"Such Resonance!"

The Crone with the eldest aura stepped forward then, towards the Shadow King, offering a slight bow of the head in reverence.

"His blood sings true, your Majesty. He is the Catalyst. It is time to read what remains of the prophecy."

The King scowled for a moment, appearing almost displeased before offering a curt nod and turning towards his guards and his wife.

"Leave us," he commanded.

Though the Queen of the Shadow Plane knew her place, she hesitated—casting a pained expression towards her son. She had not prepared him for this. Even if she had known... there was no way one could ever prepare a child for what was to come. Her eyes drifted to the ornate raven skull that hung around his neck and she released a shaky exhale, still lingering. She could only hope it would be enough.

"Helena!" the King barked.

With one final, apologetic glance at the pale, dark-haired boy who bore the eyes of his father, the Queen turned and left in silence, flanked by what remained of the kingsguard. Helena did not allow her tears to fall until she was well beyond her husband's line of sight.

The Shadow King took several slow, measured steps towards the Throne of Hel, the dark seat of power—his rightful place. It was not until the room was emptied, leaving only the Crones and his trembling heir, that Dagon designed to speak again.

"You are certain?"

"Yes, my king," they sang together, harmonizing with strange euphoria. "Yes, at long last, He has arrived! It is time!"

After an immeasurable length of silence, the Shadow King nodded once more.

"Proceed."

The young prince could barely process what happened next, as he'd had no idea what to expect. Every heir to the throne had failed this test before—stronger men, better men, more ruthless men, more *deserving* men. All who came before him had apparently lacked the inexplicable qualities the Crones had been seeking from their blood. But bony hands, meaty hands, warm-yet-trembling hands took hold of his limbs, picking him up off the ground and laying him face down on the obsidian altar.

He felt the aetheric power of the inlaid runes begin to activate, the thrumming of magick coursing through the air as his arms and legs were splayed apart and bound to each corner of the table with leather straps.

There is no room for fear in our bloodline, the prince repeated to himself, over and over. *There is no room for fear in our bloodline. There is no room for fear, Father is right there, I am not alone.*

He was the heir apparent to the throne of Hel, and he would not cower from his duty.

That wellspring of courage ran dry once one of the Crones stripped him of his tunic, exposing his bare flesh to the cold stone and he began to writhe in discomfort.

"Be still!" they commanded, and suddenly the boy could not move at all.

Tendrils of shadow began to reinforce the leather bindings, locking his limbs in place. The youngest of the Crones flitted across the room, returning with a pot of black ink and what appeared to be some sort of stylus or quill... with a razor-sharp tip.

In his panicked confusion, the young prince did not understand what was happening until the Crones began to carve into his back, starting at the very top of his shoulder blade. At first, it was not unlike the self-inflicted pain as he had cut into his palms for the offering. And then it began to *burn*.

As one of the Crones continued to cut into him, pausing only to dip her tool back into the acidic ink, the others began to cackle and hiss out their morbid approval, drowning out his cries. They read the words aloud, as if his body were an open tome.

"Betwixt the realms where balance has been upset, a debt must be paid. Those who have stolen life and spread filth will pay their due tenfold," one whispered.

"Vitality shall be restored to the Plane of Shadows. That which plagues us shall be banished within an age," the other replied.

The Shadow King tapped one foot with clear impatience. He knew this much already, they were simply reiterating the first foretelling. Thunder rumbled through the mountain as the storm drew near, yet another omen to be interpreted.

"Yes, yes!" the Crones hissed in unison as a bolt of lightning shot through the sky. "One shall wield All, the other shall wield None."

The eldest Crone spoke out alone now.

"He who has been chosen, this star-split soul, shall be the Catalyst to this prophecy of mirrored fates. He is our reckoning. The other, our deliverance. Together, they are our salvation."

"*The other*?" the Shadow King snarled, growing irritated.

He paid no mind to his son, whose sobs had grown audible, instead focused on his own mounting frustration. Though he knew that the Crones spoke in riddles, that understanding did little to keep his temper in check. Very little ever did.

"What do you mean, *the other*? We were promised *one* Harbinger. One weapon."

"No, my king, no," the youngest Crone crooned before succumbing to a fit of mad giggles, her wild eyes rolling back into her skull as she clutched at her temples with ink-stained fingers. A trickle of blood ran down her chin unceremoniously as she returned to the tattooing of the prophecy, their dark magicks interpreting the fate of the prince simultaneously as the story was cut into his flesh.

"There is another…"

"A Catalyst and a Conduit," the others chanted. "All and none, all and one. Mirrors, my King. *Mirrors*. Not one Harbinger, but two—one yet to be reborn! Two fates entangled, another entwined. The Source, it gives and takes and gives and takes and gives and takes. They are life and death. They are the cycle, preserved. They are vengeance and mercy, incarnate."

"Mercy?" the Shadow King repeated, eyes narrowing. "There shall be no mercy for that which has been wrought upon our kind. Keep going. What is to come next?"

"Father, *please!*" the boy cried out, his voice hoarse, choking on a sob as the pain grew unbearable. This was agony unlike any he had ever known.

The flames within the room flickered, several candles from the chandelier snuffed out by the growing winds that were seeping through cracks and crevices in the stonework.

"*Silence*, boy. I did not raise you to be weak. You will face your fate."

The Crones continued to carve into his flesh, meticulous and unforgiving, the ears of all three seemingly deaf to the pleas of their crown prince.

"Ah, yes, your Majesty. The threads of fate bleed ever so freely from the flesh. The path is clear. Our chosen Catalyst must find the Conduit before his ascension of the throne. Only then can destruction rain down upon the souls responsible for our suffering."

Three times, the boy lost consciousness to the pain as his blood mixed with ink and ichor.

Three times, the Crones revived him with smelling salts, requiring his cognizance in order to complete the prophecy.

"Wake up, my prince," they crooned. "Your blood won't sing unless you're awake, little one. We're not done yet. It hurts, we know. It always does, wresting the threads of fate away from the Source…"

None of their words made any sense to him, and yet he saw both malice and understanding glittering in the eyes of his father as he peppered the ancient women with questions. And every time the Shadow King asked for more, it was the prince's flesh that paid the price.

"How will we know when the next Harbinger is born? Where will we find him? How will we identify him?" the King demanded, his penultimate inquiries.

Dawn was soon approaching, which would turn the Crones to

stone until the next nightfall. Such was their curse. To remain so close to the Source came at great cost to what had once been three mortal women of Scáth.

"A seed shall soon be planted within the heart of our enemies, your Majesty. Bearing fruit that will leave poison on their tongues and burn the aether from their veins. In the realm where few can wield one, He must find the one who wields all."

The Crones began to grow weary, and their tender, whimpering canvas was on the cusp of losing consciousness yet again, but the Shadow King had one final question.

"And you are absolutely certain that it's him? *This* child? Of all the heirs who have come before him, this is who the Source has selected?"

It was the eldest of the Crones who replied, her tone curt and clipped. They were offended to have their divine gifts called into question, as it was known: the Crones of the Tower always spoke true. *Always.*

"Yes, your Majesty. We are certain. The blood can sing, but it cannot lie. The prophecy could not have been read from the aether of any other. The boy is our salvation."

Slowly and meticulously, the eldest Crone undid the ties that had kept the child bound—both physical and arcane. He remained there on the table, light-headed and listless even as the stylus was put away. An attendant appeared out of nowhere to drench his wounds in some sort of black, foul-smelling medicinal liquid. It burned even worse than the ink had, and yet now, he didn't even flinch.

For once, the Shadow King experienced a small swell of pride towards his son.

"All will kneel before the Harbinger of Hel one day," the middle, more matronly Crone supplied, gently cupping the boy's cheek as she offered him water.

"Even you, my King," the youngest of them added, a wicked

gleam in her pitch black eyes as she handed the Shadow King a scroll of parchment. A copy of the prophecy for his records.

"Even you."

CHAPTER ONE

ARKEN

Find yourself, Arken. You're ready. It's time.

That haunting whisper caressed my ear again as I began to stir—a familiar, yet foreign echo carried by the salt-laced gales as I woke up to perfect darkness. Perfect darkness, and a thick, whorling mist in the air that felt... odd, somehow. A bit eerie. It was a touch too heavy on the inhale, the hazy vapor shrouding me in shadows. My skin prickled with an uncomfortable degree of self-awareness, the strangest sense that I was being watched.

What was... Where was I...?

"Ah, good. You're awake. I thought I was gonna have to prod at ya with the broomstick again."

I blinked. Oh. Right. I had fallen asleep on deck earlier, having spent my day lounging around like a cat in the afternoon sun. I had been perfectly content to laze about for hours on end, soaking in that late summer warmth and watching wispy clouds drift across an endless cerulean expanse. Now, there was only the silver light of the moon overhead, her glimmering halo glowing softly against a smattering of starlight.

"In the middle of the night? That's just rude, Conrad," I groused, pushing myself up from the pile of potato sacks that had served as my makeshift bed.

"Storm's coming."

Well, that would explain the mist, at least. I tilted my head towards the deckhand as I proceeded to run my fingers through my hair, combing out the sleep snarls. Gods, I was in desperate need of a haircut. These soft brown waves were pretty enough, but they had grown much too unruly over the last few weeks. The length was nearly impossible to manage without access to a mirror. Slowly, I began to process the implications of the old man's clipped observation.

"A storm? Here? Aren't we just now passing Luxtos and Stygos?"

"Aye."

All of the research I'd done back home suggested that the Astral & Umbral Isles had some of the most mild waters in the entire realm of Aemos. If anything, we should have dealt with a few thunderstorms up north as we left Samhaven nearly six weeks ago, but we had gotten lucky. So far, we had experienced fairly smooth sailing. As smooth as one could hope for over such a long journey.

"I'll head back down below deck if it gets too bad, then," I promised, hoping to buy myself just a little more time in the open ocean air.

Technically, that's where I should have been regardless. Below deck, alongside the rest of the passengers who had purchased their tickets from Samhaven to Pyrhhas. But somehow, I had managed to endear myself to the ship's crew within about a week of our voyage, so as long as I kept out of their way, they let me sneak up here to my heart's content.

"You should head back down *now*," Conrad countered, his expression grim. "Before it even hits."

The grizzled deckhand offered no further explanation, which was nothing new. He was the taciturn type. Still, I followed his gaze to where it had affixed itself just above the horizon, and then I understood.

This was going to be one Hel of a storm.

Though the skies were crystal clear overhead, whorling clouds had begun to gather in the east, and the full moon was wrapped in her stunning silver halo—a telltale sign of an incoming front. Not that I needed either of those signs to know that the inbound tempest was dangerous. Each breath I took was heavy with mist, salt, and a touch of pure aether as it crackled through the air like static. I could practically *taste* the rising fury of the elements.

That probably should have frightened me. It did not.

"Come on, Conrad. You know that I can handle myself just fine up here."

All I received in response to that assertion was a scowl.

"*Please?* I've always wanted to see an aetherstorm like this up close," I whined, pouting in excess and batting my eyelashes for dramatic effect.

The old man let loose a heavy sigh, rubbing at his temples as he so often did when my stubborn side came out to vex him.

"You're a reckless one, little star-seeker. It's gonna get you killed if you're not careful. But fine. You can stay, *for now*, under two conditions."

I raised a challenging brow, but allowed him to continue without protest.

"One, let the record show that there's no rescuing you if you fall off the damned ship. We'll leave you behind and let you sink down into the Abyss in a heartbeat."

They would *not*, but I grinned and nodded in agreement regardless.

"Naturally."

Conrad held up a second finger, still scowling at me, clearly unphased by my enthusiasm.

"Two, the next time I tell ya to go down below—you listen. No arguments."

I made a face, displeased with any sort of clause against

arguments. I was good at arguing. I *liked* to argue. But I did have to acquiesce that Conrad knew these seas like the back of his hand, and this was my first seafaring voyage... ever. All of the tomes, journals, and lectures in the world couldn't make up for what I lacked in direct experience.

"Fine. But if you send me below over a light drizzle, you'll never hear the end of it, old man."

Conrad chuckled.

"You're only gonna be in my hair for a few more days, Arken. I think I'll survive."

That was true. After six long weeks of travel, we would soon arrive in Port Sofia, and I could finally seek entry to Sophrosyne: The City of the Gods.

◊ ◊ ◊

The storm hit within the hour.

Angry gales of wind whipped past me so violently now that my skin felt raw, and the wooden planks beneath my feet were becoming dangerously slick. I had given up trying to remain on the prow, as my well-worn and now-sodden leather boots were *not* helping in the matter of my staying upright.

All of that aside, the storm was gorgeous. I continued to marvel at the sheer force of the tempest, utterly fascinated while I clung to the mast of the ship with a desperate death grip. As the next roaring rumble of thunder rolled in, I was both enthralled and terrified.

I was a *smidge* reckless, yes, but I wasn't stupid. I knew this was risky, yet even in such adverse conditions, I much preferred to be above deck. I would take wind-chapped skin, rope burns, and a little bit of downpour over the stale musk and miserable wailing that awaited me below.

A vast majority of the other travelers on board were the sons and daughters of the elite and noble families of Atlas—though noblesse, I was not. Most of them were aged anywhere from thirteen to somewhere in their early twenties, like me. Many of us also had the same final destination, but that was where our similarities seemed to end. My so-called peers had grown up in such comfort and luxury that stale food, occasional turbulent waters, and a general lack of privacy made for the most dire of circumstances.

They were constantly worked up and whining, as though the last six weeks were the worst days of their lives. If they weren't bemoaning their fates and cursing their parents for sending them to the Arcane Studium in the first place, they were bickering amongst themselves and hurling insults at one another over a myriad of House dramas. As if any of them played a part in the successes or failures of Atlassian politics.

I really couldn't stand it half of the time, and so I had made a habit of spending as much time as possible on deck. I tried to make myself useful where I could… or at the very least, I seemed to keep the crew entertained.

"You can't avoid them forever, star-seeker," Conrad had reminded me the other day. While I got along just fine with the other sailors, he and I talked the most. We had bonded over my interest in his hand-drawn star maps, and how the sailors charted their courses based on known celestial bodies. Thus, the nickname.

"Can't say I like the brats much either, but you're all headed to the same place, are ya not?"

On one hand, he was correct: Almost everyone on board was on their way to Sophrosyne as a prospective student, hoping to be accepted into the Arcane Studium. On the other hand, Sophrosyne was the largest city in Atlas. Surely I could find more like-minded company, if I so chose?

But that's hardly what I was looking for.

There were quite a few things that I *was* looking for in Sophrosyne, but connections weren't really on the list. I had other priorities. Priorities that I had avoided thinking too hard on as of late, lest my nerves eat me alive.

I focused my attention back on the weather, though the winds were growing so strong now that the storm was almost equally as anxiety inducing as everything else. The onslaught of saltwater was starting to feel like pins and needles cutting into my skin. I could hardly see a thing, blinded by the downfall and angry ocean spray—when suddenly, a massive flash of Light aether came out of nowhere. It was followed almost immediately by thunder, not a low rumble this time but a sharp crack, as if the very skies were being split open.

Shit, I thought to myself. I could feel the residual aether in the air intensify, which meant that the lightning had struck far too close for comfort. I hadn't seen where it landed, but my suspicions were confirmed when I heard Conrad bellow out an order. The one that I had promised not to disregard.

"Arken! Go. *Now.*"

I waited for a break in the waves before I let go of the ropes, and took one last gasping breath of fresh air—choking on the rain as I dropped back down to the cabins below.

✧ ✧ ✧

It was quieter down here than I had anticipated, but not by much. Those who were not yet sleeping were shivering and bickering over blankets, and they paid me no mind as I sought out a familiar corner in the bunks. Sighing, I wrung as much moisture out of my hair and clothes as I possibly could by hand, before wrapping myself up in a threadbare blanket of my own.

The lightning continued to surge through the skies every few minutes, always followed by that vicious thunder, like the maws of the Abyss were opening up and groaning beneath us. The waves were getting choppy, and I had to push myself up against the wall as the ship began to heave and rock violently in various directions. The worse the storm got, the more of the young ones woke up and started to cry out in terror.

Too much.

It was all becoming too much. I had never done well in tight spaces, but the incessant whining, the erratic nature of the storm, the stale air, thick with the musky scent of far too many body odors combined... I grit my teeth, and every time the ship would jostle and jerk, my muscles would tense up in an effort to steady myself and avoid being flung across the cabin. I was too damp. It was too warm. My hair and clothes were sticking to my skin, rubbing and itching and *gods,* the children. They just kept *screaming.*

Every sensory detail was becoming more uncomfortable than the last, driving me to the brink of madness. There was a reason why I would have rather braved the storm.

I couldn't breathe. I should have stayed home. It wasn't worth it. All of the knowledge, all of the answers, all of the arcane expertise in the world wasn't worth the crushing pressure in my skull. Wasn't worth the weight on my chest threatening to—

Breathe, Arken, I reminded myself. *Breathe.*

As I closed my eyes and took a deep breath, I pushed the pungent taste aside. Instead, I focused on the subtle buzz of aether in the air, tugging it towards me—drawing it inward. I felt the warmth bloom in my chest as my Resonance stirred to life, heeding my call as I gathered the Light aether from all around me. Claiming it. On the exhale, I looked down at my fingertips, resting on both knees, and marveled at the way they glowed softly, illuminating this dark little corner of the cabin, just for me.

I had been doing this since I was a little girl and still, the comfort that my Resonance brought me was unparalleled. It was a gift—and a somewhat rare one, at that. Something I hoped to hone further at the Studium, gods willing.

That comfort was cut short by the grating sound of Percival Zephirin's voice across the cabin, decrying our doom with a degree of entitlement that only he could possibly muster at a time like this.

"If we die on this godsdamned ship, my father will have your heads!" the lordling shouted up towards the deck above.

What a poorly-crafted threat. If we were to die in this storm, so would the ship's captain and crew, leaving no heads to roll. Regardless, his outburst left some of the younger Resonants in shambles, and the cacophony of wailing intensified.

Gods, I hated that man—the sniveling heir to the House of Gales. Not that the others on board were much better. Why had I even subjected myself to this fresh Hel? I felt more isolated on this ship than I ever had in the Brindlewoods. Maybe Conrad was right, and this was all I had to look forward to...

But no. That couldn't be. Amaretta had come from the Studium, after all. There would be more to Sophrosyne than just brats and bickering. There had to be. And so with every deep inhale—and each slow, measured exhale—I remembered my purpose and why the destination was almost certainly worth one relatively brief, uncomfortable journey.

You're ready, Arken. It's time.

As my breathing fell into a slow, comfortable cadence, I closed my eyes again and allowed my anxious mind to untether from these dank quarters, instead falling into the comfort of my memories.

Memories of pine, of moss, and of sunshine.

CHAPTER TWO

KIERAN

I entered the holding cell at a leisurely pace, casually examining my fingernails.

A man was currently shackled to the wall in said cell, struggling against his chains and spouting off a colorful slew of profanities, but I paid him no mind. Instead, I turned my attention to the man in uniform who had been threatening the captive's life just before I walked in. Deep within the catacombs of Sophrosyne, the stone felt damp and dark—downright dreary compared to the brilliant light of the city.

"Report," I barked at Hans Deering, my second-in-command.

"The fucker refuses to give us any answers. Claims his information was good the first time around. Can't be bought, won't name a price for the truth."

My eyes flickered briefly towards the man in chains: Alistair Corvus—an old informant of mine.

"Now, now, Corvus," I purred, meeting the prisoner's beady, frantic eyes.

I slowly withdrew one of my daggers from the holster at my hip, and gently ran one fingertip across the edge of the blade.

"Everything has a price. It's just a matter of if you'll pay willingly, or if we take it by force."

"You won't do shit, *Aetherwhore*," the prisoner seethed. "I already know that your precious Elders won't allow you to kill me, and even if I did have the intel you wanted, I would take it to my grave."

"Despite popular belief, that can be arranged, Alistair," I shot back.

"Errr. Captain, he's Pyrhhan," one of my lieutenants hedged.

"And?"

"And so we need to defer to the House of Embers on sentencing. Per the Elders."

I knew that, of course. This entire conversation was for show, crafted with the intention of making Corvus sweat.

"If that's the case, why have we not handed this fine gentleman off to the Pyrhhan Guard?"

"We tried to arrange an exchange of the prisoner, and their response was that without documented evidence of his involvement in the kidnappings, he is to walk free. No transfer necessary. Lord de Laurent's direct orders."

I resisted the urge to roll my eyes. That part was news to me.

"Well then," I mused. "If the illustrious Lord of Embers wills it, I suppose our hands are tied. We'll have to let him walk free."

"Kier—I mean, *Captain*—you can't be serious," Hans sputtered. I shot him a warning glare as he temporarily broke character, forgetting his assigned role as the honor-bound guardsman that Alistair Corvus expected him to be. "We *know* he was involved, we just don't have the—"

"We have our orders, Deering," I replied sharply, unlocking the prisoner's shackles. The warning in my tone was only partially for show. Sometimes this asshole forgot that I knew my way around a godsdamned interrogation scene, even if it was rare for them to call me in for one these days. I had trained my men well.

Corvus' entire body sagged in relief as I released him, and he rubbed at his chafed wrists as I gave him about three seconds of respite. Within a single breath, I let my Shadows gather, and with a flick of my wrist, bound the man against the stone wall again. He cried out in panic.

"Hey! The fuck is this? They said—"

Tendrils of stygian smoke began to tighten around his wrists and ankles, keeping him in place far better than the steel ever could.

"Oh, don't you worry your pretty little head, Alistair," I replied, a wicked smile spreading across my face as I took pleasure in his discomfort. "We'll release you. Eventually."

My commander would nail my balls to the wall for this little song and dance once he caught wind of it all, but so be it. I trusted my men, and if they said that Alistair Corvus was tied to the disappearance of a young boy, snatched from the safety of our city? The bastard was guilty. The Lord of Embers could get fucked.

Documented evidence... Seriously? Did he expect the culprit to scribble out his dastardly plans in a secret diary or something? There had been no witnesses, save one. This prick.

"Lieutenant Fairchilde," I called out to my third, who was standing guard outside. "Send a note off to Fen, let her know we're in need of a cleric. Preferably one of her more... discerning acolytes."

Right on cue, Jeremiah let out an irritated groan. He was a far better actor than Hans.

"I tire of these games, Captain. Can we not just send for the Overseer and be done with it?"

At the mention of the notorious Elder, our captive began to writhe in panic, just as I'd hoped. I glanced back at him and chuckled softly. He was right to be afraid.

The Overseer was said to be one of the oldest of the remaining gods—and that he could wrest any thought he wished straight out of your head and replace it with one of his own. If we were to request his presence, this investigation would be over within the next thirty seconds... but where was the fun in that?

I cocked my head to the side, watching Alistair struggle.

"You seem more afraid of the Overseer than you are of us. A smidge short-sighted, don't you think?" I asked, spinning the dagger between my fingertips for creative emphasis.

"He's an *Aetherborne*, Vistarii. Of course I'm more afraid of that bastard. He is a *god*. You're just a... a bootlicker. A sadist and a filthy godsdamned Conduit."

"I am technically only *one* of those things," I argued with a casual shrug. "And what you fail to understand here, Corvus, is that the Overseer would be a mercy."

I waltzed up to the man with measured steps, close enough now that he could strangle me, if only the poor bastard wasn't bound in place by my arcana.

"Sure, your own mind may incriminate you enough that you rot in the prisons of Pyrhhas for the rest of your days... but it really is a humane method of information retrieval, all things considered. He would just pluck the details we need right out of your ugly head, and leave your mind, body and spirit intact. I won't be quite so kind."

Malice glittered in Alistair's eyes as a bead of sweat slipped down his grimy temples. There were dark circles forming under his eyes. My men had most assuredly done a number on this man long before I'd arrived, and yet he still hadn't cracked.

"And unfortunately for you, the Overseer is, funnily enough, *overseas* at present. So let's try again, shall we?"

As I tightened my left hand, the aetheric bindings on his wrists began to dig into the man's flesh—I could feel it in the resistance of the arcane energy. With my right hand, I slid the dagger so softly against his grizzled throat that it could've been a caress, had it not drawn the slightest trickle of blood.

"Who actually took the child?"

The coward before me said nothing.

"Come on now, Alistair," I crooned. "Give me what I want, and we can make this quick."

"What do you care, Vistarii? What do any of you even care?! The brat isn't even Pyrhhan, and he's sure as shit not from Sophrosyne. Just some over-privileged snotrag from Vindyrst," Alistair snapped.

Be that as it may, the Elder Guard had a commitment to the safety and well-being of anyone behind our walls. It didn't matter where they came from—Sophrosyne was a melting pot, filled to the brim with students and visitors from across the realm. I raised a brow as the asshole continued to try to appeal to my sense of reason.

"I mean, do you even *realize* what atrocities that little shit's father has committed against his people in the mountains? Of course not. All the while, the courts and Houses are doing fuck all about it with their thumbs up their arses, playin' politics!"

It was then that I realized that even though my men had confirmed Alistair Corvus' status as a Pyrhhan citizen, there was the slightest hint of Vindyrst in his accent.

So this was personal. That was going to be a problem. It was difficult to alter the minds of men who thought their actions were justified, no matter how heinous their ideas of retribution were. Difficult, but not impossible. Glancing down at the blade in my hand, I liked my chances.

"So you thought that the child needed to pay for the sins of his father?" I challenged through grit teeth. I knew where this conversation was going, and had already lost my patience for it.

"The way I see it, we're just culling the problem before it becomes another one."

Yeah. There it was.

"Wrong answer, my friend. Wrong fucking answer. Because the way I see it, the 'problem' in question? The one you're trying to 'cull'? That's just a child. He's only eleven. An eleven year old *kid.*" I spat. "And for that?"

I shoved the dagger into his thigh and pressed one hand over his mouth to mute the agonized screams. One of Fen's clerics would be on their way soon enough.

"For that, Corvus... I *will* break you."

CHAPTER THREE

ARKEN

The walls that encircled Sophrosyne were made of gleaming, polished limestone that sparkled in the sun. Somehow, they displayed no signs of aging or erosion, even though I knew they had stood there for centuries.

As our guides herded us through the Western Gates, my mouth parted in gentle surprise when a ripple of tangible power brushed against my skin like a low hum. *Wards.*

I don't know why I was surprised by the sensation. Of course the City of the Gods would be warded. Even the smaller port cities of Samhaven carried that same buzzing, protective arcana.

And Sophrosyne was far more than just a city.

It was technically an independent city-state, an enclave within the territories of Pyrhhas that had retained its sovereignty when the Atlassian Houses were formed, several hundred years ago.

More importantly, it was home to the most prestigious college of arts and sciences that one could attend: The Arcane Studium. It was here that a Resonant could become a Conduit, learning to channel their elemental abilities into the complex arcana of the gods themselves—or at least something akin to it. We mortals would never be able to access the near-limitless powers of creation that our ancient, immortal ancestors once had.

The woman who led us through the gates and directed us towards the annex of a larger building was so tall and lithe that, at first glance, I had almost assumed she was one of the nineteen immortal patrons of this city.

I wouldn't have been particularly surprised if I saw a pair of pointed ears and glowing eyes staring back at us as she turned, but alas. There were no pointed, feral fangs in her smile either. While our guide was stunning, she did not carry the telltale signs of our Elder species. Our physical differences were supposedly just happenstance, a random byproduct of evolution—but I envied the beauty of the gods, even if I'd only ever seen it depicted in paintings.

No matter, I reminded myself. I would face them soon enough.

Our guide reiterated this after gathering us all in the foyer. Her feminine voice sparkled as it echoed off the white marble columns of the entryway and the matching tiles, just as polished as the city walls.

"Those of you who have been selected for today's round of trials, please be seated in the aisles to your right. Those of you who have been assigned to tomorrow's round, please form an orderly line here," she said, gesturing to the podium to her left. "I will distribute vouchers for your room and board tonight. Please bear in mind that you are expected to stay within this particular section of the Western district of the city until you have completed your trial."

"What happens if we don't stay in this particular section?" A thin, reedy voice rang out to challenge her. I didn't even have to turn around to know the speaker would be deathly pale, with thin blonde hair and limpid blue eyes that lived beneath a permanently furrowed brow.

Of course it would be Percival who had to ask, who somehow couldn't read between the lines and deduce what seemed rather obvious to me. Had he not felt the wards?

"You are welcome to try to enter the city on your own and see what happens, young Master Zephirin," the tall, elegant woman said with a wry smile. "But I highly recommend against it. We would rather not send you back to the House of Gales in pieces."

"*Tsk,*" was apparently all the young Master Zephirin had to say about that—and I resisted the urge to roll my eyes.

Eventually, all of the prospective students who were not taking their trials today made their way outside of the annex, presumably to anxiously meander about this small section of the city. I offered a silent prayer of thanks to the Source that I was selected to take mine today, as my nerves were already beginning to fray.

Those same questions I had harassed Amaretta with before I ever set sail for Sophrosyne continued to swirl around my mind.

What if the Elders could sense that I was hiding something? What if they didn't, but found me unworthy of being a Conduit anyway? What if I failed their tests, whatever they may be? What if I was sent back home? What would I even do with the rest of my life if that happened? What if I never figured out what I was, why I was like this?

What if, what if, what if?

I chewed furiously at my lower lip, one leg bobbing restlessly against the tiles as I waited, and waited, and waited in this shining, open room that had become far too quiet for my liking. You could hear a pin drop in here. Occasionally, the slender woman behind the podium would call out a name, and if I had to guess, we were being called up in order of our elemental Resonances, because it certainly wasn't alphabetical.

"Arken Asher," our guide's voice finally called out. "Please proceed past these doors, where one of our scholars will run you through the details of your trial. Best of luck, young Resonant."

✧ ✧ ✧

With a single deep breath, I pushed through those heavy annex doors and on the exhale, found myself within a small, but elegant antechamber. Sitting at a desk in front of yet another set of doors, these ones larger and somehow even more ornate, was a stout and elderly looking gentleman who almost immediately reminded me of Amaretta. They looked to be about the same age, and there was that oddly familiar twinkle in his eye…

"Welcome, Miss Asher," he said as he rose briefly to offer a small, polite bow. "I am High Scholar Wallace, and I will be handling the introduction to your trial, and the subsequent onboarding paperwork, should you succeed. Please, take a seat."

The man gestured at an expensive looking, velvet-lined wingback chair across from his desk. As I sank into the plush cushion, he continued on.

"Before I explain what comes next, I just need to run through a few basic questions, is that alright?"

My voice cracked a bit as I spoke, but I managed to reply. "Yes, of course."

"Your full name?"

"Arken Asher."

"No middle name?"

"No, sir."

Not as far as I was aware, anyway. One of the many mysteries of being abandoned at birth.

"Your age?"

"Twenty-two."

"Your Resonant element of aether?"

"Light."

And Shadow. And Fire. And Water. And Earth. And Air. But he didn't need to know that. Amaretta made me swear on my life to keep them hidden here.

"This is quite exciting," he exclaimed. "It's been some time since we've seen a new Light Resonant come through these doors. Over twenty years now!"

I blinked.

Gods. I knew that both Light and Shadow had become increasingly rare Resonances these days, but twenty years? Perhaps I would be receiving more than just a small amount of extra attention during my time here. I hadn't planned for this. I would have to find a way to skirt some expectations.

I offered the scholar a nod and a weak smile, all the while trying to prevent my leg from frantically bobbing again and exposing just how nervous I really was.

"And does Resonance run in your family line?"

"Ah, I wouldn't know. I was adopted."

The old man gave me an understanding, apologetic smile before continuing on.

"Are you aware that, should you pass your trial, you will be expected to receive an arcane brand on the inside of your dominant wrist—a sigil that will both allow you entry to Sophrosyne and prove your status as a Conduit and student of the Arcane Studium?"

"Yes."

"And you are aware that said sigil will prevent you from discussing any matters that are considered selective or exclusive knowledge of Sophrosyne and the Studium?"

"Yes."

The Trial itself was known to be one such insight that was exclusive knowledge of the gods and Conduits alone. As such, none of us Resonants truly knew what to expect here. We were all going in blind.

"And do you consent to this?"

"Yes."

"Last but not least, please specify your territory of origin."

"Samhaven. The Brindlewoods," I answered.

"Ah, you certainly are a long way from home now, aren't you? Tell me, does Amaretta Sinclair still live around those parts?"

I blinked in surprise. "You know Amaretta?"

"Indeed! I take it you're familiar as well…?"

"Yes, actually. She's my… Well, she raised me. Amaretta is my mentor. Practically the reason I'm here today," I explained.

"Oh, how absolutely marvelous!"

The old man clapped his wrinkled hands together with an emphatic nod.

"What a small world we live in, Miss Asher. The next time you see her, you must tell her that Ambrose Wallace sends his warmest regards. We studied together when we were your age, you know. I took over her position when she retired."

So he was a cleric, then. Yeah, that checked out. It would explain why he reminded me so much of my mentor, at least.

High Scholar Wallace nodded again with even more enthusiasm before peering at me from behind his spectacles, which had fallen quite low on his nose now due to said nodding.

"Well then. A Light Resonant from the Brindlewoods, raised by none other than the illustrious Scholar Sinclair. I expect great things to come from you, young one. Great things! But oh dear, I do digress. Let me explain how we will proceed with your trial," he said, offering a slight, apologetic wince for having so clearly strayed off-script.

Honestly, I had been grateful for the distraction, but it was time to focus. I had to do this. I had to get into the Arcane Studium. I was thousands of miles from home, having traveled for over six weeks on that gods-forsaken ship, just for the chance…

"In a few minutes, you will enter the Hall of the Seeing by passing through these doors behind me, and you will speak with the Nineteen. I trust that Scholar Sinclair provided you with some insight on the Aetherborne?"

I nodded. Indeed, I knew a great deal about the last nineteen gods residing in our realm, though Amaretta had informed me that I would learn much, much more once I began my studies. There were things even she could not disclose. Perhaps due to the arcane brand.

What I *did* know was that those same nineteen Aetherborne—the gods, as some mortals called them, or Elders, as they called themselves—were both the rulers and the benefactors of this city-state.

While they were neither omnipotent nor omnipresent in the way that some of the more religious zealots of this realm believed the Aetherborne to be, there was a reason we called them gods.

Beyond being the elder species and the first known intelligent life form on Aemos, they were exceptionally powerful beings who had held great influence over the people of Atlas, over humankind as a whole, and for all of history as we knew it.

And they held my fate in their hands today.

"Before you enter, you will select one of these three vials before you and drink the elixir within. While I cannot specify what any of the elixirs do, I can say that there is no wrong selection. They are all perfectly safe for human consumption, and you will be carefully monitored throughout your trial to ensure that remains the case. Your safety and well-being are of the utmost importance to us," Scholar Wallace explained calmly.

"Alright," I said slowly, with vague apprehension. I hadn't really expected to imbibe any strange liquids today.

"What happens after that is entirely up to the Elders, so I am afraid I cannot offer much guidance there. The trial is tailored specifically to the individual, you see."

Ah. So they make it personal when they take your measure. No pressure, then.

I grimaced.

"I am sure you'll be just fine," he said, a sweet attempt at reassurance. "And do keep in mind that even if this trial does not go as you may hope or plan, most are welcome to re-apply for entry to the Studium after a ten-year period."

I was far from reassured. If I had to wait another ten years for access to the endless font of knowledge that was the Arcane Studium, I would lose my mind. Sure, I could attempt to find my answers elsewhere, but when? Where? *How?*

I had scoured the city of Elsweire for clues whenever Amaretta and I would take trips and found nothing of import. The libraries of Novos were rumored to rival even Sophrosyne, but that was practically worlds away from me now—a literal separate continent. I simply did not have the means to travel that far, at least not any time soon.

I had to pass this trial. I had to start searching now.

I eyed the glass bottles that were laid out before me with suspicion.

Maybe it's poison.

I shook the intrusive thought from my head, and selected the vial on the left, turning it over in my palm and awaiting further instructions.

"Any moment now, this orb here will glow, signaling the time for you to enter—ah! And there it is."

The crystal ball nestled beside a globe and stack of parchment on his desk, which I had presumed to be purely decorative, began to glow with soft, warm light.

"Please go ahead and drink that now, and then you may enter the Hall. Your trial awaits, Arken Asher."

I carefully uncorked the crystal vial and knocked back its contents as if the liquid was a shot of the whiskey I'd shared on occasion with friends back home. It had a similar burn on the way down my throat, but tasted more... botanical. Herbal, maybe.

Here goes nothing.

CHAPTER FOUR

KIERAN

We released Alistair Corvus on the border of Sophrosyne and Pyrhhas before the break of dawn, mist still blanketing the forest floors of the Wyldwoods as the man stumbled home in shambles. Though our clerics had healed every last physical wound he had sustained during questioning, there was a certain delirium present in his frantic, beady gaze as he looked back, and I knew that I had kept my promise. I broke him.

If only I could bring myself to give a shit.

No man on this plane of existence or the next was ever truly innocent, no hands among us ever truly clean... but this one's had been particularly filthy. Stained in blood and greed, among other things. Over the course of several hours, quite a few admissions of guilt had slipped past the merchant's lips, confessing his involvement in the Pyrhhan black markets, the distribution of dangerous and illegal substances, and, most disturbingly—his participation in the flesh trade in recent years.

He'd been a buyer, not a seller, and he swore up and down that his *purchases* had always been of age. That they had been *"willing."* I had my doubts on the latter point, but it was hard to lie about such things with a dagger in your thigh. For that reason he still drew breath, though I knew his freedom would be short-lived.

We had recorded every last confession, signed and sealed with the intent to deliver the information to the Pyrhhan Guard by sunrise. Corvus would spend the rest of his pathetic existence behind bars, that much I knew.

Justice served between the territories in Atlas was a tricky thing, particularly when we got involved. Every territory from Samhaven to Pyrhhas operated independently, answering only to their respective Houses. That said, the Atlassian Houses were put in power by those that ruled over Sophrosyne today: The Elders. The gods.

The Elders who would admittedly *not* approve of what I'd done to that man over the last few hours, but I was well-acquainted with operating outside of standard protocol for the Elder Guard. I was also perfectly content to sacrifice what little remained of my own morality, so long as it kept my city safe.

Tonight though...

I had failed. There had been some sort of block placed on Alistair's mind that had legitimately prevented him from confessing anything related to the Jerricks boy—an unfamiliar sort of arcane bind that even I couldn't unravel, nor could my blades. Every time we had even come close, the merchant's eyes nearly burst from their sockets as he screamed bloody murder, and then would promptly lose consciousness. Eventually, we had to relent.

Though I had direct confirmation that he was the last person seen with the missing child, holding Corvus any longer than twenty-four hours would be considered a breach of several treaties, and the last thing I needed was to have Pyrhhan scouts sniffing around our business. They were our allies, and any breach of trust that severe would cost me my position.

Letting him go was still infuriating.

After directing a few of my reports to look into some of the names Corvus had given up in association with his *other* crimes, I returned to my horse and rode back into the city with haste. As the wind whipped around me, a rare voice of self-defense and reason spoke in my mind.

You and your men did all you could with the information you had. It had been a long shot, anyway. The boy's been gone for weeks.

A more familiar voice bit back.

Doesn't fucking matter if your best isn't good enough. His blood is on our hands.

Whose blood, though? The blood of Alistair Corvus? Or the Jerricks boy? That was yet to be determined, I supposed. We hadn't found a body. The kid could still be out there. As for Alistair's survival... That wasn't really my problem anymore.

I focused in on the cadence of my steed's gallop, numbing my anger and frustration, and by the time I'd arrived at the stables, my failure was properly compartmentalized. I had a solid list of next steps prepared in my head. All of which would have to wait, because if I wanted it done right, I needed to get some semblance of rest first.

The problem was that after the last twenty-four hours, I would be hard pressed for sleep. Not without a distraction, at least. And so I went hunting for one.

◇ ◇ ◇

I was not a man of many vices.

I had a rather... *stringent* upbringing. One that bred a great deal of self-discipline and regiment, but ascetic I was not. I rarely drank to the point of inebriation, had never willingly touched an ounce of any drug in my life, and I was not a betting man... but I was still a man, one with as many carnal cravings as the next. Perhaps more.

Probably more.

I was not a man of many vices, but to say that I often overindulged in the *one* vice that I allowed myself might have been an understatement.

This tavern was not one of my regular haunts, but I knew it had a certain reputation, and pickings would be slim at nearly six in the morning. After ordering a single round of ale and getting comfortable at a corner table, I began to scan the room for possibilities.

A woman who looked to be in her thirties glanced over at me from across the bar, and I allowed my gaze to flicker over her briefly. She was attractive, if not a bit thin, but there was a tell-tale droop in her expression. A dull sort of glassiness to her gray-blue eyes that told me all I needed to know. She was drunk off her ass.

No, thanks.

Given my own proclivities, I could hardly judge those who found solace at the bottom of a bottle, but I preferred my quarries conscious and consenting. I continued my casual scan through the tavern, which was surprisingly busy for six in the godsdamned morning. I supposed the place had earned its reputation after all.

That was both convenient *and* inconvenient for me, because sure—there were plenty of bodies in the building, but most had seemingly entered the night before. And many were chasing away their hangovers with another round or three. I could only sympathize with the poor barkeep who was surrounded by shuffling feet and slurred speech.

This was, admittedly, not my sort of place.

My line of work was not particularly suited for… *relationships*. Or any sort of long-term commitments, for that matter. But I liked to fuck—hard and often. And while my tastes in participating parties weren't exactly particular, I held myself to certain standards with who I chose to take home, whether that be for an hour or an evening. Never much more than that.

This much alcohol didn't play nice with enthusiastic consent, or decent sex for that matter. And bad sex… Well, that wasn't much of a distraction, now was it?

"Looking for someone?" A low voice called from my left, just as I was about ready to take my leave.

A handsome man with dirty blonde hair and hazel eyes that glinted green in the low light was leaning casually against the table beside me. His head was cocked with a curious grin, and he made no efforts to conceal the slow once-over he was giving me. I took advantage of the opportunity to do the very same, and I liked what I saw.

Not anymore, I'm not.

"Oh?" A lighter, more feminine voice called from behind him, a manicured hand snaking around his waist. "Who's this?"

"A good time," I replied, taking a sip of my drink as I gave them both a slow, methodical glance, studying their body language. Reading their signals. They were far from subtle.

The femme who had just joined us also made no efforts to conceal her interest, either—biting down on her painted lip as her eyes roved hungrily from my face, to my neck, to my groin. She twirled a single, strawberry blonde curl with one finger, and though her eyes were also hooded, it was with lust over liquor—and I chuckled softly. She was pretty, though I was more interested in her partner at the moment.

I knew what they saw when they stared me down—a handsome face, a hint of danger in my scars and tattoos, a well-toned physique. A toy to be used, perhaps, but I was down to play. That's what I was here for, after all.

"You know, I was sort of hoping you'd say that," the man said, his grin spreading slowly. His partner's eyes lit up like a sparkling solstice pyre, practically vibrating with anticipation.

Talk about an easy target. What was that saying again? A bird in the hand is worth two in the sack?

"Your place, or mine?"

CHAPTER FIVE

Arken

The warmth of whatever liquid I had just swallowed was coating my throat like a syrup, but aside from that physical sensation, I didn't feel any different as I entered the next room... until I saw them.

By the Fates.

Seventeen... Eighteen... Nineteen. I sucked in a breath. All nineteen of the Aetherborne were here today.

Apparently, that was not always the case. The Elders did not often leave Sophrosyne, but they would travel overseas on occasion. You only really needed one Aetherborne to approve your entry to the Arcane Studium. Because of this, I had almost been bracing myself for disappointment, half-expecting to meet a few of the Elders at most. But nineteen pairs of glowing eyes were staring me down as I walked into the Hall of the Seeing.

"Welcome, Arken Asher," a sweet, melodic voice called out from the center of the dais where all nineteen Elders sat before me.

There was an unfamiliar lilt present in her voice, an accent that I couldn't quite place. A female Aetherborne, one I presumed to be the Speaker, beckoned me forward with long, pale fingers adorned with ornate silver rings.

I proceeded forward with delicate steps against shimmering

white tile until I reached the very center of the room, where the symbol of the city-state was inlaid in gold. Six circles overlapped one another, and each represented an element of aether, with a seventh circle in the center connecting them all in representation of the Source itself. Together, they formed what almost appeared to be a flower with six petals in the center, not unlike the white lilies that grew naturally all over the continent. It was also known as the Seed of Creation, and it was the official emblem of Sophrosyne and the Arcane Studium—both of which were synonymous with the Aetherborne themselves.

I personally recognized it as the silver tattoo on the inside of Amaretta's left wrist, which had faded with age but still glowed gently from time to time. If all went well, I would soon bear that same mark that would identify me as a Conduit.

Upon arrival to the center of the room, I lifted my gaze upon the dais before me where the Aetherborne sat in silence.

All nineteen of the gods had titles specific to their roles within the Convocation and their arcane specialties, if I could recall correctly, though the details of what they all could do had been obscured over time. I had a feeling they preferred things that way.

The Speaker, the Oracle, the Priestess, Justice, Temperance—I had seen them all depicted in paintings and etchings in books, and yet nothing could have captured their breathtaking, ethereal forms as they appeared before me now.

"I am the Speaker," the woman in the very center confirmed, her voice a pleasant song. It was so lovely, easy to listen to, and almost as entrancing as her beauty.

The Speaker was tall and slender, as they all were, with pale porcelain skin and long, pointed ears that peeked out behind thick waves of silver-white hair. She wore a complimenting sleeveless white gown made out of layered panels of sheer, semi-iridescent Irrosi silk, cinched at the waist with a silver cord and a broach that mirrored the symbol beneath my feet. Her eyes were such a pale blue that they appeared almost as silver as her hair with the wisps of aether flowing behind each iris, creating that otherworldly glow.

Gods, she was like pure aether. As the stunning immortal spoke, I could see her elongated canines flash and glint in the light, and felt myself shiver.

When I was younger, I thought that the stories of the gods having fangs was an embellished detail designed to scare children and remind us of their power. It was true, though. Those teeth were sharp as Hel and must have served some predatory purpose in an age long past. I should have probably found them fearsome for that reason, but they were actually rather pretty, in a dangerous sort of way.

I had always been attracted to danger.

They were all so entirely stunning. It was both enchanting and suffocating to stand before them in my plain mortality.

"We welcome you to Sophrosyne, young Resonant."

"Thank you kindly, Speaker. I appreciate your time and consideration."

Amaretta had instructed me to carry myself with grace and formality before the Elders without being overly reverential, and though I was so nervous that I thought I might faint, I somehow managed to speak the words clearly.

"What brings you to Sophrosyne, young one? What is it that you hope to seek from the Arcane Studium?"

That felt like a loaded question, though that was probably the point.

"Knowledge. Insight. Growth," I answered honestly, unsure of how specific they wanted me to get here. For a moment, I felt slightly lightheaded. The Speaker's lips curled into a slight smile.

"You may be seated at any time, should you need it," she said, gesturing to a small bench behind me that I hadn't noticed before. I nodded.

"And what is the nature of the knowledge and growth that you seek here, Resonant?"

As I could not tell her the full truth, I decided to go with... truth-adjacent.

"In all honesty, Speaker, I do not yet know the answer to that question. Having been raised by a retired scholar, I know there is a wealth of knowledge here, far beyond my current understanding of the world. I grew up in the woods, and so I come eager to learn, but without any one specific path in mind. All I know at the moment is that I would like to strengthen my Resonance, learn arcana, and hope to see where the rest takes me."

"Ah yes, your Resonance..." she mused softly after nodding along with the rest of my explanation. "It has been quite some time, by mortal standards, since a potential Light Conduit stood before us. Several decades, I believe. Am I correct, Alexei?"

The male Aetherborne to her left, dark-skinned with wine-red eyes, nodded slowly. If I could recall correctly, the god she referred to as Alexei was known as The Archivist. He was just as stunning as the Speaker and the rest of the Convocation. It was becoming quite clear to me why there were still some mortals who looked upon our living ancestors and saw divinity.

"Twenty two years," he said, voice slow and thick like honey.

A coincidence, I told myself. *Just an odd coincidence.*

"The pursuit of knowledge for the sake of knowledge is a path we honor and respect, and you need not justify it. We are pleased to see another Lightbearer seek entry to the Arcane Studium."

There was that term again—or was it a title? Lightbearer. One of the other Resonants on the ship had called me that, but I was unfamiliar with the origin.

"Tell me, Arken," the Speaker continued. "At what age did your Resonance manifest?"

"I was just about twelve when it first appeared."

An instinctive lie. It had manifested much earlier than that. I offered a silent prayer to the Source, willing that the Speaker wouldn't be able to detect the untruth.

"And how old are you now?"

"Twenty-two."

The Archivist exchanged a glance with the Speaker, as they too noticed the coincidental timing of my birth and the last known arrival of a Light Conduit. I tucked that observation in the back of my mind for future research. Perhaps it wasn't quite a coincidence, if the gods themselves took note of such things.

Seemingly out of nowhere, that strange sense of lightheadedness returned in waves, and I had to blink a few times to steady myself, shifting weight from one foot to the other.

"And you have been able to access Light ever since the first manifestation?"

"Yes, ma'am."

A light, sparkling laugh fell from her lips.

"Oh, you are far more polite than some of your peers have been today. It is comforting to know that at least some of our children retain their manners. You may call me by name if you wish, young wise one. I am known as Elura; the Speaker and the Eleventh Elder of the Convocation."

I dipped my head in a slight bow.

"It is an honor," I breathed.

When I raised my head again, my eyes wandered over the other eighteen members of the Convocation, all of whom continued to sit in silence and perfect stillness as Elura spoke. Every last one of them gazed back, studying me intently with ancient, seemingly all-knowing eyes.

Those haunting eyes were all aglow in various colors—some of which we humans did not seem to inherit. Lilac. Crimson. Copper. Though I envied the beauty of their brilliance, it was the depth of the eons carved within that was truly breathtaking. Somehow, you could see how thousands of years had passed before those eyes, though most of the Aetherborne did not appear to be any older than thirty.

The long pointed ears and the sharp fangs were the most obvious features that they did not share with their mortal descendants, but it was the eyes that made the truth of their immortality apparent.

I lowered my lashes again, tucking my chin towards my chest in a show of respect. I had regained my bearings, no longer feeling dizzy, though I did notice a slight throb in the back of my head beginning to form. What the Hel was in that elixir, anyway? And what had been the damn point of it, other than making me feel slightly sick?

"We will be concluding here shortly, Arken, but first we would like to measure the strength of your Resonance in its current state. Are you sure you don't wish to be seated?"

Concluding? Hadn't we just started?

"I'm fine standing, thank you. What would you have me do?"

"In just a moment, we will remove all Light from these chambers. You may find it more difficult to summon your Resonance when this happens, but what we would like you to do is try and illuminate the room to the best of your ability. Do not hold back. We want to witness your full strength, without hesitation. Understood?"

That was all? This was the trial that I had been so worked up over for the last six weeks of travel? I just had to use my Resonance with some extra effort?

"Understood," I answered, despite my disbelief.

Surely, this was too simple. I hadn't known what to anticipate here, but I had expected something more challenging than just proving I could summon Light with a basic example.

"Are you ready?"

I nodded once, still confused. There was a knowing look in the Speaker's eyes, as if she knew exactly what I was thinking. She almost looked... *amused.*

"Then you may proceed."

And before I saw a single member of the Convocation even so much as blink, the room went black. Pitch black, ensconcing us all in total darkness.

This was a different kind of darkness—it wasn't anything like the familiar shade of nightfall, though I could still sense the aether all around me. This was Shadow, but it was heavy. Oppressive, even. As if there were layers of it weighing down on me. Nineteen layers, perhaps? It certainly felt like it. There wasn't even an ounce of Light aether that I could draw from...

Well, fuck.

Anxiety began to pulse as I attempted to draw on my Resonance and felt nothing at first. It was then that I realized that I was enshrouded in both total darkness and total silence. I couldn't hear a single whisper of ambient noise—no rustle of clothes or breathing outside of my own. If I concentrated, I could probably hear the sound of my own heartbeat as it steadily elevated.

Breathe in. Breathe out.

One of the last lessons Amaretta had taught me before I left had been about the concept of aetherflows, and how supposedly Shadow aether was the strongest resource for Light arcana. But that... that was arcana. Not Resonance. There was a difference.

Resonance was what came naturally to mortals born with it, the clumsy channeling of existing aetheric energy drawn from our surroundings. The aether in our bodies allowed us to attune to one element—or all six, in my case—and allowed us to essentially channel that element. With enough practice, we could learn to command its form and shape. When I toyed around with my dancing lights against my fingertips, I was pulling that Light aether from my environment. It became mine, but it remained Light.

Arcana was the conversion of one element of aether into something else entirely, drawing upon the pure aether in our veins to transmute that elemental energy at will. It was true control. True manipulation of the lifeblood of the universe. The complex science and spellwork of the gods.

I wasn't trained. I didn't know how to do it, only knew the very basics of theory at best. I hadn't even paid full attention when Amaretta would...

But I could do this. I had to.

I had to.

I took a deep, slow inhale of breath and held it, tasting the purity of the air as it filled my lungs. I flexed my toes inside my boots, shifting my stance slightly so that I felt grounded, focusing on the power I could feel from the Earth below me. I tried to steady my mind the way that I had been taught, releasing that breath slowly, but my pulse was quickening instead of slowing.

What if I failed?
What if I succeeded, but it still wasn't enough?
What if I somehow exposed my secret?
Did they already know?
Was this a trap?
What if? What if? What if?

How easily these fears found me in the dark, wriggling beneath my skin, biting into flesh, the venom of panic slipping into my bloodstream. I could hear my own breath grow ragged, unaware of exactly how much time had passed.

Was there a time limit? She hadn't said, but surely they wouldn't wait on me forever in the dark.

Again, I tugged at my Resonance and felt nothing. Was this the purpose of the elixir? Some sort of blend of herbs that blocked my aether, making the trial a test of strength and will? Or was I just choking under pressure, buckling under the weight of what I wanted so badly?

I felt as though I stood on the precipice of fate, the next step into a new life just out of reach. If I fell back now, what would be left for me?

Could I really go home to the Brindlewoods and pretend that it was enough, now that I had sailed through the Western Seas? Now that I had ridden through the lush hills and grasslands of Pyrhhas, and gazed upon the sparkling City of the Gods?

No. I really couldn't.

I wanted answers. I wanted more. I wanted to live and to learn and to find whatever it was that had been calling me here, whispering sweet nothings in my ear for years and years.

Find yourself, Arken. You're ready. It's time.

I was going to pass this godsdamned trial if it killed me.

With another sharp inhale, I tugged hard against that core of arcane energy I knew I held within. It was mine to command, and I felt the familiar prickle against my fingertips as power awakened, answering my adamant call. This time when I pulled, the Shadows came.

Drawing in this form of aether did not feel the same as drawing in my well-acquainted Light. Though I had felt Shadow before, I had never used it with intention. Such was the case with every element for me, except for Light. This energy was cold and smoky, feeling foreign and much less pliant than the warmth of Light as I willed it towards me with outstretched fingers. There was a slight opposition—a tangible resistance that tried to suggest this element was not mine to wield, that this power didn't belong to me.

But *it did*.

All six of them did. For whatever reason.

I had manifested this darkness before, accidental or not. If I could hold it like this, I could convert it. If I could hold it like this, it was mine. I pushed up against that internal resistance, gritting my teeth as I strained against an invisible barrier in my chest. A small bead of sweat formed on my brow as I struggled to use the power I had been wielding with ease for the last ten years of my life.

Gods. Why was this so fucking hard?

My chest was beginning to tighten and constrict, head

throbbing and throat dry as the Shadow aether I held continued to resist. I could feel its chaotic nature tangling around and whipping itself back and forth inside of me, refusing to bend to my will. Nausea roiled in my gut and I fought off the urge to release it all. To just give up and let the Shadows go.

Stop, I commanded—as if the aether was a sentient beast. As if it could hear me. Somehow, the chaos stilled long enough for me to take another deep, heavy breath. I shut my eyes out of habit, not that it made a difference here. But the feel of my lashes against my cheeks was calming all the same.

Aether was aether.

If Light could fade to Shadow, Shadow could grow into Light. Night into day. Dusk into dawn.

You are the master of your fate, Arken. You always have been.

That hum of power beneath my skin surged as I smiled at the memory, those encouraging words from my mentor. Warmth pooled in my chest, gentle and familiar. I could almost taste the sunshine and the fresh forest air on the exhale, and then suddenly, the Hall of the Seeing was illuminated by pure, blinding Light aether.

Holy Hel.

I did it. I actually did it.

A delighted, somewhat childish peal of laughter escaped my lips in shock as I opened my eyes and saw what I had done. Orbs of shimmering Light aether were floating overhead like makeshift constellations, the glow of those tiny stars permeating through heavily conjured Shadow like it was nothing at all. Without instruction or tools, I had used arcana. Not my Resonance. *Arcana*. I had cast a *spell*.

Even the most impassive of the nineteen Elders before me had their eyes raised to the ceiling, some of them even looking slightly surprised.

"Most impressive, young Conduit," Elura murmured, still

looking towards the Light above.

Conduit?

I blinked back the tears that had already started to well up in my eyes as she spoke the words that forced them to spill forth regardless.

"Welcome to the Arcane Studium, Arken Asher."

CHAPTER SIX

KIERAN

I woke abruptly to three sharp raps at my door. Blinking slowly and still disoriented, I realized that I had fallen asleep at my desk for something like the third time this week, poring over the latest reports after my early morning indulgence. Sometimes even the best distractions weren't quite enough.

While the Jerricks case was the first kidnapping we'd seen in Sophrosyne proper for the last fifty years, the other territories had been experiencing an alarming uptick in similar crimes. Always children or teens. Always relatives of people in power—noblemen, merchants, or even Atlassian Court leadership. And they were always Conduits.

If it were simply a matter of missing Conduits, the answer would be painfully obvious: blood cultists. There were still a number of them left in Atlas, convinced that they could unlock the power of the gods if they consumed enough aether directly from the blood of a Conduit, or even a Resonant human. It wasn't common knowledge, for obvious reasons, but sometimes their reckless experiments even worked... but only for a moment. The fleeting power gained was always of little consequence, as they died quickly, and they died screaming.

The next series of raps at my door became louder, more

insistent—and I recognized the cadence immediately.

Shit.

"Vistarii! I know you're in there. Get your ass up."

I groaned as I rose from the chair and made my way across the room, opening the door to a *very* disgruntled looking superior officer.

"Morning, Commander Ka!" I offered cheerily, with what I hoped would be a disarming smile.

"What have I told you about sleeping here, Kieran? It's your day off, for fucks sake."

"I know, I know. In my defense, I hadn't *planned* on falling asleep here, we just had a long night with the suspect last night and—"

"I'm electing to ignore that," the commander said, his eyes flickering from my face to the blood spattered sleeves of my coat.

"Then, by the time I wrapped up a few other dalliances, there were more reports to review..."

Hanjae Ka scowled and then sighed heavily—clearly he was already over my shit.

"Anything of note?" Hanjae inquired. Loath as he was to admit it, my commander was an enabler of bad habits when it suited his own needs.

"Two missing in Samhaven. One in Ithreac. No signs, no calling cards, no ransom demands. All we've really managed to gather so far is that they seem to be targeting particularly talented Conduits, or precocious Resonants. The last two taken were Shadow Conduits as well, and Markus and Theia have expressed serious concerns over the security of the Astral & Umbral Isles the next time Theia makes her way to Sophrosyne."

"They can get in line. Vindyrst is breathing down our fucking necks about the Jerricks boy, and the rest of the Atlassian Courts seem to be waiting on the Elders to come step in and solve this for them," Hanjae groused.

I sighed. While that wasn't exactly *our* problem as the Elder Guard, it was still a frustrating expectation. The Elders made their stance on intervening with mortals quite clear. We, the mortal guardsmen, served the city-state of Sophrosyne, the Arcane Studium, *and* the Nineteen, and yet the entire continent of Atlas had a tendency to rely on us for strategy and matters of collective regional security.

"We've also received word that the first Light Conduit in the last twenty years just got accepted into the Studium."

A Light Conduit? *Holy Hel.*

"Yes," Hanjae confirmed, reading my expression. "It's a big deal, and the Elders have requested that we keep a close eye on things now that she's arrived. She and the Makar girl could easily become the next targets, so keep your men vigilant. Keep looking. Acquire your information by any means necessary, *within reason*, but Kieran?"

"Yeah?"

"Get started on the rest of that *tomorrow*."

"I'm fine, Hanjae."

"Commander Ka," he corrected, narrowing his eyes. I resisted the urge to roll my own. Hanjae only ever pulled rank on me when he wasn't in the mood to argue.

"And I don't give a shit how bright-eyed and bushy-tailed you're feeling this morning after your *dalliances*, Captain. Go home. Take a damn bath. And wash that fucking coat."

"Yes, sir."

✧ ✧ ✧

Though I swore up and down to Commander Ka that I'd go straight home and rest, that had been a bold-faced lie. Though to be fair, he probably knew it.

On paper, my title in the Elder Guard was the Captain of Scouting and Reconnaissance. In practice, I was more like their spymaster—and I had several informants to meet with and pay off on my way back to the townhouse.

I withdrew a small fortune's worth of Lyra from our coffers before leaving headquarters and made my way over to the Merchant's Quarter with heavy pockets, paying no mind to the way they'd jingle every now and again when the pouches jostled. Though I could have easily slipped into the Shadows and remained unseen, I kept my stroll casual and enjoyed the warmth of the morning sun. I would be so lucky to encounter a thief with the balls to fuck around and find out. Let them make my day.

Alas, Sophrosyne was indeed home to some of the best and brightest minds in the realm, none of them stupid enough to attempt robbery against an armed guardsman. As such, my walk remained rather uneventful until I rolled up to my first stop: Duncan Falk, a butcher with connections to the Pyrhhan Black Market.

Yes, even the region of Pyrhhas, shining star of the Atlassian Courts, had its own seedy underbelly—and Falk was in bed with some of their key players.

"Falk," I greeted the heavyset man whose bald head had already begun to glisten as the cool air of morning gave way to the warmth of early afternoon sun.

"Ay, Vistarii. I have your order in the back, come, come."

Falk nodded to his apprentice before leading me away from his stall in the open-air market, back towards the small shop where we typically did business. It was a slow afternoon, so he locked the door behind us for privacy without hesitation.

"Listen, boss, imma cut to the quick with ya. I know yer men have been looking into that Jerricks boy, yeah? An' I put out feelers, but no bites. Somethin' has most of my people skittish these days, but no one's talkin'."

"That's unfortunate," I murmured.

"And uhh, respectfully, sir, I'm not sure if ya really helped matters by lettin' Corvus go. Not sure what y'all did to the man, but uhh, he's all sorts of banged up in the head now..."

I raised a brow.

"Yeah. Well. You know. Folks are gonna be spooked."

I nodded. "That's to be expected, I suppose. As things settle down, though, I'd like for you to keep putting those feelers out. Flesh trade, blood cults... I'm looking for people who are explicitly interested in Conduits. If you catch wind of buyers, I want to know immediately."

"Yessir, you got it."

I withdrew two pouches of Lyra and tossed them his way. The man gave me a quizzical look, as I'd just tossed him double what I typically paid him for information.

"For this week, and consider the rest an advance for your swift call the next time you catch wind of anything. You know how to reach me."

"Aye, Captain. Always a pleasure."

I wasn't sure I'd call it that, but I didn't mind working with the butcher. Despite his harrowing appearance as a massive man, often found in bloodstained clothes and wielding a meat-cleaver, he was actually fairly harmless. His connection to the Black Market was purely circumstantial—his father was the criminal who built those relationships, and when he died, he'd passed them down to the "next in line," hoping that Duncan might one day follow in his nefarious footsteps.

Alas, as far as my background research could tell, the worst crime Duncan Falk had ever personally committed was coming up short on his taxes.

✧ ✧ ✧

After I wrapped things up with Falk, I made my way over to a nearby tavern where a familiar buxom, raven-haired woman was tending to the bar. As I entered, the woman narrowed her eyes, placing her hands on her hips. She was in her late thirties, maybe early forties at most—and vivacious as ever.

"And just who do you think you are, strolling in here like you own the damn place? We don't offer discounts to men in uniform, you know—we charge them extra."

"You're looking rather stunning today, Roshana. Is that a new dress, or do you just make everything look that good? Oh, and hello to you, too."

As per usual, she cracked under the compliments and dropped the act.

"Hey there, handsome. You want the usual?"

"Please," I answered with a smile.

My "usual" here was whatever Roshana had on deck as this week's lunch special, often delivered with a fat stack of intercepted missives and stolen notes from her little songbirds. Roshana's tavern doubled as a pleasure den for those with deep connections and even deeper pockets. It wasn't as if sex work was illegal in Sophrosyne, but it was so heavily regulated and taxed in the city that it was... hard to come by, to say the least. In the grand scheme of things, that was probably for the best, given the amount of minors who lived on campus at the Studium.

Within minutes, Roshana slid a plate of sausages, boiled cabbage, and potatoes in front of me, alongside a healthy helping of the barmaid's cleavage and a few scraps of parchment.

"Afraid I don't have much else for you, K. You're back so soon. Miss me, did you?"

"Always do," I purred, plucking an envelope that I knew Roshana had intentionally left in her bosom. That woman was insatiable.

"Can I get you anything else? Ale, whiskey, cider? Another

round between the sheets?"

"Nah," I replied. "Tempting as that may be, I can't stay much longer, Ro. A bit tied up today."

"Mmm, I do like that in a man," she replied, her smoky voice thick with innuendo. "Are you sure you can't come back to see me this evening? You know I'll make it worth your while, Captain."

"Afraid not, beautiful. I'm sure you've got plenty of other hearts to break."

"A bold claim coming from you, Vistarii," she laughed. "But you know, the new girl, Sadie—you might like a tangle or two with that one if you're craving fresh blood. I'll even give you a discount."

As the barmaid waggled her eyebrows at me suggestively, I tried not to grimace. While I held the courtesans of Sophrosyne with the utmost regard, I never quite understood the appeal of paying for sex. It was probably an ego thing. I wanted my sexual partners to want my cock more than my Lyra.

"*Tsk*. Roshana, Roshana. You know me better than that. If I want fresh blood, I'll go on the hunt for it myself."

I tossed her a wicked grin and a wink before brushing off my thighs and leaving a handful of extra Lyra on the counter for my meal. I tried not to wince as I stood—my lower back was absolutely killing me.

I really needed to stop falling asleep at that damned desk.

CHAPTER SEVEN

ARKEN

I expected the arcane brand to hurt more than it did.

According to the sailors I had befriended on the ship, tattoos in general were supposed to hurt like Hel. Many of them had artwork that had been needled into their skin with ink, and had grimaced when I asked about the experience of receiving such marks.

This was no ordinary tattoo, though.

Upon receiving unanimous approval from the Convocation to be granted entry into Sophrosyne and the Studium, the Speaker had beckoned me forward, asking me to extend my dominant hand.

The aether behind her eyes flared brighter when she murmured an incantation in the Elder tongue, running a single fingertip over the inside of my wrist in such a way that almost felt intimate.

"This will serve as your key to the city and the Studium, young Lightbearer," Elura had explained, her melodic voice soothing as a flash of sharp pain hit. Within an instant, the pain was gone.

One by one, the circles began to appear, overlapping in red, carving out the space for themselves just beneath the skin. There were no needles, no ink, no physical act whatsoever placing this sigil. It simply appeared, by the sheer will of the Elders before me. I could feel the depth of the arcana the Speaker was using as the symbol was created—binding, ancient, and powerful beyond words or understanding.

"It will allow you to pass through our wards safely, and it will prove your status as a Conduit anywhere in the world. Whether you remain here for just a few quarters, or for many years to come, those who carry the Seed of Creation are always welcome in Sophrosyne."

I watched in wonder as the tattoo began to glow with the quicksilver sheen of pure aether.

Whether it was my own, or that of the gods binding me in that moment, I did not know—but it was a fascinating sight to behold. After the glow settled, the glimmering silver remained as if the geometric pattern had been painted on—but I knew it was permanent.

I was officially marked as a Conduit.

◇ ◇ ◇

After receiving the arcane brand, I returned to High Scholar Wallace, who took down the details of my acceptance for their records. Once the paperwork was complete, the kind scholar ran me through all of the next steps of my residency here—housing information, my pre-allocated appointments for academic counsel, when my courses would start, where I could go for supplies, how to recognize members of the Elder Guard in emergencies, etcetera.

Truth be told, it was all a bit of a blur. I did my best to retain as much information as possible, but I think I was still in shock, wrapping my head around the fact that this was all real. I had made it to Sophrosyne. I had passed my trial. Me, the little orphan girl from the woods, accepted into the most prestigious arcane university in the world. I knew she had never doubted me, not even for a minute—but I still couldn't wait to write Amaretta, telling her everything.

My hands were full as I made my way back through the annex, trying to keep my bag from sliding off my shoulder while juggling several tomes and a stack of papers, pamphlets and maps. There were attendants who could guide me over to the Student's Quarter and show me around, Wallace had explained, but I was also welcome to explore the city on my own. He had also pointed out where we were on the city map, as well as several key points of interest, all of which I was eager to visit. But first and foremost...

I had a letter to open.

I found a quiet, sunny corner outside of the annex and withdrew the now-weathered parchment envelope that Amaretta had given me the day that I left home.

"Don't you dare open this until you've made it to Sophrosyne, missy. And only after you've passed your trial," she'd threatened me before I left. "I'll know. I always know!"

She always did have an uncanny ability to recognize whenever I was up to no good.

I began to open the envelope with hands still trembling from the excitement. I had to pause a moment to admire the way the new silver sigil on my wrist glinted in the sunlight, taking several deep breaths as I began to process that this was real.

Once I was ready, I took a seat on the closest bench and melted at the sight of my mentor's handwriting.

My dearest Arken,
I trust that for once in your life, you've been a well-behaved young woman and are opening this letter upon completion of your entry trial at the Arcane Studium. You wouldn't dare peek, so allow me to be the first to say—congratulations, my love. I knew you would get in.

I know that I gave you a hard time about this journey before you left, and I hope that by now, you've grown to understand that my intentions were never to hold you back... only to make absolutely certain that you were ready to walk this path. But you were—you are. *And I am so very proud of you.*

Enclosed in this envelope, you will find a pouch that contains both a key and an address to my old research studio. Though the Studium will offer you student housing, I would strongly prefer that you stay at my studio apartment instead. It's likely a bit dusty, but it's warded—and very safe. Please, make yourself at home there—if only for this old woman's peace of mind. Consider it yours, now.

Besides, I spent a great deal of time building that celestial orrery inside, and it's about time someone else appreciated my efforts! The brass was far too heavy to take with me when I left the city, but you always did enjoy stargazing, now didn't you? Take good care of it.

You will need to have the wards refreshed within a fortnight—head to Graham Kepler's arcane supply shop in the Market District and tell him that Scholar Sinclair sent you, he'll know what to do, as I have sent him a letter with detailed instructions.

Now, within the studio, there are also hidden coffers beneath the floorboards in the first closet on the left. The Lyra stashed within is for emergencies only—but remember what I told you. Trust your instincts. Keep your secrets.

And do keep in mind that I still have connections within the city. If you don't write to your poor, aging mentor on a regular basis, I have my ways of tracking you down, girl.

Be safe, my love. And be well.

Amma

Tears pricked at the back of my eyelids as I realized that as excited as I was to be here, I would miss my mentor so very much. For the first time in twenty two years of life, I was entirely on my own. This journey had been my choice, and what I made of it was entirely up to me.

As the elation and adrenaline from the trial began to fade and I followed the map to find Amma's studio, I began to realize how *terrifying* that was, in the grand scheme of things.

I had always been a fairly solitary creature, so I wasn't too concerned with the fact that I was alone in Sophrosyne. Not exactly. Back home, I had often enjoyed the comfort of my own company more than I had enjoyed being around others. It was a learned behavior, sure—but the learnings lingered, as they do when you grow up... different.

I suppose what made this all so frightening was the fact that I had no definitive strategy for what came next. I had no master plan, and no mentor to hold my hand through the process, or make me a cup of tea when my nerves threatened to eat me alive.

You're ready, Arken. It's time.

All I really had was that voice in the back of my head and this hunger in my heart, this desperate thirst that had haunted me all my life for any and all knowledge that I could get my hands on, particularly when it came to aether, arcana, and Resonance. It was all-encompassing and inescapable, a byproduct of twenty-two years worth of abandonment wounds, dangerous secrets, and never quite fitting the mold of what others expected of me.

I didn't think this was a fear of failure, though. Quite the opposite, actually. I think I was afraid of what it meant now, to have everything I ever wanted. I was already falling in love with Sophrosyne and it had only been a day. As I traversed through what I believed to be the Academic Quarter, my eyes wandered greedily, taking in every possible detail of this city and its sights to behold. At every turn, Sophrosyne was bustling with life and energy and stunning architecture.

It was a strange thing, to be afraid of my own happiness. But as I found the front door to Amma's old studio apartment and took out my key with a trembling hand, that dawning realization was becoming undeniable.

Life was a little more frightening when you had something to lose.

CHAPTER EIGHT

KIERAN

I considered myself a man of many talents, but if there was one thing that I was *particularly* good at, it was remaining unseen. Whether I was bustling about the night markets amidst throngs of people, wandering alone with my thoughts in broad daylight, or taking a midnight stroll through the Wyldwoods, it didn't matter. If I wanted to disappear—I could.

Which is why, when some stunning little thing breezed past me in the Market District first thing on a Monday morning, her head buried deep within the pages of a book, it was easy enough to step back into the Shadows and give chase in silence, sight unseen.

Her curves had been enough to set my head on a swivel, but there was something else about her that woke up a certain hunger, the prowling hunter in my veins that had been dormant for the last few weeks.

Who was she?

I had been too busy as of late to feed that borderline predatory thirst that arose from time to time, that familiar, carnal craving. Because to seduce? To charm and capture the willing, where the only reward is reciprocal pleasure? That was my personal drug of choice. And I desperately needed a hit off the woman who had just walked past me, smelling like citrus and sunshine.

I couldn't quite place the reason behind the immediate desire. Her shoulder had brushed mine as she passed, just barely—not that she'd seemed to notice. Was it that summery scent she left behind? I mean sure, she had a very appealing figure, but I had hardly even caught a glimpse of her face as it was shrouded in lengthy, dark brunette waves. If she held that damned book any closer to her face, her nose might have touched the page.

I may have been a man addicted to the chase, but the chase rarely found *me* first. I hadn't been looking for a distraction just yet though. I was still working.

You've got time.

I followed the sound of her footsteps.

She had a calm, confident gait, which suggested she either knew where she was going—someplace familiar, I'd wager—or that she had her mind set on some particular task she knew she could accomplish. Perhaps both.

The pretty little thing didn't put her book away once as she walked down the old cobblestone road, barely looking up as strangers walked past. She appeared to have a solid sense of her surroundings, weaving around anyone or anything in her way—though not keen enough to realize she was being followed. That was fair. Most wouldn't.

"That doesn't make any *fucking* sense," I heard the woman murmur under her breath, her voice soft, melodic—and clearly quite frustrated.

If I wasn't already intrigued, that wicked tongue would have caught my attention any day.

A quick glance towards the inside of her left wrist was all I needed to glean the basics—the dark-haired woman was a Conduit, and a fairly new one at that. The sigil of entry was still vibrant and fresh, with a sheen that would fade in time. In order for it to be *that* fresh, though, she had to be a part of the newest cycle of freshlings: a class of about two hundred or so.

Despite having her head buried in that book, she was making a careful beeline northeast, so she must've been heading towards the Biblyos.

The quarter hadn't started yet—the courses would begin in a few days. This one was clearly a bookwyrm already. Either she was meeting someone in the Academic Quarter, or she was getting a headstart on her coursework.

Or maybe she just liked books.

I quickened my pace in an effort to get ahead of her for a different view, curious as to what she was reading that had her cursing in annoyance. Ah. *An Introduction to Arcane Theory.*

Really?

Even I had read that one, and it wasn't particularly complex. I was fully prepared to make some snap judgments on the woman's intellect levels if an entry level textbook was enough to piss her off, but my mind went blank and my mouth went dry the very next moment—when I actually got a decent look at her face.

Fucking Hel.

A pair of wide, golden-brown eyes glanced towards the clock tower at the center of the city. Thick, dark lashes encircled them both, but even they could not block the mid-afternoon sun streaming through the skies, rendering her irises a stunning shade of gold—like liquid honey. A light smattering of freckles ran across her nose and cheekbones, contrasting with pale skin that was ever-so-slightly sunkissed. And good gods, that mouth. That mouth was going to get me into trouble.

She had full, soft looking lips that were so deeply pink that they almost looked freshly bitten—a thought that sent a strange surge of envy through my veins. Whatever had irritated her just a moment ago must have faded from her mind, because now those lips were now parted slightly with the corners upturned in a hint of a smile.

What little semblance of chivalry I had promptly flew out the window as I watched the tip of her tongue run across her lower lip—and my thoughts took a turn for the needlessly inappropriate. It was just dry outside, and hot as Hel today. But *gods be damned*, I wanted to be the one tasting those lips instead.

I needed a plan of action. I was just about to step inside to follow her when I heard a familiar voice call out to me.

"Captain Vistarii!"

Some bright-eyed recruit was nearly shouting at me from a few feet away, short of breath as they caught up. "Commander Ka has requested you return to the office as soon as possible. There's been an update on the Jerricks case."

I groaned internally. This investigation was too important to push aside in favor of getting my cock wet, and if said update was confidential enough to send a courier straight to me over a falcon or a mail sprite, I needed to get my ass in gear.

"Very well," I sighed. "I'll be in momentarily."

As I stepped back into the Shadows, I couldn't help but laugh at the look on that poor recruit's face. The moment he'd glanced away, I was gone without a trace. Most of my men were accustomed to that—I was the Captain of Scouting & Reconnaissance for a reason. The fresh blooded courier just looked dazed and confused as he searched the crowd.

Back to work, it is.

My prey would have to wait.

For now.

◇ ◇ ◇

As it turns out, the "update" in the Jerricks case was simply that we had heard back from Lord Zephirin of the House of Gales. Vindyrst had set a bounty on the heads of any individuals involved with the missing boy, but had yet to receive any sort of response, or request for ransom.

"That's it?" I asked, running my hand through my hair, still out of breath. I might've rushed along the way back, eager for any sort of break in this case.

"Apologies, Kieran," Hanjae said. "I was just going to send off a mail sprite, but the recruit—Kraiggson, I think his name was? He volunteered to deliver the message himself. I think the kid's got a little bit of a hero worship thing going on with you."

A hero worship thing? I wasn't a fucking hero.

I sighed. "I don't know what to make of any of this, Commander. It's like these kids are disappearing into thin air, and it shouldn't be that godsdamned easy to get away with something like that."

"I know. The only upside to this has been the amount of flesh traders and blood cultists who have been caught in the crossfire. I know you and your men are spread thin right now, Vistarii, but you're doing excellent work. The realm is safer thanks to your efforts."

It was the least that I could do. My commander, the Elder Guard, the city of Sophrosyne, and even the Elders themselves—they had all earned my loyalty a long time ago.

"Just doing my job, sir."

"I know that *you're* a lost cause, Kieran, but please make sure that *your men* are taking breaks."

"They do. Hey, speaking of—who manages the schedules for grunt work these days?"

Hanjae raised a brow. "Rorick, I believe. Why?"

"Eh, Deering's getting a little too big for his britches," I lied smoothly. "I lost a bet to him recently, and want to make him pay for it."

Hanjae rolled his eyes.

"You're dismissed," he said sternly. Whether my commander liked it or not, though, I could detect a glimmer of entertainment in his expression as I left.

I swung by Rorick's desk on my way back to my office and penciled myself as well as a small handful of my men down for an upcoming round of guard duty for entry-level student lectures in the Wyldwoods.

It had been a while since any of our upper level officers had set a good example for the recruits who normally got tasked with this easy work, and as boring as it was, I knew my lieutenants wouldn't really mind. Even if they did suss out my ulterior motives.

Almost every new Conduit ended up taking Larkin's introductory courses within their first few quarters, and if I was lucky...

I might just catch myself a pretty little bookwyrm.

CHAPTER NINE

ARKEN

The scholars of the Studium offered counsel to all new Conduits upon entry, where they provided a particular route of courses to take within your first year. It wasn't required, but it was firmly recommended.

The Studium and the elder city-state of Sophrosyne operated under the principle of free access to the knowledge of the gods. It was built for the pursuit of a deeper understanding of our world, so that we may study the arcane sciences that bound us and make use of this fundamental, powerful knowledge to go forth and make the realm a better place.

As such, there was no graduating from the Studium, the way one might celebrate the completion of education elsewhere. There was technically no required coursework, no enforced order of operations, and no tests that you had to pass in order to become recognized or respected. Once you entered the city and began your studies, you were a Conduit.

There were a few exceptions, of course. I imagined there was likely some type of formal training required in order to become a professor or High Scholar of the Studium, for example, but I had very little knowledge of such things. I probably should have paid more attention to Amaretta's talk of her early years here.

Sophrosyne was essentially our oyster, and we were responsible for our own individual pursuits of the pearls of wisdom in the worlds held within these walls. Ultimately, I decided to go with what the scholars recommended, starting my first year off with some foundation building courses on history, the natural sciences, and arcana.

Today, I was attending a lecture in the Wyldwoods, focused on the fundamentals of Resonance within the natural world.

It was presented by High Scholar Jude Larkin—widely lauded as a master of Bios, a true genius in this particular field of study. That said, I could not help but feel somewhat amused, biting back a smile when I first saw him approach. Our professor was a small, diminutive looking man in clean cut robes, with thick, goggled lenses and a very impressive mustache. Scholar Larkin looked like a complete caricature of a man, the very essence of what a High Scholar *should* look like. It was delightful.

Larkin led our group down the streets of Sophrosyne to the Eastern Gates, where several men from the Elder Guard were waiting to escort us into the woods.

Though many of the monsters and other dangerous beasts of the world had been culled from the natural areas which surrounded our city, it was not without risk to go into the Wyldwoods alone. Typically, these guards were tasked with the overall protection and peace-keeping within the city, but I suppose sometimes they got stuck with more mundane tasks.

As the scholar took us through the bustling streets of Sophrosyne, I was admittedly not paying very close attention to his introductory notes & warnings.

I couldn't help myself—it had only been a few weeks since my arrival, and both the campus and the city itself were absolutely sparkling with life, creativity, and curiosity. I suppose that's what happens when you build an entire enclave dedicated to the pursuit of knowledge.

My mind was a greedy, willful thing, as Amaretta would say, and I was hungry for every new sight and sound, and *gods*—even the scents around me. The smell of freshly baked bread wafted by as we passed a bakery, and I practically salivated at the sight of pastries in the window, dusted snow white with confectioner's sugar.

I made a mental note of our location with the full intention to return once the lecture had concluded. It may seem like a silly indulgence, but I didn't often have sweets growing up. In our village, resources were pooled and shared amongst those in need first and foremost.

That was another unique thing about the Arcane Studium.

The Convocation graciously provided new Conduits both room and board at no cost for our first year, including a small monthly stipend of Lyra to be spent however we wished. After your first year, you were expected to do some work, anywhere within the city. Any vocation with an opening was an eligible option, so long as you were contributing to the overall maintenance and quality of life in Sophrosyne.

In turn, the city provided these businesses with the funds to see us paid for our work, all the while continuing to provide us with food and housing if we chose to remain on campus. There was also an annual pool of Lyra allocated for basic living costs, which was granted equally and universally amongst the active Conduits in study.

It was all a bit surreal to me. Sure, my village back home had operated under similar principles, but to successfully do so in a massive city-state such as Sophrosyne? I couldn't even imagine the amount of resources and organization it took to maintain such ideals.

Naturally, there were those that lived in Sophrosyne who were no longer active students, but still chose to remain in the city and make a life for themselves. These guardsmen were among them,

I imagined. I couldn't say I blamed them. With every passing day, I understood more why people around the world spoke of Sophrosyne with reverence and wonder. It truly was a city of gods.

I pulled my head from the clouds to focus on what the scholar was saying now as we drew closer to the trail that led into the forest. The towering fir and pine trees began to darken the skies, cooling the air as we reached the entry point.

"Remember, young Conduits! Stay within the group, respect the orders of the guards, and, most importantly, open your senses to the world within these woods. Allow yourselves to attune to the elemental energies around you, identifying each reflection of aether. The Wyldwoods are some of the oldest surviving forests that remain untouched by mankind, and you may find that the aether within feels stronger."

He wasn't wrong. The air around here almost felt heavier to breathe in, even more dense to walk through. The invisible weight grew with every step further into the forest. As Larkin began to explain the basics of Resonance and elemental parallels, my mind wandered off again.

I held the High Scholar with utmost esteem and respect, of course, but Amaretta had already beaten much of these basics into my brain. It was not particularly difficult to tune him out and marvel instead at the massive, ancient trees, gnarled bark covered in moss and tiny little mushrooms.

I also enjoyed watching the expressions on some of the younger Conduits' faces as they learned some of this for the first time. Surprised interest, delight, awe. In these moments, I felt as though I could begin to understand why the Aetherborne had loved us enough to dedicate their immortal lives to our safe-keeping. Human curiosity was a beautiful thing.

Human curiosity was also one of my many weaknesses, and so I continued to explore my surroundings with my eyes, as Larkin—or *Jude*, as he kept reminding us—had so kindly asked us not to do so with our feet.

"Don't look now, but one of those guards is staring at you," one of the other Conduits beside me murmured.

I glanced over at her and found her face to be vaguely familiar. I recognized her eyes, which were a gorgeous shade of sage green, like a bay leaf—particularly offset by her deep, olive skin and a head full of long, dark curls. I was fairly certain that she had been aboard the same ship that brought me here to Sophrosyne. She was one of the few other Resonants who would catch my eye and grimace when Percival was being a prick.

"Laurel, right?" I whispered, and she nodded. "Which guard?"

"Okay so full disclosure, I'm a lesbian, but... the hot one. You'll know when you look. Be subtle!" Laurel whispered back with a conspiratorial grin.

I caught a glimpse of the offending guardsman out of the corner of my gaze, giving no indication that I noticed him, unless he could see the whisper of my smirk. I was trying my best to keep it contained, but Laurel's cheeky expression was not helping in the slightest. Once the man appeared to have glanced away, it was my turn to give him a once-over.

It was one Hel of a once-over.

The guardsman was very tall, built with lean but apparent muscle beneath his coat and leathers. Prior observations had told me that certain pins and tassels on the breast of the Elder Guard's uniforms indicated rank, and his was decorated enough to suggest seniority. He had to at least be a lieutenant... or, judging by the difference between his uniform and that of the others next to him, perhaps he was a captain. There was certainly an authoritative aura about him.

What was a captain of the Elder Guard doing on minor babysitting duty?

That particular curiosity could wait though, because as I

watched him laugh at something one of the other guards said, my mind went blank. Good *gods*, he was attractive.

"See what I mean?" Laurel murmured.

I most certainly did. While the two men he was standing closest to weren't unattractive by any means, the other Conduit had a point—the captain stood out, partially because he was so tall. The man would likely tower over me if he were closer, and I wasn't particularly small in stature.

I also liked the deep, golden tan tones of his skin, and the way that his dark hair was lengthy enough on top that it fell into his face as he leaned forward into his laughter. When his more disciplined posture returned, he brushed the longer locks back with one hand and my breath caught in my throat for a moment.

The left side of his face was marred by the slash of a scar through his brow, eye, and cheekbone. It had to have come from a vicious blow, or one Hel of a sharp blade. The scarred eye in question was white and clouded, I could only assume it was now blind. The other eye was a stunningly light shade of glacial blue, noticeable even from a distance.

Whoever this guard was, he was a lesson in colors, angles and contrast, and—*oh gods*, he was looking at me again.

I averted my eyes, pretending to be focused on the lecture.

"Do you know him?" Laurel asked.

"I most certainly do not," I murmured back, though a reckless part of me very much wanted to get to know him.

I didn't come to Sophrosyne or the Arcane Studium looking for romance, or even friendship, really—but one thing was certain upon my arrival: I could spend hundreds upon hundreds of hours in this city and still only glean a fraction of the information it contained.

In all likelihood, I would be here for years to come, searching for my answers and hopefully mastering arcana along the way.

I still wasn't looking for romance, but with handsome

strangers like that walking around the place? I could be convinced to open my mind to the possibilities of a casual fling every now and again. There was more to life than lectures and dusty old tomes, after all.

Even as a guardsman, I could sense a wicked, dark sort of edge to the man that I found strangely intriguing. It wasn't just the scar, or the hint of a tattoo I could see crawling up his neck. It was just in his energy, the way he carried himself, the way he laughed. It felt dangerous, but also beautiful.

I kept stealing hungry, hidden glances in his direction for the entirety of the lecture. Sophrosyne was a big city, and he was the most attractive creature I'd encountered so far... by a long shot. The odds of encountering him again felt slim.

You have to appreciate such ephemeral beauty while it lasts, right?

Or maybe it was just that higher concentration of aether in these woods getting to my head. One or the other. Probably both.

Besides, he had been staring at me first.

CHAPTER TEN

KIERAN

I could not stop staring at that woman if I tried.

"So," Hans murmured beside me. "Is this why you signed us all up for this boring shit, K? To eye-fuck some pretty little freshling from afar?"

Jeremiah tried his best to cover up his snort with a false bout of coughing, and I elbowed him in the side for good measure.

"It's good for morale to have higher ranking officers pick up grunt work on occasion, Deering," I replied to my lieutenant, unphased.

"And it's good for *your* morale to find the most attractive creatures in the city for another notch in your bedpost," he snarked back. "Like, my gods. She's probably been here for all of two seconds and you've already got her in your crosshairs. I'm almost impressed, Captain."

At that, I couldn't help but laugh.

I had a good rapport with most of my men, but Jeremiah, Hans and I were particularly close. We kept things informal, for the most part, because I preferred it that way. True loyalty didn't require the pomp and circumstance of military formalities, and these two were probably the closest thing I had to friends.

"So, are you going to go over and introduce yourself, or what?

She keeps looking over here, and it's certainly not for our ugly mugs," Jeremiah cajoled.

I raised a brow. The two of them were perfectly good looking men—perhaps not *my* type, but they each had their way with the ladies & gentlemen of Sophrosyne well enough. Still, I did hope that my second-in-command was right.

"Nah, not just yet," I replied, still looking at her surreptitiously from the corner of my eye.

"You know he's got a method to his madness, Jer," Hans reminded his fellow officer. "And the Fates fuckin' know that it works damn near every time."

"Is that jealousy I detect there, Deering?" I shot back with a grin.

Slowly and intentionally, I pulled the thin leather cord that I used to keep my hair back and held it between my teeth for a moment. I could feel her eyes on me, and didn't bother to hold back the smirk as I pulled my hair back, tie still dangling from my mouth.

"You're goddamn right it is! I'd be hard-pressed to find anyone worth a tumble around here that isn't your sloppy seconds these days, you handsome bastard."

I snorted, flashing Hans a wink as I re-tied the length of my hair back in a quick bun, pleased to have it out of my face—and to give the attractive Conduit more to ogle, should she be so inclined.

"Maybe I'll go introduce myself first, then," Jeremiah suggested. I knew from his tone that the man was joking, but something inside me still bristled at the implication. *Odd.*

"You're welcome to try," I replied breezily, shaking off that unusual flare of jealous energy. "Unlike Hans here, I don't mind sloppy seconds. Or thirds, for that matter."

The two men continued to volley jests and insults back and forth for the rest of the afternoon, most of them at my expense. Though I had indeed signed us all up for lecture duty as an excuse to observe the golden-eyed beauty I had encountered the other day, it was also just a nice excuse to give my men a break.

The growing number of disappearances across the continent was taxing on us all. It took a great deal of effort and coordination to retrieve intel from other territories while also covering our own tracks, making our work absolutely untraceable as we investigated the issue. It was important that if we meddled in the affairs of the Atlassian Houses, that we were *never*, ever caught doing so. The Elders would have our heads for breaking the terms of their treaties.

Much of my work operated under the principle of don't ask, don't tell—or, at the very least, that our ends had to justify the means—and so we worked hard behind the scenes. We made our cloak-and-dagger efforts count. My specialized forces were some of the most talented and efficient men on the Elder Guard, and we solved quite a few complex problems over the years behind the scenes.

Which is what made these disappearances all the more frustrating.

We hadn't figured out *shit*.

Weeks had turned into months now since the first child had been taken from Samhaven, and we *still* had no concrete evidence or solid leads. Even our above-ground efforts to collaborate with the other territories' military forces had proved useless thus far. It didn't help that most of them were bumbling fools, playing their part to wield a sword and look scary in exchange for a healthy salary. The continent hadn't seen war in decades.

Truth be told, I was exhausted. A day of monitoring the Wyldwoods, which were relatively safe these days, was a much needed breath of fresh air. Literally.

And then there was *her*...

The freshling was more of a figurative breath of fresh air, I supposed. It had been a long time since I felt so immediately attracted to a perfect stranger. For me, attraction often developed over a round of drinks and good conversation. I could find beauty in the mundane, so long as the mind was engaging and clever.

I had no idea whether this little Conduit was clever—or engaging, for that matter—and I didn't even know her name, much less her mind. Eventually, I would have to find an excuse to run into her in a less formal setting, because unless I legitimately stalked the woman, there wasn't much I could do with a physical description alone.

Not that I was entirely above the idea of stalking her from the Shadows... but no, not yet.

"You joining us at the tavern tonight, boss?" Jeremiah asked, interrupting my train of thought.

"He fuckin' better be! You still owe me a drink, Vistarii. I won that bet fair and square," Hans griped, pointing two fingers at his eyes and then one back towards me. Cute.

"Yeah, yeah, I'll be there. Go run a quick lap around the perimeter, will you?"

It wasn't really necessary. Don't get me wrong, the scholars had good reason to employ our services out here, but we weren't even a kilometer deep in these woods, and most of the dangers one might encounter were prowling around much, much deeper. I just needed to buy myself a little more time to be alone with my thoughts, and to catch a few more glimpses of the pretty little Conduit uninterrupted.

The two men groaned, and I gave them a charming smile in response.

"That *is* an order, you two. Get going."

As the two men left, I stole another glance at the girl with that glossy, dark brown mane out of the corner of my eye, only to find that she was already staring back at me.

Though she was on the complete opposite end of the clearing, I could've sworn I caught her blushing as she looked away.

Excellent.

CHAPTER ELEVEN

ARKEN

I kept thinking about that guardsman throughout the day, and I didn't like it.

Sure, he was devastatingly attractive, but he was hardly the first man that I'd ever set eyes on or even taken interest in since I'd arrived in Sophrosyne. Or woman, for that matter. There were thousands of people to encounter every day here, and plenty of them were attractive. I hadn't even spoken two words to this man. I didn't even know his name. Why did I want to know his name?

Gods.

This was absurd. I needed to go eat, or study, or *something*. Clearly, I was out of sorts.

As I made my way towards the dining hall, I busied my mind with thoughts of what I'd actually learned from the lecture.

Certain elements of aether were considered parallels to one another: Fire and Water, Air and Earth, Light and Shadow. These parallels made it easier to draw from one to produce the other, due to their opposing natures. Scholars believed this had something to do with where they fell on the known spectrum of aether. It was theorized that pure aether could be broken down into elemental... fractals? Shards? Something like that.

It was pure aether that flowed through our veins alongside

the blood, and so it was pure aether that we returned to the Source whenever we mortals passed on. The aether used in arcana, however, was but a fragmented version of this pure, primary source of power and life.

Professor Larkin had explained it better, but I had admittedly been distracted.

Essentially, what I knew from Amaretta was that elements were merely parts to a whole when it came to aetheric energy, and certain elements worked best together, the spellwork was stronger when you used them accordingly.

That wasn't to say that you couldn't draw from Fire to produce Earth arcana—aether was omnidirectional in that way. It was just easier to produce results by using parallels, and for mortals? We needed all the help we could get compared to the Aetherborne.

When I reached one of the dining halls on campus where the Studium offered basic daily fare for students, I was a bit bored with what they had available.

I was a bit bored in general, really. After the lecture in the Wyldwoods, Laurel had invited me out to some networking event at the Biblyos tonight, but I told her I had other plans. It was a lie, of course, but the idea of rubbing elbows with a bunch of sons and daughters of the noblesse made me itchy. I liked Laurel, but she felt more like an exception—almost everyone else that I had encountered so far had been more of the same from my experience on the ship. Not that I had exactly gone looking for anything beyond a few stray conversations with my classmates so far.

As I deliberated over the leafy, spinach-heavy main course, the sudden impulse struck me. Why not skip the salad offerings, and pass the remainder of my evening by partaking in one of my favorite hobbies instead? Obviously, I wasn't the most social of creatures, but I did love to observe others from afar. And it was a perfect night for people watching.

I knew there was a tavern just a few blocks south, so I took off in that direction, buzzing in anticipation.

It may sound like a dull thing, just watching other people go about their evenings. But I found it fascinating—particularly in new places, and Sophrosyne was still quite new to me. I had so many patterns, turns of phrase, and common habits to learn from the locals.

Perhaps I felt drawn to this as a hobby because I often felt so different, so other in comparison to... anyone else I knew. I had felt that way for most of my life, even before my strange Resonances had manifested—though if that didn't confirm it, I wasn't sure what else would.

It was as if I was missing one small, but integral piece of being a human. So it had become a habit, a game almost, to mirror certain behaviors and try to slip into some semblance of normalcy. If I could parrot those around me well enough, I could surely pass myself off as somebody perfectly average. Just another Conduit.

Nobody would suspect that I had something to hide. Nobody would suspect I was different. Not in the ways that mattered.

I wasn't about to go down that rabbit hole, though. To The Clover it was.

◆ ◆ ◆

When I reached the tavern, I knew I had made the right choice. It was toasty warm inside, with a blazing fire in the center hearth of the large room, filled to the brim with busy, raucous energy. Various groups of people shared flagons of ale amongst themselves, talking, laughing, dancing, arguing.

This was exactly what I was looking for. I made my way through the crowds to seek something other than spinach for my evening fare. Leaning over the counter to catch the attention of the barkeep, I ordered a simple meal of meat and potatoes, waiting to retrieve it before finding myself a small, unoccupied corner table and settling in. Over a slow sip of cider, I began my observations.

A burly man across the room was trying to impress an attractive older woman leaning against the wall, and I watched intently out of the corner of my eye. I had been caught staring one too many times in the past, so I had learned how to be subtle about it. The older woman was clearly skeptical, but not entirely disinterested in whatever it was the man had to say. Meanwhile, he was preening and overconfident, finding the subject at hand to be most impressive.

With enough practice, it was easy to read people like this. It showed up in the crook of a smile, the glimmer of an eye, whether they were leaning in or out, what direction they were oriented towards. Body language had always been fascinating to me, and I had grown rather skilled with its interpretation over the years.

I snorted under my breath when the burly man ordered himself a shot of liquor, only to set it aflame before taking it down. Why was I not surprised he was a Fire Conduit?

I had set my attention on the older woman, ready to interpret her particular reactions to the Fire Conduit's showboating, when suddenly someone bumped into my chair hard, leaving me eye level with their groin and cursing under their breath.

"So clearly, I was—ow, *fuck!*"

"Um, sorry?"

I could hardly see whoever stood before me because they were still so... close.

"No, no, that was my fault, I apologi— *Oh.*"

Oh?

I looked up at whoever was speaking.

Oh, indeed.

It was that damn guardsman. He was out of uniform, but I would recognize that face anywhere now. I nearly had it memorized. Gods, that was embarrassing to admit, even to myself.

"I would expect a captain of the Elder Guard to be a little more aware of his surroundings," I said with a sly smile, taking a sip of my drink.

He raised his eyebrows for a moment before returning the smirk and craning his neck towards the two men he'd been conversing with just a moment ago.

"I'll catch up with you two later," he called over his shoulder.

I glanced at both men behind him. They were the same pair that had been with him in the Wyldwoods, I was fairly certain—and now that I got a closer look, I had to admit that this trio was a sight to behold together. All handsome in their own right, though the captain still blew them both out of the water.

I definitely recognized the man on the left, with that rich, warm brown skin of his, the tidy goatee, and his dark brown hair that had previously been pulled back into a thick bun atop his head earlier this afternoon. Now that he let it loose, I could see that it was even longer than his captain's—the wavy, curling tips brushing the bottom of his ribcage. He was smirking now, green eyes twinkling with intrigue as he crossed his arms.

The taller man beside him carried himself differently. He was pale, and compared to his companions, he looked downright *ghostly*. Up close, I could see that his face was also littered with scars—but none so striking as the man who was still invading my personal space. There was a harsh one across the bridge of his nose, though, beneath stormy gray eyes that looked rather exasperated at present.

"You still owe me a drink, Vistarii," the first man said, rolling his eyes as if this was something that happened often.

The guardsman who they had just called Vistarii—*a last name, maybe?*—dug into his pockets, pulled out a single gold coin and flipped it towards the man who had complained.

"Enjoy it, Hans," he chuckled.

Great. His voice was attractive, too—all low and slow and deep. There was a slight rasp to it, as well, which I found obnoxiously sexy. As if the man needed any more advantages when he looked like *that*.

I couldn't help but notice he *still* hadn't moved away from where he'd bumped into me, so I was still uncomfortably close to his groin. And good gods, he was tall.

Once the other two men had headed off to the bar, the familiar guardsman finally took a step back, making it easier for me to see his face.

"Well hello there, Little Conduit," he started with a smile and a curious tilt of his head. "How do you know I'm a captain?"

Little Conduit?

I was hardly *little*, and besides, he didn't look all that much older than me. He had to be in his mid-to-late twenties at most. He could be slightly older if he was a Conduit. We aged slightly slower than the average human due to the higher amount of aether in our bodies.

I raised an eyebrow as he helped himself to the seat across from me, and answered his question with one of my own.

"How do you know that seat's not taken?"

He tilted his head again.

"Is it?"

"I mean, no, but—"

"Ah, so you're just changing the subject, then."

You know, I wasn't sure I particularly liked this man.

"I could tell based on your uniform," I explained, feeling like this should have been a little more obvious for someone of his rank and status. "Seems like a couple of those fancy tassels and pins indicate a position of leadership."

"That's a pretty specific detail to pick up on for a freshling. You must have been paying very close attention, considering I was several yards away from you the entire time."

"Freshling?" I asked him, ignoring the second implication and the smirk it had earned me.

"Fresh blood. Baby Conduit. First-year. You're brand-new to Sophrosyne, are you not?"

"Do you keep track of all the comings and goings of the members of the Studium? That sounds exhausting," I replied, mildly irritated by his suggestion that I was the equivalent of an infant.

"No, though I am very observant," he replied. "Besides, you were in an entry level lecture this morning. Jude was covering the basics. Even if you weren't paying much attention," he added with a wink.

He had a point there. He was also irritatingly perceptive. I sighed.

"I mean yes, I suppose you can say I'm still new here. I arrived about three weeks ago, but I'm also *very observant*," I replied, mimicking his tone.

"Clearly," he said, raising an eyebrow again. That glacial blue eye was drifting a bit, examining me as if he were taking my measure. I could feel my cheeks warm under his gaze.

"Last I checked though, not everyone here is a Conduit," I challenged.

"True, but the vast majority of us are. And almost anyone attending the Studium is. I'd put money on you being of the majority, as opposed to, you know, the less-than-one percent of the student body that is non-Resonant."

Us. So he was a Conduit as well. Interesting.

"That would seem like a safe bet, statistically speaking," I acquiesced, taking another sip of my cider.

"So I'm right then? You are a Conduit."

His smirk grew, as if he took a certain pleasure in being right. He did seem the type, honestly.

"Yes, of course I'm a Conduit!"

My reply came out more exasperated than I had intended, but surely he could reach such simple conclusions on his own. He gave me a cheeky grin again, as if he could tell he was irritating me. As if he was doing it on purpose.

"What kind, though?" he asked, looking amused and rather pleased with himself after my outburst.

"An observant one, apparently," I answered sardonically.

At that, he actually laughed—and I let myself appreciate the sound of it in spite of my vague annoyance. It reminded me of the low rumbles of thunder, if thunder could sound so inviting. The warmth in his expression after that laugh left me feeling just a hint more generous.

I raised one hand above the table, slowly wiggling a few fingertips and allowing the Light to flow forth and shimmer just long enough to answer his question, releasing it back into the aether before anyone else could notice. For a moment, his face went entirely slack, though he quickly recovered.

"Holy shit," he said. "So much for statistics, eh, Little Conduit? You are the definition of an outlier."

He wasn't wrong there, either. I had known that Light and Shadow Conduits were rare when I set sail for Sophrosyne, but it wasn't until I had actually arrived at the Arcane Studium that I began to grasp just how increasingly rare we had become over the last few centuries.

As a few scholars had already pointed out to me, there were only a handful of Shadow Conduits present in the city—and only one known Light Conduit, who split her time between Sophrosyne and the Astral & Umbral Isles, home to the House of Light & Shadow.

There were other Light Conduits in the world, of course—but it was just the two of us in Sophrosyne at any given moment, apparently. I had yet to meet her.

I ignored his question, which was clearly rhetorical.

"So, do you often find yourself tripping over chairs, joining people for their meals uninvited, and then asking them invasive questions without even introducing yourself?" I asked the stranger with an arched brow.

"My apologies, freshling," he offered with a slight, sarcastic bow of the head. "Kieran Vistarii, Scouting & Reconnaissance Captain of the Elder Guard, occasional babysitter of lectures, and local asshole who trips over the chairs of *very attractive* women. At your service."

"That's a bit of a mouthful."

"So I've been told," he purred, eyes glimmering with something wicked and alluring as that smirk slid back into place.

Gods. I was beginning to think that damned expression lived permanently on the man's irritatingly attractive face. It suited him well, though—curling up the left and exposing the slightest of dimples and his sharp jawline. And if he didn't think I caught that innuendo...

It's going to take more than that to make me blush, Captain.

I turned his name over in my head like a smooth stone, studying the way it fit him. *Kieran Vistarii*. Dark, alluring, intriguing.

"And you are...?"

"Arken," I answered, pretending not to be flustered by the compliment that had taken me an extra moment or two to process. *Tripping over the chairs of very attractive women?* I probably was blushing now. "Arken Asher."

"Well, it was a pleasure to meet you, Miss Asher. I really ought to be joining my men now before Jeremiah drinks Hans under the table and I have to carry that poor bastard home again. But I figured it was only fair to offer you some company in exchange for your forgiveness over my apparent lack of coordination," he said.

Did he really think several minutes of his time was such a gift that he could offer it as currency in exchange for his transgressions?

He was so cocky, but I held my tongue. Mostly because I liked it.

As he stood up and slid behind me in order to return to his friends, Kieran leaned over my shoulder.

"I do hope you enjoy your time here in Sophrosyne, Arken," he purred, his mouth dropping dangerously close to my ear.

That tone of his was far too explicit to be used without intention, and my toes might have curled a bit in my boots.

Fucking Hel.

"Thanks?"

I was too tongue-tied to think of something clever, and as he walked, or rather, sauntered off to the other side of the tavern, I could've sworn he was chuckling to himself. I felt a pang of regret, almost wishing that I had asked him to stay and join me for a drink.

Dangerous.

If I was lucky, that would be the last I'd see of this man for a while, because he'd essentially ruined my plans. No amount of people-watching would interest me more than Kieran Vistarii, but I would be damned if I let him catch me staring.

Again.

CHAPTER TWELVE

KIERAN

Jeremiah and Hans were absolutely howling with hysterics, slamming their palms against the table so hard that their flagons of ale threatened to spill over.

"She's the fucking *Light Conduit?!*" Hans cackled, wiping tears of laughter from his eyes. "Oh, I am so sorry about your dick, Captain, but that's too damn good."

"Keep your voices down, you drunk bastards," I growled.

The discovery had already put me in a foul mood. My favored game of seduction had just been cut terribly short by the realization that my commander might actually fucking murder me if I tried to take the most rare Conduit in Sophrosyne to bed.

Arken, she'd said her name was. Arken Asher. It was a lovely name for a lovely woman, and I found myself wanting to speak it out loud again just to savor the taste.

It was an effort not to groan in frustration and bang my head against the table as my lieutenants changed the subject, prattling on about some recent rumor that the House of Clay had, yet again, drawn the ire of the Zephirins.

This was supposedly the second clash between their Houses this month. What else was new, though? Drawing the ire of the House of Gales was neither difficult nor abnormal with Cecelia as their Lady. Kole was decent enough as a Lord, but his wife? That woman was a piece of work. I didn't make a habit of keeping up with the Atlassian Houses for several reasons these days, but I remembered that much from my father. This was hardly an interesting conversation.

My conversation with that Little Conduit, however...

Fates be damned.

A part of me almost wished that I hadn't met her now.

It had taken nearly all of my good sense to walk away from that table before inviting her to bed, and I'd nearly slipped up in the end. She was just so fucking alluring, and I didn't know what it was about her, but *damn*.

She really was beautiful, all big golden eyes and dark brown hair, pale skin, kissed with light freckles. That godsdamned mouth. I was immediately attracted to her when we'd first crossed paths near the Biblyos, unbeknownst to her. The attraction had only intensified from across the clearing back in the woods. But up close? *Fates above*, she was something else. A stunning little seraph—if a seraph could evoke such unholy thoughts.

I'd had to consciously, intentionally block myself from thinking about exactly what came to mind when she was looking up at me like that with those doe eyes from that particular... angle. And I certainly hadn't wanted to show my hand that early.

But beyond the immediate physical chemistry I felt around her, she was so godsdamned *clever*. Her mind was quick as a whip, immediately ready for the sort of banter that left me weak in the knees. Under any other circumstance, I would gladly allow this beautiful creature to be the death of me for a night.

Staying my hand and putting distance between us was for the best for a multitude of reasons. Yes, my commander would kick my ass from here to Samhaven if I made myself an enemy of someone we would likely have to keep tabs on in the future. But also, the last thing I needed, personally, was to piss off a woman who would likely acquire a great deal of power and influence among the Houses later in life.

Both Light and Shadow Conduits tended to end up in the spotlight in Atlas, in one way or another. I already had one enemy among those Lords and Ladies, and was not looking for another one. Arken hadn't necessarily seemed like an easy woman to piss off, per se, but she sure was easy to irritate. Playfully, of course. That had been fun.

A little *too* fun, because I wanted more.

Thankfully, I could take solace in the fact that avoiding her would be easy enough. I didn't have to worry about the dark desire I had to encircle her Light like a moth to a flame, even if it was growing stronger by the minute.

Silver linings, I supposed.

Is it though?

I wasn't in the mood to go there. It was time to find my next distraction.

CHAPTER THIRTEEN

ARKEN

The Fates were trying to kill me.

It wasn't even two days later that I found myself stumbling into a certain guardsman, yet again.

"Are you following me, Arken?"

That irritatingly attractive voice came out of nowhere as I'd been waiting in line for breakfast.

"Fuck!" I yelped, jumping out of my skin.

I had finally made my way back over to the bakery, with the intention of a croissant and maybe even one of those little pastries for later. I had been lost in a daydream when that low, gravelly purr returned right next to my ear again. Did this man have no concept of personal space whatsoever?

Gods above and below.

A chuckle that was already starting to sound familiar fell from his mouth as I whirled around to face him.

"My, my. Such language..."

His words were admonishing, but he was grinning, clearly amused by my reaction... or my profanity. I swore like a sailor more often than not. Amaretta hated it.

"Where do you even learn such foul language, Arken?" she'd often cluck irritably. *"Certainly not from me."*

No, not from her.

Not from anyone in particular, really. But even back home, I liked to watch people from a distance, observing the mundane little things they'd do and say when they thought nobody else was paying attention.

The stable hands, for example, often exchanged tales of their filthy exploits whenever they'd return from a night or two in the city. The men were hardly careful with their language when mucking out the stalls and describing their most recent rounds in the sack. Apparently in Elsweire, you could find women who offered their bodies in exchange for a fistful of Lyra, if you knew where to look. It was all a bit crude and vulgar.

Still, I liked the way certain words rolled off the tongue.

I shrugged at Kieran, who was still grinning at me like a fool. There was no use pretending that the curse had been an anomaly, and my vocabulary sure as Hel wasn't going to change any time soon with him sneaking up on me like that.

"You clearly came in here after I did, so who's really following who here?" I asked him pointedly.

"I think you've been scoping out my breakfast patterns. I come here almost every day."

"You must think awful highly of yourself if you think I'd go through all that trouble just to talk to you again."

"And yet here we are, talking again," Kieran said, flashing his oddly sharp teeth.

"Indeed. By sheer coincidence."

"So she claims," he chuckled again. He seemed to be in a particularly good mood this morning.

"Wouldn't it reflect rather poorly on you as the Scouting and Reconnaissance Captain if you could be so easily followed and monitored for your breakfast habits?" I asked.

"You've got me there, Little Conduit."

Ah, wonderful. That irritating nickname had stuck.

"I recommend the croissants, by the way," he added. "They're divine."

"I didn't ask, but I had already been planning on getting one, so don't get too excited when you see me taking your recommendation," I said, trying—and failing—to resist the urge to glance back at him.

Gods, he was attractive.

"It's too late now, I'm completely ecstatic," the guardsman replied, with an irritating glimmer of amusement in his eyes.

"You're completely demented," I replied, rolling my eyes.

"Such a rude mouth you have," he laughed. "It's impressive, really. What other tricks do you have up your sleeve, freshling? Or is it just your wicked tongue that sets you apart?"

"My tongue is not the only thing that—You know what? I'm not finishing that sentence," I hissed, getting the sense that I'd somehow walked into one of his traps.

He looked like he was about to keel over, laughing out loud in the middle of this tiny pastry shop. And yet again, I found myself disarmed by the sound of it. Of that welcoming rumble of thunder. The man was as dangerous and alluring as an aetherstorm.

After catching his breath, Kieran slipped past me, sauntering up to the counter to pick up a small brown box tied up with string. He must've ordered ahead.

"I told you, I'm a regular," he said with a wink, headed straight for the door. "Have a nice morning, freshling."

But naturally, the attractive guardsman added one more comment in passing on his way out. "You *and* that wicked tongue of yours."

Gods, I hated him.

✧ ✧ ✧

After picking up breakfast and surviving one particularly rude interruption, I made my way over to the Biblyos.

Earlier in the week, I made plans with a fellow Conduit from my Bios lectures, Laurel Ansari, to get together for a study session. Though I typically preferred to study alone, I liked Laurel. After the lecture in the Wyldwoods, the charming, extroverted Earth Conduit had made a habit of sitting next to me in class, often making sly but good-natured jokes under her breath that made me bite the insides of my cheeks to avoid laughing out loud. Poor Scholar Larkin.

"Change of plans, Asher," Laurel informed me as soon as I found her on the front steps, tossing her mane of bouncy black curls over her shoulder and flashing me a wicked grin as I walked up to her. "It's far too nice out to spend all afternoon inside studying plants."

I could hardly disagree. It was rarely this warm, this late in autumn—or at least it hadn't been back home. It was more likely for Atlas to see early cold fronts than this balmy breeze. My classes this week felt empty, as if half of my fellow Conduits had taken off early for a weekend on the Pyrhhan Coast.

"That so? What are we up to today, then, Miss Ansari?" I asked, amused.

"Mischief and nonsense."

See, this was why Laurel and I got along.

"Any particular flavor of mischief?"

Laurel reached into her bag and pulled out a dark green bottle. "Strawberry."

I snorted. "Day drinking it is."

In all honesty, I felt a tinge of relief. I felt comfortable enough around Laurel so far, but a hint of alcohol in my system often helped me loosen up around the presence of others. A light buzz was a balm against my social anxieties, and that strange sense of inhuman otherness that so often plagued me in groups.

"Don't forget the nonsense," Laurel added.

"How could I possibly?" I laughed. "What nonsense are we up to this afternoon?"

"How opposed are you to heights? And a bit of harmless breaking and entering?"

"Color me intrigued," I replied with a grin. I was in—so long as we didn't get caught.

"I knew I liked you, Lightbearer. C'mon," she said, tugging at my hand and taking off towards the back entrance of the Biblyos. "I'll show you my secret route."

As it turned out, Laurel's "secret route" involved the two of us sneaking through a restricted floor, climbing up some questionable looking scaffolding, and trying not to laugh every time the bottles clinked together in Laurel's bag. Because of course she brought two.

Once we got ourselves situated up on the rooftop of the Biblyos, Laurel spread out a small blanket and sat down, stretching out her legs and motioning me to join her.

"The view is great and all, Asher, but if you gawk on the ledge for too long we're gonna get our asses caught. Come, come. Let us sunbathe and get drunk."

I would have to be cautious about the *drunk* part of that plan. Tipsy, maybe—but sometimes when I got too inebriated, my Resonances would start to get a smidge too comfortable. The ones I normally kept hidden got tempted to come out and play. I'd had one too many close calls in the Brindlewoods, back when I was still learning my limits—and it was sheer dumb luck that I never got caught. I liked Laurel, but that didn't mean I could trust her with this. I couldn't trust *anyone* with this.

I watched with a little bit of awe as Laurel twirled her fingertips over the neck of the first bottle of wine, the cork simply popping out with ease.

"Earth Conduit, remember?" she laughed. "Corks are made

out of bark. Or something."

"Convenient," I said with a smile, taking a seat beside her.

"It's a neat little party trick. Here's hoping I learn how to do some things that are *slightly* more useful while I'm here, though."

"What's your area of focus?" I asked, taking that first thread for potential conversation and artfully weaving it away from myself. "Arcana?"

"Trade," Laurel replied with a grimace.

"Not your first choice, I take it?"

"I mean, if I had it my way, my only field of study would be *women*," Laurel said with a sly smile.

"But I'm the eldest daughter of the Ansari family. The eldest child. And so I'm expected to take up my father's mantle as the High Advisor of Trade to Lord Ymir one day."

"Oh! You're from Samhaven, too?"

"Yup. Yvestra. You?"

Ah, it would make sense for the Ansari family to live in the capital city if her father worked in the House of Torrents.

"The Brindlewoods."

"No shit? Like one of those small villages out there?" Laurel asked, curiosity clearly piqued.

Most people in Sophrosyne didn't know villages like mine even existed.

"Mhmm," I said, pausing to take a swig of strawberry wine—pleased to find that it was sparkling. I loved the feel of effervescence on my tongue. "Exactly."

"Wow. What was *that* like?"

"Quiet," I mused. "Slow."

"Gods, I bet. No wonder you scampered off to Sophrosyne. Did you just need an escape from the boredom?"

Something like that.

Now didn't feel like the right time to delve into the nuance and complexity of the feelings that brought me here.

"Basically," I replied instead.

"Well, I'll drink to that," Laurel said, pulling the second bottle of wine out and popping the cork with ease. "Cheers to reckless escapism, my friend."

"Hey now," I countered. "Who said it was reckless?"

"You followed a strange, charismatic woman on a quest to get drunk on the roof of the Biblyos. I'd say you have a bit of a reckless streak."

"Gods, Ansari," I laughed. "Give a girl some warning before you read her for filth."

But she certainly wasn't wrong.

"It takes one to know one," Laurel explained with a wink. "Though, speaking of filth... Have you taken a tumble with the sexy guardsman yet?"

"Who, Kieran?"

"Oooh, *Kieran*. Of course the bastard would have a sexy name, too. So I take that as a yes?"

I rolled my eyes. "No. I did run into him this morning at the bakery, though. I regret to inform you that he is still devastatingly attractive."

"And you haven't taken him home yet because...?" Laurel asked, flicking a pebble at my forehead with irritating accuracy. Damned Earth Conduits.

"First of all, that's the second time I've even had a face to face interaction with the man," I argued. "Second of all..." I trailed off.

"Girl. Don't tell me its nerves. I saw the way he was looking at you in the Wyldwoods. He wants you. Like, *bad*."

Did he?

You and that wicked tongue of yours...

Maybe.

"I mean, it's not necessarily nerves so much as..."

"As what? Spit it out, Asher," Laurel prodded. "I need to know this. For science. Consider this me studying Bios. The mysteries of human willpower, if you will."

I sighed. "I haven't slept with anyone since my ex, back home."

"Ah, I see. Sounds like there's some baggage with that one?"

"With Grays?" I sighed, running one hand through my hair. "Absolutely. I'm pretty sure she still hates me."

"*Grays*, eh? That's a femme name. Am I to believe Miss Asher goes both ways, then?" Laurel smirked.

I grinned. "I most certainly do."

"A victory for all the sapphics in Sophrosyne, honestly," Laurel replied, raising her bottle as if it were a toast. "But, apologies. I got us off track. The Grays situation—you wanna talk about it?"

Not particularly, I thought to myself. I generally tried to *avoid* thinking about Graysen. Everything about that breakup had been inevitable. And everything about it had been my fault.

"Nah, not really. It's old news at this point. But I'm also not looking for a relationship any time soon."

"Fair enough. I'm not much for long term commitments either," Laurel replied easily. "I fully plan to sample my way through the city... For now, at least."

"Just for now?"

"Yeah, well. My parents are still Hel-bent on trying to set me up with an 'advantageous marriage.' Archaic fucks. My father apparently has some loose agreement with the Lord of Clay that I might marry his heir, Anders—with the right trade agreements in place."

"Gross."

"Yeah. I was so annoyed about him springing that shit on me the day before I left, trying to sell me off like cattle. I didn't even bother telling him that if I had to settle down with a fucking Cragg, it would be *Hanna*—not Anders."

"Would that bother him?" I frowned. Same sex pairings were almost as common as heterosexual relationships, especially among the noblesse.

"Nah, I just didn't want to encourage the auctioning of my own agency. I'm sure Mama will course correct that eventually. And on the bright side, Hanna Cragg is hot as Hel."

"I do like a woman who has her priorities straight," I cackled.

"Only damn thing that's straight about me," Laurel agreed, clinking her bottle against mine.

Maybe an hour or so worth of casual conversation and quippy remarks passed us by until Laurel and I both fell asleep, lazing around like cats in the sun. I stirred first, though—and decided to let her rest just a little while longer. Meanwhile, I meandered over to the edge of the building again, my mind wandering through the haze of strawberry wine and the balmy breeze.

Life in Sophrosyne was... different from what I had expected. Back home in the Brindlewoods, I had pictured myself a shut-in, furiously thumbing through books and researching all day and night. Before I set sail for the City of the Gods, my intentions had felt so singular:

Find out who—or *what*—I really was.

I certainly hadn't pictured myself making fast friends, flirting with dangerous and alluring men, and getting drunk on rooftops. But maybe this was what I actually needed, for now. A sense of belonging. Something I'd never quite found for myself, even back home... because I was born alone.

According to Amaretta, they found me in the woods. Alone, abandoned as an infant, in the middle of the night on a full moon. Somewhat unusual, sure—but she told me people abandoned their children all the time for a multitude of reasons. Shame, poverty, fear.

"It wasn't your fault, Arken. This world can be cruel to new parents, especially those of lower stations. We don't know their story, but I do know this: *It wasn't your fault.*"

If only I believed her.

If only the circumstances of my birth were the strangest, most mysterious thing about me. Perhaps if that were the only damning evidence surrounding my existence, I could have been content to stay home, comfortable with our slow and quiet life in the woods. But it was not—and I never had been. Because I was born alone, I was born hungry, and I was born... *different*.

There was something wrong with me. Something dangerous.

My Light Resonance manifested first, but it came too early, and it was too strong. I had barely been a toddler when I had first displayed signs of being a strong Resonant, my chubby little fingertips glowing every time I wanted something from my surrogate mother. Precocious, she'd called me. That's how she had explained it to the others, too. Light Resonance was rare these days, and perhaps it just manifested a little differently from the other elements. It's not like the people of the Brindlewoods had much of a frame of reference.

To this day, Light was still my strongest aetheric bond. It was what came naturally to me, my default wellspring of arcana. But it was not the only one.

Perhaps it was a gift from the Fates that my other Resonances didn't manifest until I was old enough to understand how to hide them. Fire came first, then Air, when I was eleven. Earth and Water showed up within the week I turned twelve, and finally, Shadow. On the day I turned thirteen.

It had only taken me one glance at the sheer terror in my mentor's eyes that day to understand that this secret of mine was a dangerous one. And Amaretta confirmed it the moment she made me promise to keep it hidden... to keep them *all* hidden. Everything except the Light. She couldn't explain why, not in full. Something about the tattoo on her wrist, she'd said, kept her bound to secrecy on certain matters. They were typically things that related to the complexities of arcane science. I understood that, now, glancing down at my own wrist, where the arcane brand glistened in the sun.

I just wish I understood the rest.

I did know one thing though. My priorities were starting to shift. There was still a hunger in my heart, a desperate thirst for any and all knowledge I could get my hands on about aether, arcana, and Resonance. I didn't think I would ever truly escape that need, that thirst for answers... the craving had just been dulled. Sated by something else.

But I had also realized that the pull, the tug that I had felt, drawing me away from home and into the unknown in the first place... it hadn't just been the abandonment wound, or my lack of self-identity. Beyond needing answers, I had just been craving bigger and better things. Craving *more*.

And *gods*, Sophrosyne was more.

Every day, I found something new to fall in love with about the city. Slowly, but surely, I was coming out of my shell, stepping into the person I had been too afraid to reveal in the Brindlewoods because there had been no one else like me. Not just because of my secrets, either. Here, I was surrounded by similarities—surrounded by potential. The burden of my secret felt less heavy surrounded by so many like-minded individuals, by so much knowledge and history and art and *Resonance*.

I glanced back at Laurel, who had thankfully rolled over in her sleep. Even her deep golden skin was prone to burn, though, and she was tempting the Fates at this point. I got up from my perch, and went over to poke her with my wiggling toes.

"Pssst. *Laurel*. Wake up. I may be a Light Conduit, but I can't control the sun. You're frying like a fish, woman."

Laurel groaned, flicking a pebble at me with astounding accuracy yet again.

"Fine, fine—suit yourself. I'm sure you look good in red," I teased, tossing the pebble back.

"What if I had been dreaming about your sexy guardsman, hmm? The cruelty to just wake me up from such bliss!"

I burst out laughing. "Oh my gods, were you really?"

"No, I was dreaming about Hanna Cragg."

"Of course you were."

"*Hey!*" a third, unfamiliar voice shouted out, interrupting our conversation. "What the actual Hel are you two doing up here?"

Oh, fuck.

CHAPTER FOURTEEN

KIERAN

I absolutely loathed dealing with the Lord of Embers.

If my random encounter with Arken at the bakery had been the highlight of my day, this was essentially the very opposite. Another child had gone missing, this time from Pyrhhas, and the figurehead of Atlassian leadership had just arrived at our doorstep to discuss the matter.

Fucking phenomenal.

I had several bones to pick with Lord de Laurent, leader of the Atlassian Courts and the House of Embers, but first on my list was how he'd just strutted into the Elder Guard headquarters today like he owned the damn place.

It was true that Sophrosyne was embedded right within the heart of Pyrhhas. His territories touched every edge of our borders—but we were still an independent entity. The Courts ruled over every square inch of Atlas *except* this city-state, and yet he still waltzed in here, carrying himself with that same presumptuous authority that he always did, demanding to speak with High General Demitrovic.

"I'm afraid that won't be possible, Milord," Commander Ka replied. "General Demitrovic is en route to Ithreac to speak with the Lord of Clay about *their* disappearances."

"Unfortunate," de Laurent replied. "Is there anyone else I can speak with on the matter? I would like to know the latest details. Anything that I can brief the Pyrhhan Guard about to help tighten security would be appreciated."

"Our Scouting Captain is probably the most knowledgeable on the current state of things, sir," Hanjae explained, and I blanched. "Vistarii! Come, brief Lord de Laurent on the latest we have on Jerricks and Gillespie."

Oh, godsdamnit.

Even from the second floor alcove where I currently stood, I could see de Laurent's lip curl with disdain. That motherfucker *hated* me.

The feeling was mutual.

"Certainly, Commander. I'll be down in just a moment."

As I came up behind de Laurent and his attendants, I shot Hanjae a dirty look. Commander Ka didn't like the leader of the Atlassian Courts any more than I did, and this was definitely his way of avoiding spending any more time with him than necessary.

I ran the High Lord through all of the latest information my men had gleaned about the disappearances, keeping things mostly surface level and taking care to avoid revealing any of our sources that might draw suspicion to just how deep my network of spies ran across the continent. Still, the intel I was providing would be of use to his men. I had no interest in seeing the people of Pyrhhas suffer, regardless of my personal feelings about their lord.

To his credit, he and his men asked clarifying questions and managed to keep things respectful, despite their obvious discomfort as tension crackled between us.

That was, until we wrapped things up in the war room and I prepared to take my leave. As his assistant began to gather up their maps and notes from the meeting, the pale, regal looking man turned towards me and leaned in close.

"Oh, and for the record, Captain," he hissed under his breath.

"I'm well aware of the state you and your men left one of my citizens in before his release. Whether Corvus is convicted in the future or not, it would serve you well to know your place."

My palms prickled, eager to show the arrogant asshole exactly where my place was, should we ever go toe to toe again. But I kept my temper in check, not in the mood to get flayed alive by my commander for assaulting an honorary High Scholar of the Arcane Studium... especially considering he was arguably the most powerful man in Atlas. Even if he was an over-privileged little prick.

◆ ◆ ◆

The whiplash between my serendipitous encounter with Arken and my less-than-fortunate foray with the Lord of Embers left me feeling vaguely unmoored for the rest of the afternoon. There was a strange taste in my mouth. A familiar restlessness. An urge to escape.

Fuck it. You've got time to kill.

Sometimes, it was a comfort to simply slip back into the Shadows. I had a number of quiet, hidden places throughout the city where I could easily disappear and observe, and I often chose to do so whenever I was feeling... *off*, like this.

One of my favorites, though, was not a place that I had discovered, so much as one that I had *created*—and had done so before I ever became a guard. Back when I was still studying at the Arcane Studium, my brother and I used to climb an old, gnarled oak tree. It just so happened to be near the Elder Guard's headquarters, but tucked away snugly against one of the city walls. The ancient oak was tall enough that you could see nearly half of the Administrative Quarter, if you knew where to sit.

Though my brother and I were no longer on speaking terms, I

still came back here from time to time. Something about it helped clear my head—and godsdamn, did my head need clearing right about now.

My mind was a seasick, swimming cocktail of frustration and temptation. Lord de Laurent never failed to raise my hackles.

It would serve you well to know your place.

The urge to wring his pale, pedigreed neck had yet to fade, so I focused on the lesser of two evils: The temptation.

After discovering that the freshling from the Wyldwoods was the godsdamned Light Conduit, I had resolved myself to leave her the fuck alone. Hanjae had made himself clear: A new Light Conduit in Sophrosyne was a big deal. There hadn't been one in over twenty years, and some scholars had even started to fret that Light Resonance was a dying gift. Shadow Resonance was rare, too—but not like that. There were at least a handful of new Shadow Resonants who turned up every year to take their entry trials. But Light Resonants? Practically unheard of in my time here. It was no wonder the Elders themselves had requested we keep an eye on this one.

If only she weren't so easy on the eyes. *Gods*, she was gorgeous. I had tried to forget it, honestly. But then I had to go and run into Arken at the bakery this morning. And the moment I was in that woman's presence again, I forgot all about my endeavor to avoid her. I had been drawn in yet again, and that string of profanity she let loose when I startled her? Source be damned.

Arken fucking Asher.

It was far too much fun to tease her. Watching that pretty, filthy mouth of hers twist in irritation was just...

The musky scent of wyldweed drifted past, distracting me from my wicked reveries before they could even begin. That was probably for the best. I really, really needed to leave that poor woman alone.

A pair of younger guardsmen had just strolled up to the tree at a lackadaisical pace. I didn't recognize them, which meant they weren't in my unit, so I resisted the urge to bark at them both when I realized they were the source of that dank stench, exchanging hits off a joint, clearly attempting to remain unseen.

"Pretty ballsy if you ask me," one of them was saying with a smirk, in between a deep inhale. As he spoke again, wisps of blue-green smoke bled from his mouth. "I'd expect that shit from a more tenured student, not a pair of bright-eyed, pretty little freshlings."

I rolled my eyes. They had better be on break.

"So they were just up on the fuckin' roof of the Biblyos?"

"Drunk off their asses, apparently."

The pair chuckled, and I raised a brow. I wasn't sure why either of them found this to be newsworthy information. It was an unseasonably nice day, with half of the Studium already running off to the beach for the week's end. It was hardly a surprise to hear that those who remained were getting up to some nonsense. Although, the Biblyos? That was kind of impressive.

The massive library was probably one of the tallest structures in the city. How the Hel did a couple freshlings manage to get up there?

"Oh, wait, fuck—you missed the best part, Kent," the guardsman crowed. I pocketed the name away in my mind for reference later. "You're not gonna believe this, but according to Andrea, one of the culprits? The brunette one we saw? That was the fucking Light Conduit."

Immediately, I sat up from where I had been leaning lazily, shifting myself forward. Arken had done *what now*?!

"No shit? Girl's been here for what, a month? Sounds like trouble, that one."

They had no idea.

In one fell swoop, I leapt from my perch in the tree, landing gracefully to the left of these idiot gossips and startling the ever-living shit out of them both. They recognized me on sight and immediately started scrambling to hide the joint.

"Hello, boys," I said with a wolfish grin.

"Shit!" Kent muttered. "I mean, uhh—Greetings, Captain Vistarii!"

"*Greetings*," I parroted, letting my eyes narrow for show. Just to make them sweat a little bit.

"I don't think that I need to remind you two that smoking in uniform is *strictly prohibited* by the code of conduct, do I?"

"No, sir," the other man stammered out. "Apologies, sir, it won't happen again."

"Consider yourselves lucky that you're not one of mine. I'll cut you both a break this time," I said evenly. "Under one condition."

For whatever reason, that offer seemed to make them *even more* anxious, and my grin widened.

"Err, what's that, sir?" Kent asked uneasily.

"The freshlings you two were talking about. Which holding cells does Andrea have them in?"

"Uhh, they're at the Eastern Gates, I think?" Kent said, looking confused. "Why?"

"Don't you worry your pretty little head about that, Kent," I replied easily. "Now put the godsdamned joint out and get your asses back to post."

"Yes, sir!" the pair chanted, looking both shocked and relieved as I took my leave, headed towards the Eastern Gates.

Ten minutes later, I was breezing down the stairs of the eastern city walls. I had no good reason to be here, honestly—except the errant hope that our little criminals had not been released quite yet. Even so, this was a direct contradiction of my resolution to stay away from Arken...

It might have been a weak resolution to begin with.

We had a number of temporary holding cells scattered throughout the city, intended to quickly and safely remove threats from the public eye when necessary. In all likelihood, the two Conduits had already been released with a firm slap on the wrist and maybe a note on their student records, but on the off chance they weren't...

I nodded to one of the guards as I passed through, rounding the corner, and then I heard a vaguely familiar voice.

"This is such bullshit," a woman who was decidedly *not* Arken was moaning. "Since when is having a nice little picnic in the sunshine against the laws and regulations of the Studium?"

My lip quirked when I saw Andrea cough, attempting to mask her snort of disbelief.

And that's when I heard her laugh—sparkling, melodic, and sweet.

"I think when the 'picnic' is really just several bottles of wine, and the 'sunshine' in question is acquired via breaking and entering, *Laurelena*," Arken replied sarcastically. "Namely the breaking and the entering. We *did* climb up some questionable scaffolding."

Gods, I liked her snark.

Andrea saw me out of the corner of her eye and began to turn, but I shook my head in silence, pressing a single finger against my lips. I was enjoying this banter of theirs.

"I think certain laws should have exceptions when the weather's this nice," Laurel responded. "Can they really blame us for wanting to take advantage of the heat wave?"

"Oh, brilliant, Ansari," Arken laughed. "Have you considered going into politics? I think you might have a knack for sensible policy-making."

"And I think you might have a knack for getting yourself into trouble, Little Conduit," I purred as I made my overly-staged entrance.

It was an effort to keep a straight face as I caught Arken's eye through the bars. The utter disbelief on her face was hilarious.

"Go ahead and release Miss Ansari, here, Andrea," I ordered smoothly. "And escort her back to the Student's Quarter."

"Yes, sir. And the other?"

"Oh, I would like Miss Asher to remain for some additional questioning. I can take it from here, though. You can return to your scheduled post."

Andrea shrugged, knowing better than to question a superior officer, and proceeded to unlock the cell and guide Laurel Ansari towards the exit. She handed the key off to me after closing the barred gate again, and once her back was turned, I couldn't help but flash a smirk. Arken's eyes narrowed.

I waited for a few moments, simply staring back at the little Conduit in silence until I was certain Andrea was out of earshot.

"Well, well, well," I finally said, leaning up against the bars. "Somebody's got a rebellious streak."

"You have got to be fucking kidding me," Arken groaned. There was that tongue again, wicked as ever.

"Additional questioning? Really, Vistarii?"

"*Captain* Vistarii," I corrected. "And it's just protocol. You are a criminal, after all. You could be dangerous for all I know."

"If you don't already know, I have to question whether or not you have the skills to support your title, *sir*," Arken spat.

I had to disregard the way hearing that last part of the sentence made me feel if I had any hopes of remaining coherent.

"My, my, Miss Asher. A filthy mouth and sharp teeth? I do like that in a woman."

"And would you like to know what *I* would like, Captain?" Arken asked. Her voice was excessively sweet and delightfully saccharine, tilting her head with wide eyes—false innocence. Oh, she was *so* annoyed with me already.

"Absolutely, I would," I replied with a grin.

In more ways than one.

"I would like to not be stuck in a holding cell for some arrogant bastard's amusement. Pray tell, what sort of stupid questions do you need to ask me before I can return to my previously pleasant afternoon?"

I bit down on the inside of my cheek in an effort to avoid laughing out loud.

"Give me a moment to think," I mused, tapping my chin.

"A moment to think? About what, exactly?!"

"What sorts of stupid questions I should ask you, of course," I replied.

"Are you serious right now?"

Good *gods*, she was easy to rile up.

"What's your favorite color?" I asked, pretending not to hear her.

"I don't have one," she groaned, tossing her head back against the limestone, eyes rolling toward the ceiling.

"Pick one."

"I don't know, black?"

Unexpected, but I could work with that. Being irritating was one of my many talents.

"If we're being technical, black is not a color. It's the absence of color."

Arken just stared incredulously for a moment, blinking as if she wasn't certain I was real. Surely she wasn't that drunk.

"Green, then," she said, finally.

"Phenomenal. While we're on the subject, do you prefer green grapes, or red?"

"I'd prefer you to be at the bottom of the godsdamned Western Sea right now."

So fiesty.

"Please answer the question, Miss Asher," I said with faux seriousness. "This is simply protocol."

"I don't like red grapes," she said.

"Just red wine?"

"It was strawberry wine, thank you very much," she replied primly.

A vague flash of irritation passed through my mind, prompting my next question.

"And what, *pray tell*, gave you and Ansari the genius idea of getting drunk on the top of one of the tallest buildings in Sophrosyne? Do you have a death wish?"

"Errant impulse," Arken said with a shrug.

"There are better ways to feed your reckless streak, you know," I informed her.

"Just as I am sure there are better ways for you to be spending your time this afternoon, Captain," she replied coolly.

"Oh, I'm not so sure about that," I chuckled. "I'm having a great time. Did you enjoy the croissant earlier?"

"No. It was terrible."

I could tell from her posture and the slightest shift in her expression that Arken was just being stubborn now.

"Oh, you're an awful liar, Little Conduit," I crooned through the bars. "It's kind of cute though. Does your nose always scrunch up like that when you lie?"

She let out a heavy, exasperated sigh, rubbing at her temple.

"Headache?"

"I'm fine."

"Please tell me that you ate more than just that damned croissant before downing a bottle of wine on a rooftop," I groaned.

"Unfortunately, I've just been informed that I'm a bad liar, so… can't help you there, Cap." Arken muttered.

My gaze darkened.

"Look, if you're going to be a degenerate in my city, can you at least use some common sense? Alcohol, heights, and an empty stomach don't play nice together."

"I was hardly even tipsy," she argued.

"Yeah? How's your head feeling right about now?" I

countered.

"Funnily enough, this headache only began when you showed up."

I couldn't help it, I had to laugh. I would have to let her go soon, because the woman clearly needed to go get some food and water in her system, but I found myself hesitating. Selfishly craving just a little bit more time in her presence.

"What's your favorite number?"

"Thirteen."

Interesting.

"Oho, you answered that one quickly, Miss Asher. Any particular reason?"

Her expression clouded for a moment, and then hardened. She clearly knew the answer, but she wasn't going to tell me.

"Nope."

Thought so.

"Well, for what it's worth, that's my favorite number, too."

"Congratulations," she muttered sardonically.

I leaned over and unlocked the cell door, offering an exaggerated bow as I swung it open, allowing her to walk free.

And it took damn near all of my willpower not to offer her an escort home—if only because it would be far, far too tempting to watch her from the Shadows afterwards. After that whole exchange, I couldn't trust myself to behave.

Arken glared at me as she pushed herself up from the bench, though she held my gaze even as she started to walk away.

"Behave yourself, Little Conduit," I called out, smirking as she turned to take her leave.

Arken simply tossed her hair, the dark brown waves swishing past her shoulder blades, and offered me a smirk of her own.

"No promises, Captain."

Trouble, indeed.

CHAPTER FIFTEEN

ARKEN

I was developing a newfound appreciation for the subject of Arcane History.

After over a month in Sophrosyne, it came as no surprise to me that my preference of study had been in the more practical subjects thus far—I was a tactile learner, and making legitimate use of my Resonances was significantly more engaging.

Even though I had only learned the very basics of arcana so far, everything that I was learning to do with Light, I was able to replicate with the other elements—my hidden Resonances—in the privacy of Amaretta's studio. It had been exhilarating to see what I could do with just a little bit of guidance and technique.

Though I had always enjoyed reading historical texts back home, now that I had a taste for arcana, I was finding most of my courses on things such as history, Bios, and anthropology to be a bit dry in comparison. But today, I was enraptured, utterly engrossed as High Scholar Sykes spoke on a subject that I had been wholly unaware of for my entire life: the history of the Cataclysm.

Before the scholar had began our lecture, she explained that what we were about to learn qualified as knowledge exclusive to the Studium—and sure enough, when I glanced down at my wrist, I could see the silver tattoo begin to glow with that strange

Aetherborne arcana, a spell with complexity beyond my novice understanding.

"Today, young Conduits, you will learn about a great sacrifice," Scholar Sykes began. "And a truth that is not kept concealed for the sake of posterity or control, but rather the overall safety of Aemos and her people. You will most certainly have questions, but I ask that you hold on to them for the latter half of the session, when we break out into discussion groups."

Over the course of the next hour, High Scholar Sykes wove a tale so intricate and beautiful that it almost felt as though it was a sort of faerie-tale, not a true recounting of history as we knew it.

According to the mythos of the creation of mankind, the Elders loved us deeply, and by default—because we were their children, after all. But beyond the fact that our species had been born mortal after some strange circumstance of evolution, we were also *different* from the Aetherborne—and they loved us for that, too.

Our lives were shorter, and thus we were more ephemeral creatures by nature. In time, the Elders discovered that the first humans were far more emotional, passionate, and creative than their progenitors—within their shortened lifespans, they innovated, they explored, they created art and music and laughed and screamed and cried and *loved*, all so viscerally.

In their own immortality, the Aetherborne had grown stagnant as a species, having a tendency to crystallize over the eons. It made sense, when you thought about it. With enough time to experience anything and everything this plane of existence had to offer, one might begin to lose that inherent curiosity and thirst for *more*. Such was so with the Aetherborne, where even the most exhilarating emotions and experiences had grown blunted, dulled over time.

And then we mortals came along, all loud and bumbling and breakable—and we reminded them of a youth long forgotten. As an inadvertent consequence of our birth, we'd restored humanity to the realm of Aemos, and thus we were named: Humans.

In those earlier days where Aetherborne and mankind were more equal in number, they had collectively decided to watch over us. They were our protectors as the human species began to grow and develop, because they thought we were worth protecting. They did not find our mortality to be a flaw, but rather quite the opposite. Aemos had always been considered the Plane of Life, and to them, we were symbols of that more fleeting, cyclical vitality.

It was that desire to protect us that led to the formation of the Convocation.

Several hundred years after the birth of humankind, the Cataclysm took place. There was a great, unnatural upheaval of aether that occurred as a result of a lack of balance. For everything that humans offered that was beautiful and good, we were also deeply flawed. As our population exploded, so did the growth of senseless war, violence and death. The plane struggled to preserve itself in our wake, and the Cataclysm began—leaving Aemos on the brink of ruin.

The aetherstorms that occurred as a result of this expedited cycle of life and death caused chasms to form between the very planes of existence. Rifts tore from the void space in between realms—from the Abyss—and summoned forth beasts and plague and chaos that even the gods did not know how to handle.

When all seemed lost, and the threat of extinction of both species seemed inevitable, it was said that the Source herself intervened. The Aetherborne experienced a moment in time referred to as "The Awakening"—an otherworldly connection of every living mind and soul of the immortals, which allowed them to collectively decide how to save us all.

Together, the gods determined that in order to close the chasms and restore balance to the plane, a majority of the Aetherborne's arcane power would need to be condensed and shifted into the hands of a select few. Somehow, the majority of the surviving Aetherborne conceived a method to give up most of their aether, and thus their *immortalities*, just so that they could amplify the strength of those who had been selected to deliver our realm to safety.

The methods used were understandably kept secret and even though this information was guarded by our arcane brands, the scholar did not go into detail about how it had been done. Perhaps even she did not know. Either way, that transfer of aether dramatically increased the power of its recipients, allowing nineteen souls to quell the calamities that were threatening to end all life on Aemos. They were able to mend the tears between worlds with pure aether, temporarily wielding the true powers of Creation as if they were extensions of the Source itself.

Those nineteen Aetherborne were the very same who served on the Convocation to this day. The Elders that I stood before on the day of my trial were the very ones who saved the world, built the Studium, and led mankind into an era of innovation and safety.

I could understand, now, how religion must have developed over time, though I was a secularist myself. It made sense that some still worshiped the Aetherborne as gods, imagining them to be omnipotent, exalted beings. It was hard not to be awestruck—emotional, even—over just how much our forefathers had sacrificed just to ensure our survival. And perhaps the immortals could have survived the Cataclysm, but the humans most certainly would not have.

It was easier, now, to understand the intent and the inherent selflessness behind the Arcane Studium. To understand why the Nineteen would still be so willing to teach us, to offer such free and fair access to their knowledge.

After all they had given us, after all they had lost—the Aetherborne didn't want humankind to simply survive.

They wanted us to *thrive*.

✧ ✧ ✧

The discussions with my peer group after the lecture were less than satisfactory.

A majority of the other Conduits seemed appreciative of this new revelation, at least *slightly* grateful for it—but very few of them appeared to be as moved by the gravity of it all. A few were even skeptical, suggesting that High Scholar Sykes spoke with a little too much reverence on the subject, biased in favor of the Aetherborne.

I knew that history was biased—always written by the victors—but if the Aetherborne wanted to be worshiped or admired for what they had done, why would they keep the knowledge of what happened restricted to attendees of the Studium?

I had never fully understood why many humans seemed to have this slight, lingering resentment towards the Elders. Was it envy? Or misunderstanding?

I also continued to ponder over the philosophy behind it all, questioning whether or not we as a species had given enough back to the Elders or to Aemos as a whole. A majority of us had no idea what our lives, our futures, our potential—what it had all cost our living predecessors.

Would that change anything, if it were common knowledge? Would we live differently, if we understood how fragile existence truly was?

I was so lost in thought as I made my way through the halls that I didn't notice that someone had stopped right in front of me until it was too late—I ran straight into them, dropping my texts and notebook in the process.

Well, that was embarrassing, I thought to myself before I

opened my mouth to apologize to whoever I'd just run over.

Once I saw who it was, however, the apology dissolved on my tongue.

Seriously? Again? What was he even doing in this quarter?

"Thousands upon thousands of souls in this city, and yet here I am running into you again, Captain. Did you stop in front of me on purpose?" I scowled at him in accusation, bending over to pick up my books.

"I may have, yeah," he laughed. "In my defense, I was surprised to see you, and sort of expected you would look up eventually before knocking straight into someone."

"Surprised to see me? A student, leaving a lecture hall? I'd argue I'm more surprised to see you here. Are you sure you're not following me?"

"The guard meets once a week in the amphitheater for general briefings. I can assure you I didn't come all this way just to harass the best and brightest minds of Sophrosyne," he said with a smirk.

"Just me, then?"

"You seem pretty bright to me, Little Conduit. A little uncoordinated, maybe, but rather clever."

Not clever enough to avoid running into this gods-forsaken man, apparently.

I didn't have anything against Kieran, but I also couldn't stop thinking about him. And these random encounters absolutely weren't helping the matter. Especially not when he kept complimenting me like that. His attention stroked my ego to no apparent end, and that was... dangerous.

I sighed.

"Long lecture?" he asked.

"No. Well, yes. It was lengthy, but it was interesting. It was just intense... I hadn't realized how many details from our histories were kept exclusive to the Studium," I explained.

"Ah, yeah. The Cataclysm, I presume?"

I nodded.

"Heavy shit," Kieran agreed. "Though if it helps, that's probably the most jarring revelation you're going to face here. Probably."

"That's a relief," I said. "I think I can only handle one apocalyptic shift in my understanding of reality per academic quarter."

He chuckled.

"That's fair. Are you headed off to another lecture?" Kieran asked.

"No, I'm done for the day. Why?" I asked, curious where he was going with this.

"Wanna grab lunch?"

Oh.

Well, that was unexpected. And it seemed as though the ever-meddling Fates were making it damn near impossible for me to avoid this man, so...

"Sure, why not?"

I had nothing else better to do.

CHAPTER SIXTEEN

KIERAN

I didn't know what possessed me to ask her such a thing.

Lunch? Really, Kieran?

I had already decided that pursuing Arken wasn't an option, no matter how attractive she was. I didn't really do the whole "friendship" thing either, outside of a few closer connections with my fellow guardsmen. So why was I bothering with this? I had my moment of fun when I kept the poor woman in that cell for my absurd questioning. Why couldn't I just leave her alone?

It's not like I was a misanthrope by nature, and I had nothing against the woman herself—I enjoyed good company and good conversation as much as the next person. It was what followed in the wake of those things that I tried my best to avoid.

The expectations of consistency. The desire for commitment or plans. The pursuit of deeper connection.

It was far too risky for me to allow myself to get close to anybody here, and so I had developed some specific rules of engagement. I was doing just fine in keeping a casual circle of work acquaintances and a string of one-night stands—and nobody suspected a thing, because I was damn good at the performance. Charisma in the hands of the clever was one Hel of a defense mechanism.

So why in the ever-loving fuck was I inviting some innocent, curious looking Conduit to join me for lunch?

Calm down, I told myself. *It's one casual meal. It's not like you're taking her out on a date. Relax.*

I sighed internally, supposing my subconscious had a point. It wasn't that big of a deal, and Arken was an entertaining presence. I think I had gotten a rise out of her almost every time we'd encountered each other thus far.

Entertaining, indeed.

"So, where are we headed?" she asked casually, following my lead as we made our way towards the northern half of the Studium.

"I take it you're not in the mood for the standard student fare?"

She made a face and I laughed, her scrunched expression suggesting that she'd quickly gotten bored of the repetition of the Studium's dining halls. I couldn't say I blamed her, either—the scholars were more focused on nutritional benefits than they were on actual flavor. That said, it was all free and you couldn't really look a gift horse in the mouth.

"Gods, please, no," Arken groaned.

"Don't fret. I know a place," I assured her. I had a feeling she would enjoy Corrine's—the small café that was hidden between the pockets of administrative buildings near the Biblyos.

"Oh?"

"Just trust me, freshling."

Arken rolled her eyes at the term, and I laughed again. I seemed to laugh often around her, and it was a breath of fresh air in contrast to my habits of more apathetic brooding.

"I think you'll like it. Come along, Little Conduit."

At a casual pace, the stroll from the amphitheater to the café took ten, maybe fifteen minutes.

"So what's your story, Asher?" I asked her as we wove our

way through the crowds. "What grand ambitions bring you to Sophrosyne?"

She shrugged. "Can't say that I have any."

I raised a brow. "I don't believe *that* for a minute. Nobody comes to Sophrosyne just for the Hel of it. Where did you come from, anyway?"

"Samhaven," she replied, nonchalant.

As I looked back at her, I saw her eyes drift around the city with that same sparkle of fascination and wonder that seemed to have a permanent place in her expression. Like anyone and everything was worth a second glance.

"Okay, but *where* in Samhaven?" I inquired. "That's a rather large territory."

The corners of her mouth upturned with the subtle hint of a smirk.

"Yes, though it *is* smaller than Pyrhhas," she observed.

"Are you avoiding the subject on purpose, or do you simply delight in being difficult to talk to?"

"A bit of both, really," she replied cheekily.

I resisted the urge to audibly groan.

"You are a *maddening* woman to try and get to know."

Her sly smirk only widened. "Does that mean you're *trying* to get to know me, then?"

So it would seem. I shouldn't be, and yet here we were.

"Is that such a crime?" I countered.

"You tell me, Captain. You're the local law enforcement, are you not?"

Arken snickered as I ran one hand through my hair in faux frustration. In reality, I was rather entertained by this, completely charmed by her quick wit. She really was something else.

"The Brindlewoods," she finally answered.

"So you're from Elseweire."

"No," she corrected, frowning slightly. "I'm from the

Brindlewoods. Literally. I grew up in a small, nameless village right in the heart of the forest. It was several hours out from the port."

Interesting.

"So what brings a small woodland creature like you out from the forests, into one of the largest cities in the world?" I inquired.

"Curiosity," Arken answered. As if it were that simple. I rolled my eyes.

"It's okay if you don't want to share details, Little Conduit," I said. "You can just tell me to fuck off and mind my own business."

"I'm telling you the truth, you pushy bastard," Arken retorted, though she was still grinning.

I smirked back. Baiting her was far too easy, and *far* too entertaining for my own good.

"It's hard to explain," she continued. "The slow, simple life was all that I knew, but I was never satisfied with it. And it probably didn't help that I was raised by a retired scholar of the Studium. Honestly, I blame her for the fact that I ended up *here* in particular... but I think I was bound to make a run for it eventually. I've always been a bit restless."

That did explain quite a lot, particularly in how Arken seemed to carry herself. She was very clearly intelligent in the academic sense of the word, but she was also incredibly grounded. She seemed far more down to earth than the vast majority of her peers.

"That probably seems terribly naive," she confessed. "To leave behind all of that safety, security, and comfort for what must seem like an errant whim."

"On the contrary," I replied. "I think it's proof that you're wiser than your years. Stability is a fleeting thing, and often overrated. It takes a lot of courage to follow your instincts like that."

"Hmm. An interesting perspective," Arken mused. "I suppose time will tell if it was instinct, or simply *impulse* that took me so far from home."

"I'm guessing that for someone like you, those two things are one and the same."

"Someone like me, eh?" Arken replied. "What makes you so sure about that?"

I grinned.

"We have more in common than you might think, Little Conduit."

◆ ◆ ◆

Once we arrived at the café, Arken took one look at the pastel storefront shrouded in wisteria branches, and turned to me with a raised brow.

"*This* is your first choice for lunch?" she asked, a touch of surprise in her voice.

"I'm offended, Miss Asher. Are you assuming I'm the type to let my masculinity stand in the way of Sophrosyne's best sandwiches?"

"I mean, yes," she admitted. "You don't strike me as the type to frequent such a pretty place."

"Are you suggesting I'm not pretty? Rude." I replied, leading her into the shop.

The feigned expression of offense that I wore earned me an adorable giggle from the Conduit, and an unexpected frisson of pleasure ran through me at the sight of her smile.

Off-limits, Kieran. She's off-limits. Move it along...

It was a nice enough day out, so once we'd ordered and retrieved our food from the counter, we sat down to eat on the small patio outside, and continued our earlier conversation about the Cataclysm.

Arken was, understandably, still processing the revelation of what really happened to Aemos. The truth of the Elders was a heady concept—why only nineteen remained, and why the Arcane Studium was truly formed. Most mortals—most of the *world*, really—believed that the Elders were just a collective of the last remaining gods, and that Sophrosyne was where they chose to settle. They thought that the Arcane Studium was just a university, albeit a highly prestigious one.

They didn't know that the Convocation of the Nineteen carried both the aether and the burdens of *hundreds*, if not thousands of their fallen brethren, the remnants of our immortal predecessors' power flowing in their veins. The mortals that often spoke poorly of the gods—those who took issue with their stance of neutrality in the modern age—they didn't even know how much was *sacrificed* to preserve mankind as a species, let alone their freedom. And even though Conduits learned about it by default as part of their introductory studies here, a vast majority of them didn't seem to *care*—but Arken did.

Her mind was utterly fascinating, and I was hanging on every word as she rambled through her thoughts on the matter. She barely took a breath, but every insight was surprisingly complex, nuanced, well thought out, and deeply empathetic. Arken seemed to view our history like a living, breathing entity. She talked about the past like it was something of great importance to consider, not just a forgone conclusion. Her frenzied enthusiasm for it almost reminded me of Viktor—though I promptly pushed *that* thought out of my mind.

Even as we strayed from the topic, there was something mildly unsettling about the conversation. Perhaps it was just that Arken saw the world in many of the same ways I did, which was… rare, to say the least. And somehow, we just kept stumbling into one another. Repeatedly. *By sheer coincidence*, as she claimed.

Interesting indeed.

"So," Arken said, interrupting my train of thought. "Croissants for breakfast. Sandwiches for lunch. Do tell, Kieran.

What's your evening meal of choice? You do seem to be a creature of habit."

I shook my head, disregarding the way it felt to hear her say my name out loud.

"You're making some bold assumptions, Asher," I countered.

"You didn't even have to give Corinne your order," she replied. "And you said yourself that you're a regular at the bakery."

Okay, that was a fair point, but I didn't actually come here every day—unless it was late winter, in which case I absolutely did. In my defense, Corinne's soups were unparalleled, and a bowl of tomato bisque paired with a cheese sandwich on a cold day? Divine.

Arken, on the other hand, was picking small bites out of a fluffy scone, seemingly quite content with the meal and her warm tea.

"Perhaps I'm just a memorable individual," I suggested.

She snorted, practically choking on her food.

"What? Are you suggesting I'm not memorable? You wound me!"

I continued to feign offense—but Arken didn't take the bait. She was too clever for her own good. And mine, really.

"Mm, it's hard to gauge how memorable a man can even be when you *repeatedly* run into him," she replied with a sly grin. "I'll have to get back to you on that. But you'll have to stay away long enough to become a memory in the first place. You're certainly a noteworthy stalker, though."

It was my turn to snort, and I crossed my arms with raised brows, challenging her notion that our repeated encounters were by design.

"I'm hardly a stalker, freshling. If I was stalking you, trust me when I say that you wouldn't even know."

"I thought we'd already established that I'm quite observant," she noted over a sip of tea.

"You are indeed, I'll give you that." I laughed under my breath. "But you still wouldn't stand a chance."

Arken looked mildly offended by that assertion, which was cute.

"How can you be so sure?"

"Aside from being a verifiable specialist in reconnaissance?" I laughed, gesturing at my uniform coat.

"I mean, is there another reason?"

Hmm. Decisions, decisions. I paused for just a moment, deliberating on whether or not I should show her now, or let her figure it out on her own.

I chose to be self-indulgent for once, knowing that her reaction would entertain me. With a smirk, I lifted one hand lazily, calling towards the aether within. I pulled from the arcane energy of the sunlight and the gentle breeze, converting Light and Air to smoky tendrils of Shadow. There, in the palm of my hand, they formed a shifting, dark orb of energy in my palm.

"Holy Hel! You're a Shadow Conduit?!" Arken crowed, almost shouting in surprise.

Something like that.

I stifled my laughter, giving her a wink. Thankfully, this corner of the Academic Quarter was fairly quiet this time of day. It was no secret that I was a Shadow Conduit, but there were only a handful of us in Sophrosyne these days. And I really wasn't one for unnecessary attention.

Still, her reaction had been worth it. I was beginning to like *her* attention, specifically—whether it was necessary or not.

"I am, indeed," I replied.

There was something about the way Arken studied the ball of umbral arcana in my palm, with hungry fascination and intrigue in her golden eyes, that was doing very, very distracting things to me. She looked utterly transfixed, and then vaguely disappointed when I exhaled and let the Shadow return into the aether.

When her gaze returned to me, those gorgeous eyes were still glimmering, a shy half-smile curling up one side of her face.

Gods.

"I am so godsdamned jealous of you right now," she confessed.

"Jealous?" I asked incredulously.

Why? She was the rarer one between us. Light Conduits were almost unheard of.

"I've always found Shadow to be the most interesting element on the aetheric spectrum," she explained.

"What makes you say that?" I asked, legitimately curious.

"Shadow just feels so... constant. Eternal, compared to some of the other elements. Darkness is this constant presence in life, no matter where you are. Even in the Light of day," Arken said gesturing above us where the wisteria branches and their handing flowers were casting shadows on us both.

"And then when you consider everything that Shadow seems to *represent* to humans—even though we fear the darkness, it can almost be comforting to know—"

She broke off for a moment, looking sheepish. "Sorry. I'm veering off into poetics and philosophy here."

"No, continue," I said gently. "What's comforting?"

The way this woman saw the world was so godsdamned refreshing. It was fascinating to listen to her slip back and forth between casual speech, and a much more formalized, academic voice. She had an impressively elegant command of language, especially considering she had only been attending the Studium for mere *weeks*. I knew of only a few others who could make the transition between tones so seamlessly.

"Well, I've always seen it like... Okay. If you go swimming or seafaring, you'll experience an absence of Earth aether beneath your feet for a while, right? And clearly, we're all blind in the absence of Light aether in the dead of night. Fire has to be summoned, and Water may be present in our bodies but it's not readily available no matter where you are otherwise, right?"

I nodded, vaguely understanding where she was going with this.

"I don't think I've ever been in a circumstance where there was no Shadow aether to be found. Because even in broad daylight, I cast my own shadow. I can sense that energy and its presence."

Her gaze drifted from my eyes to her lap for a moment as she paused to think.

"To me, that almost suggests that there's darkness in all things, by default. Even if it's slight, just barely noticeable, Shadow is a constant in life. And I suppose that just resonates with me."

"And why is that?" I asked softly.

Her fingers worried absently at the hem of her sleeve as she spoke, pulling at the threads. A nervous habit, perhaps?

"When you think about what Shadow represents—what humanity has attributed to darkness, even though we know that aether has no true emotional ties—we associate Shadow with things like... pain, or grief, *emotional* darkness in the context of poetry and art," Arken continued. "And as humans, it feels like we fear those things in life just as much as we fear that total blindness in the dark. And yet it's inevitable, is it not? Darkness is as inevitable as Shadow in life, and I find that to be more comforting than unsettling, for whatever reason."

For a moment, I just stared at her. A strange blend of awe, appreciation and discomfort—feeling somewhat exposed by her insights.

A Light Conduit, comforted by the Shadows.

An unfamiliar swell of emotion was brewing in my chest, but I kept that side of me in its designated vise grip. Compartmentalized it, locked it away. Tossed the key into the Abyss. Yet even so, I was fascinated by this woman. I wanted to know so much more about her. Despite my better judgment, I wanted to know *everything*.

People who saw the true inevitability of pain and suffering

in this world had often experienced enough of it to harden themselves, developing walls to weather that storm. Arken was still so very open, so soft.

How?

"I can't say that I've ever thought about it like that," I replied. "But I'm inclined to agree with you. That said, Light is just as incredible. It's nearly as constant as Shadow, and you are much more rare than I am around here, Little Conduit."

Arken seemed to visibly relax, her smile turning serene, as if she'd been anticipating that I wouldn't take her seriously. *Strange.*

"I do hope you're prepared for an onslaught of Shadow-related questions if you make a continued habit of stalking me," she said with a coy smile over another sip of tea.

Don't tempt me with a good time, Little Conduit.

Because Source be damned, that was tempting. The impulse to make her a habit was already stirring, alongside an even darker desire to stalk the poor woman from the Shadows. I had trained myself out of such curiosities a long, long time ago, and yet...

"I've got quite a few questions for you, myself," I murmured.

"Like what?"

Arken tilted her head in surprise, as if she hadn't expected such a thing. For such a clever creature, she seemed to have a stunning lack of self-awareness when it came to how godsdamned *alluring* she was.

I chuckled.

"I'm not sure we have time for that this afternoon," I said, though I wished it weren't the case.

"Oh, come on, Captain! At least ask me *one*."

She wasn't forcing my hand, per se, but I didn't want the conversation to end, either. I decided to go for the low-hanging fruit, something that was top of mind after listening to her speak for the better part of the last hour.

"Where did you study before coming to Sophrosyne? Did you

go to preparatory courses in Elseweire or something?"

Arken laughed.

"I didn't."

"*Bullshit*," I challenged. "There is no way this is your first round of formal education. You speak like a seasoned scholar half the time."

At that, she snorted, though a corner of her mouth crooked upwards. There was a glimmer in her eyes that suggested she knew damn well how intelligent she was. *Gods*, as if I needed another reason to be attracted to her.

"I told you, I was raised by one! My caretaker, my mentor—Amaretta, she used to be the High Scholar of Clerical Studies here. She moved back to Elseweire when she retired, and then found that she preferred a more quiet life than the city could offer. Eventually she found her way and settled in with the village."

"Even though we lived simply out there," Arken continued, "She still had quite the collection of texts. And she never truly lost the urge to teach. I think I received an academic lecture for breakfast almost every day."

That certainly made sense. I noticed that she said *caretaker*, though, and not mother, which only left me with more questions.

Unfortunately, though, I had to go. Both literally and figuratively.

I had work to do, running my men through plans for a few scouting missions around the outskirts of the city and monitoring the movement of a rather troublesome group of humans. Occasionally, they would attempt to harass guests of Sophrosyne as they came and went, and their numbers had been steadily increasing as of late. Nevermind the fact that we still didn't know much about their intentions.

But I also had to get out of here before I set my mind on legitimately stalking this woman and asking for her entire life's story.

I sighed as I stood up.

"Alas, I have a shift starting soon, and answering all of the questions in your pretty little head would most assuredly make me late," I said, bowing my head in slight apology. "Until our next random encounter, Miss Asher."

"*Random*," she laughed, making air quotes with slender fingers. "But hey—thank you for lunch, Kieran. I'm glad I ran into you... this time."

"Any time, Little Conduit," I called over my shoulder, blanching slightly as I walked away.

Now why in the *actual fuck* would I say something like that?

Fates help me, this girl was trouble.

CHAPTER SEVENTEEN

ARKEN

That night was the first time I dreamt about Kieran Vistarii.

By the time I woke up the next day, I barely remembered anything, but I did distinctly recall that he'd been in it. That man, his smirk, and his Shadows.

Fucking Hel.

While our lunch had been perfectly pleasant, and I'd legitimately enjoyed his company, the fact that I was already so eager to see him again was... a problem.

Sure, there was nothing wrong with making friends while I was here at the Studium, but there was a distinct urge to be more than friends with him. And that? That just couldn't happen.

It was one thing to consider dating casually around Sophrosyne, to enjoy myself in my spare time. It was another thing entirely to consider dating an extremely attractive, extremely perceptive scouting captain of the Elder Guard who would be duty-bound to report my secret to the Convocation if he ever discovered it. And as a Shadow Conduit? He could easily discover it, if I let my guard down. The urge to let my guard down around him was a little too strong, as is.

As much as it pained me, as much as I really didn't want to, I set my mind to actively avoiding places where we'd already encountered each other. This was rather irksome for my sweet tooth, but I could find other restaurants, shops and cafés to frequent. It was a big city.

Several days passed, and it seemed like so far, my efforts had worked. Three days went by, then four, then five, and I had yet to run into Kieran again. For some reason, I wasn't particularly pleased with my own success, and found myself more moody than anything else.

I knew that he hadn't really been stalking me, but a pathetic part of me had wished he would. There was no avoiding it at this point: I was lonely.

I missed home, I missed Amaretta and all of her lectures and clucking about. I missed the children of the village and the way they'd ask me to participate in games of tag and hide and seek, even though I was twice their age and size. I even missed the stable boys and their dirty minds, if only because it was all so familiar.

Sometimes, I even missed Graysen.

I hadn't really found a niche or a social group at the Studium. I had made a single friend in Laurel Ansari, sure, but the woman was a social butterfly. She was constantly preoccupied, and we only had one course together.

Occasionally, I would share classes and familiar nods with some of the people who had been on the ship with me when we'd arrived in Sophrosyne, but people such as Percy weren't exactly thrilling to be around. That was the thing, I supposed. A great many of the Conduits attending the Arcane Studium, at least in my current route of coursework, came from exceptional privilege, and I found that hard to relate to.

It was common sense, honestly. While any human with Resonance could make the journey to Sophrosyne and seek entry to the Studium, said journey was often long and arduous—and long, arduous journeys were expensive. Had it not been for Amaretta's generosity and connections, I would have never been able to purchase my ticket for the journey from Elswiere to Port Sofia. And there were many in this realm that had far less than I ever did, even in my simple village life.

When you took into consideration the rarity of Conduits—who were only a small fraction of the overall population—and then divided that small fraction by those who had the means to even make it out to Sophrosyne, it shouldn't have surprised me that so many of my peers were the sons and daughters of exceptionally wealthy and powerful families.

It left me homesick in a very odd sort of way. I never quite fit in the village either, but at least I knew how to play by their rules. At least there was common understanding, a sense of community, and mutual aid.

I knew next to nothing about Kieran or his upbringing, but he was easy to talk to. In our few exchanges, I felt like I could relate to him more than anyone else I'd encountered so far in this city of gods and scholars. Whether that was because he was a guard and not a student, or because of how naturally it had felt to build a rapport within minutes of meeting the man, I wasn't certain. I really didn't know what it was that drew me to him, specifically. It was likely many things at once.

I mean Hel, he was even a Shadow Conduit, my parallel on the spectrum of aetherflows. Perhaps I could blame the compelling nature of his presence on science alone. I had far too much pride to actively seek him out now, but maybe I'd stop trying to avoid him entirely.

If I got lucky and ran into the guardsman again, I would simply focus on being his friend. Surely, we could be that much. We couldn't ever be more than that, but I could at least use a friend.

No harm in that, right?

✧ ✧ ✧

Apparently I'd been lying to myself when I said I had too much pride to seek him out. It only took a few more days for my loneliness to get the better of me.

I had tried this week, I really had. I went out of my way to converse with a few peers before and after class, forcing fake smiles and dull conversation in hopes of finding somebody else who I clicked with in the same way Kieran and I had. Preferably someone whose company I could enjoy without wanting to jump their bones.

I even managed to hunt down Laurel, who I barely saw outside of our Bios lectures lately. The poor woman had looked way too overwhelmed with coursework for me to dare pester her for some company. Her latest girlfriend also shot daggers at me with her eyes the minute I'd said hello in the Biblyos, which was awkward to say the least.

I hated every second of this miserable reminder that I was the odd one out in a sea of thousands of other people from all over the world. It wasn't that I was shunned, disliked, or singled out—I generally found that people were friendly, polite, and even nice, especially when they heard that I was a Light Conduit. But I found it hard to stay interested in conversations about ambitions, about how our budding arcane expertise would one day convert to comfort and riches, or the latest petty disputes between those in power.

It was becoming clear to me that in order to fit in around here, at least with the students who were my age, I would have to put up a bit of a facade. I'd have to don a polite little mask and participate in a song and dance I still hadn't really mastered, and in the meantime, hold my true self back—biting down on the snark, the enthusiasm for the mundane, the simple pleasures of a girl from the Brindlewoods of Samhaven.

And the thing was... I had no real interest in trying to fit in. There wasn't an ounce of drive within me to maintain that facade, to keep the ribbons on that mask tied. I wanted companionship, not acceptance from the noblesse. Even if I could never be entirely open with anyone here, I at least wanted easy conversations, some laughter and fun in between all the coursework and my efforts to find answers to impossible questions. I wanted a certain degree of comfort, a certain ease—the ability to be some semblance of my true self.

And I think I had found that in Kieran.

I couldn't help myself. I asked one of the guards about him on my way home from class.

Our few encounters had been happenstance, and if I didn't actually seek Kieran out, I wasn't sure I'd run into the man again. It had been sheer dumb luck that we'd repeatedly run into each other before in a city-state of thousands. So when I spotted a guardsman who looked fairly young and naive, I figured I might as well ask him.

"Hey there. I'm looking for Captain Vistarii, are you familiar?"

I flashed the guardsman what I hoped was a charming smile.

"The captain? You're looking for Kieran?"

"Yes, is he around?"

"Erm, no. We're not really able to provide that information to strangers, even if he were. Sorry, miss, it's just protocol."

"That's fine. Would you be able to give him a message, perhaps?"

"Eh? I mean, I suppose we could, yes. No guarantees on timing or an answer, hope ya can understand."

"Of course. If you do encounter him any time soon, could you just let him know that I was looking for him? My name is Arken. He'll know who I am."

He raised an eyebrow, but nodded.

"Arken. Got it. Will do, miss."

He was giving me the strangest look, as if it was extremely

abnormal for anyone to be asking about his captain. Kieran didn't really strike me as a solitary creature, though. He was far too charming and extroverted. Surely, people had come around for him before?

"Thanks, uhh?"

"Grant Kraiggson, miss. I should be headin' back now."

"Thanks again, Grant."

He dipped his head respectfully before striding off towards the gates.

I wasn't sure what to expect next. I had next to no information on where he lived, where his typical station was for work, or what his habits were outside of the occasional bakery or café run. Truth be told? I knew very little about Kieran at all, other than the few basics I had gleaned from our conversation the other day. My little observations from every chance encounter.

He was young for a captain, implying high degrees of skill and martial prowess. He was a Shadow Conduit, and had at one point been a student here in Sophrosyne. He was tall, clever and devastatingly attractive. He had a nice voice and a penchant for poking fun at me. He liked croissants and cheese sandwiches. That was about it.

Not particularly helpful information to track someone down and attempt to befriend them.

I cringed, realizing that it all sounded a little pathetic, even in the privacy of my own thoughts. Because here I was, the bright-eyed new student, chasing down a literal senior guardsman of Sophrosyne in hopes to, what? Hang out more?

But I liked Kieran, and I was tired of pretending that I didn't. I was tired of pretending like I hadn't clearly found a kindred spirit in that cocky bastard.

And so it was decided, then. The next time I ran into Kieran, I'd invite him to lunch again.

Just friends. Just lunch.

That was fairly harmless, right?

CHAPTER EIGHTEEN

KIERAN

I spent the next few days absolutely losing myself to my vices.

I could not get that godsdamned woman out of my head, and that was... exceptionally unlike me. It was so unnerving that I felt like I could crawl out of my skin every time that she crossed my mind, and I found myself taking a different person to bed every night just to attempt to drown her out.

By the time a week had passed, I was starting to get bored. All of the hedonism had grown excessive, and truthfully? I just needed a break. That was also unlike me, but in all fairness, I also typically paced myself a little better when it came to sleeping around.

The worst part? It didn't even fucking work.

Shadow is a constant. I find that more comforting than unsettling.

Even though I had gone well out of my way to avoid bumping into her again, I was quickly finding that Arken was haunting me more in her absence than her presence. Her voice echoed through my mind at the most inconvenient times. Including when I was sleeping around.

What the fuck is it about her? Why her, *Kieran?*

I didn't have a good answer to that.

I was starting to think that maybe I should just invite

Arken to bed and get it over with. I could deal with one potentially-scorned-ex-fling leading the House of Light & Shadow one day. I already had the Lord of Embers ready to slit my throat, what was one more regret?

It wouldn't be a hard sell. She would say yes. I knew she was just as attracted to me as I was to her, and not just because I was a cocky bastard—though I was that, too. But rather because of how she reacted to me, physically.

When seduction becomes a game, you learn how to pick up on those kinds of cues, and she'd given me plenty of them. So why was it that I couldn't bring myself to seek her out and play the game?

Because she wouldn't put up with your shit the next day, and you'd have to hurt her just to keep her away.

Yeah, basically.

I wasn't in the business of breaking hearts—I didn't let anyone even remotely close enough for that to become a problem. But even still, plenty of people conflate sex with attachment, and I'd been an asshole to one too many men and women who had pushed the envelope. I'd been brutal on those who had dared to ask more from me than just a night's worth of distraction.

When my sexual exploits got the wrong idea, misinterpreting my adamant walls as some childish act of playing hard to get, I'd often have to make use of what was running through my veins alongside the blood and the aether.

Venom. Cruelty. Ruthlessness.

I didn't particularly enjoy making use of those things... most of the time. But it was necessary. I would never be anybody's lover, just a damn good night or two.

For reasons I couldn't fully comprehend, I was violently opposed to ever doing that shit to Arken, though. The idea of tears in those pretty little golden doe eyes? Caused by me? Intentionally? It kinda made me sick to my stomach.

If I couldn't push her away afterwards, I couldn't fuck her.

And when I was around her? I very much wanted to fuck her. But the premature guilt was already right there, ready to eat me alive if I even so much as kissed her.

Gods, I wanted to kiss her, though.

My subconscious was reeling at these stupid little thoughts every time they cropped up. I couldn't believe I was seriously fantasizing over a kiss. What was I, fourteen?

Literally what the fuck is wrong with you?

I didn't have enough time to go down that list, though. I had to get ready for work.

As I washed my face and got dressed, I reminded myself that I was doing the right thing in holding my ground. As unpleasant as the experience may be, the right thing to do here was to continue avoiding Arken like the damn plague, and to suffer about it in silence.

It was ultimately better for the both of us, because whether the Little Conduit enjoyed her time in the Shadows or not, she would not enjoy her time in mine.

There was nothing comforting about the beasts that hid within that darkness.

Even if I wasn't a miserable son of a bitch, it was far too dangerous for me to want... what I wanted from her.

Everything. Anything.

Fucking Hel.

◆ ◆ ◆

By the time I made it to my shift monitoring the Eastern Gates for the night, I was in a foul mood.

It must have been very clear in my expression, because most of my men gave me a pretty wide berth, asking questions and confirming post details, but not much more. That was probably for the best.

"Hey, Captain?"

One of the newer recruits, Grant Kraiggson, made his way over to me, blissfully ignorant of my current mood.

"Yeah?"

"It's probably not important, but some dark-haired woman came up looking for you earlier this afternoon. Asked if any of us had seen you recently. We followed protocol, of course—didn't give her any info. But does she sound familiar? Pale, maybe 5'5, big brown eyes, uhh, kinda cute?"

I set my jaw to avoid a very irrational response to this poor kid, who was catching me on the worst night to receive this exact information. It wasn't even jealousy that had me simmering, it was the crude description. *Kinda cute?*

Unless there was some other short, deliciously soft, doe-eyed woman I'd accidentally ensnared recently and didn't know about, Grant had to be talking about Arken, and she went well beyond "kinda cute."

She was so godsdamned hot that it had been ruining me for a week straight.

"She said her name was Arken. Anyway, just wanted to see if you knew her, and if you wanted us to tell her anything if she comes 'round again. She seemed pretty intent on finding ya."

I exhaled through my nose, unsure of what answer I wanted to give. A very stupid part of me—one that was most definitely thinking with the wrong head—was ecstatic that Arken had sought me out.

"If she comes back again, you can give her my schedule. But please report back if you do so. Immediately."

Whether that was so that I could anticipate her, or change my schedule entirely to avoid her, I wasn't sure yet.

"Yes, sir."

He paused for a moment, expression obviously curious, but

torn. Clearly debating whether or not the risk was worth the reward.

"If you're about to ask me about her, I highly recommend that you reconsider. If you'd like your evening to remain pleasant, that is, Kraiggson."

"Yes sir. Sorry, sir."

I sighed.

"Get back to your post, please."

◆ ◆ ◆

I couldn't sleep that night, and I really wasn't in the mood to go out on the town and fish for another distraction, so it was just me and the tea kettle, screaming to ourselves at midnight.

For just a moment, I allowed myself to consider alternatives to this helscape of a situation I was in, forcing me to avoid one single woman like the plague. And somehow, struggling with *that* so much that I was driving myself insane.

Because the Fates were cruel bastards, and I would inevitably run into her again. If I didn't sort myself out, there was no way I could keep my hands to myself the next time we crossed paths.

There was just no way.

I could seduce Arken and maybe let her stick around afterwards, keeping her at an arm's length and avoiding any further depth to the relationship. But my instincts told me Arken was far too perceptive for that. She seemed like an emotional creature, and to ask her to follow my "no feelings" rule probably wouldn't end well.

Yeah. She would inevitably call my bluff, and then I would have to be the asshole. The precise scenario I was trying to avoid.

I could keep sleeping around until I found someone else to obsess over, taking her place in my mind... but the odds of that were impossibly low, considering I had never felt like this before. Besides, I'd just be trading one problem for another.

You could just be her friend, you pervert.

I took a sip of tea and mulled it over in my head.

Though the initial thought wasn't nearly as appealing as the idea of Arken tangled up in my sheets, it did offer its advantages.

I could have more than just one night. I could spend enough time with her to hopefully calm down and regain the ability to think about literally anything else. I could enjoy her company without fear of inevitably crushing her spirit. I could allow myself to be just a little less alone.

But all of these were inherently selfish reasons to seek out her friendship, and I didn't even know what she wanted. She could very well have sought me out for something else entirely. She could be interested in the very same things that I was currently obsessing over the thought of.

Admittedly, I liked the idea of her wanting me like that, problematic as it may be for this plan. I also liked the idea of that mouth on my—

Get ahold of yourself, Kieran.

I groaned inwardly at my inability to stop finding every excuse to picture her naked. Among other things.

I was a degenerate, but even I understood that she was so much more than something to screw.

Arken was charming and charismatic and smart—smarter than me, that's for damn sure. Beyond the book smarts, she was clever and intuitive, never taking things at face value.

For reasons beyond my comprehension, she seemed to enjoy my company. She even came by looking for me.

I had to ignore the warmth that bloomed in my chest, and the distant feeling that was reminding me that I had skipped the alternative that I probably wanted most. I downed what remained of my tea for the night and shook it off. That was an impossibility.

There was no use wasting time wanting what I couldn't ever have.

We could be friends, though...

I was still mulling it over. Even a friendship with her was not without its risks for both of us.

Was it worth it?

CHAPTER NINETEEN

ARKEN

I was studying in the Biblyos one afternoon, entirely engrossed in my notes when suddenly, I felt a gentle peck at my left hand.

I blinked twice before processing the fact that a small raven was now resting atop my stack of tomes, looking at me expectantly with strangely intelligent eyes. It tapped its tiny foot, where a small scroll of parchment was tied up with twine. I unraveled it to find a note that had to be from none other than Kieran.

__I'm terribly bored, Little Conduit. What are you up to?__

The raven continued to rest atop my books, waiting. It was staring at me as if it knew to anticipate a response. *How did a bird even get in here?* I sighed, rummaging through my satchel to pull out a pen.

__I'm studying. How did you even know where to find me? This isn't helping your case against being a stalker, you know.__

Upon receipt of the parchment with my scribbled response, the raven simply disappeared into a puff of smoke and Shadow.

Well, that explained it. That wasn't a bird at all, it was a mail sprite—a conjured bit of complex arcane energy, summoned by Conduits to deliver correspondence within the city. Some sprites were even powerful enough to take letters across the continent, though often that sort of spellwork would cost you.

They usually weren't quite so realistic-looking, often more semi-corporeal and elemental in nature, but Kieran was clearly a man with an eye for detail. That sort of thing took a great deal of power and finesse, though... I could practically taste the aether in the air when the raven returned.

There's a chance that I looked up your aetheric signature in the Archives. Wanna go on an adventure?

Gods, the audacity of this man. At least that saved me the trouble of seeking him out for lunch, though. It would seem that the interest was mutual... though that hardly excused the literal crime of pulling up private information from my files in the Archives. Rolling my eyes, I tore off another scrap of parchment to send my reply.

That seems like a gross misuse of administrative power, Captain. And as exciting as that sounds, I have class soon.

Poof. The mail sprite was back within moments, as if he was waiting on my replies with bated breath.

Skip. I'll make it worth your while.

I bit my lip, praying to the Source that I wasn't blushing at his phrasing. That damned man had a way of making even the most perfectly mundane sentence sound intimate.

Aren't you supposed to be some sort of authority figure around here? Should you really be the one to suggest that I start breaking the rules and blowing off my education?

Five or ten minutes must have passed before I received a response. I couldn't help but fidget in anticipation, paying very little attention to the notes I was skimming. He had spoiled me with such quick responses earlier, and I hated how eager I already was to hear back.

Breaking the rules can be fun every now & again.

Seriously? He made me wait that long for yet another vague one-liner? I swore under my breath and attempted to shake off his idle distractions. I had work to do, and sure, maybe I was already ahead in this course, but that was no reason to skip my lectures on the whims of a handsome stranger.

"Shoo," I murmured to the mail sprite, flicking my hand through its tiny, false raven effigy with a flicker of Light, causing it to dissipate back into Shadow.

"Now that was just rude," a low, velvety voice murmured from the stacks beside me. Lo and behold, the aforementioned handsome stranger was slinking towards me with a feline sort of grace and a cocksure grin.

"Besides," he continued. "Something tells me that you don't always follow the rules, now do you, Little Conduit?"

I gave him a withering look as I glanced up from my notes. Regardless of our prior encounter in the jail cell, he had no idea how accurate that statement was.

"Yeah, didn't think so," Kieran said, reading my expression for what it actually was. Interest. "So... How about a field trip?"

"You're a menace," I groaned, silently cursing the Fates. I didn't have the willpower to resist this man *in person*.

"I'll take that as a compliment."

"You take everything as a compliment, you cocky bastard."

His answering grin was admittedly infectious.

"Fine," I conceded. One missed lecture wasn't going to kill me. "Where are we going?"

"A museum," Kieran replied simply.

You've gotta be kidding me.

"Seriously, Vistarii? Your idea of rebellion is to have me skip class... to go to a *museum*?"

Truth be told, I was delighted. I loved museums. I loved the study of history and arts and all the stories one could unravel from within the archives. But the fact that this was his idea of an adventure as well? *This* was how he wanted to spend his time off? That's what caught me off guard.

"It's a quiet sort of rebellion, I will admit," he mused, tapping his chin.

I just stared at him incredulously for a moment.

"Just trust me on this one, Little Conduit. Allow me to be your tour guide for the day—I have a feeling you'll like what I have to show you."

I had a feeling I'd like damn near anything this man had to show me.

Fucking Fates, Arken. Get it together.

Thank the gods that Shadow Conduits weren't mind readers. I pictured myself being doused with cold water just to calm down before responding.

"Lead the way, then, Captain."

◆ ◆ ◆

I wasn't sure what to expect as Kieran led me through the bustling streets of the Academic Quarter, away from the Biblyos and towards the center of the city.

Though I peppered him with questions along the way—*What kind of museum? Didn't he have anything better to do? And just how in the Hel did he find my aetheric signature so easily?*—the man gave nothing away.

"Just trust me," he said again. "I'm taking you to one of my favorite places in the city."

Ten minutes later, we arrived at a tall building, several stories higher than those in our immediate surroundings, though it was still white limestone, much like the rest of the buildings in this quarter.

I struggled to make out the letters carved into the marble facade above the large entryway, as they were written in a very flowery iteration of the ancient Elder script.

"It's the Museum of Arcane History," Kieran supplied.

"Wait, can you read Aetheric?"

"I can, actually," he replied.

Of course he could.

"But in this case, I just know the names of almost every building in this quarter. I know most of this city like the back of my hand."

"Did you grow up in Sophrosyne?"

Kieran glanced away for a moment, suddenly interested in the grit underneath his fingernails.

"Nah, I grew up in Pyrrhas, but very close by. And I've lived here for... Gods, I think it's been five years now? Maybe six."

"Ah, okay."

Only five or six years, and already a captain of the Elder Guard. There was more to Kieran's story, it seemed. Much more. I resisted the urge to pepper him with further questions as he led me down a series of halls. Instead, I turned my attention back to my surroundings. He seemed a bit closed off about his past, and I could respect that. I had my own secrets, after all. Things that I preferred to keep close to the chest.

"It's rather empty, isn't it?" I observed. I could hear our footsteps echo, but not much else.

"That's why it's one of my favorite places in the city," he explained. "For whatever reason, this museum doesn't see much foot traffic during the week."

"I wonder why not," I mused, thinking out loud.

"I'm not sure, actually," Kieran said with a shrug. "But it does make for a nice place to unwind after a long day."

"Aw, have you had a long day, Captain? It's barely noon," I teased, glancing toward a room that looked to be filled with old globes, maps and star charts.

As I started towards it, Kieran caught me by the hand—and I felt my breath catch in my chest. There was something about the sensation of it, the warmth. I hadn't really been touched by anyone in... quite some time. In those scant few seconds, I memorized the roughness of his calloused fingers as they'd wrapped around mine. The sensation was lovely, and it left me wondering what they might feel like against my cheek.

"This way first," he said, interrupting my reverie and nodding his head towards a hall to the left.

Wordlessly, I let go of his hand and followed him into a large, seemingly empty room that was absolutely flooded with natural light pouring in from the skylights above. It was only when we'd made our way into the center of the room that I realized it wasn't empty at all—but rather, the walls were the exhibit here. It was one massive, sweeping mural.

I strained my eyes again, attempting to read the plaque that was, again, carved in Aetheric.

"The... Mur... *Mural*, I'd assume, so... The Mural..." I murmured under my breath.

"They call it the Mural of Creation," Kieran offered. "It's the Elder's depiction of the universe."

Oh. Wow.

I took several steps towards the wall in front of us, marveling at the whorls of color, the elegant brush strokes that had somehow captured the beauty of the cosmos—not in an exact sort of way, but the artist had somehow managed to capture the *essence* of the night sky as the backdrop to several scenes. I tilted my head back just enough to take in the full picture, having been immediately distracted by details.

"It's... the Source..." I breathed.

Kieran nodded, taking it all in beside me.

"Some of the Elders depicted it as this massive cluster of silver crystals, others shaped it more as an entity, a divine feminine form, if you will," he explained quietly.

In this case, the artist had chosen both.

An ethereal looking female figure with eyes of pure silver sat atop a veritable mountain of what appeared to be crystalline aether—faceted with glimmering iridescence. A quicksilver liquid spilled from her cupped hands, the streams of pure aether parting and weaving throughout the rest of the mural with such painstaking intricacy. As if they were the very threads of fate.

It was the most stunning work of art I had ever seen in my life.

"Incredible, isn't it?" Kieran said, still speaking softly even though we were the only ones in the room. There was something odd in the tone of his voice, though. Something unexpected.

It was admiration, I realized as I nodded in agreement. It was *reverence*.

Despite living in an era of relative peace, there was no denying that Kieran was a soldier. He carried himself with that lethal grace, and clearly bore scars to prove what he'd survived over the years.

But beneath the surface... I could've sworn that I saw glimmers of an artist. I caught glimpses of a man who valued beauty, and creation. Whether that was *because* of the bloodshed he'd witnessed over the years, or in spite of it—I wasn't sure yet. But it fascinated me all the same.

He fascinated me.

"Do you know that the Aetherborne don't believe in reincarnation?" Kieran inquired.

"They don't?"

That was news to me. It was the most widely-accepted theory among humans—that our spirits would return to the Source of All Life alongside our aether, allowing us to be born anew in the next cycle of rebirth. I was surprised to hear that the gods disagreed. Those cyclical concepts of growth and decay—that inherent need for balance preserved—it was all practically embedded in the laws of arcane science.

"They do not," Kieran confirmed. "At least, that's what the history texts claim. They say it's how the concept of the Fates was born."

As I turned to look at him, his eyes continued to roam across the mural. There was a certain sort of... nostalgia in that glacial gaze of his now, as if Kieran was recollecting a familiar old story.

"Tell me more?" I requested, my voice coming out a bit breathier than I'd intended, exposing the fact that I was hanging on every word. The corners of his mouth curled upward, though he kept his eyes affixed to the painting.

"It's uncertain whether or not this applies to humankind, but the Elders at least seem to believe that they themselves do not reincarnate. The theory of the Fates predates that of rebirth," he explained. "Because back before the Cataclysm, it was quite rare for an Aetherborne to die."

I nodded, my eyes drifting back to the whorling patterns and brush strokes.

"So rare, in fact, that they would dedicate certain patterns in the stars to the fallen to honor their names—the constellations. But it went beyond symbolism for those ancient Aetherborne, I think. They believed that as beings of pure aether, while their bodies were immediately absorbed by the Source, that their souls would remain among the stars above."

I felt a sharp, familiar tingle at the tip of my nose, the one that always meant I had tears welling up in my eyes. I tried to blink them back, embarrassed.

"And so their fallen brethren would find new purpose," Kieran continued. "As celestial beings, ascending beyond the heavens. It's said that from there, they could reach the Source herself, weaving her threads of Fate to guide the paths of the living by her will. Watching over Aemos for an eternity."

I thought of the Cataclysm, the Awakening, and the Aetherborne's sacrifices. How many souls they must believe still watch over us all, thanks to that fateful day alone. Again, I had to blink back tears, feeling oddly emotional about it all.

"That's somehow both beautiful and terrifying," I admitted after a few moments of shared silence. "The notion of... eternal protectors. The thought that the Fates might actually be real."

At some point, I realized, Kieran had taken his eyes off the mural. He'd been watching me, instead. But there was no judgment to be found on his face as I brushed the stray tear back with my knuckles—just a soft smile. A gentle understanding.

"Yeah," Kieran said after a slow exhale. "Yeah, it really is."

✧ ✧ ✧

We spent the remainder of the afternoon on a lighter note, meandering through the quiet halls as Kieran guided me towards exhibits of interest. It was a massive building, though—by the time the sun began to set, I think I'd only managed to see a quarter of what they had on display.

So much history, so much knowledge, so many artifacts and slices of the past, preserved. It was astounding.

As we left the museum, though, an uncomfortable anxiousness started gnawing at the back of my mind.

Kieran had called this little excursion an "adventure," and it had been a good one. Truthfully, the entire day had been lovely—but did he consider our little *adventure* to be a date? Because it could easily have been interpreted that way, and even though I was painfully attracted to the man... I also really didn't want to lead him on. It wasn't fair. I had to say something.

"Hey, Kieran?"

"Mm?"

"I really enjoyed today. But... before we spend any more time together, can I just ask you something?"

"Go for it," he replied easily, flipping a single gold coin that he'd drawn from his pocket.

"Are you okay with keeping things platonic between us?"

For a moment, Kieran looked oddly taken aback, as if he hadn't expected this conversation at all.

"I mean, I'm sure you don't get this a lot, huh?" I laughed nervously. "It's nothing personal, I just... I don't think I'm ready to settle into anything serious right now. My whole world just expanded in a flash, practically overnight—but I really enjoy your company and—"

"*Arken*," Kieran interjected. "Hush. You don't have to explain yourself. Honestly, you just saved me from an awkward conversation that I wasn't looking forward to. I don't really do the whole... *relationship* thing," he explained.

It wasn't lost on me how he'd said the word *relationship* with clear disdain, but looked almost apologetic about that as his glacial eye searched my face for a reaction.

"I would like to be your friend, though. I don't really do that much, either... But for you, I think I'll have to make an exception."

I felt all of the tension I'd been holding in my shoulders melt down, ignoring the smallest part of me that felt disappointed. Still,

I exhaled in relief. That was significantly easier than I expected.

"I do still need a tour guide," I mused, fluffing my hair and trying to maintain the casual energy he'd so graciously provided for us.

"Oh, I am an *excellent* tour guide, just you wait."

And there it was again. There was a certain lightness, an ease Kieran brought into every conversation, and I found myself craving it. The comfort of being understood.

"I do have to ask, though," he said with a sly half-smile creeping up one side of his face. "Is it because I'm terribly ugly?"

I barked out a laugh. "Oh, shut up, you preening peacock. You know damn well how attractive you are."

"Even pretty men enjoy a good stroke to the ego every now and again," the cheeky bastard replied with a wink. "Among other things."

"*Platonic*," I reminded him.

"What? You can give platonic handjobs. I've given plenty of them."

I resisted the urge to ask for details.

"In your dreams, Vistarii."

"Perhaps," he grinned. "You're not half bad yourself, Asher. I'm pretty sure you'll be giving me a run for my money on disappointing all the men in Sophrosyne soon enough."

"And women," I added.

"Oh?" he raised a brow and his grin widened. "We'll just add that to the list of things we have in common, Little Conduit."

That list of his was growing rather fast.

CHAPTER TWENTY

KIERAN

The next day, I found myself meandering through the Market District with my lieutenants.

Given the nature of our work and respective responsibilities, it was rare for Jeremiah, Hans and I to get off early, and rarer still for all of us to get off-shift at the same time. And so naturally, we took advantage of it—making our way from the Guard Headquarters to the other side of Sophrosyne, searching for a bite to eat.

Admittedly, I was lost in thought. I kept letting my mind wander back to yesterday's impromptu trip to the museum with a certain Little Conduit.

Well. Maybe *impromptu* was a bit of a stretch.

After well over a week's worth of deliberating, reconsidering, and arguing with myself, I had honestly given up. I could no longer help myself, considering the universe seemed Hel-bent on ensuring that Arken and I would repeatedly run into one another. No matter how much I endeavored to leave that poor woman alone.

It wasn't until after she and I had our conversation about keeping things platonic that I realized I had a perfectly acceptable excuse to remain in her orbit. Hadn't Hanjae asked me to keep an eye on her? I could do that.

With pleasure, Commander.

The only issue was that now the dam had broken through. I'd given in to impulse, and now I would be hard pressed not to pester Arken Asher on a daily basis. I mean, I had resisted the urge thus far... today, at least. I had left her alone for a solid twenty-four hours. Still, my mind kept wandering back to those little moments at the museum yesterday, those oddly comforting signals that maybe, *just maybe,* this friendship thing was actually a good idea. For the both of us.

We just had so much in common. I was an excellent mirror, able to parrot the mannerisms and behaviors of others to make them feel at ease—a very useful skill in my line of work. Around Arken, though? I didn't have to. Our similarities were genuine, and strange as that was, as hard as it was to fathom.... It was nice.

Even without those eerily common threads—and those wide, golden eyes that stared straight through my soul—Arken was clever. Charming. Entertaining as Hel. And I had a *little* too much fun messing with her head, teasing her for the childlike wonder she still managed to retain over seemingly ordinary things.

Like a room full of dusty old star-charts, for example.

"You *really* like astronomy, don't you?" I had teased Arken yesterday after we had moved on from the Mural of Creation.

"Is it that obvious?"

"A bit," I'd laughed—though I could hardly say I was surprised.

That was why I had brought her towards that exhibit, after all. It wasn't particularly hard to deduce that a Light Conduit transfixed by Shadows might be drawn to something as alluring and enchanting as the night sky.

"I've always loved the stars. Though, the moon and I have more of an... antagonistic relationship," Arken had replied.

"And why is that, Little Conduit?"

"Because I can never sleep under a full moon," she huffed.

"It's infuriating. Every damn month. Amaretta always said it was because I was born under a full moon."

"So was I, actually," I'd informed her, surprising even myself over being that forthcoming.

"*Really?!*"

As I said... Those odd little similarities between us just kept stacking up.

"You're in an awfully good mood today, captain," Jeremiah said, eying me with suspicion.

"Why do you say that like you're worried about me?" I asked, smirking.

"I mean..." my lieutenant trailed off, letting his expression say the rest—to which I just rolled my eyes.

"I had an unusually good day yesterday. Simple as that," I replied.

"So you got laid?" Hans interpreted.

"That's hardly an *unusual* occurrence," I shot back with a wink. "Well, I mean—perhaps it is for *you,* Deering..."

Jeremiah snorted.

"Oh, fuck off! The both of you!" Hans sputtered.

"You'll kick that dry spell any day now, buddy," Jeremiah laughed. "You know, as soon as you learn how to manage your own expectations."

"What are you trying to say?!"

"Nothing, nothing," Jeremiah said in a reassuring, cheerful tone. "You're a perfectly handsome bastard, Hans. Just *maybe* stop immediately going for the most sapphic woman in the room, and maybe then you can get some."

"It's a curse, it's not my fault," Hans moaned. "It's not like there's any way to tell at a glance! How am I supposed to know that I'm flirting with lesbians half the time?"

"A hint," Jeremiah joked. "If they're ogling *other women* at the bar the whole time, they might not be interested in the likes of *you.*"

"Excuse you," Hans said. "Bisexuality exists. Look at *him!*"

When I glanced over, Hans was pointing a brown, calloused finger in my direction.

"I do indeed exist, bisexually," I acknowledged. "Neither of you assholes are creative enough to conjure me up in your imaginations."

"If Hans could conjure up anything, it would probably be a lesbian," Jeremiah said.

"Alright, enough about *my* sex life, you sneaky bastard. The cradle robber's over here trying to make jokes."

Cradle robber?

I raised a brow, peering over at Jeremiah for context.

"Ignore him," Jer muttered.

Before I could press him for details, I felt the hair on the back of my neck prickle as my body reacted faster than my mind—my neck snapping instinctively towards the Western Gates, towards the sound of commotion. Shouting.

What the fuck?

"Did you two hear that?"

My lieutenants paused, listening—and then quickly met my eyes. I gave them both a brief, terse nod, and the three of us were off, sprinting northwest towards the source of the disturbance. Within minutes, we arrived at a bit of a scene.

A small crowd had formed just outside the entrance to the Guest's District of the city. A pair of novice guardsmen of ours appeared to be trying to reason with a small cluster of Pyrhhan noblesse flanked by several stiff-looking bodyguards—also Pyrhhan.

Oh, joy.

I jerked my head towards the throng of what appeared to be more common folk. *Angry* common folk.

"Sort that out, will you?" I murmured to my lieutenants before striding towards the party of Pyrhhan nobles with confidence. "I'll handle these ones."

As I approached, I quickly recognized two men in particular—Master Levi Mirkovic, High Advisor of Trade within the House of Embers, accompanied by his cousin Gidgeon, the Viscount of the Eastern Pyrhhan territories of Freyston.

"Good afternoon, gentlemen," I offered with a slight bow of the head. A show of respect that was, admittedly, just for show.

"Oh, thank gods," one of the younger guardsmen began. "Captain, there's been—"

"Captain?" Levi interrupted, his lip curling with a sneer. "Good, I'm glad the Elder Guard had the sense to send someone with appropriate authority to handle this situation. Your men have left much to be desired, *Captain*."

"I am *so* sorry to hear that, Advisor. How can I be of assistance?" I simpered smoothly, hoping that I bit back enough of the sarcasm in my tone that it wasn't blatantly obvious.

I had never cared much for the Mirkovics. Especially not Levi—the man was a fucking twat.

"You can *assist* by arresting these miscreants immediately," Levi demanded, shoving a finger towards the group of commoners.

As he did so, flickering embers encircled his wrist. Clearly, the Fire Conduit's temper was getting away from him.

"I'm going to need a bit more information before I can proceed with any of that, Master Mirkovic," I said smoothly, turning back to the freshling. "Brief me on the situation, Kraiggson."

"Yes, sir. According to the Mirkovic party, this small group of Pyrhhan citizens began to follow their traveling caravan just as they passed through from Freyston into our territory. Once they had made it onto neutral ground, the Mirkovics claim that they started harassing their party, namely the Viscount and the High Advisor."

Hardly a crime that warranted arrest in Sophrosyne.

"We *claim*? It's the truth! They threatened to assault me!" Levi interjected, those flickering embers around his coiled fists beginning to grow, stoking themselves into flame as he shook with rage.

The High Advisor of the House of Embers looked as though he was ready to pounce against his own godsdamned constituents.

"With all due respect, sir, I'm going to need you to settle down," I warned. "I can assure you that no harm will come to you or yours within the safety of our city."

I stepped over to one of the Pyrhhan guards while Levi continued his tirade towards anyone who would listen... which was essentially just the Viscount and the poor younger guardsman who didn't know any better.

"Did you witness any legitimate threats of assault or harm, corporal?"

I was fairly familiar with the rank and file of the Pyrhhan guard, recognizing their status immediately based on uniform.

"No, sir. They were causing a scene, but it was mostly just an airing of various grievances," the Pyrhhan guard explained. "They maintained a reasonable distance. We didn't even notice they were following us until we passed the border."

"I see," I said, glancing back towards that small group of townsfolk.

I could only presume they were from Freyston, if they had a bone to pick with the Mirkovic family. It was a clever move, really, to wait until the noblesse had passed through into the territories of Sophrosyne before beginning to cause a ruckus. Clever... and a little bit *too* calculated, for what appeared to be a gaggle of disgruntled farmhands.

"Deering," I called out, motioning for my second-in-command to join me momentarily.

"Captain?"

"I want you to take down their names—all of the Pyrhhan

folk who were following the Mirkovics. Once we have their information, they're free to go."

"Free to go?!" Levi snapped, craning his overly-long neck towards me, his gaunt features fixing themselves into a portrait of disbelief. "Surely, you must be joking."

"I'm afraid the Elder Guard does not hold authority to arrest Pyrhhan citizens without due cause, Master Mirkovic," I replied simply. "Without evidence or a direct order from the Lord of Embers himself."

"Useless," Mirkovic sniffed. "Trust that Lord de Laurent will be hearing of this soon enough."

The High Advisor picked a stray bit of lint from his shoulder before glaring back at me. His eyes narrowed.

"You look... familiar. Have we met before, Captain?" he inquired.

"Nope," I lied cheerfully, beckoning his group towards the Western Gates. If Levi Mirkovic didn't remember me, I much preferred to keep it that way.

"Do enjoy your stay in Sophrosyne," I offered with a dazzling, forced smile—not that any of them could tell the difference. "And be sure to let us know if we can be of any further assistance. I trust you know where to find the Guard."

Before any of the Pyrhhan pricks could respond, I turned on my heel and made my way back to my own men.

"All sorted?" I asked.

"Yes, sir," Hans replied, handing me a small sheath of parchment which I promptly pocketed for later.

I would have to have my sources in Pyrhhas keep a close eye on these ones. I had a feeling that there was more to this little protest than met the eye.

"In that case, you're all free to go. But a word to the wise," I offered. "If you're going to start fights with your figures of authority... Consider sticking to Pyrhhan territory, where the worst thing waiting for you is just a wealthy, *mortal* man. Got it?"

It was a bit of unnecessary intimidation, if I was being honest—but I wanted this crowd dispersed quickly. No disrespect intended to the Pyrhhan Guard, but the colors of the Elder Guard did have a tendency to foster more... compliance, so to speak. Even in the other territories, the gold emblem on our coats always served as a reminder of who and what we stood for. The Seed of Creation represented more than just the ultimate balance between blood and aether, life and divinity. It reminded them who we reported to at the end of the day. Who we served.

The Aetherborne.

We were the sworn sword & shield of the City of Gods, after all.

"Well then," Hans said, after Jeremiah had dismissed the younger guards and the three of us made our way back into the city. "That was interesting."

"You can say that again," Jeremiah muttered. "Sort of strange though, wasn't it? You don't often hear about protestors. Not in Pyrhhas, of all places."

Exactly.

Despite my own personal opinions on leadership within the House of Embers, Jeremiah was right on point. The people of our neighboring territories were, generally speaking, very well taken care of. Pyrhhas had been peaceful, content and thriving for decades. *Yet another reason to raise suspicion*, I thought as I toyed with the parchment in my pocket.

"We'll be looking into it," I said. "And here's hoping that the Mirkovics went straight to the Admin Quarter for business or some shit, I do *not* want to deal with that asshole again today."

"What a prick," Hans agreed.

Besides, the last thing I needed was for Levi or Gidgeon to take a closer second look at me any time soon, lest any old memories stir up.

I had been having a damn good week, and I was simply not in the mood.

CHAPTER TWENTY-ONE

ARKEN

I could feel my own excitement radiating off of my skin in waves. Aside from the entertainment of Laurel's company, I rarely found myself looking forward to much of anything in my Bios lectures these days—but today was an exception.

Today, we were visiting the Irrosi Arboretum.

The fact that I had yet to discover this place on my own was a true testament to the sprawling expanse that was Sophrosyne, reminding me just how *massive* the city-state truly was—and how many secrets must be hidden behind its gleaming white walls. Because the Arboretum stood tall, located towards the very center of the Studium grounds, with a large, domed glass ceiling that glittered in the morning sun.

The building itself was a work of art, the intricate Irrosi architecture stunning to behold—but it was what it held within that truly took my breath away. The moment we stepped through the towering double doors inlaid with stained glass, I felt as though I had been transported to another realm—another plane of existence entirely.

High Scholar Larkin offered me a wry smile at my quick intake of breath, a hushed silence passing through the rest of our class as we were suddenly surrounded by a riot of color—vivid neons, soft pastels. It was darker inside than it had been outdoors, and yet the whole space was aglow, illuminated by natural phosphorescence. And while I had read about the towering mushroom forests of Irros, seeing it for myself was...

Fucking Hel, this was unreal.

Massive, spongey fungi sprouted up from the grounds, their stalks as wide and towering as the thickest of oaks in the Wyldwoods. Their caps were so broad and large that they could serve as the rooftop of a small cottage. Swirls of glimmering spores were drifting through the air like stardust, and for a moment I held my breath. Somewhere in the distance, I could hear faint clicks and cracks that were reminiscent of splintering glass.

For those first few moments, all I could do was stare in awe, mouth agape until Laurel let out a low whistle, nudging me with her elbow to get my attention.

"*Psst.* Arken. Beautiful bookwyrm alert."

"Hmm?"

"Greetings, young Conduits!" An unfamiliar voice called out. "Please rest assured that it is perfectly safe to breathe freely without face coverings—these glowing spores of the *Amacita Luxpharia* are not toxic or harmful to humans in any way. The same cannot be said of it's cousin, though, the *Amacita Lunaeris*—but that particular species is not kept here."

A beautiful bookwyrm, indeed.

The man in question, currently waxing poetic on these Irossi native mushrooms, was a stunning specimen himself. He was tall and tan, beaming with a friendly grin that lit up his entire freckled face. His green eyes glittered with enthusiasm as he clapped High Scholar Larkin on the back with familiarity.

"It's good to see you, Jude."

"Students, I would like you to meet Scholar Thompson, the lead researcher here at the Arboretum," Larkin said. "He has graciously offered to guide our tour today, so please utilize his expertise as the rare resource it is, and ask plenty of questions!"

"The real rare resource is whatever shampoo that man uses," Laurel murmured under her breath. "Look at that *hair*."

Ever the astute observer when it came to anyone remotely attractive, Laurel wasn't wrong—the scholar's hair was a deep chocolate brown, sleek as all Hel, and had to be longer than mine. Good gods.

"Oh, please," Scholar Thompson replied to Larkin, cheeks flushing a bit. That made his freckles more pronounced, which was sort of adorable. "You flatter me. But hello there, students. You can call me Ezra, and I will be your guide this afternoon. As Scholar Larkin is well aware, I jump at any opportunity to discuss regional biomes. Irrosi horticulture, in particular, is a specialty of mine."

As we proceeded through the first wing of the building, Scholar Larkin droned on about some of the basic details of the tropics of Irros. I focused on taking in the sights and sounds, though I occasionally pulled out my notebook to scribble down some of the more nuanced details as Ezra weighed in. I had to admit, the man knew his mushrooms.

"Watch your step!" A voice called overhead as we approached the second wing.

Wait. Overhead?

When I looked up, I almost yelped in surprise. One of the researchers—a Water Conduit, I realized—was floating above us, seated atop a massive bead of swirling liquid.

Holy Hel, you could *do* that with arcana? Literally *levitate*?

"Don't try this at home, folks," he said, peering down at us with a grin. "Ready when you are, Addie!"

I watched on in quiet fascination as the Water Conduit began working in tandem with another researcher, the one he'd called Addie. She'd been standing a few feet away at the base of one of the largest mushrooms. As it turned out, Addie was a Fire Conduit—evidenced by the fact that she began tossing small bursts of Fire arcana overhead, sending them hurtling towards the gills of the massive mushroom canopy.

What on Aemos was she...?

But the floating Conduit worked in perfect synchronization with his companion, tossing out small orbs of Water aether to douse every flame, which in turn dispersed a fine, warm mist throughout the air around us.

"In order to maintain the right environment for the flora and fauna of Irros to flourish here, our groundskeepers have developed this unique method of dispersing heat and moisture into the air," Ezra explained. "El and Addison often work in tandem to bring the mist straight up the gills of these majestic mycelium, where it can be most readily absorbed."

How fascinating.

"*Majestic mycelium?* Is this man for real?" Laurel whispered, rolling her eyes.

"Hush, you," I shot back under my breath. "This is interesting."

As I watched the groundskeepers go back and forth with this synchronous little flow of Water and Fire, my fingers began to tingle. That familiar itch was back, the urge to emulate the arcana myself. I wouldn't even need a partner, and the spellwork seemed simple enough...

I sighed heavily, clamping down on the impulse before anything could manifest.

Not now, Arken. Not here.

Most of the time, this secret of mine was manageable enough, but I still hated it. I hated having to shove my other Resonances down in public, severing what felt like such a natural connection to the elemental world around me. I hated having to hide something that seemed so harmless on the surface, but became something insidious, something dangerous when you stopped to consider the implications. I hated not knowing what it *meant*, that I could do these things.

Huffing again, I tugged the Light towards me instead. I slipped my hands into my pockets to avoid drawing attention to myself, and let that familiar glow wash over my fingertips. Even without the shimmering visual feedback, I took comfort in the sensation of using at least *some* of my Resonance, in feeling what was mine. Embracing the part of me that I didn't have to hide.

"Oh, drats," Scholar Thompson muttered to himself as we approached the third wing of the sprawling arboretum. "I nearly forgot. Before we proceed with the rest of the tour, are any of you arachnophobic? Don't be shy, it's a perfectly common fear, but if you don't enjoy spiders... you might want to excuse yourselves now."

"If you don't enjoy spiders? Who the Hel *enjoys* spiders?" Laurel whispered. "Also, did he seriously just say "drats"?"

"Will you leave that poor man alone? If you're scared, you can always hold my hand," I teased.

"I never said I was afraid of them," she sniffed. "I simply tolerate their existence."

"You say that now..." I mused, knowing what was to come next. "And for the record, I enjoy spiders."

"You would."

"It's just about feeding time for our little friends, so they'll be getting more active overhead as they leave the nest," Scholar Thompson said, looking up, and my eyes followed suit.

"Holy Hel," I breathed.

There had to be thousands upon thousands of strands of wispy, iridescent spidersilk draped from every corner of the ceiling. The thin, pliant cords extended down from the tops of every tree and mushroom cap to form various structures—tunnels, hammocks, makeshift ladders and webs of all sorts.

I started to lose focus on the lecture, finding myself hypnotized by the patterns in the silk and the way that glowing spores and droplets of dew seemed to cling to every strand, glistening like jewels, like berries from the bush. It wasn't until that strange clicking noise from earlier returned and Laurel jolted beside me that I snapped out of the enchanted haze. The clicks and crackles were louder now. Much louder.

"Holy shit! What the fuck is that fucking thing?!" Laurel squealed, gripping at my bicep.

Ah. There it was.

"Language, Miss Ansari," Scholar Larkin chided sternly. "But can anyone answer her question?"

Unlike Laurel, I had spent the whole night prior studying up on Irrosi biomes. Partially because I was excited for this, and partially because it was the only way I could even *attempt* to get my mind off a certain guardsman after he'd walked me home.

"*Latrodectus lustrae*," I offered as one of the giant, crystalline looking arachnids started skittering out from the nest. "Those are Astral Spinners."

"Indeed! Very good," Ezra said, breaking into a wide grin, as if a smidgen of class participation had made his whole damn day. "This one is Elorei, one of our young adult female Spinners."

Elorei was making her slow descent from the gills of the mushroom canopy and I watched in near disbelief that a single, thin thread of spidersilk could bear the weight of such a large, translucent carapace. Again, it was one thing to read about these things, but to *witness* them...

I found myself hanging on Scholar Thompson's every word as he detailed the uses for their silk, how it was harvested, and the seemingly symbiotic relationship between the Spinners and the mushrooms themselves. To Laurel's credit, she held back most of her snark for the remainder of the lecture... though she would still occasionally snort when my hand would shoot up, begging Ezra for more details.

What could I say? I just really liked mushrooms.

◇ ◇ ◇

Long after the lecture had concluded and our class had dispersed, I found myself lingering in the arboretum, still utterly fascinated. Every corner and crevice had something new, something worth scribbling notes about in my journal—much to Laurel's chagrin.

"You don't have to stay here with me, you know, Laur."

"I know. But damn. You're really into this shit, aren't you?" she asked.

I nodded. "Yeah, I am."

"I know you said you don't really have plans for the future yet, but... have you ever considered becoming a scholar? I'm sure you could specialize in Bios, join the ranks with our pals Jude and Ezra."

I paused for a moment, tapping my chin with my drawing pencil, and then shrugged.

"There was a time where I thought I might go that route," I admitted. "When I was younger, all I wanted to do was follow in my mentor's footsteps and become a High Scholar one day. But not so much anymore. I love nature, it absolutely fascinates me, but it's more of a personal connection. And I'm not much for teaching. Though I suppose I could become a researcher... I can't say that path particularly appeals to me, though."

"Does that ever bother you?" Laurel asked, her expression unreadable as she took a seat on the stump next to me.

"Which part?"

"The... not knowing what comes next. The lack of a larger life plan. Not that there's anything wrong with that, Ark. I think it's cool that you're just here to learn. It's just such a foreign concept to me. I can't quite wrap my head around it."

"It used to bother me a lot, actually," I confessed. "Back home.

The uncertainty of not knowing what I really wanted used to drive me insane. But I swear, the minute I arrived in Sophrosyne, something in me just sort of settled. It felt like I was where I was supposed to be."

"Aw. That's sort of beautiful, Ark," Laurel said softly, smiling. "I'm happy for you, even if I do envy your ability to just... live in the moment."

"It's funny, when we first met, that was actually what I admired about *you*," I told her. "I thought you just seemed to float around with ease, like a little social butterfly. But there's more to you than meets the eye, Ansari."

Laurel snorted.

"Yeah, well, you know. It's easy to play that role when it's your social life that's keeping you sane. Sure, there's more to me than meets the eye, such as: the constant state of stress I'm living in these days," she said. She kept her tone light, though I could hear the edge of tension.

"You wanna talk about it?" I asked, keeping my tone neutral and unimposing. I didn't want to pressure her... I was just opening the door.

Laurel shrugged before releasing a heavy sigh.

"My family expects me to be in and out of the Studium within two years. An "accelerated path," so that I can come back home and start to apprentice under Baba and Lord Ymir again. It's like... It wasn't enough that they've been grooming me for my entire life, right? Just because I was the first child to pop out of the womb. This High Advisor role has belonged to the eldest Ansari for centuries, and it's afforded my entire family so much comfort, so many opportunities... So who am I to break that chain?"

"Do you want to?" I asked, continuing to sketch, though I was actively listening. I found that it put most people at ease if you didn't stare at them while they bared their soul, and it was easier for me to focus on deeper conversations when my hands were occupied. "Break the chain, I mean."

"That's the thing," Laurel said. "I don't think that I do. I mean, before I ever came to Sophrosyne, I had already studied trade at the College of Torrents. I had already worked with the Merchant's Guild, attended multiple trade summits—and believe it or not, I'm actually good at that shit, Ark."

I arched a brow, but let her continue.

"I know, I know, you wouldn't picture me in a room full of stuffy old viscounts and merchants, but I can actually hold my own with them. And I like that. I like knowing that I can make a difference one day. That I might guide Lord Ymir towards policies that serve Samhaven well."

I had teased Laurel on several occasions about how she should consider a future in politics. I hadn't realized that in a lot of ways, that's precisely where she was headed. A role of influence amongst the Atlassian Courts.

"Godsdamn," I murmured. "That's actually pretty incredible, Laur."

"Thanks," she sighed.

"It's also an incredible amount of pressure to be under when you're so young. You're what, twenty?"

"Yeah. I guess I was sort of hoping that I would have a little more time, you know? A little more freedom, maybe. Room to breathe. I'm afraid that the next two years will come and go in no time at all."

Suddenly, I understood so much more about my friend and the antics of sleeping her way through the city. I had already gotten the sense that it was some sort of a reclamation of personal autonomy, considering the Ansari family's plans for an arranged marriage in her future. I could see now that it went beyond a small rebellion, though.

Laurel just wanted to experience everything she could out here... while she still could.

I decided that I would endeavor to be less difficult when the woman tried to drag me out for drinks, dancing and rubbing elbows with our peers.

"Gods, Ark, I'm sorry to just dump that all on you at once. You're really easy to talk to, you know that?"

"I get that a lot, actually," I laughed.

It was such a strange contradiction. Though I often felt like a spectator, an outsider looking in on the human experience, I had also studied it. My empathy became an obsession sometimes, an urge to dig deep. A selfish impulse to sink my teeth into what made other people tick, as if it might explain what I was lacking. And I could often taste the emotional wounds of others long before they ever revealed them out loud.

Though that was also why I had a tendency to keep to myself. It was overwhelming, *feeling* so much all the godsdamned time. I could never seem to turn it off. To then inadvertently collect the burdens of others, to experience that weight alongside them whether I liked it or not, to feel their emotions as if they were my own... It was a lot.

Very few people that I had encountered in life were worth that headache. People like Laurel, like Kieran... they were exceptions.

"Lost in thought over there, Asher?" Laurel teased. "Or just very focused on capturing that mushroom with flawless precision?"

"Both," I laughed, finishing up my sketch of an unfamiliar cluster of fungi. "Definitely both. Gods, I love mushrooms."

"Um, I think you mean *majestic mycelium*," Laurel said with a smirk, mimicking Ezra's mannerisms.

Wistfully, I wished I had brought my watercolor kit so that I could capture the pale lilac hues of the stalk and the vibrant, lacy little skirt that was a deeper violet. Instead, I tried to commit the colors to memory so that I could go look it up later.

"Okay, Asher. The lecture wrapped up an hour ago. I love you to death, but I'm starving, and I get the feeling that if left to your own devices, you'd stay here sketching until nightfall. Come on."

Rising to her feet, Laurel plucked my journal out of my hands, ruffling my hair affectionately.

"If we must," I sighed.

"We must," Laurel replied, handing my journal back. She seemed much more at ease now that she had gotten some of that shit off her chest. "All this mushroom talk has me craving that chanterelle & thyme galette from the Arrowhead."

At the mention of food, my stomach rumbled and I realized that, yet again, I had forgotten to eat breakfast. Laurel gave me a pointed look, as if she knew, and reached down to tug at my arm.

"Come along, bookwyrm. My treat."

CHAPTER TWENTY-TWO

KIERAN

Jeremiah and Hans were prattling on about something unimportant, or at the very least, something *uninteresting* again. For a pair of grown ass men, they sure got themselves deeply invested in the Atlassian rumor mill.

I had distanced myself from the nonsense of the political elite a long time ago, and didn't particularly care to reinvest my time or energy into that shit unless I absolutely had to. And sometimes I did have to, due to the nature of my work—but this was not one of those occasions.

Who the fuck *cared* that some heiress from Vindyrst had run off with another House heir? And who could blame her? The Zephirin family was not unlike the Mirkovics: it was filled to the brim with notoriously awful people.

I was about to say as much when I stilled, my ears pricking up when I heard a familiar, sparkling peal of laughter several paces behind us. Another round of louder giggles told me all I needed to know. That was most certainly Arken and her partner in crime, Laurel Ansari.

"Isn't that your captain?" Laurel was whispering, in a hushed tone that was far from subtle.

I smirked at the way Laurel seemed to emphasize the "your" in that sentence—apparently blissfully unaware that the Conduits in my cadre of the Guard were trained to use our arcana for enhanced hearing. I paused mid-step, pretending to examine the available goods at a nearby stall, and resisted the urge to turn around. As much as I wanted to see her pretty face, I was having fun eavesdropping.

"Isn't that *your* Conduit?" Jeremiah parroted beneath his breath, nudging my shoulder as I pretended to listen to the vendor hawk his wares. Meanwhile, Arken and Laurel were deliberating on whether or not they should approach us.

"I think we should invite them."

"Oh gods, don't you dare," Arken replied with a stern whisper. *"He's with his lieutenants, Laur."*

"So?"

"So leave them alone! They're probably working."

"I can think of a number of petty crimes we could commit to get their attention," Laurel laughed.

"Do! Not!" Arken hissed.

"We're off duty, actually," Hans called over his shoulder with a wicked grin, and I groaned. "So hold off on any criminal activity, if you'd be so kind."

Leave it to Deering to ruin my fun in favor of the attention of a pretty woman. As the three of us turned around to greet Arken and her friend, I found myself mildly startled.

While Ansari's shrewd gaze traveled between my men and I with intrigue, Arken was staring at me. Just me. And when our eyes met, she smiled—not the tight-lipped, performative gesture that I'd seen her offer others before by way of greeting. No, this was an all-out grin, her straight white teeth sparkling in the sun.

Fucking Hel.

It had been less than twenty-four hours, but that smile of hers lit me up the same way it had yesterday. For a moment, it felt as though we were standing in front of the Mural of Creation again...

not some hawker's stand for trinkets and knick-knacks.

"Does that mean you three are free to accompany us for a late lunch, then?" Laurel asked. "I'm not going to name names, but *someone* here forgot to eat breakfast. We're heading over to the Arrowhead Inn."

Jeremiah and Hans glanced back at me, both clearly interested, but they waited for my answer. I had a feeling both of my lieutenants were chomping at the bit for a closer look at the woman who had managed to ensnare me into a casual friendship. Especially after our conversations earlier about the "awfully good mood" I was in today.

I shrugged. "Sure, why not? If you two don't mind the intrusion, I can't say we had anything better to do," I replied, and my men exchanged a grin. "Lead the way, Miss Ansari."

As Laurel began to stride south with confidence, Jeremiah and Hans quickly fell into an easy conversation with her, leaving Arken and I to meander several paces behind.

"Well, hello again, Little Conduit," I purred. "Long time no see."

"Indeed," Arken replied, a hint of that wry smile remaining. "Did you miss me that much already, stalker?"

"Naturally," I said.

Though I kept my tone light, it wasn't a lie. I started missing Arken's kind company the moment I'd dropped her off at her studio last night, which was both unusual and somewhat disconcerting. But I had given up on trying to stay away from her.

"Did you miss *me*?"

"No," she laughed, though I made note of how she glanced away briefly, her cheeks coloring as she said it. "But I do miss the museum already."

"We could always go back," I offered. "Though there are quite a few other spots I'd like to show you first. You know, as your official tour guide to Sophrosyne."

"Oh? Do you have a list or something?"

"Perhaps I do," I mused noncommittally.

I did. I absolutely did have a list of places I wanted to take Arken around the city, and that list had been growing by the hour every time I passed by something or somewhere I thought she might enjoy.

"So what were you two up to this afternoon?" I asked. "Besides skipping breakfast."

"Oh *gods*, not you, too," she groaned. "Spare me the lecture, Captain. This just happens sometimes when I get excited. We had a Bios lecture."

"You got so excited over a lecture that you forgot the most important meal of the day?" I teased.

"In my defense, it was a lecture at the Irrosi Arboretum. A smidge more exciting than Larkin's typical talks."

Okay, yeah, that would do it—the Arboretum had been on that ever-growing list of mine. I felt oddly satisfied knowing that I had figured her out, to an extent.

"Fair enough," I said. "But you best be intending to get some food in your system before you and Ansari start drinking on rooftops again. We've been over this."

The inn her friend was guiding us towards wasn't far off now, and Laurel paused for a moment, allowing us both to catch up to the group.

"You are *not* allowed to monopolize all of her attention today, Vistarii," Laurel informed me, eyes narrowing.

I offered a slight bow of the head, extending open hands in acknowledgement of her demand. I couldn't deny that, given the opportunity, I would have done exactly that. Hans let out a low whistle, eyebrows raised, clearly impressed by anyone who had the audacity to order *me* around.

We entered the inn as a group and got ourselves situated at a small table before I stood, offering to order us drinks at the bar as

Arken happily fell into animated conversation with Laurel, Hans and Jeremiah.

The drinks were mostly an excuse to familiarize myself with the layout of this establishment, as I had never actually been *inside* the Arrowhead Inn. It was important to me to identify every exit, gauge the room, and also to be strategic about where I would be sitting. My lieutenants already knew my preference for corner tables, and had thankfully picked one on the left hand side of the room. In many ways, I could rely on my Shadows to make up for the loss of vision in my left eye—but I was much more comfortable when I didn't have to utilize that arcana constantly, especially in a social setting.

"It's interesting that the Guard has secondary uniforms," Arken was saying as I made my way back to the table, several flagons of ale in hand for my lieutenants and Laurel. The Little Conduit had politely declined any alcohol on an empty stomach, which pleased me more than I cared to admit.

"Secondary *what now*?" Jeremiah was asking with a raised brow, before glancing back at me. "Oh."

"That's his secondary uniform, alright," Hans snickered. "Or, as I like to call it, *bait.*"

"I heard that," I said, dropping off the ale.

"Is he wrong, though?" Laurel challenged, seeming amused. "Seems to me like that tunic of yours is awfully low-cut. Ill-fitting, or intentional, Vistarii?"

I grinned wolfishly, resisting the urge to catch Arken's eye even though I could feel her gaze traversing over me with newfound intrigue.

"Now, now," I purred. "I can't expose *all* my methods of acquiring delicate information."

Hans wasn't wrong, though. Not in the slightest. My attire today, like most days, was crafted and donned with intention. Unless I was doing more routine work such as guarding the gates, or babysitting a lecture, it was rare to catch me in the official uniform of the Elder Guard. I was recognizable enough as is, what with the massive facial scar, a pretty face, and a mild degree of notoriety—so anything that might help me keep even a *slightly* lower profile was conducive to my work.

And as far as the "low-cut" tunic was concerned, well, that was intentional too. When it came to the acquisition of information, it was all too easy for me to rely on baser human instincts. I wasn't afraid to use every tool in my arsenal to get things done. It was a simple truth: lips were loosened by attraction—and I was perfectly content to let myself be ogled when it lent me such advantages in the field.

As Laurel and Hans returned to slinging pointed barbs back and forth, I took notice of a small group of guardsmen who had just entered the room. Jeremiah appeared to notice them with interest, as well.

"I'll be right back," he murmured to us as he placed his napkin on the table. "I want to check in with Kraiggson."

"That's one way to phrase it," Hans snorted, his expression knowing as he took a large quaff of ale. It didn't slip my notice that he was strategically avoiding my sharpened gaze.

The fuck was he talking about?

Laurel tilted her head in curiosity as well, to which Hans only shrugged as my other lieutenant took his leave and waltzed up to the bar. I continued to chew on the warm hunk of sourdough bread that had accompanied my lunch of rabbit stew, beginning to piece certain implications together.

I tuned in and out of the conversation at the table, mostly watching Jeremiah now.

As he was conversing with Grant, one of the younger guardsmen in our scouting unit, the man was smiling—laughing. At ease. I continued to observe in careful silence, noting the way he leaned into the other man, the tips of his pale ears tinged with a deepening pink.

Ah. Cradle robber indeed.

Jeremiah had a godsdamned crush on a freshling. And under any other circumstances, I might have been happy for the man, but—

Arken yawned, stretching herself out while seated on the bench beside me. All it took was one brush of her ample thigh against mine, and suddenly my train of thought was entirely derailed. A small groan of relief escaped her mouth as she worked out whatever kink in her posture had been bothering her.

Good gods, that sound.

I took a needlessly large sip of my water and returned my focus to the conversation at hand… to the best of my ability.

"So, as I was saying. I really don't know what's got the Zephirin's all worked up over this. I mean, *if* they're as worked up as people say," Hans was saying to Laurel.

"Oh, trust me. *They are,*" Laurel confirmed.

Ugh.

"I cannot believe you're still talking about this shit," I groaned, pinching the bridge of my nose.

Arken's quiet snort was the only validation I needed.

CHAPTER TWENTY-THREE

Arken

I, for one, found it endlessly amusing that Hans Deering, a highly respected lieutenant in the Elder Guard of Sophrosyne, was so very invested in the latest romantic scandal between the Houses. Apparently, Penelope Zephirin, second heir to the House of Gales, had recently run off with Johan Ymir—the son of Lord Gabriel Ymir of Samhaven. This was apparently a big deal. Kieran, however, did not seem to agree.

"Listen here, Captain. You might have grown up in the peace of Pyrhhas, but some of us come from the messier Houses. Let us bask in the hometown drama," Hans shot back, rolling his eyes at his captain.

Laurel cackled.

"Are you from Vindyrst, then, Deering?" she asked.

"Unfortunately," Hans replied with a grimace.

"So it should come as no surprise to you that even though Kole is the acting Lord of the House, it's Cecelia who runs that whole show, yeah?"

"Quite. A toast to the Lady of Gales," Hans said sarcastically, raising his glass.

"No chance in Hel," Kieran muttered under his breath, before turning towards me.

"Do you want anything to drink now that you've actually got food in your system, Little Conduit?"

"I wouldn't mind some cider, if they've got anything local," I said, smiling. "I'm not picky."

Though I, like Kieran, had no real interest in the political direction of conversation, I was having a good time. The mushroom tart that Laurel had brought us here for was indeed worth the trip, and the past few days in general had been rather pleasant.

Kieran nodded, briefly touching my shoulder as he stood. The brush of his fingertips was so subtle that it was likely unintentional... But that didn't stop it from distracting me entirely from the conversation at hand. It wasn't until the captain was halfway across the room that I managed to tune back into Hans and Laurel's gossip session.

"Obviously the woman is *ruthless,* you know that. And she's *constantly* butting heads with Lord Ymir in private. Like, let's be real, none of the other Lords and Ladies can even stand her. So it's not like Penelope had a long line of suitors, anyway. Just between us? I think the real reason why Lady Zephirin is so furious is that she'd been trying to groom Pen to be some perfect bride so she could negotiate a proposal from the Lord of Embers."

Hans snorted.

"A second-born heir, matching with the most eligible bachelor in Atlas? Is Cecelia *high*?"

Laurel shrugged. "Lord Ymir speaks very highly of the High Lord de Laurent. I doubt that her position within the House of Gales would matter much to a man like him, but he *is* notoriously picky. Every attempted advantageous pairing fell through when he was younger, I guess... And now, the man simply doesn't date."

"We have *got* to hang around more often, Ansari," Hans said with a wicked grin. "You clearly have *all* the insider information."

Laurel feigned a curtsy while remaining seated.

"See, Ark? At least *someone* here appreciates my socialite expertise!"

I shook my head gently, still bemused.

"I'll be right back," I promised.

All of the ice water that I had gulped down when we first arrived had run straight through my system, so I excused myself to find a restroom while Hans and Laurel resumed their chatter.

◇ ◇ ◇

After washing up, I was about to round the corner and return to the main dining room of the Arrowhead Inn when I heard Kieran's voice, dropped low and deadly serious.

"You know I trust you, right, Jer?"

I should have kept walking. This conversation was clearly none of my business—Kieran had pulled his lieutenant to the quiet side of the inn for a reason.

Unfortunately, when my curiosity and my moral compass went head to head, it was often a coin toss on which would win. Adding in my absolute fascination with Kieran meant the game was rigged. I continued to eavesdrop, like an asshole.

"I know," Jeremiah was murmuring back, tension clipping into his tone.

"Why haven't you said anything?"

"It's not that serious, Captain. We haven't..."

I heard Kieran exhale slowly.

"Don't bullshit me, Fairchilde. I saw the way he was looking at you. Grant Kraiggson is very clearly into you. Are you saying that's unrequited? When you literally just up and left lunch to approach him at the bar? Come on now."

"No, sir. It's not necessarily unrequited, but that doesn't matter. I acted on impulse and I apologize. I shouldn't have approached him. It won't happen again."

"Jer, if you're interested in the man, I'm not here to judge. Sure, he's a little young, but that's not my concern. But I do need to know your intentions... *before* anything escalates."

"He's my direct report, sir. That would be an abuse of authority and a breach of policy. Things won't go any further."

Kieran groaned.

"I'm not trying to lecture you here, Jer—though you're doing a damn good job at lecturing yourself. I'm trying to extend an *offer*. We can always talk to Hanjae. Grant's a fairly fresh recruit, it wouldn't be difficult to get him shifted to another unit so that he's *not* your direct report."

"I'm not gonna upend this man's career just so that I can fuck him, Kieran."

"His career?" Kieran clucked. "Kraiggson is a shit scout and you know it. He'd honestly be better suited elsewhere. But I can't in good faith keep him under you if he's going to end up... you know. *Under you*."

I bit my tongue, resisting the urge to laugh. Abyss take me.

"I told you, I would never abuse my authority over him. It's not right."

"I know you wouldn't, Jer. But that sexual tension alone could create risks that I'm not comfortable with in our cadre. Just think on it, alright? Keep your head on straight. Think it through, and keep me posted."

"Yes, sir."

"It's okay to move on, you know," Kieran said, his tone slipping from authoritative to... something much more gentle. "It's been a long time. He would want you to be happy."

At that, the conversation seemed to end, and once I heard footsteps head in the opposite direction, I rounded the corner—only to run headfirst into Kieran, who was leaning casually against the wall.

Shit.

"Hello there, little eavesdropper," he purred, eyes gleaming.

"Shit. I'm so sorry," I stammered out. "I didn't mean to—"

"Don't be," Kieran interrupted, shrugging. "I trust your discretion. But we are going to have to work on your stealth skills, methinks. You were hardly subtle."

"Still, I had no right to hear any of that," I said, grimacing at my own behavior.

Kieran shrugged again. "If I wasn't comfortable being overheard, I wouldn't have had the conversation in a public space, Arken. It's no big deal."

I'm sure that I was bright red, regardless.

"It's very admirable," I said softly. "The way you handled that. What you were offering Jeremiah."

Kieran glanced back across the room, his icy gaze flickering to our corner table where his lieutenant had rejoined an animated conversation with Laurel and Hans. Laurel was spinning a single gold coin on the table, likely starting up some sort of drinking game. I shook my head, smiling.

"Admirable? Nah," Kieran replied. "I'm just doing my job. As both his captain, and as his friend. Jer... Well, he hasn't really expressed interest in anyone since his last heartbreak. Caleb. It's a long story, but it's been years. So if he's actually into that freshling, I'd much rather open a few doors to make the relationship appropriate, rather than expect him to hold back his feelings for the sake of policy."

For somebody who spoke of *relationships* and *commitment* as though they were dirty words, Kieran sure seemed to understand the nuanced nature of such things. And he clearly had empathy for Jeremiah and his position. I couldn't help but wonder why a man so intuitive, so emotionally intelligent and insightful, felt the need to avoid companionship like a plague. Not like *that* was any of my business, either.

"Still, there are plenty of leaders who would have responded to that shit with a lecture and a write up, nothing more," I said. "It's no wonder the three of you are close. They both really trust you."

"You have *got* to stop saying nice things about me, Little Conduit," Kieran laughed, pushing himself off the wall. "It's going to go straight to my head. Come on, let's get you that cider."

After we rejoined our friends, the five of us remained at the Arrowhead Inn for several more hours—eating, drinking and laughing. It was a surprisingly easy dynamic. Though Kieran and his men led wildly different lives from Laurel and I, we were all fairly close in age. Like Kieran, Hans and Jeremiah were only in their mid-twenties—and we all had more in common than I expected.

Once the sun began to set, Laurel declared her intentions.

"Alright, you fucks. As delightful as this place is, I'm in need of harder liquor and hotter women to flirt with."

"I'll drink to that," Hans replied heartily.

"Come join me at The Clover?" Laurel asked the table, though she turned on the puppy-dog eyes when she caught my gaze in particular.

I groaned, shaking my head.

"You guys go have fun, I'm tapping out for the night. I need to catch up on my notes and get some rest, I've got an early lecture tomorrow."

"I'll walk you home," Kieran offered.

It wasn't lost on me how Hans and Jeremiah exchanged a *look* over that, though neither of them said anything.

"I hardly need a tour guide to get back to my apartment," I said quietly, mostly to Kieran. "Why not join the others?"

"Not really in the mood," Kieran murmured back while the rest of the group began to get up. His lieutenants stretched and groaned over the discomfort of the hardwood benches where they'd been seated, but I had a feeling they'd be fine as soon as they got to The Clover.

"Suit yourself, Captain," I replied, keeping my tone even despite the fact that I was secretly delighted for the company.

If there was one thing that man did *not* need, it was an ego stroke.

◆ ◆ ◆

"Thank you, Arken."

Kieran's eyes had gone a bit distant as we were walking together, effortlessly weaving through the bustling crowds of the Market District with his guidance.

"For what, exactly?" I teased. "You're the one who picked up the tab."

Much to Laurel's chagrin, Kieran paid for all our food and drink before anyone else had time to even so much as reach for their Lyra. It didn't escape my notice that he tipped the wait staff generously. And I found that what was once a simple, if not *slightly obsessive,* curiosity was quickly morphing into a deep admiration for the man that was Kieran Vistarii.

The more I observed, the more I found to appreciate about this man who was once just a handsome stranger. The more time we spent together, the more I began to wonder why he only seemed to have two people in his life that he was even *remotely* close with. And the more he and I spoke, the more I had to wonder what made *me* an exception to a lifestyle that seemed to be so carefully crafted to keep people at a distance.

After a brief pause, Kieran answered.

"It's rare that I get to see those two so at ease and relaxed. It was good to see them let loose a little. They had fun."

"I doubt I had anything to do with that," I replied.

"No, you did. You definitely did."

Catching my eye and my clearly puzzled expression, Kieran laughed.

"I act differently around you," he explained. "More like a *person*, and less like their captain. And I've just been in a better mood lately, which is also arguably your fault."

I prayed to the Source that the low light of dusk would mask my flushing cheeks.

"Adding you and Laurel to the mix seemed to let them relax. And with how stressful things have been for us lately... It was a relief, to say the least. I worry about them. So thank you, Little Conduit."

I shrugged, still uncertain if that was *my* influence. If anything, it was probably Laurel's.

"Anytime, Captain. But I'm surprised you didn't join them at The Clover. They'll be even more at ease once Laurel gets going. That woman is a menace on the dance floor."

Kieran chuckled.

"I'm sure, but that's not exactly my scene. They deserve to let loose without their captain's watchful eye from time to time."

"You don't drink much, do you?" I observed.

"Nope," he replied. "I'm not a fan of dulling my senses. And honestly? It fucks with my depth perception even more than usual."

Kieran gestured to his blind eye in explanation. That made... perfect sense, actually. As tempting as it was to ask him how that wound even happened, I held my tongue. There was no need to be invasive.

"So what do you do to unwind, then?" I asked him instead.

He cocked a brow, smirking.

"I read. I run. I train. Among other... physical things."

I tried my best to disregard the low rasp present in his voice as he spoke, causing visions of such *other physical things* to swim through my mind.

"Though I'll admit, you don't strike me as the type who drinks often, either."

"No, not particularly," I mused. "Mostly in social situations. Also, Laurel is a bad influence."

Kieran gave me a doubtful look.

"Something tells me you're not so easily influenced, Miss Asher," he said dryly. "I'd wager you can be bad enough all by yourself."

"Perhaps," I said with a grin.

As the sky darkened, I found myself distracted by the twinkling constellations as they peeked through the clouds. For a moment, I forgot that Kieran was at my side as I paused, sighing wistfully and staring up at the sky.

"There's that look again," Kieran chuckled.

"What look?" I asked.

"The same look you had the entire time we were at the museum yesterday. The fascination. The *wonder*. You see beauty in everything, don't you?"

Gooseflesh raised on my forearms, and I wasn't sure if it was due to the chill of the breeze, or the fact that his words left me so exposed.

"Doesn't everybody admire the night sky?"

"No. Not like you do."

Gods. I almost wanted to press him for details, demanding to know what he meant by that... But I also wasn't about to fish for compliments from Kieran. The man made me blush enough as is.

"It's hard not to be fascinated," I murmured, eyes still affixed to the heavens. "Especially considering what you told me yesterday. I keep thinking about it."

"About which part?" Kieran asked, perfectly patient. As if my distraction didn't bother him in the slightest.

"About the Aetherborne and how they mapped out the constellations in the names of the fallen. That whole concept of the

Fates existing among the stars, guiding our paths... I don't know. It stuck with me."

I glanced over at him just in time to catch a quick grimace. "What?"

"It's nothing, Little Conduit. Go back to your star gazing."

I huffed out a sigh, pouting in his direction. "Tell me."

Kieran's gaze shifted from me, back up towards the skies I had been admiring.

"I'm not sure if I believe in the Fates. Or in fate, in general."

"At all?"

He shook his head, exhaling slowly.

"Why not?" I asked, legitimately curious.

"For starters, I'm not particularly religious," Kieran said, still staring at the sky. "I'm actually more of an anti-theist, truth be told." His expression had gone blank. Distant and unreadable. "And to me, the concept of fate and faith tend to go hand in hand. Both require you to believe in some unseen, all-powerful force at play, with very little evidence to prove its existence."

We were aligned in that respect, but I let him continue.

"Don't get me wrong, I think the Elders' story of creation is profound. But I'm also dead set on carving my own path. Fuck the Fates."

"I don't disagree. But I have to wonder... Do you think the Aetherborne truly believe in that mythos?"

"According to what I've read, yeah. It's not supposed to be a parable—they legitimately don't believe that immortal souls reincarnate. They just... linger. By design of the Source."

"Hmm," I replied. I had finally managed to tear my eyes from the darkness above, just as the streetlamps nearby began to flicker—the arcana activating, setting the streets aglow.

We started walking again, and I chewed at my lower lip, pondering the possibilities.

"What's on your mind now, Arken?" Kieran asked as we were

approaching my block.

"I like your take on fate. On carving our own paths," I admitted. "That resonates with me, and yet I still find myself drawn to the concept of these fallen gods, weaving our threads, guiding the way. I can't explain the appeal, though. I suppose it could be that if even the *Aetherborne* believe in such things, I'm more inclined to consider the possibilities? But those two considerations exist in conflict..."

"Are you saying that you believe everything the Elders claim?" Kieran teased. "I pegged you for more of a skeptic, bookwyrm."

I snorted. "A bold accusation coming from a man who swore an oath to protect and serve those very same Elders."

"I swore my oath to *Sophrosyne*," Kieran corrected, winking at me. "Not just the Aetherborne."

"Semantics," I scoffed, waving a hand around flippantly. "You still answer to the Nineteen."

"Sure," Kieran said. "And I respect the Convocation and their beliefs. I hold the Elders in high regard... But that doesn't mean I follow them blindly. Nor do I think they're infallible."

I frowned at the implication, intended or not. I was not so naive.

"I never said they were *infallible*," I argued. "But you do have to consider their lifespan. The Elders have been alive for well over a thousand years, have they not?"

"So they say," Kieran replied easily, his tone free of that initial skepticism.

"I'm more inclined to believe assertions of our history from those who witnessed it first hand. They are the primary sources, after all," I said.

"History is always written by the victors, though," Kieran murmured. "And I trust the Aetherborne. But I'm still not certain if our fates are truly written in the stars."

"Now who's veering off into poetics and philosophy?" I

teased, elbowing him gently in the ribs as we arrived at my doorstep.

"Guilty as charged," Kieran laughed, leaning in to my jab slightly.

Silence fell between us for a moment, the air thick with tension. A part of me wanted nothing more than to invite him inside, yesterday's agreement to keep things *platonic* be damned. I watched his gaze drift from my eyes to my mouth as my teeth grazed my lower lip, a nervous habit.

"You have a good night, Little Conduit," Kieran breathed, his voice a low rasp that sent heat straight towards my lower belly, desire pooling up from an endless wellspring.

Fucking Hel.

"You too, Captain," I replied softly, rifling through my satchel to find my keys before I could act on the stupid, reckless impulses running rampant in my brain.

"Let me know when you're ready for our next adventure," he said, turning back towards the street, smiling over his shoulder. "You know where to find me."

It took everything I had in me to resist the urge to catch his arm and pull him closer. No matter how much I wanted him, I knew damn well that if I acted on those feelings I would regret it.

Even so, I spent the rest of my evening in mild torment, haunted by the kiss I couldn't bring myself to steal.

CHAPTER TWENTY-FOUR

KIERAN

A week or so had passed since I took the Little Conduit to see the Mural of Creation, and yet as I was lazing about in bed on my day off, I found that my mind would still wander back there, seeking quiet pleasure from the memory of that day, *and* the one that followed.

I was a lucky bastard.

It wasn't until after we'd arrived at the museum that I realized our first little adventure could have been very easily misconstrued. It was my way of saying *fuck it, let's be friends*—but I was so accustomed to keeping people at arm's length that I didn't even realize that I had taken her on the equivalent of a date. *Again.*

And yet she was the one to set the boundary for us, with total transparency. It would seem that like me, Arken didn't do relationships, which essentially made her the perfect companion.

A companion...

My connection with her was different from the ones I had with Jeremiah and Hans. I had a good rapport with my cadre, and I trusted those two with my life, but she was just... something else.

It was the look in her eyes as she beheld the mural that had truly struck me. If it wasn't for that, I probably could have written off that trip as a one-time thing. I could have gone back to avoiding her. But that sense of awe, the way she absorbed the weight of every brush stroke, every detail woven into that grand picture...

I'd had a feeling she might enjoy it, but I hadn't realized that she would see the mural the exact same way that I had, the first time I encountered it. Looking beyond the surface, finding the most intricate details to admire and appreciate. It was the same way that she looked at the sky, too. And sometimes, it was the same way she looked at *me*.

Gods, the way that woman made me feel seen sometimes was downright terrifying. And yet it was also invigorating. I had kept to my Shadows for so long. And I couldn't lie to myself—I still wanted her. Carnally. But I could get over that. And when I couldn't... Well, I had my left hand and an active imagination.

I was about ready to put that active imagination to work when I heard an aggressive tap at my bedroom window.

An owl that looked like it had been carved out of stone sat on the windowsill with a stiff envelope in its beak. It had a black wax seal embossed with Commander Ka's emblem, which meant it was important. I gave the sprite a gentle pat on the head in thanks as I retrieved the letter. They weren't truly sentient, but it still felt like a nice gesture.

Well, there goes my day off.

The missive was a summoning for all officers of the Elder Guard to report to headquarters at once.

High General Demitrovic had returned.

◇ ◇ ◇

The air was thick with tense, anxious energy as the upper ranks of the Elder Guard began to convene in the large meeting hall, taking their seats one by one and murmuring amongst themselves.

It wasn't often that we were all called together at once for a formal meeting with the High General, who was the pinnacle of leadership among us. General Demitrovic answered only to the Elders themselves.

Actually, outside of our annual ceremonies and reviews, I wasn't sure I could even recall the last time I'd been summoned to this sort of off-the-cuff conference. I scanned the room while walking over towards where I'd spotted Jeremiah and Hans, but Demitrovic had yet to arrive. Commander Ka stood at the dais, looking worse for the wear. Troubled, even. That was... unusual.

What was going on here?

"Do either of you know what this is for?" I murmured quietly to my lieutenants as I took a seat beside them.

They both shook their heads.

"Rorick mentioned he'd heard a rumor that the reason Demitrovic went to Ithreac to meet with the House of Clay himself was because there was a high-risk lead on the disappearances, though. Not just to make nice with the Courts."

That could very well be true. In fact, it seemed the most plausible reason to gather us all here. If that were the case, he must've found something worthwhile.

Finally.

The tension in the room grew taut like a bowstring as the clock struck noon, and High General Jin Demitrovic made his entrance.

He cut an imposing figure as he stepped into the room, the towering white-haired man still wearing the more official garb of the guard—the type of armor and leathers we wore when going into a known fight. His silver pauldrons were shined to perfection, but they still bore the dents and slashes of a man who had seen combat. Who had actually gone to war, unlike a majority of us who served in the guard today.

I took note of the fact that he still wore his traveling cloak as well, a dusty gold shade indicative of being a representative of Sophrosyne. Clearly, the man had not taken even a moment's pause since his return, which meant...

A deep, grizzled voice filled the room, authority ringing through his tone clear as day.

"Guards, take note that what you are about to be briefed on is highly confidential. This information is not to be dispersed amongst your regiments without an explicit directive from your commanders. Is that understood?"

The replies were immediate, and in unison. "Yes, sir."

"As you are all aware, in the last several months, forces across the entirety of the continent have reported an uptick in kidnappings. At first, there seemed to be no common thread between them, save the fact that none of those missing had yet to be found. The Atlassian Courts, however, have been leaning on us for guidance and strategy, and with the help of our scouting units," the general paused, offering me the slightest dip of his chin.

My chest swelled with pride at the subtle recognition as the man continued on.

"We started to piece together similarities between each case. Every missing person was a child or young adult, connected to the noblesse in some way. We assumed this meant there were political motives at play here, and yet we have not received any demands of ransom or signs of extortion. It was also noted that every missing person thus far has either been a known Conduit, or a highly skilled Resonant."

While I knew all of this, a majority of the other branches wouldn't have had access to this information yet, and so the room started buzzing with hushed whispers.

"With no signs of blackmail, we'd been investigating the potential involvement of the flesh trade, blood cultists, or even a threat from overseas. We looked into movements in Irros, Novos and Exxem—all to no avail. Though we have not fully ruled out the possibility of foul play from beyond the continent."

This was news even to me. While I had been involved in

some of those more external investigations, it was mostly just due diligence. We had no reason to believe that any of the other nations of Aemos would be hostile. Save the Deadlands of Exxem where people lived a more nomadic, tribe-based lifestyle, trade was open and thriving between all continents. This realm had known peace for several ages.

"However, the reason you have been gathered today is not to recap what we already knew. I am here to share what we learned while I was in briefings with the House of Clay. I must warn you, the news is... disturbing, to say the least. I will remind you that this information is confidential, not only within our ranks, but when interfacing with those of the Atlassian Courts."

"Yes, sir," the room echoed again.

"We have reason to believe that there is unrest brewing across the continent. Namely, amongst mortals who are neither noble nor Resonant—those who consider themselves to be the least privileged members of Atlasssian society."

Those who *considered themselves* the least privileged? Come on now, Demitrovic.

I held our general in the highest esteem, but took issue with his wording and tone. It was a simple, empirical fact that non-Resonant humans without wealth or power had access to the least amount of resources in this world.

"This is nothing new," the general rumbled. "However, it would appear that the beginnings of a network are being built across the territories. As accusations against certain members of the Courts rise, as does a feeling of solidarity between the common folk of Samhaven, Vindyrst, Ithreac, and even Pyrhhas. The Isles of Luxtos and Stygos are not immune, though they are less likely to succumb to the same... pressures."

That's because there were no nobles in Luxtos & Stygos outside of the Lord of Shadows and the Lady of Light, as the isles were too small to need additional magistrates. Markus Makari and

Theia Frey were good leaders, kind and generous to their people. I would be shocked to see the Isles involved in this anytime soon... but there had to be more to this story.

"During my time in Ithreac, one of the missing children was discovered dead. Strung up from the tallest tree in the Red Valley, considered to be a sacred space to the House of Clay. The child was... mutilated. With a note nailed," Demitrovic paused for a moment, visibly upset. He swallowed thickly before continuing. "The note was nailed to the child's forehead. A note that read, 'Blood is thicker than Aether.'"

I felt sick to my stomach.

"Upon investigation, the Ithreacian clerics declared that the child had only been dead for several hours. They had kept him alive up until some predetermined moment—whether it had to do with my arrival or something else entirely, I do not yet know. But it is because of this most grievous offense that we have convened with the Elders. The Nineteen have approved that we call for a defensive alliance between the territories."

Holy shit.

"While we were previously operating on an honor system between the other forces of Atlas, we will now be seeking more official lines of communication, and working alongside the Atlassian Courts to keep tabs on the growth of this unrest, to prevent any unnecessary violence, and hopefully, any further losses."

It was a big deal that the Elders would allow us to get involved in such an official capacity, considering how firm they were on their stance of neutrality in the conflicts of mankind. The Aetherborne had been directly involved in establishing that new order of mortal leadership across Atlas, and the elemental houses had maintained said power and territories ever since with minimal influence from these Elders, or so we were told.

The Aetherborne established two caveats when the Houses

began their rule over the continent. The first was that Sophrosyne would remain its own independent entity, existing under the temporal and diplomatic jurisdiction of the Nineteen.

The second caveat was that the city-state of Sophrosyne would remain neutral in the face of any future mortal conflicts. They would train Resonant mortals in the art of their arcana if they were deemed worthy, they would offer counsel to the mortal leaders when it was sought, but they would not step between mankind and its own destruction. Not again. That said, if there was one thing the gods valued more than their neutrality, it was peace. At the end of the day, we were their peace-keepers, after all.

As Demitrovic ran the room through more details—and some of the upcoming summits we would be expected to attend as a result of these alliances—I couldn't help but wonder if all of this shit could have been avoided if the Atlassian Courts would just do their fucking jobs.

I supposed it wasn't my place to throw stones from a glass house, considering my own privileges, but *gods*.

The Elders were not infallible, and I feared they might have made a mistake when they established the ruling families of each House to be highly Resonant bloodlines. As a result, generation after generation, it was Conduits who led our people. Less than five percent of the population, making decisions that impacted the majority of non-Resonant humans.

It was easy to forget that though arcana was a beautiful, powerful thing, it was becoming increasingly rare as time went on. If the Houses didn't start taking better care of their people, we could soon find ourselves entirely overrun, chased out of power by the common folk.

Despite my loyalty to Sophrosyne, I couldn't quite say I'd blame them for it. Not when there were people out there who were starved for resources, who were just trying to survive, while the politicians of Atlas lined their pockets and amassed power just for show and ego in their idiotic internal squabbles.

Though part of me was relieved just to have *some* form of a lead or explanation behind the mysterious disappearances, a much larger part of me was preparing for things to get much, much worse.

✧ ✧ ✧

By the time I made it home that night, I was so beyond exhausted that I was about ready to collapse at the door of my townhouse. But at least I hadn't fallen asleep at my desk again. Hanjae would be proud.

My mood had taken a turn for the pessimistic and foul as I found it hard to shake the image from my mind. Righteous, valid anger or not, there was *never* an excuse to mutilate a fucking child. I didn't drink often, but found myself craving the harder stuff.

If only I wasn't so godsdamn tired.

As I reached for my keys, I realized that there was something glowing on my porch. What in the actual *fuck* was—

Oh.

It was a fox.

Not a real fox, but one that appeared to be made of Light aether. It looked as if it were molded out of the starry constellations of the night sky, and it was... sleeping? With a small scroll of parchment in its mouth. It was sort of adorable.

This had to be Arken's mail sprite.

Stepping over the glowing, semi-corporeal canine and into my townhouse, I unraveled the scroll to confirm my suspicions.

My turn to harass you, Captain. Hope you had a decent day off.

She'd kept it short and sweet, clearly just looking to show off her latest skill in complex arcana. And to be fair, I was impressed. Mail sprites weren't particularly easy to summon, or maintain for however long the fox had been waiting for me.

I started boiling water for tea before scribbling back.

Well, well. Look who learned something new in class today. It wasn't much of a day off, unfortunately.
The fox is cute.

I didn't have the energy to think of much else, but still found myself smiling despite the day I'd had as I sent *my* sprite back to her. Let her little friend take a break for the evening.

Isn't he precious?? His name is Bluebell.

I shook my head as I poured myself a cup of tea, still deliberating on the idea of finding something stiffer at the bar down the road. Instead, I wrote back to Arken.

Of course it is. Apologies in advance if I fall asleep on you, Little Conduit. It's been a long day. I am quite impressed that you're summoning mail sprites within a day of learning how, though.

I could hear the teasing tone as I read her quick response, absently wondering what she was doing up so late. It had to be nearly two in the morning.

What, is it supposed to be hard or something? I haven't quite figured out how to make him look real, like your raven. How in the Hel do you do that?

She *would* notice something like that.

I'm going to go out on a limb here and say that patience isn't your strong suit. I think Bluebell looks very pretty as is, but I'll teach you, if you like.

Her response was immediate.

Yes, please!

I chuckled softly, fairly certain that she just wanted an excuse to show off to her peers or the scholars.

I'm free after four tomorrow. Swing by the guard headquarters in the admin district, and we'll put young Bluebell to work.

Yawning, I began to stretch and shrug out of the uniform I'd put on in haste earlier this afternoon.

Excellent... I'll stop pestering you now that my ulterior motives have been met.
Rest well, Captain.

I fell asleep before I could even reply to her, quill still in hand, hoping that her dreams were as sweet as this newfound, unexpected friendship of ours.

CHAPTER TWENTY-FIVE

Arken

Today's lecture in Arcane Theory was hitting a little too close to home.

The subject matter at hand? The difference between human Resonance and the magick of the Aetherborne.

"It has yet to be determined whether the difference is primarily physiological, or if it's more based in the compatibility of the magicks themselves, but one thing has been proven: The human form cannot sustain itself on aether alone," the scholar droned on.

It was once theorized that the only limitation on human Resonance was the amount of aether we held in our bodies. Unlike the gods, we needed blood to live—our hearts and organs relied on the more mundane, organic fluid as a means to transport oxygen, circulate nutrients, and carry away the waste products of our slowly decomposing bodies.

It was a bit morbid to think about it that way—but that was the primary difference between the humans and the Aetherborne, was it not? Their flesh was eternal, their bodies did not age or degrade with the passing of time, and no blood ran through their veins—only aether.

"Any questions thus far?" the scholar inquired.

Several hands shot up, and she started calling on individuals from the amphitheater. I kept taking my notes, but my ears perked up at a certain query.

"Are there any theories as to why humans can only attune to one element? Resonant mortals have less aether in our bodies than the gods, but it's still pure aether, is it not? In such a circumstance, shouldn't we just have the same range of power as the Aetherborne, but to a lessened extent?"

"Ah, an excellent consideration. Does anyone here know the answer?"

The room fell silent, so apparently not.

"The more popular theory, of course, is that Resonance is impacted by genetics. Perhaps the first generation of humans had been impacted by random chance, but it became more predictable over time. We have clear examples of family lines producing the same Resonances over generations, with the most noteworthy being the ruling families of the Courts," she explained.

This was true. It was also how each territory became somewhat synonymous with a certain element of aether: Samhaven and the House of Torrents, Vindyrst and the House of Gales, Ithreac and the House of Clay, Pyrhhas and the House of Embers, Luxtos & Stygos—the Astral & Umbral Isles, and the House of Light & Shadow.

"The second theory takes into account the more random nature of some Resonant births, and has us consider the possibility that when a child is born with enough aether in their veins to be Resonant, there is a certain developmental period where their Resonance has yet to be determined. This theory purports that a Resonant attunes to the strongest density of aetheric energy that they encounter first during that period of aetheric maturity."

That seemed like a weaker argument, though. Perhaps one developed to excuse streaks of infidelity among the ruling Houses, but what did I know?

"Both theories, of course, rely on the base concept that the ratio of blood to aether is what limits us to a single element, which is all but proven at this point."

Something about that explanation didn't entirely add up, but before I could start to mull over why it wasn't sitting right in my brain, my train of thought was interrupted.

"But what about the legend of the Harbingers?" A young male student interrupted. Merrick, I think his name was.

Harbingers?

The younger Conduit's eyes were wide and fearful as he continued on. "I mean, according to the Irrosi, a mortal *could* be born with the power of the gods! But when that happens, it's supposed to be a sign of the end of days, right? Because it would break all the laws of arcane science, disrupt the balance, and trigger a second Cataclysm. A single Harbinger could kill us all."

My stomach lurched. *It's just a story*, I reminded myself. *Just a stupid legend that you've never even heard of.*

And he was probably exaggerating. Embellishing.

"Such things would be better discussed in a cultural history or anthropology course, Merrick. We do not study myths and legends here, only science," the scholar said firmly.

"Apologies, ma'am."

The damage had been done, though. I struggled to pay attention to the rest of the lecture, and found myself getting increasingly frustrated with my wandering mind. Amaretta would be reeling to know that I put any sort of stock into some old Irrosi wives tale, but I couldn't help but feel spooked—haunted by even the slightest of chances…

Because every legend had its origin, every tall tale carried some kernel of truth, some spark of inspiration that was anchored in reality. Such was the nature of storytelling.

So what if there was some truth there? Was I *that* dangerous? Did my parents know? Is that why they left me behind in the woods that night? Could it be possible that my parents knew what

I was, and just couldn't bring themselves to save the world? Was that why they had abandoned me out there in the wilderness? In hopes that someone—*or something*—else might do it for them?

I shook my head and took a deep breath, trying to let go of the paranoid and intrusive thoughts. I could always look into the legend later, find more tangible evidence or context to soothe my nerves.

Thankfully, the remainder of the lecture resumed free of any more damning theories about my existence.

✧ ✧ ✧

My classes wrapped up for the day around half past three, which left me with a bit of a conundrum.

Kieran told me to meet him at four, and the Elder Guard headquarters were about ten minutes away from the lecture hall. My apartment was about twenty minutes in the opposite direction, though, if I wanted to drop off my things and freshen up. I was essentially trapped between being awkward and early, or late—and I hated being late to anything. I sighed, really wishing that I'd thought ahead.

Why, though? Who are you even trying to impress?

I cringed at the internalized snark, realizing that even though Kieran and I had agreed to keep things platonic, I still found myself wanting to impress him. I was going to have to get over that sooner or later.

It didn't help that I hadn't been with anyone else since arriving in Sophrosyne. I had flirted, had a few close encounters at the tavern once or twice, even exchanged a kiss or two with pretty strangers in the city. But I hadn't slept with anyone since Graysen. I had barely even thought about Grays since leaving the Brindlewoods, and we had broken up long before I left for

Sophrosyne, so to say that I was in a bit of a dry spell was an understatement. That explained a lot.

I was able to find the guard headquarters without issue, and had been about to seek someone out to direct me to Kieran's office when, speak of the daemon, I heard his voice booming from the grassy fields behind the main building.

"Again!" he shouted, and I followed the sound to find where he was training a group of younger looking men and women—fresh recruits, I'd presume.

I settled in on a nearby bench, content to flip through my notes and steal glances at them all glistening with sweat in the midday sun. Kieran smiled when he caught my eye a few minutes after I'd arrived, glancing towards the clock tower with a raised brow. *You're early,* he mouthed. I shrugged and nodded towards my textbook to indicate I didn't mind waiting, but he still jogged over in between a round of sprints.

"Hey you."

"Hey," I replied with a smile. "Class ended early today, but I'm in no rush. Is it alright if I just hang out here until you guys wrap up?"

"Yeah, of course. I think you might be distracting my recruits though," he said, still breathing hard. It seemed like he often joined his trainees in whatever drills he was running them through, and I wondered if that was expected... or just Kieran being Kieran.

"Ah yes, distracting them with my feminine wiles," I replied sarcastically, glancing behind his shoulder where a small gaggle of prospective guardsmen were indeed standing together, eyeing us both, and giving each other slight nudges.

"Exactly those. It does give me an excuse to make them work harder, though," he grinned. "Speaking of which, please hold."

I raised a brow.

"If you've got time to ogle her, you've got time for another lap!" he shouted across the field, his voice taking on a low rumble of authority. "Get on it, freshlings!"

I bit my lip, trying not to laugh. At least I wasn't the only one who got assigned dumb nicknames, though I had a feeling that my other one was a little more exclusive.

"It's gonna be about another twenty minutes or so here, and then I'll clean up and we'll head out, okay? Hang tight. Your academic education will resume shortly, Little Conduit."

Yeah, that nickname. It had sort of grown on me over time, though. I'd found the diminutive irritating at first, but these days it felt friendly and affectionate, and only made me blush sometimes—depending on how he said it and in what context.

I also couldn't help but notice the way Kieran's voice softened into a husky rasp when he was directing it towards me instead of the recruits... but maybe that was just because he was out of breath.

"I'll be here," I chirped cheerfully.

As he jogged back towards the center of the field, I attempted to return back to my texts, reviewing the notes I had taken on the theory of arcane fractals and opposing aetherflows.

The key word there being *attempted*. I found it fairly difficult to focus on my academia as Kieran shrugged off his uniform jacket, revealing the black sleeveless top he wore underneath and the way it hugged his torso.

I was only human. Given the choice between the intricacies of the aetheric spectrum and the deep golden tan of the scouting captain's muscled arms—now freely exposed and glistening with sweat as he dropped to the ground and held himself in a plank position...

I was going to look respectfully.

He was instructing his recruits to mirror his pose, counting down from sixty. My abs hurt just watching them. Just when I felt like this couldn't get any more distracting, Kieran hopped back up to his feet with an irritating degree of effortlessness and grace.

"Keep it up!" he called out with that same sharp, authoritative tone.

I had to admire the nuance he was able to command among his men, because while there was no doubt an aura of seniority and leadership that he carried about him at work, he was also encouraging and respectful. You could tell that he was pushing these recruits to challenge them, not to break their spirit. That wasn't always the case when it came to people in positions of power, and I admired him for it.

Though speaking of admiration...

I swallowed hard as Kieran stretched one arm behind his back, biceps flexing. He was still watching his recruits as they held their planks with pained expressions, but I was watching *him*.

What struck me first was how much of his tattoos were visible now that he had taken off his jacket. Even from a distance, the dark black ink embedded in his sun-bronzed skin was a stark and mysterious contrast. The strange, jagged markings peeked out beneath his shirt, appearing to cover the entirety of his right shoulder blade at least, creeping up one side of his neck. If I had to guess, it was some kind of script... but with so much more of Kieran on display right now, I could not be bothered to wrack my brain to guess the language.

My gaze drifted over him lazily, and I realized that his trousers had slipped down dangerously low on his hips. That skin-tight undershirt of his was riding up just enough that I could see... Gods, I could see a lot. Too much. This was just rude, really. Had he been carved out of fucking marble?

I really should've just looked away, but instead I was hungrily studying the toned dips of his hip flexor muscles, and that thin trail of black hair traveling from his navel to... well. *Lower.*

Fates above, I needed to stop staring. As I quickly glanced back up and attempted to recover, Kieran caught my eye... and winked.

Fucking Hel.

That man was a menace to society.

CHAPTER TWENTY-SIX

KIERAN

That woman was going to be the death of me.

Shortly after I caught her staring, I wrapped up with the recruits—a few minutes earlier than I had originally intended—but I was in need of a cold bath after watching her bite down on her lower lip. She had been so blissfully unaware that I had been looking back at her that I almost let her get away with it, too. Almost.

Platonic, I reminded myself. *We're keeping things platonic.*

But there had been plenty of other fit, sweating guards for her to make eyes at on the field—plenty of them shirtless and plenty of them attractive. Any one of them would have fallen on their swords for her attention, too, but she'd been staring at *me* when she bit that lip.

Yeah. A cold bath would be necessary before I could come back out and tutor her in the magickal, inane art of realistic-looking mail sprites.

Gods.

I was getting better at tempering my degeneracy around her, but it was a little easier to play off as friendly flirtatiousness when she wasn't *staring at my fucking groin.* That image of those pretty golden eyes going hazy and half-lidded as they rested on my torso was going to haunt me later in the best of ways. I pushed down the impulse to act on the attraction in any other way than that private fantasy, though. We both knew better.

That said, I wasn't sure if sticking the pair of us in close quarters like a study room in the Biblyos would be in either of our best interests today. Perhaps I could put off the lesson, and instead play tour guide again... but where to take her?

I pondered on it as I strolled into the bathing rooms and stripped out of my sweaty clothes, thankfully having calmed down a bit as I stepped into one of the tubs, hissing with relief as the cool water sluiced the heat, sweat and grime of training off of my body.

I could take her to another museum, but most of the museums in the northeastern quarter were much quieter and more enjoyable in the mornings.

Another day, then.

There was always the arts district, or going for a meal—though she'd been nibbling on some grapes as she'd "studied," and I wasn't particularly hungry yet, either.

Another idea came to mind... Hans was stationed at the Western Gates this afternoon, so I could swing it without issue. It was just about the perfect time of day for it, too.

I smiled to myself as I toweled off and got dressed in clean, civilian clothing. She was going to like seeing Sophrosyne from above.

◇ ◇ ◇

"So," I began, strolling up to where she was still seated beside the fields, flipping through her notebook. "How would you feel about skipping the lessons today in favor of another adventure? As your official tour guide to Sophrosyne, I must say that this one comes highly recommended."

"You know, I'm starting to think that your friendship might be a detriment to my education, Kieran."

That was entirely possible.

"What if I told you that the adventure involves us sneaking around a bit?"

A spark of intrigue flickered in her eyes, as I had anticipated.

"You have my attention."

"Excellent. Follow me, Little Conduit."

Instead of cutting directly through the city, I took the longer route, leading her through the backstreets of the Administrative Quarter, towards the Archives.

"Do you often train the new recruits?" Arken asked me along the way.

"Actually, no. I was standing in for Rorick, another branch captain, as a favor," I explained. "Why? Any of the freshlings catch your eye?"

She snorted, pausing a moment to pick up a quartzy-looking pebble off the side of the road and held it up to the sun.

"Ah, no—of course not," I supplied. "The woman is clearly more interested in rocks."

Though if that were the case, it would make our little field trip all the better.

"I collect them," she said, with the slightest hint of shyness creeping into her voice. It would seem the Fates had smiled upon my plans.

"Pebbles? Crystals? Any manner of rock?" I inquired with genuine interest.

"I typically stick to anything small enough to fit in my pockets. Not just rocks, though. Anything pretty, with a good texture or pattern. Things that sparkle. Uncommon bits and bobs. My mentor used to poke fun at me for it, calling me her little raven."

Absently, I raised my fingers to my sternum, reaching for a necklace I no longer wore.

"So if you're not typically training, and not typically standing guard at lectures, what is it that you normally do for the guard, Kieran?" Arken asked.

I winced. Probably should have prepared myself for that one. I didn't often put myself in situations where people had enough time to try and get to know me better, but here we were...

"Most of my work is confidential," I admitted. "I run a subsection of the guard dedicated to scouting and reconnaissance, obviously. The reconnaissance side of things was built more for a time when the territories were at war. So in times of peace, that typically means going out and looking for anything that might threaten Sophrosyne or its people. Proactive peacekeeping, if you will. I'm afraid I can't go into much more of the details."

"I mean, that was a perfectly good answer on its own," she said easily.

I supposed she was right, though I felt strangely compelled to tell her more. It would be nice to get out of my head like that, to talk about my day to day, but Arken didn't need to know what troubles and horrors were brewing behind the flawless facade of the city.

We passed by the Northern Gates, and I nodded in acknowledgement to those on duty as they quickly corrected their posture and attempted to look busy. I managed a straight face, but Arken noticed and could hardly contain her own giggles.

"You're pretty young to be a captain already, aren't you?" she asked, tilting her head in careful consideration as we passed them.

"Yeah," I replied, trying to keep my tone light. I didn't particularly like talking about exactly why that was. "I worked hard."

"Can I ask... why? I mean you can't be much older than me, right?"

According to my ill-gained research, Arken was twenty-two.

"I'm twenty-five, yeah."

I swallowed the growing irritation and discomfort, knowing that she was only curious. I picked through the skeletons in my closet to find the most authentic answer I could muster to her first question.

"And it's not as complicated as you might think," I lied easily. "I love this city. I want to see it protected."

It wasn't entirely a lie, but it wasn't anywhere near the full truth. Regardless, the trusting woman nodded, offering me a soft and understanding smile.

"Though speaking of people who are ahead of the curve, how are your classes going? Learn anything of interest today?"

We had almost reached our destination, but I was eager to change the subject.

"Oh," she murmured.

The energy in her voice had dropped, just enough to be noticeable. Out of the corner of my eye, I saw her bite at her lip nervously.

"No, not really."

Hmm.

"We'll have to fix that, then," I replied, placing my hand on the small of her back to gently guide her as we approached a small entrance in the massive limestone walls that encircled the city, several feet in front of the Western Gate.

From the distance, I caught the eye of my lieutenant who was stationed there and nodded once in acknowledgement. He would give me shit for this later, but then again, Hans Deering would give me shit for breathing if he found the right angle.

"Am I even allowed to be in here?" Arken asked as we stepped inside the wall's interior, where several flights of stairs ascended within.

"In theory, no. In practice... also no. Remember what I said about sneaking around?"

Her eyes widened, and I chuckled.

"Don't look so worried, Little Conduit. My men are the ones on guard at the gate tonight, none of them will tattle," I teased.

"I'm going to kick your ass if this "adventure" ends with me getting tossed in a cell for trespassing again, Vistarii," she threatened as we began to climb the stairs.

I smirked.

Oh, I would truly love to see her try.

CHAPTER TWENTY-SEVEN

ARKEN

This staircase was, unfortunately, a prime example of how I couldn't kick Kieran's ass if my life depended on it.

By the time we'd reached the top, I had to take a moment to catch my breath. Meanwhile, my tour guide hadn't even broken a sweat, the fit bastard. That wouldn't stop me from threatening him, though.

"You ready?" he asked, extending a hand. Whether it was to guide me or steady me, I took it, and pretended that the sharp breath I sucked in was just because I was winded. It certainly wasn't the warmth of his rough fingers against mine, or the comforting nature of his firm grip. Of course not.

The stairway had led all the way to the very top of the wall, offering a birds-eye view of the entire city within, and behind us, the rolling hills and forests of Pyrhhas. It was absolutely breathtaking. I tried to take a moment to pause and enjoy the view, but Kieran tugged at my hand, pulling me towards the Northern Gates. There, two massive limestone walls met at a wide angle, and I felt the surge of aether before I saw anything.

Whoa.

Nestled in between where the two walls met was a massive, floating chunk of crystal, oddly reminiscent of the one from The

Mural of Creation. The jagged, uncut gem sat atop what almost looked like a pewter brazier, also floating. Several sigils were carved in the stone beneath it, glowing softly with a blue-green hue—the telltale sign of Aetherborne arcana.

"What *is* that?" I asked in awe as we approached.

"It's a wardpoint. They're made of astral quartz and some rare, arcane conductive ore mined from caverns in Luxtos and Stygos. There's something about those two materials that can help contain and preserve the specific arcana that the Elders use to place wards. There's one of these at every corner of Sophrosyne—six in total. The wardpoints make it so that they don't have to come up and re-cast the protective magicks every other week. Sophrosyne is a pretty big city to keep constantly warded."

I never really thought about that—hadn't considered that warding arcana might be so complex that even the Aetherborne couldn't preserve it with one single cast.

Then again, we had learned that the wards around Sophrosyne weren't your average elemental barriers. They weren't like the basic wards a strong Conduit might be able to set up. There were all sorts of alarms and detections woven into our city's security system, including the one that would only allow you to pass through if you had the arcane tattoo that acted as your key.

"They're so pretty," I breathed, entranced by the iridescent shimmer of the astral quartz and the thrumming power of the arcana it clearly contained.

"I figured you might like them. Considering how buckwild you get over normal rocks," he teased.

I ignored him and the weight of the several "normal" rocks I currently had in my pockets. The pebble I had found on the way here was not alone.

"Though, do me a favor and don't go around telling people about them, alright?"

"Who would I even tell?" I laughed.

"I dunno. Laurel?"

"Laurel is far more concerned with a different element of Earth at the moment. You might even say she's lost in the Craggs."

Kieran snorted, catching my drift.

"I know, I trust you. And while you really aren't supposed to be up here, it's not like they're some particularly dangerous secret. I would just prefer to keep my balls where they are, and my commander would probably feed them to me if he knew I was taking civilians up here."

"Do you take people up here often?" I asked, trying to mask the disappointment in my voice.

"Nah. Just you," he replied.

The disappointment dissipated, replaced by a warmth that I tried to ignore.

"I'm surprised that these aren't one of those secrets that the Aetherborne keep bound by the brand," I mused.

"Truth be told, I think that's by design. Anyone who discovers that the wardpoints exist would probably make the assumption that they're a weakness, right? Most people would default to thinking that if you disable them somehow, you'd take the city wards down."

"Yeah, that was my assumption. Is that not the case?"

He shook his head.

"The wardpoints preserve the arcana, and thus they store a whole Hel of a lot of it at once, allowing the spellwork to trickle out over time. If anyone were to disable a wardpoint, several things would happen," he explained, walking around the quartz to examine it from another angle.

"For starters, the Aetherborne would be alerted, and good fucking luck to whatever poor bastard made that poor life decision. But also, disabling the device would simply release all of that stored arcana at once. The wards would get stronger, not weaker—albeit temporarily."

How fascinating.

"You'd be surprised at how much the Convocation keeps hidden in plain sight," Kieran said. "Knowledge is power, as is the artful omission of it. Allowing the masses to know most of the truth while withholding some key details is an unfortunate element of public safety."

A certain darkness passed through his expression as he said that.

"Why is that unfortunate?" I asked, curious about the tinge of bitterness behind those words.

Kieran sighed, leaning over the parapet and gazing off into the distance.

"Call me idealistic, but I don't like the willful deception."

"Is it really deception, though? It's certainly not malicious," I replied, interested in his perspective.

"A lie by omission is still a lie," he said with a shrug. "I don't know, I'm certainly not one to talk here, but..."

I tilted my head, listening intently.

"There are a lot of things that I know about Sophrosyne that most of the general public doesn't know, Arken. Things that most of this city will never know, and it can get burdensome at times."

I had a feeling that we weren't just talking about the wardpoints, now. I had always suspected Kieran's job was... intense. It was written in his scars, the way he carried himself, the way that he held almost anyone at an arm's length. I couldn't pretend to understand, but I wanted to.

"I guess I just don't like the assumption that the rest of the city—*this* city, of all places—can't be trusted with a clearer picture. It's not that I think everyone should know everything, but..."

Kieran took pause, glancing at me before returning his gaze to the skyline. As if he were second-guessing his next words, unaccustomed to saying things like this out loud.

"Do you remember what you asked me that day? When you

learned about the details of the Cataclysm?"

I nodded. I only remembered because I had been embarrassed about that emotional outburst later, the one that had come up as I feverishly discussed my thoughts on the lecture that day.

"Why do they keep it a secret?" I had asked. I had been angry, in the heat of the moment, thinking about all the times I had heard mortals speak ill of the Aetherborne, pissing and moaning about how the gods were useless these days. *"Don't you think that mortals might behave a little differently if they knew the full truth of things? Don't you think things might change if they knew what the survival of our species had cost the Elders?"*

The way Kieran had looked at me then was similar to the way he was looking at me now. Like he saw me in full. Like he understood. I had never met anyone else who looked at me like that when I spoke.

"I remember," I said softly.

"Sometimes, I just have to wonder whether or not it's always for the best. We keep so much hidden for the sake of safety, and I often wonder if the ends always justify the means by which we do so."

I didn't need much of an imagination to gather what those means might be.

"Sometimes, I wonder if given the chance, the people of Sophrosyne—of Atlas, in general, really—if we could just *do better*."

I tore my gaze from the glimmering wardpoint, walking over to join him at the parapet and taking in the gorgeous view at his side as I reflected on his uncommon philosophical musings.

From this high up, I could see almost the entirety of the Wyldwoods, the tips of those towering trees bending gently in the breeze. Just past the forestry, I saw where the Pyrhhan Strait cut through the region, threading out into an estuary by the rocky coastline to the west. The sun was just beginning to make its late afternoon descent, casting the sky in hues of pink and orange, the wispy clouds above looking like handspun sugar floss.

"I'd like to think that we could," I finally said after a couple minutes of silence. "Do better, I mean. Given the chance."

"Maybe I'm just a hopeless idealist, but I'd like to think so too, Ark," he said, keeping his eyes fixed on the skyline.

If Kieran was an idealist, then so was I. No matter how many well-documented centuries of greed and warfare existed in the histories of mankind, I did believe that we were inherently good, or at least that the goodness outweighed the wicked in us all. I also believed that much of those conflicts were born from disparities that could have been mended peacefully if more people had access to the resources they needed.

I could see now why even some willful omissions of truth might bother Kieran, considering he so clearly believed in the core message of Sophrosyne, that knowledge is power. To omit access to that power was to leave gaps in our defenses in favor of artificial walls, operating under the assumption that we couldn't handle or behave ourselves.

I was sure that, in his mind, keeping certain secrets felt like failing to protect his people, because he was failing to prepare them... And I truly couldn't imagine what that weight felt like.

"I'd like to think so, too," he repeated, this time glancing back at me.

Something in his gaze felt distant, unreadable in a haunting sort of way. Like his body was here in Sophrosyne, acting as an anchor to his mind as it floated off in the distance, to some place that was very, very far away.

I probably should have found that unsettling, but instead I just felt drawn to it.

Like I wanted to join him there.

CHAPTER TWENTY-EIGHT

KIERAN

The walk back to Arken's apartment was quiet, but the silence between us felt comfortable.

Every now and again, I'd steal a glance at her to make sure she felt the same way, confirming it in the soft, serene expression she held as her eyes wandered over the beauty that was Sophrosyne at night.

Our conversation on the wall left me more introspective than usual, if not a bit unsettled. Even though I'd kept all confidentialities in check, I hadn't opened up to anyone like that in a very, very long time. I felt a certain ease around Arken, one that I would have to be more actively aware of going forward, I realized.

I wasn't against opening up with her to an extent—I knew that was part of friendship, but I was still treading dangerous ground. There were some things that I simply couldn't share with her, and would never be able to share with anyone.

That said, I was nothing if not a master at compartmentalization, so I'd figure it out. I had only been thrown for a moment, because opening said compartments was atypical behavior... but I couldn't lie to myself and pretend that I hadn't felt some relief, like I had released just the tiniest amount of pressure in the back of my head.

"Hey, Kier?"

My ears perked up, both eager for the distraction and the odd satisfaction of hearing her shorten my name with any sort of familiarity.

"Yeah?"

"How familiar are you with myths and legends?"

I raised a brow, curious as to where she was going with this.

"I'm decently versed in them, I suppose. I mean, clearly I have a penchant for museums and secret scraps of Sophrosyne lore. Why do you ask?"

"Have you ever heard the Irrosi legend about the Harbingers, and a second cataclysm?"

A sudden weight plummeted in the pit of my stomach.

Why was she asking about that legend, of all things?

"I'm familiar, yes," I replied, keeping my voice even. Casual. "Did they cover that in class today or something?"

"Not exactly. They were talking about the differences between mortal and Aetherborne magicks today, and some guy brought it up as a side tangent. I wasn't sure if they were exaggerating, or making some shit up," she explained.

"Well, I mean, most legends are made up—stitched together with inaccuracies and misinterpretation," I replied.

Though this one was an exception...

"I beg to differ, but I'll put that particular argument on hold," Arken said. "But... Do the people of Irros really believe that? That some errant Conduit could come along and upset the aether of the world again to such an extent that it would bring about another Cataclysm?"

Clearly, this was Arken's latest hyperfixation. I sighed internally. Leave it to her to get wrapped up in the concept of the end of days.

"I couldn't tell you—I've never been to Irros, and haven't studied enough anthropology to know whether or not that's still a commonly held belief."

"Oh."

I glanced over at her to find her staring into space, chewing at her lip.

"They're just stories, Ark," I said.

Or nightmares.

"Ah, yeah. I know," she replied. "Every now and again, I just get struck by some reminder that the world is a much bigger place than I could have ever truly fathomed. As much as Amaretta taught me back home, it was always so self-contained to that tiny little village. Legends and myths like that were just as distant as the stars in the night sky. Here in Sophrosyne, they feel... closer to reality, somehow."

Yet again, I found that I completely understood how Arken saw the world.

"Sometimes being here makes me feel like I spent the last twenty-two years of my life in ignorance. Asleep, even. And now, it's like I'm finally waking up," she said. "From a very dull dream, I might add."

I laughed gently.

"I'm not sure that feeling ever truly goes away," I said. "I'm not even in active study anymore, and the absolute depth of knowledge stored within these walls still knocks me on my ass sometimes."

"Glad to hear *something* can knock you on your ass sometimes, Captain," she teased, her spirits clearly lifting.

"You'd be surprised," I said. Sophrosyne wasn't the only thing knocking me off my feet as of late.

"So I assume you used to study here, too?"

I rolled up my left sleeve, showing her my wrist where the Seed of Creation was still visible, marred by a few light scars and scratches.

"I studied for about a year or so before I decided to join the guard," I explained. "Prior to that, I had been trying to follow in my brother's footsteps, focusing on politics."

I could taste the regret on my tongue the moment those words passed my lips. I really needed to be more careful around her, godsdamnit.

"You have a brother?"

"Had."

I didn't like using that clipped, brusque tone with her, but this was a hard line for me.

"Oh. I'm so sorry," she said softly, assuming the worst.

"He's not dead," I replied quietly. I wasn't about to let this conversation go much further, but I could give her the bare minimum explanation. "We're just not close. Not anymore. I'm essentially dead to him. We haven't spoken in years."

Her brow furrowed. I could see the curiosity, the blend of analytical and emotional calculations happening behind her eyes as she tried to imagine what could have caused such a deep cut in a bond like brotherhood. I sighed heavily.

"I know you're about to ask me why, or what happened, and I promise that it's nothing against you, but I really don't wanna go there, Ark," I said.

The concern cleared from her face almost immediately as she nodded.

"That's alright," she said. "I understand."

I exhaled, feeling relieved. This wasn't the first time that I had slipped up around her—around *Arken*, of all people—an inherently curious woman. But she never used it as an excuse to dig any deeper, never pressed me for details. She always seemed to respect my boundaries without question. Somehow, that made me want to give her just a little bit more. A small token of my appreciation.

"Ultimately, I joined the Guard because I love this city. I love Pyrhhas and Atlas, but Sophrosyne in particular... I've always loved it here. The people, the vibrancy, the ideals—they're all worth defending. I wanted to do something meaningful with my life, and I'm proud of the path I chose and how hard I worked to get here. I don't take pride in a lot of shit, but this is one of the few things that I really, really do."

She was quiet for a moment as we kept walking, quickly approaching the cluster of private apartments where she lived. Instead of accepting the free housing offered by the Studium, Arken had inherited her mentor's old studio. Not that I should know that, but I'd pocketed more than a few details from her file when I'd gone searching for her aetheric signature.

"Thank you, Kieran," she said softly.

It was like she *knew* that wasn't something I'd ever told anyone else. But I had to ask. "For what?"

"For giving a shit. Protecting what you love. And for being an excellent tour guide, sneaking me places where I'm not supposed to be without getting me tossed in a jail cell again."

I laughed, appreciating that last addition.

"Getting tossed in a jail cell costs extra, actually. The first time is free, but after that it's more of an add-on package to my services," I replied.

She smirked. "I didn't realize I was being charged for your *services* in the first place. Am I running up a tab as we speak?"

"Nah, you can keep your Lyra. You pay for my tour guide services by putting up with me in the first place."

"You also still owe me a lesson in conjuring a better mail sprite," she reminded me.

"And I'm going to keep ignoring that in favor of more exciting excursions," I informed her. "You're going to give poor Bluebell an inferiority complex."

She laughed as we stopped walking, having arrived at her studio.

"Goodnight, Kieran."

"Sweet dreams, Little Conduit."

As I walked back to my townhouse that night, it was the first time in a long time that I didn't feel the need to go searching for some sort of distraction to get out of my head.

My mind was quiet.

It was a temporary balm, I knew. A fleeting comfort, one that I didn't dare let myself grow accustomed to.

But it was a comfort, nonetheless.

CHAPTER TWENTY-NINE

ARKEN

The remainder of my first quarter at the Arcane Studium had passed by rather uneventfully, leaving me restless and bored.

I spent most of my free time with Kieran these days, but work had been keeping him busy as of late. New investigations seemed to crop up constantly, leaving very little free time for our adventures, though we snuck them in where we could. In lieu of his company this week, I had taken to studying and practicing my arcana with refreshed fervor.

For the last several days, I had spent every spare hour holed up in my studio, attempting to apply all my learnings with Light to the other elements, the ones I kept hidden. It was admittedly exhausting. Tonight in particular, I had worn myself to the bone, yawning and stretching as I padded around the kitchen in search of a certain tea blend, one that Amma used to make for me after long days of foraging in the forest. My muscles were a bit sore.

Arcana seemed to take its toll on the body, which was hardly surprising. I'd been at this for hours, practicing the incantations and gestures, poring over tomes. I was just about to draw myself a hot bath and get ready for bed when I heard a few urgent, desperate-sounding knocks against my front door.

"Arken?" A frantic, muffled voice called through. "Ark, are

you home?"

That sounded like... *Laurel?*

I quickly rushed over to the door, wrapping my robe around my otherwise naked body as I dashed across the room.

"Laurel," I said as I opened the door to the tearful face of a friend. "Are you okay?"

She immediately burst into tears and I tugged at her arm, pulling her inside.

"I'm—*hic*—I'm so sorry to barge in like this, there's just, I don't know who else—I just," she said in between small, hiccuping sobs.

"Hey, shh. It's alright, it's no trouble. C'mere, Laur," I said, wrapping my arms around her, fearing for the worst as she shuddered against my chest. "Take your time. We can talk when you're ready."

Fifteen minutes and several warm cups of tea later, Laurel began to explain what happened.

"I got a letter from Lord Ymir today, on behalf of my parents. They were apparently too indisposed to—well, it doesn't matter. My little brother is gone. Stolen. Amir was just *taken* from the streets of Yvestra, and he's just disappeared without a trace. Apparently, he's been gone for weeks. *Weeks*, Arken! And nobody told me until now!"

"Oh my gods," I breathed.

"Lord Ymir apologized on their behalf but I'm still so furious with my parents. How could they not take two godsdamned minutes to send a sprite? The only reason Ymir is reaching out is because there have apparently been similar disappearances elsewhere, and he wanted me warned, in case our family is a general target. They might even assign me a personal guard. What in the Hel is happening?"

"And they still have no idea where he is? Or who was involved?"

"No," she sniffed. "I guess our nanny had her head turned for a fraction of a second. He couldn't have just wandered off, they were in the middle of the markets and he wouldn't have gotten very far. Somebody had to have taken him, but there hasn't been a ransom or anything."

My heart sank.

Without a ransom, it seemed more likely that Amir had been stolen by people who intended to *keep* him. The Ansari family was *very* wealthy and *very* well-connected, so if the culprits had demands, surely they would have made them by now.

I prayed that the Fates would be kind, and that Amir would be found soon. While I had no true siblings of my own, I could still empathize. The other children of the Brindlewoods were still so dear to me, and I thought of them often.

I would be in tatters if I was in her position.

"You're staying here tonight, Laur."

She tried to argue, claiming that she didn't want to impose, but all I could think about was how I would feel if I had to spend a night like this alone. I refused to take no for an answer, and instead tossed her a pair of my pajamas and drew her a bath.

I brought over my little tray of pebbles and crystals, my tiny hoard of found items since I'd been here, and left them by the tub.

"You know, just in case you feel like throwing something," I said with a small smile.

As an Earth Conduit, I'd often catch Laurel spinning sand or pebbles around her fingertips as a mindless, anxious habit. The last time I'd seen her, she was arguing with an ex and ended up with little bits of quartz orbiting around her head. Honestly? I was surprised she hadn't just lobbed them at the woman instead... I would've.

"I appreciate you," she said softly.

I nodded and stepped away to give her some privacy—time and space to process this alone.

About half an hour later, her voice startled me from dozing off.

"Hey, can I steal a couple blankets?"

I was lounging on my bed, reviewing some notes from a lecture earlier today, and raised one brow at the inquiry.

"You are not sleeping on the couch, Laur. Get your ass over here," I said, pushing myself over to one side and patting the empty space in my bed.

"Ugh, I love you," she murmured appreciatively, crawling in beside me. You didn't often have to tell Laurel something twice, and I liked that about her.

She picked up a light novel from the stack at my bedside table, and for a while the two of us just enjoyed some calm, quiet time together. Simply existing in one anothers' orbit. As it started getting late, Laurel turned to me with a strangely wistful, apologetic looking expression.

"I'm sorry for doing this, Ark."

"What do you mean?"

"I dunno, I can't help but feel like I'm taking advantage of your kindness. We haven't seen each other in weeks, and it's shitty of me to just burst into your apartment with my troubles when I've hardly been there for you."

"I've been perfectly fine, Laurel."

"I know, I know. You can take care of yourself. It just sucks that we don't have any courses together anymore, and I worry about you going all... hermit on us. I should reach out more," she said.

I laughed quietly, patting Laurel's head. It was sweet that she still worried about me, but I had adapted to Sophrosyne quite well.

"There's nothing to apologize for, or worry about. Kieran wouldn't let me hermit if I tried, he's constantly dragging me all around the city whenever he's not working. So if anything, I've been bad at keeping up with *you*."

"How is that going, by the way? Are you and the sexy guardsman *official* yet?"

I resisted the urge to groan or roll my eyes. I knew that she was asking this as a means to distract herself from Amir, but I understood and played along.

"No, we're just friends."

She raised a brow, looking skeptically towards the ceiling since she couldn't quite face me in her current position.

"You told me, *verbatim*, that you wanted to fuck that man on sight when you first met. The few times I've seen you two together, he looks at you like... *Gods,* he even *looks* like he's fucking you every night, Ark. You're telling me the two of you still haven't?"

I sighed. "It's not like that."

"Bullshit," she immediately shot back.

"Okay, okay," I acquiesced. "There is obviously some mutual attraction, but I'm not looking for a relationship! And Fates know that he isn't, either."

"Alright, fair," Laurel reasoned. "I feel like he's my primary competition in the taverns."

I snorted. I was sure he was.

"Sex would just complicate things, and his friendship means a lot to me. I asked him if we could keep it platonic. It's a mutual agreement."

"Mmm, I still don't buy it," Laurel said plainly. "I think the two of you should just bone and get it over with."

Honestly? Sometimes I felt the same way.

I had no doubt that he and I would have great sex, but I didn't know how to explain that the idea of sleeping with Kieran was vaguely terrifying.

Some rewards weren't worth the risk.

It wasn't like I hadn't had my fair share of casual tumbles with pretty strangers. I could have sex without feelings involved, but shit often got messy as soon as I started to care about anyone.

I had broken one heart back home—watched the way my love transformed a soft, gentle woman into something vicious, hard and cruel.

Sometimes I wondered if Graysen had softened again in my absence. For her sake, I hoped so. She deserved to be happy.

Kieran and I had obvious chemistry, but I had my reasons for keeping him at arm's distance—reasons I couldn't really get into with Laurel, either. But also...

He wore it well, kept it all hiding in plain sight, but I *knew* there were wounds beneath that man's armor. There was a dark and deep pain that all of the charisma and cocksure energy in the world couldn't quite hide, held within that glacial eye. I only caught glimpses of it sometimes, but I knew Kieran had his own reasons for keeping things platonic between us.

I would not let my own insatiable impulses introduce any more troubles or complications into that man's life. Not when his companionship was such a gift, something I had so sorely needed.

Laurel prodded at my side with a fingertip, rousing me from my introspective thoughts.

"Nah," I replied. "Not when there are plenty of other, less complicated options. Who's your latest quarry, hmm?"

"*Fates*, don't get me started on Cypress. She's completely gorgeous and well-connected, but has the emotional availability of a boulder. I actually asked her if I could come over tonight and talk, and she said 'Sorry, I'm going to bed early.'"

"Excuse me?! Did you tell her it was an emergency?"

Abyss take me, I really hated the noblesse. Even if that was Laurel's taste in women, the lack of empathy was astounding.

"Yeah. I told her I had gotten really bad news and needed someone to talk to. That was her response. I guess she has some important dinner party tomorrow and needs her beauty sleep."

"*Laurelena Ansari*, please break up with her so I don't have to get into a fistfight with some socialite."

"I'll get around to it," she said, her voice starting to soften as she got drowsy.

She was resting her head on my stomach, basically using me as a pillow as I ran my fingertips up and down her arm the same way Amaretta used to comfort me as a child when I couldn't sleep. The scene would probably look romantic to a stranger, but unlike my weak excuses about Kieran, Laurel really was just a friend.

What I loved about Laurel was the fact that she was just as comfortable as I was with the concept of platonic intimacy. There was no confusion in this, as she snuggled into my torso for additional warmth beneath the blankets. She was like me, understanding that sometimes *closeness* was a much-needed comfort, one that we could give each other without sexual ties or mixed messages. We were both just very physical creatures, craving touch. I had no doubt that was another reason why Laurel probably outpaced Kieran in her appetite for new partners, and truthfully? I admired her for being so unrepentant about it. So completely and unapologetically *herself*.

Maybe that's why she and I became such fast friends, whereas I struggled to connect with almost anyone else here in Sophrosyne. Laurel and I were just cut from the same cloth in many ways. I did wish that she and I could spend more time together, but her coursework was charted in a pretty opposite direction from my own. She had family obligations to study the path of a trade leader, and I had very little interest in mercantilism myself.

But even if our paths continued to diverge, I would always be there for her. Always. She had been my first friend in Sophrosyne, and I was a sentimental sap, grateful to have been there, to have provided some semblance of comfort in her moment of need.

CHAPTER THIRTY

KIERAN

Hans looked deeply uncomfortable as he stepped into my office, unannounced and unexpected.

"Hey boss?"

"Yeah?" I asked, glancing up over the stack of paperwork I'd been brute forcing my way through.

When I'd been offered the position of Scouting & Reconnaissance Captain last year, Hanjae had failed to mention how much godsdamned paperwork was involved. And Hans was approaching with even more in hand. *Lovely.*

"You're going to want to read this one first," he said quietly, handing me a scroll.

Ah, fuck.

The scroll in his hand bore the official seal of the House of Torrents—a missive from Lord Ymir in Samhaven.

"Another one?"

"Yes, sir," Hans replied, his voice particularly morose as he handed off the missive. I quickly scanned over the message.

Young boy, age 8... Taken in broad daylight... No leads... Relative of an attending student... Formally requesting support from the Elder Guard, as the young woman may be another, future target... Earth Conduit, first year... Family Name: Ansari.

"Shit," I hissed, dropping the parchment as if the letter had been penned in acid instead of ink.

I understood now why Hans seemed so upset—he knew as well as I did that Arken was close to Laurel. The young spitfire had befriended her right around the same time that she and I met, and though Arken often lamented the lack of time they were able to spend together, Laurel had come around on more than one occasion to hang out with Arken, myself, and my lieutenants at the tavern.

Hans and Laurel had always gotten along well. They had similar senses of humor. If Laurel wasn't so obviously sapphic, I was fairly certain that my lieutenant would have made a move by now.

And the latest lost child—no, the latest *stolen* child was... Laurel's little brother.

Fucking Hel.

Nausea rolled around in my gut, oily and thick. What could I even say to them? To either of them?

By now, I was certain there would be whisperings amongst the noblesse, hushed concerns spreading as high ranking families started noticing a pattern. Our alliances between territories had done our best to quell too many rumors and avoid a mass panic, but that only went so far. Still, I was under direct orders to keep *everything* I knew about this situation under lock and key.

"This says the child has been missing for several weeks," I croaked. "Do we know if... Does she know?"

I hadn't seen much of Laurel this month, but it was odd that Arken hadn't brought this up. The woman respected my boundaries, and had the patience of a saint, but...

Hans ran one hand over his face for a moment in exasperation and then nodded.

"Yeah. About that. They told her *today*."

"The fuck?"

That didn't make any godsdamned sense. Hans winced at what had to be a dumbstruck expression on my face, and continued to explain.

"Apparently, her parents were so wrapped up in the initial investigations that they just... completely failed to communicate with her. Failed to communicate with anyone, really."

What a shitty excuse.

"It wasn't until the Samhaven forces recommended a bodyguard for each remaining sibling that the Ansaris seemed to even recall that they had more than one kid at risk," Hans continued. "And now I guess Lord Ymir himself has petitioned to see if we could assign one of *our* men to the job for Laurel, since the Novosi Guard has already offered that for her sister, Lakshmi, while she studies abroad."

The Novosi Guard had less to lose, though, offering their services like that. They had an entirely different system of government up there.

"Did we accept?"

"Hanjae's running it up through Demitrovic. The Ansari family offered loads of Lyra in compensation, which complicates things even if we were to deny the funds. They're trying to sort through the optics before we make an official decision."

Right. Of course.

"We'll keep an eye on her regardless," I murmured, mostly to myself—but Hans still nodded solemnly.

This was going to get real complicated, real fucking fast. If the other Houses caught wind of even the *implication* that the Elder Guard was accepting funds from the Samhaven noblesse to keep one of their most wealthy families safe, that was the beginning of a political shitstorm. The Elders would withdraw our involvement in these investigations so godsdamned fast—leaving the Atlassian Courts to fend for themselves.

As much as I would love to watch a bunch of greedy

politicians flop and flounder while trying to solve their own problems—problems that were a direct consequence of their own actions, mind you—I still couldn't stomach that. Not when children's lives were on the line.

I mean, Fates above, Amir was only *eight*.

"Make sure that if we do monitor Ansari in the meantime, though, Hans—that we keep it very much under the table. I don't even want to involve the commander right now."

"I doubt Hanjae would be opposed," Hans replied. "It's not like it would take much effort on our end."

"No, but plausible deniability could work in his favor if shit goes south with the Houses. Don't involve the rest of the cadre, either. I just want you, Jer, and myself on this one. We'll keep our ears to the ground. Sophrosyne is safer than Yvestra regardless, and I doubt anyone will be stupid enough to strike right under the noses of the Aetherborne."

"Godsdamn right," Hans agreed.

"Do you mind briefing Jeremiah on this? He should be running patrols tonight," I said, running a hand through my hair.

"Can do. I take it you won't be joining us for lunch later, then?"

"Not today," I replied. "I've got plans with Arken."

Hans snorted audibly, and opened his mouth to make some smartass remark—but it immediately snapped closed when he saw my darkening expression. A rare show of tact from the impulsive, mouthy bastard.

"Get back to work, asshole," I muttered.

"Aye, Captain."

CHAPTER THIRTY-ONE

ARKEN

The next morning, I walked Laurel home.

As the two of us were wading through the crowded Market District in relative silence, there was so much I wanted to say. So many words of comfort that I wanted to offer my friend, but they all turned to ash on my tongue as I realized I could promise nothing.

I was never good at pleasantries or telling lies for the sake of other people's comfort. In truth, there was no reassurance to be found here, nothing sincere that I could give. Nothing *true*.

There was nothing sane about this scenario, and we both knew that. All I could really offer was to hold her hand as we walked together in the cold air—and to make sure she knew she wasn't alone.

"Don't be a stranger," I murmured, kissing the top of her head as we reached her apartment. "I'm here if you need me."

"Thanks, Ark," she sniffed. "I really appreciate that. I appreciate you."

There was a certain thinness to her tone and the weak smile she offered as she turned to go that left me lingering.

"Hey, Laur?" I called out hesitantly before she pulled her keys out from her coat pocket.

"Yeah?"

"Would you like me to stay? Keep you company for a bit?"

Laurel shook her head, though her eyes softened a bit at the offer. "No. Thank you, though. I think... I think I just need to be alone for a little while."

That, I completely understood.

"Of course. I'm just a mail sprite away, though, okay?"

She nodded once before heading inside and I exhaled heavily, not realizing that I had been holding my breath.

◆ ◆ ◆

As I meandered home slowly, I tried to wrap my head around who could do such a heinous thing.

Who would steal a *child*? And *why*? To what end? Perhaps it was just my own naivete that left me so shaken. Amaretta had warned me long ago that life in the cities was different, that there were criminals and soulless creatures out there who preyed upon the weak. She had been concerned that there would be those who mistook my softness for weakness, and had all but beaten certain safety practices in me before she ever let me explore Elseweire.

I was beginning to think there was a reason she gave me her old research studio, too, as opposed to letting me stay in the student apartments. A reason beyond her typical motherly paranoia, that is. Perhaps not even Sophrosyne was entirely safe from such mortal monsters.

A slight shiver ran down my spine at the notion.

I took a detour on my way home, unable to resist the temptation to wander through one of the nearby gardens. There were a handful of floral hedge mazes scattered throughout the city, but I knew that this one had a small swinging bench beneath curtains of hanging wisteria—a lovely place for quiet contemplation.

Every few meters, there were enchanted slates on pedestals that contained puzzles, riddles and other mind-teasers. Upon success, the hedges would part and grant you one pathway closer to the center. If you got the answers wrong, the hedges turned you around instead, completely obfuscating your progress. Complex, but delightful spellwork—crafted by the Elders, I had to presume.

Many of my classmates seemed to hate this place, claiming it was a headache and a half and not worth the effort. But I spent hours here, particularly whenever I needed to clear my head. The puzzles reset every week.

It only took me about twenty minutes to arrive at the center this morning, and I eagerly claimed my prize: To sit quietly by myself, swinging gently and staring into space, letting my mind go blank. The water fountains had been replaced by fire pits during the winter months, and I was grateful for their warmth.

At some point, I had closed my eyes, focusing only on the swinging sensation and the way it reminded me of calm nights on the ship where the waves had rocked me to sleep, back and forth.

"What's on your mind, Little Conduit?"

Kieran had appeared out of thin air, joining me on the bench with two mugs of tea in hand. It used to startle the shit out of me, the way he would creep up behind me without warning—but I had grown accustomed to the way he seemed to move in silence. I had almost expected him to show up this morning, even though we hadn't planned to meet up until noon.

"I'm worried about Laurel," I said quietly, thumbing the small stone in my pocket as I so often did when anxious. Though I wasn't looking at him, I felt Kieran stiffen briefly, and then release a heavy sigh.

So he knew, then.

"Yeah," he said, voice strained. "That's fair."

"I know you can't talk about it," I said, fixing my gaze on the horizon in an effort not to search his face for answers that I knew I would not find. "But could you at least, maybe... Ah, nevermind."

"At least, what?"

"It isn't fair of me to ask," I replied. "I know the rules."

"You are almost always the exception to my rules, Arken. What is it?"

I did my best to ignore the warmth blooming in my chest, the way it always seemed to whenever Kieran let slip the fact that I was special to him in any way, shape or form. He was so charismatic that it was easy to forget that the man let a scant few people even remotely close to his personal life.

"How long have you known?" I asked, hoping like Hel that my tone didn't sound accusatory. I wasn't entitled to his privileged information, but...

"I found out this morning."

"Oh."

It wasn't fair for that to be such a relief—but it was. It really was.

"I wouldn'tve kept that from you," Kieran murmured, and I leaned my head against his shoulder for a moment, as if to channel my appreciation in silence.

"Could you at least tell me if there's... any hope at all? For Amir?" I asked softly, shrinking a bit with shame for having asked another question.

Did I even really want to know? Was that a burden I was prepared to bear, even for Laurel?

"There's hope, Ark," Kieran said, keeping his voice low as he wrapped one arm around my shoulders, offering me that second mug of tea which I had forgotten about.

I took it gratefully, immediately comforted by the warmth of the ceramic against my palms. It had been so cold this morning that I could see my breath along the way here. The scent of cloves and cinnamon was an immediate balm against my fraying nerves.

"We're doing everything we can," Kieran said. "I promise."

This left me with more questions than answers.

Why was the Elder Guard so involved with a crime in Samhaven? How did he know already? What exactly did he do as a Scouting & Reconnaissance Captain, to be so aware of what was happening in territories beyond Sophrosyne?

I *knew* his duties extended beyond training new recruits and running patrols with his squadrons—the two things I often got to watch from afar—but I also knew better than to ask for details.

"I wish I could tell you more," he sighed, as if he could read my mind. "And I wish I had better news for Laurel. I can't imagine what she's going through."

"She's pretty fucked up right now," I admitted. "Quiet. Somber. It would almost be funny, how absurdly out of character that is for her... if it weren't so frightening. They say she might be assigned a personal guard... that she could be another target."

"Yeah," Kieran said. "I know."

"Would it be one of your men?" I asked after a deep sip of tea, the warmth of cinnamon and cloves coating my tongue. "Am I even allowed to ask that?"

"You can ask me whatever you like, freshling, I just can't always answer," Kieran reminded me. "But yes. It would likely be someone from my unit."

I allowed myself to take the slightest of comforts in that. If any of the guards could keep her safe, it would be one of Kieran's own.

"Good," I murmured, staring at my boots. "That's good."

Kieran and I sat in stark, but somewhat comfortable silence for several minutes before he spoke again.

"So what are your plans for the rest of the morning?" he asked, and I shrugged.

"Not much. I was just going to go home and study before meeting up with you for lunch later. You showed up too early, stalker."

I tried to keep my tone light, playful as we so often were, but the words came out a bit more brittle than I intended.

Kieran still smirked at the accusation, though, and for a moment the weight of the last twenty-four hours seemed to lift from my chest as his pearly white teeth gleamed, peeking out from behind his lips.

"I don't see you complaining about the personal tea delivery service," he replied smoothly, without missing a beat. He was right, of course. This was exactly what I'd needed.

"That said, I did promise Hans and Jer that I'd review some of the new combat training protocols they've been working on. You wanna come with?"

"Am I allowed to?" I asked, raising a brow.

Most of Kieran's men didn't seem to mind whenever I hung around, but training protocols with his lieutenants seemed like privileged information, and I didn't want to push my luck.

His smirk stretched into an all out grin, seemingly entertained by my hesitancy.

"I'm more of an 'ask forgiveness' than an 'ask permission' sort of man these days. Come along, Little Conduit. Let's go give the boys a chance to show off."

CHAPTER THIRTY-TWO

KIERAN

When I arrived on the training fields with Arken in tow, my lieutenants exchanged a look, but said nothing. By now, they were accustomed to her presence, even if my excuses to bring her along were often flimsy at best. I appreciated their trust immensely, for a variety of reasons. Today in particular, though, because I just… had a certain sense that Arken was in dire need of a distraction.

"Congratulations, gentlemen," I called out jovially. "You get a much prettier audience than usual today. I picked up a stray Conduit on the way here."

Arken snorted, jabbing me in the ribs with her elbow as she waved to Hans and Jeremiah. Simply accidental on her part, I'm sure. They waved back to her before resuming their light sparring session.

"We're just warming up, Captain," Jeremiah said, barely containing his smirk. "Give us a few."

I led Arken over to the other side of the field where a few sets of raised benches offered a better view. I smiled as I heard her snicker beneath her breath at the volley of quips the two men shot back and forth as they parried one another's strikes.

"You three seem so close," she said as we took a seat. "I can see why, too. They're fucking hilarious."

"Who, Hans and Jer? Yeah. They're my second and third in command in the scouting unit. We've spent a lot of time together over the years," I explained.

"Which is which?"

"Hans is second. Jer is third."

"For some reason, I would've thought it was the other way around."

I snorted. That was a valid assumption.

There was a reason why I was so close to these two men in my cadre in particular—I had been the one to promote them both in the first place, hand-selecting them as my direct reporting officers within our unit. There was also a reason why Hans was second-in-command.

Hans Deering was a royal pain in my ass, but he was also an exceptional fighter. He was among the minority within the Elder Guard in that he was *not* a Conduit. The man was completely non-Resonant—but he had learned how to adapt to what he perceived to be a weakness by developing his own combat style, designed to exploit the weaknesses of Conduits in particular. He had spearheaded this project.

A majority of combative arcana required both verbal and somatic casting, particularly if it was complex spellwork—and Hans was one fast motherfucker. I'd watched him dodge and disarm multiple Conduit guardsmen within mere moments by finding ways to bind their hands during training exercises. He'd often take advantage of the aether-resistant materials in his arsenal, too.

His Novosi bolas in particular were a pain in the ass to avoid. Deering knew that even the well-trained Conduits of the Elder Guard were overly reliant on their arcana, and he exploited every last ounce of comfort to make them regret it.

Within weeks of working with the man, I'd known that I wanted him at my side. I caught some shit for it, even from some of my fellow officers—which irritated me to no end. There were other non-Resonant men within the guard, and they had to work two or three times as hard as others for a scrap of recognition. I took pride in elevating Hans, not just to set an example but because he fucking earned it.

Jeremiah was different—the polar opposite to Hans' raucous energy. He was an exceptionally talented Fire Conduit, but in the beginning, I honestly couldn't stand the man. I was naturally skeptical about training Fire Conduits for stealth roles in the guard in the first place, because their combat styles were often too flamboyant, too easy to trace. Beyond that, Fairchilde himself was very stoic and standoffish, quiet—and wouldn't often engage even when I tried to bait him into conversations. There may have been some personal biases at play, but the work that we do requires trust, and I wasn't sure that I trusted him.

Funnily enough, what changed my mind was seeing him train with Hans.

The average Fire Conduit took advantage of their blazing fists, shields and aetherblades to force their opponents to give them a wide berth. I'd been intrigued to find that Jeremiah kept his flames to a low, flickering ember—preferring to fight in close quarters. I thought Hans was fast? My third in command was *even faster*.

In studying the two together, I quickly learned that Jeremiah was a master at counter-calculations, and had developed his own combat style to counter Hans on the fly. Jer would *intentionally* expose himself with what Hans might parse as a weakness—an opening. Within moments of an attempted strike, Hans found himself disarmed. Every time. Anyone who could knock Deering on his ass without even using their arcana was an absolute force to be reckoned with.

"Lost in thought over there, Captain?" Arken teased.

"Guilty as charged," I replied. "I was just thinking about what made me select these two as my second and third in the first place."

"And that is...?" she asked.

"You're about to find out," I said, pride creeping into my voice.

"Oi!" I called out. "You two ready, or what?"

"Been ready, Cap. We were just waiting on you two to wrap up the chit-chat," Hans snarked back, swinging his bolas around casually.

"Royal pain in my ass," I murmured under my breath, and Arken giggled.

"Alright smartass, show me what you've got, then!" I called out.

With a curt nod, Hans and Jeremiah began their presentation. Jeremiah did most of the talking and I was grateful for that, all things considered. Jer was the more tight-lipped of the two, and wouldn't inadvertently reveal some detail that left Arken with more questions.

Even though Arken was now aware of Amir's kidnapping, she had no idea how many others had been stolen. Nor did she have any idea about the potential anti-Conduit rebellions that were forming, and I very much preferred to keep it that way. If it became more of a prevalent issue, maybe I could explain... but that would be treading some dangerous ground. In the present moment, though, she didn't even seem suspicious—only fascinated as Jeremiah put on an intentionally more flamboyant display of arcane combat, emulating what the average Fire Conduit might look like in a hand-to-hand scenario.

It was an effort to keep my eyes fixed to the training grounds, as opposed to watching her watch them, but I had to settle for stealing glances every time she sucked in a small breath of excitement. Was she really not bored by this? Sometimes, the woman still managed to surprise me.

Focus, Kieran.

I dug my nails into my palm a bit, letting the sharp bite draw my attention back to my lieutenants. I needed to approve this training exercise before they presented it to my commander, and it was important. It may have been a smidge short-sighted of me to bring along such a distracting creature, but I wasn't about to kick her out now. Instead, I pointedly kept my eyes on Hans, watching him move through the exercise.

This was obviously his area of expertise, and it showed. I nodded in approval as he went over the drills intended to help Conduits identify their blind spots. He had done additional research into patterns of the Elder Guard—as well as some of the regional forces—and had even broken it down by the behavior of each type of Conduit.

Air and Water Conduits, for example, had a tendency to be more ranged attackers, so he had developed some exercises to identify common casts from across the field and how to disable them with ranged weapons or stealth units depending on the scenario. Fire and Earth Conduits were often more close-range fighters, so the drills were focused more on direct disarmament.

I made a mental note to place an order with the armory for more Novosi bolas, should these methods be approved. They were really quite handy in both circumstances.

"No specific training against Shadow or Light?" Arken murmured with a hushed tone, obviously not wanting to interrupt.

I shook my head. "No. We're rather rare, remember? It would be a waste of resources to train for such a niche situation."

"Ah," she replied, her brow furrowing. "Right."

"Besides, if any of the lower ranking guardsmen were up against a soldier trained in Light or Shadow, they'd be kinda fucked regardless."

"Why's that?" Arken asked.

"We can blind people pretty damn easily, Little Conduit," I explained, briefly casting Shadow across her eyes. Though I quickly released the arcana, she still shivered gently.

"Oh, gods. I never even thought of that."

I chuckled under my breath. I mean, why would she have? The only inherent violence I'd ever seen out of Arken was when I annoyed the shit out of her and she started throwing those bony little elbows around. It was far too early for her to have enrolled in any Physical Arcana courses, if she ever even chose to. And in an era of relative peace, Physical Arcana had grown increasingly uncommon for students who weren't planning on military service.

In any circumstance, the rarity of our arcana was sort of a blessing in disguise—at least when it came to battle. Entering combat blind was a nightmare.

Finally, it was Jeremiah's turn to put his skill on display. He also managed to impress me, running through some experimental Physical Arcana tactics that would allow Conduits to disable their fellow magick-equipped enemies as well. It was all reliant on speed, so he had worked with Hans to develop a few drills that really seemed to push the limits on how fast one could cast certain spells that would bind hands or mouths, or otherwise incapacitate. That was more of a long shot, highly dependent on the arcane prowess of the individual, but we'd take every advantage we could get.

"So are you gonna keep sitting on your ass, boss? Or are you gonna come try this shit out yourself?" Hans asked with a smirk.

Arken snorted, and I rolled my eyes as I rose to my feet.

"Far be it from me to deny you an opportunity to get fucked up," I replied, cracking my knuckles.

It was my turn to show off.

CHAPTER THIRTY-THREE

Arken

A flicker of excitement shot through me as Kieran made his way onto the field.

Despite how often Kieran and I spent time together, it was rare for me to see his arcana on display. And from what I knew about Kieran's area of expertise, Shadow work was inherently stealthy and hard to track, anyway. I supposed that was what made him such a perfect candidate for his position in the Elder Guard.

That, and the undeniable evidence of his skill, which was already on display.

Every time Hans struck, lunging forward with incredible speed, Kieran managed to sidestep him even faster. Impossibly fast. It took several minutes of watching this to even parse what was happening—Kieran was strafing into Shadow, somehow—his entire body becoming briefly incorporeal, allowing him to practically *blink* into a slightly different location.

Holy Hel.

Eventually, Jeremiah joined Hans, and it was two against one. Though it was difficult for me to tear my eyes away from Kieran and his Shadows, I was also enthralled by the way his two lieutenants moved in tandem, so flawlessly fluid as they circled their captain like falcons on the hunt. These supposedly new training drills looked more like a well-rehearsed performance. A perfectly choreographed dance between some of the most dangerous men in Sophrosyne.

It was violence and grit teeth and grunting and sweat—but there was also something captivating about it. Something beautiful.

My respect for the Elder Guard deepened as I continued to watch from a distance. With every strike and parry, these three were putting their dedication on clear display. These were men of honor, men who put the protection of our city above all else. You didn't *move* like that, you didn't train that hard without something to fight for.

A strange, gnawing sensation began to grow in my belly. It was envy, I realized. I envied these men for their fierce loyalty, their drive, and their strength of will. I envied their ability to protect what they loved so deeply. I envied their *power*. I was already developing both skill and prowess in wielding my own arcana, but I couldn't do *anything* like this. I hadn't ever considered the possibility of even *needing* to—a privilege of growing up in an era of peace.

How much had these men sacrificed in order to keep that peace?

I heard Hans bark out a laugh, boastful and raucous. After what must have been nearly twenty minutes, he managed to catch Kieran's left hand with his bolas. I watched with fascination as the Shadow aether that had coated that hand like a glove faded out, disarming his dominant hand.

"Nice work Deering," Kieran said to his second, though I could already see a wicked smirk forming. "But I'll bet you all the Lyra in my coat pockets that you can't do it again."

"Challenge accepted," Hans replied, eyes glittering.

Jeremiah took several paces back, pulling out his water skin and wiping sweat from his brow. "That's all you," he said with a grin, clearly wanting to make Hans work for his prize.

Despite my surge of irrational jealousy, I also found a small kernel of relief watching the boys fight. Kieran said that if Laurel became a target—if she was in any danger like Amir—that one of his men would be assigned to her as a personal guard. His cadre extended beyond just Hans and Jeremiah, but I was certain that anyone who trained under these three could keep my friend safe.

It was then that I realized I wanted that capability, too. What if one day, Kieran wasn't around? What if Laurel was at risk, and all I could do was flash a few shiny orbs of Light in an attacker's face? I could hardly stomach such a weakness.

I wanted to be stronger.

◇ ◇ ◇

Once the three of them wrapped up for the afternoon, Kieran and I had the rest of the day to ourselves. As we meandered through the Market District, looking for lunch, I decided to ask him about what continued to tug at the back of my mind.

"Hey Kier?"

"Yeah?"

"How do people even learn all of that?" I asked, pausing for a moment by a baker's stall to peer over their selection of bread.

"Learn what, exactly, Little Conduit?"

"That sort of arcana. Combative. Defensive. All of it. It looked so complex."

Kieran chuckled, drawing a few coins from his own pocket to purchase a pastry.

"That's because it *is* very complex. It's called 'Physical Arcana,' freshling, and there are courses on it. Though, they're usually only available for third year students and above. Unless you join the Guard, of course, in which case we train you ourselves. Why?"

"I wonder if I could test into them early. Entry exams are coming up, after all..." I trailed off, touching my chin.

"Into a third year course?" Kieran asked, one eyebrow raised. "I mean shit, if anyone could pull something like that off, it would be you, Ark—but why? What's the rush?"

I glanced away for a moment, flushing slightly before Kieran nudged me, handing me half of his croissant.

"I just... don't like the idea of being so defenseless," I muttered.

"You're not defenseless, freshling. You're surrounded by some of the most intimidating motherfuckers in the city," Kieran laughed. "I would argue you're one of the safest people in Sophrosyne by association."

I sighed.

"And while I *appreciate* that," I said pointedly, "That's hardly an excuse to be complacent. We're not always together, you know."

Whether I liked it or not, Kieran would always have much higher priorities.

"Hey," Kieran said softly. "Is this about Amir, Arken? Because I promise you, you're safe here. Yvestra isn't nearly as warded as we are."

"It's not about Amir, exactly," I said slowly, trying to calibrate my thoughts. "It's more like... What the Hel could I even do if Laurel got attacked one day, and we were alone? I'm not a fighter, and neither is she. All we could do is run."

Kieran nodded thoughtfully, chewing on a bite of his food.

"Sometimes, the best thing to do in those situations *is* to run, Arken. There's no shame in that. In such a hypothetical, highly unlikely situation, you *should* run. Run, and find me."

"And if you're not around?" I asked quietly.

Kier seemed to deliberate on this for a moment before nodding again. "Fair point, and well-made as ever. But if you want to test into Physical Arcana, I've gotta warn you: It's a two part test for

Conduits. You'll have to prove arcane aptitude, which you've got in the bag already. But you'll also have to test for physical strength and endurance. Arcane combat is incredibly taxing on the body. They won't let you start until you pass both exams."

Ugh. Now *that* was an obvious obstacle—I had never been particularly athletic. Sure, I had the stamina to walk through the forests for hours on end, but I doubt that's what he meant by endurance. It certainly wasn't strength.

"You're going to try to test in anyway, aren't you?" Kieran asked with a smirk.

"You know me so well," I crooned, punctuating the remark with an elbow to his side. He pretended to stumble, lightly bumping into one of the merchant's stalls.

"I know that you're stubborn as Hel, which is all I really needed to know," he replied. "But if you're truly dead set on this, I can help, you know. I can put together a light training regimen for you, help whip you into shape. Results *not* guaranteed by the end of this quarter, but we can try."

I grinned.

"Deal."

CHAPTER THIRTY-FOUR

KIERAN

Several weeks later, I received a summons from my commander while I was in the middle of my weekly rounds.

After I wrapped things up with Roshana, I made my way back to HQ. Before I could even raise my fist to knock, I heard my commander call through the door.

"Come in, Captain Vistarii."

I knew damn well that he had very expensive wards set up to alert him of the presence and identity of visitors (or eavesdroppers) nearby, but that didn't make it any less alarming. I could have sworn that he took advantage of it sometimes, just to be as ominous as possible.

"Afternoon, sir," I said as I stepped inside his spacious office quarters, closing the door behind me. I felt the slightest brush of aether as the wards re-sealed and soundproofed the room automatically. Convenient, that. I almost wished that I could justify the Lyra for that complex spellwork in my own office, but considering I could do the same thing manually using my own arcana, it felt a bit frivolous.

"Please, take a seat," Hanjae instructed, motioning to the chairs across from his desk. The broad expanse of wood was littered with maps and missives.

Though his tone was friendly, it was also more formal than usual, and my pulse quickened. Immediately I began to run through a mental checklist, trying to remember if I had done anything particularly egregious under the table as of late. Was I about to be disciplined? Did one of my men fuck something up?

Gods, I hoped that nobody was hurt.

"The training program that your lieutenants put together has been approved. We took it all the way to High General Demitrovic for review, and he's pleased that we've managed to come up with a counter-strategy to the rebel threat so quickly. He sends his regards."

I blinked, momentarily caught off-guard. *Regards* from the High General? That was just about the closest thing you could get to praise from the stoic, strategic mastermind who led the Elder Guard.

"That was fast," I murmured, more to myself than anything. Introducing new training regimens often took weeks, if not months to be fully approved.

"You and your men are doing excellent work, Kieran. If I may speak plainly, your unit consistently outperforms the others when it comes to mission success rate, and you're often leading the charge on significantly more complex and delicate matters. That is no small feat," Hanjae began again, clear approval passing through his stern gaze. "You're still young, Vistarii, but I have to ask. Have you considered what's next in your career path?"

"With all due respect, sir, the success of my unit has less to do with me and more to do with my men. They're highly skilled and doubly dedicated to the work we do—all of the credit belongs to them."

"That's not what your men say, Kieran. Nor is that what's been observed." I opened my mouth to argue, but my commander continued before I could interrupt. He knew me too well.

"Yes, your *hand-selected* group of individuals are exceptional,

I do not deny that. You're also a natural born leader, and you've built a culture of deep trust and respect. And every single one of them attributes their recent successes to you. There is a reason I promoted you so early on in your career, Kieran—and you've clearly risen to the challenge."

My skin prickled with discomfort, unsure of how to process this unexpected turn of conversation. I had braced myself for bad news, not... excessive compliments. I took great pride in my work, yes—it was one of the few things that I took seriously. In many ways, defending Sophrosyne was my life's purpose. To hear I was doing it well was an honor, and yet I struggled to attribute these outcomes to anything *I* had done right. And a natural born leader? No. Certainly not. Quite the opposite. I had been born a coward, though I'd fought tooth and nail to overcome that. If anything, I was just following a few good examples that I had lucked into having over the last decade or so.

Commander Ka seemed to be studying me closely as I sat in silence, trying not to ruminate on certain memories that threatened to escape their assigned compartments, locked away in the back of my mind.

"I don't mean to put pressure on you, Kieran. As I said, you're still young—the youngest captain the Elder Guard has ever seen, as far as I'm aware. But if you *are* interested in furthering your career, elevating your rank in the years to come... that is something we could begin to train you for as early as next month. There will be opportunities for you to sit in on some higher level discussions soon."

My mouth ran dry. I knew he hadn't intended to put me on the spot, but if Hanjae was already considering setting up training, he likely expected an answer from me sooner rather than later. *Fuck*.

"I must admit, Commander... when I joined the Guard, it was not for the sake of personal ambition. I was just looking to serve and protect the city I love. To put my talents to good use."

"I know exactly why you joined the Guard, Kieran," Hanjae replied quietly.

That was unfortunately more accurate than I would have liked it to be. Commander Ka understood my motivations more than anyone. He knew why I had worked so hard, he knew exactly what led me to climb rank so fast and so young… and so I held my tongue.

"There is also the matter of my men. As you said, the Scouting & Recon unit tends to handle the most delicate missions, and they're often the most dangerous. If I were to advance… I'd need a damn good captain to take my place. To keep them safe. Neither Deering or Fairchilde are fully ready to take that on, and I would need more time to train them. Especially now."

As I trailed off, there was a glimmer of admiration that passed through Hanjae's expression, and my gut churned. What he didn't realize was that there was also an extremely selfish part of me that knew moving up from captain to commander would obliterate any semblance of free time that I had.

Six months ago, that would have been a welcome adjustment, truthfully. I had already often found myself staying late and working overtime on purpose back then. Work was a welcome distraction from the empty hours I had previously spent alone. And I enjoyed my work. I really did. It was just that lately, I had been enjoying something else far more.

Selfish bastard.

"Nothing needs to be set in stone today, Captain," my commander replied. "I'm simply gauging your interest. I want you to know that your talents have been recognized by my peers and superiors. They're seeing the potential in you that I always have."

He had always thought far too highly of me.

"I am not opposed to the idea, Hanjae. I swore an oath to serve, and I stand by that oath—my loyalty belongs to Sophrosyne, sword and soul," I said slowly. "I just need a little more time to think. I haven't exactly thought that far ahead in the future."

He gave me a curt nod, though I could see the understanding in his eyes, and appreciated that more than he would ever know. He was the only mentor I had left, and despite all of my self-doubt and loathing, I really wanted to make him proud. I would never live up to his expectations—or this pedestal that he'd seemed to place me on—but I could sure as Hel try.

Because now, more than ever, I owed Sophrosyne *everything* I had.

CHAPTER THIRTY-FIVE

ARKEN

"I still don't understand why you're so nervous, Ark," Laurel said, laughter in her voice as she prodded me gently in the ribs.

We were trudging through the Student's Quarter together, groceries in hand. The late afternoon air had started to chill *just* enough that I was regretting not grabbing a sweater before my friend had dragged me out to run errands.

"I mean, if you don't pass these entry exams, you can just take them again next quarter, can you not? You've said it yourself, you're not on any strict timeline here."

She had a point. Unlike her—unlike most of our peers, really—I had no particular academic plan in place. I wasn't beholden to any schedules, I had no filial obligations or expectations to uphold here at the Arcane Studium. I had the freedom to do as I pleased, which made it difficult for me to explain the nerves.

I just really wanted to start Physical Arcana. It was like a compulsion at this point. Kieran had been training me for a few weeks now, and after nearly a month's worth of daily exercises intended to up my physical endurance, I certainly felt stronger—but would it be enough? Kieran clearly had faith in me, commending my progress every chance he got, but the man was arguably biased.

"Arken? Hello?" Laurel said, jostling my arm. "Did you hear anything I just said? Gods, what is it that Vistarii calls you again? Tiny Conduit?"

Little Conduit.

"Oh, shut the Hel up," I laughed, rolling my eyes.

The first time Laurel overheard Kieran calling me that, she wore a shit-eating grin for the rest of the day, and I wasn't sure she was ever going to let me live it down.

"But no, I'm sorry. Got lost in my head there for a sec. What were you saying, Laur?"

"I was *saying*, the obvious solution to those nerves of yours is to come out tonight. Get drunk. Get laid. Preferably both."

I chuckled, pausing briefly by the baker's stall and exchanging a few Lyra for a small boule of fresh bread as we continued our stroll down the cobblestone path.

"I swear to the Source, woman. That's your solution for everything. Sex and wine."

Laurel laughed out loud, turning a few heads as we made our way back towards the Student's Quarter.

"I mean, I *am* a merchant's daughter. The best business connections are built on things like sex and wine," she informed me with a smirk.

"Ah, that explains why you cycle through your girlfriends on a semi-monthly basis, huh?" I joked. "Collecting all of those *connections*."

"Depends on who you ask," Laurel said, fluffing her hair. She paid no mind to the folks who continued to stare after her outburst of laughter. To be fair, it probably happened to her often enough that it wasn't worth noticing anymore. Everything about Laurel Ansari was infectious and entertaining.

"According to Cypress, it's because I'm a high maintenance bitch with commitment issues."

I grimaced. Knowing Cypress Glass, that was probably a direct quote.

"Remind me again why you're still dating this one, Laur?"

Her current girlfriend was a piece of work. To phrase it kindly.

"Because she's hot," Laurel reminded me flippantly, as if it were obvious. "Besides, don't act like you don't like them a little mean, too. Kieran bullies the shit outta you."

"Yeah, but I'm not *dating* Kieran."

"Whatever you two need to tell yourselves," she replied, smirking again. "Anyway, are you coming out with us tonight or not?"

I opened my mouth, only for Laurel to interrupt.

"That was a rhetorical question, Asher. I will show up at your studio and drag you out by the hair if I need to, which would be a shame because your hair looks gorgeous today. But come on."

"I dunno, Laur," I sighed. "I feel like I should probably rest up for the exams…"

It was a pathetic, half-truth of an excuse. Sure, I would benefit from a good night's sleep before putting my arcana on display for the scholars tomorrow, but the more irresponsible side of me had been hoping to pester Kieran tonight instead.

"Rhetorical. Question. Asher," Laurel repeated. "You're coming out. At least give me an hour of reprieve from Cypress and her cronies."

Though Laurel complained about her various acquaintances and friend circles, the truth was that she was one Hel of an extrovert—a veritable social butterfly who could charm in almost any setting, around any type of person. While I was decent enough at masking my own distaste or discomfort in social situations, Laurel put me to shame. She thrived in those murky waters of the political elite.

But I had spent nearly every night this week with Kieran and his lieutenants, and I knew that Laurel's constant partying was just one of the ways she was managing to cope. We hadn't talked about Amir much as of late, but I knew she was still hurting.

"Only because I love you, Laurel," I acquiesced. "And you get an hour. One. Two at best. You know how I feel about Glass and her groupies."

Laurel let out a small squeal of excitement.

"Yes! You're the best. And I swear, some of the other folks joining us tonight are halfway decent, too. Meet at my place around 8?"

"As you wish, you little party daemon," I sighed, pausing at the corner. We had reached Laurel's apartment building on the west side of the student housing complex.

"Don't you dare cancel on me," she threatened, daggers in her eyes. "I know where you live."

It was a valid threat to make, as I had certainly left her hanging on more than one occasion, like the gods-awful friend I was.

"I wouldn't dream of it. See you soon," I replied.

"See ya, *tiny Conduit*," she called over her shoulder.

"Don't make me change my mind, Ansari," I warned.

Laurel simply cackled and walked off, dark curls bouncing and gleaming in the late afternoon sun.

Gods, that woman was a pain in the ass. I adored her.

❖ ❖ ❖

Later that evening, I was pleasantly surprised to find that Laurel had made good on her promise. Some of the other Conduits who were out with us tonight were actually pretty entertaining... and attractive. It was a nice distraction.

I had been out for much longer than an hour now. Expensive wine was flowing and it had loosened quite a few things—lips, neckties, inhibitions. Laurel had unsurprisingly ended up in

Cypress' lap, while a few of their friends were volleying pointed barbs back and forth over some mutual acquaintance who had recently fallen out of favor. We were all clustered together in a more private booth in the corner of The Clover, enjoying the food, plentiful alcohol, and a local bard's set.

I could feel my interest fading, and I let my eyes wander across the tavern. I loved Laurel, I really did—and I had been having fun for the most part—but it was around this time that I had a tendency to lose interest in the conversation. I could fake plenty of things, but passing judgment over some Conduit for dating some no-name, non-Resonant farmhand? I mean, seriously? Some friends they were. What did it matter?

I took another sip of my honey-whiskey, trying not to roll my eyes.

"Do they always gossip like this?" An unfamiliar voice murmured to my left.

I turned to find that an attractive man was now seated beside me, one of the few new faces that had joined us for a night of drinks and distractions. Mason, I think his name was. Mason Park. There was a devilish sort of gleam in his dark brown, almond shaped eyes that crinkled in the corners as he smirked.

"Unfortunately, yes," I replied with a grimace, eyeing him over my glass of ice and liquor.

"How boring."

My thoughts exactly.

"You a friend of Cypress?" I asked casually.

"Gods, no," he replied. "I'm friends with Jaf—Cypress' older brother. The one who's trying to hit on the barmaid over there."

That explained why he seemed a little bit older than the rest of us. Mason nodded across the room, where Jaffrey Glass was looking to be mid-rejection from the woman tending bar tonight. Rough. My eyes glazed over a bit as Jaf returned to the fray, though I did have to laugh when Mason used his Air arcana to ruffle his friend's hair.

"Can't win 'em all, bud," Mason chuckled.

The group conversation eventually drifted away from their weird circle-jerk of self-proclaimed superiority, but my attention continued to phase in and out. I kept myself entertained by people watching, though "entertained" was probably the loosest of terms tonight. There weren't any particularly interesting groups or pairings to observe, mostly just a throng of my fellow Conduits getting sloshed and dancing the night away.

I was about ready to call it for the evening when my ears pricked up over some casual debate between Jaf and Fahra Nykos, another one of Cypress' groupies.

"Nah, guys, I'm telling you—everyone has at least *one* kink. If you think you don't, you just haven't discovered yours yet."

"Gods above, now you're just being gross, Jaffrey."

"*I'm* being gross?" Jaf barked. "Come on now, Fahra—we all know your ex had a foot fetish. Are you really gonna sit there and judge someone if they like to be tied up and spanked a little?"

I smirked behind my glass of whiskey, before realizing all of the ice had melted beneath my warming hands. I sighed, frowning for a moment. It would be so easy to refreeze the ice with a simple little spell, but the convenience of a cold beverage wasn't worth the risk of being seen. I drank my damn watered down whiskey as is.

"See, now *that's* a kink I'll never understand," Cypress mused, slurring her words just enough that Mason and I exchanged a knowing look. Laurel's latest conquest was notorious for being unable to hold her liquor.

"Like... Spanking? Ropes? *Whips?!* I don't get that shit. Sex is supposed to be about *pleasure,* not violence."

Mason Park and I snorted under our breaths in unison, and then glanced at each other in surprise.

"Oh? You've got a take on this, Lightbearer?" Cypress challenged, eyes narrowing. I didn't think she liked me very much.

Clearly, the feeling was mutual.

"I mean, there can be a very fine line between pleasure and pain," I replied, regardless. "Some people enjoy dancing on that line, if you know what I mean."

"I really don't," Cypress slurred, playing with a strand of Laurel's hair. "I mean, what does anyone even get out of that?"

The group's eyes were glued to me now, eager for a response now that I had inadvertently exposed myself as a connoisseur of kink. *Well then.*

"It depends on the person, and what role they're playing within a dynamic," I explained. "Plenty of people find the exchange of power and control arousing in and of itself."

"Sure, sure," Cypress replied. "Maybe if you're the one in charge. I get the whole power trip, ego thing. But gods, what does the receiver get out of shit like that?"

I resisted the urge to smirk and expose myself *entirely*, but still. This was something of a special interest of mine, and I didn't mind educating my drunk ass acquaintances on the nuance of power dynamics in the bedroom. I took another sip of whiskey before continuing on with a casual shrug.

"There's something to be said for the freedom you experience by giving up control for a few hours. Consciously—*willingly*—offering that up to someone else, letting them take the reins and call the shots. It's a release of responsibility, in a way, and plenty of people find that to be a relief. As for the pain... Well, some folks just like the endorphin rush that comes afterwards. Others... true masochists, mostly, actually enjoy the sensation of pain. They get off on it."

"Arken Asher, the Light Conduit with a dark side!" Laurel crowed with a wicked grin, lifting her wine glass in my direction. "Who knew you were so well versed in the kinky shit?"

I winked at her, and her grin widened.

"I mean, don't knock things 'til you try them," I replied airily, trying not to laugh as Cypress' eyes widened in shock.

"Wait, you're telling me you've *tried* that shit?" Fahra asked with hushed excitement.

"Perhaps I have," I mused, causing Laurel to burst into a fit of drunken giggles. "Perhaps I have... rather often."

"Oho, the woman speaks from *experience*," Jaf cajoled, waggling his eyebrows suggestively.

I snorted.

I was indeed speaking from experience. I had developed a taste for submission back when I was still at home in the Brindlewoods, when I was still dating Graysen. She had a bit of a *thing* for bossing me around, and over time that escalated to the bedroom dynamic between us. Since then, I had always liked sex that was rough. Demanding. Carnal.

I had indulged in a handful of casual encounters since coming to Sophrosyne, but they were few and far between. None had particularly scratched the itch right, either, though in all fairness, I had never really gone hunting for a dominant partner. I wasn't looking for a relationship, and it was rare that I met anyone who was attractive enough to distract me from the constant, devastating presence of Kieran Vistarii.

Gods, don't think about him right now, Asher, I chastised myself. *Not in this context.*

It was too late, though. As the conversation continued, I couldn't help but wonder what sort of bedroom dynamics *Kieran* was into. I had a very strong feeling he was... my type. He had even joked about his preference in honorifics a while back. But it was impossible to tell sometimes, whether Kieran was playing around for the sake of my entertainment, or if there was an underlying kernel of truth in some of the lascivious shit that fell out of his mouth oh so casually. Embarrassingly enough, I had revisited that conversation in my mind on more than one occasion...

"What, do you make them call you Captain in bed, too?"

"I prefer Sir, actually."

"Can I get you another drink?" Mason asked, interrupting my train of thought as he rose to his feet, shaking his own empty glass.

"Sure," I replied, glancing up at him. There was a glint of intrigue in his dark eyes as he gazed back down at me. "Honey whiskey, if you don't mind."

"You've got it."

As Mason wandered off in pursuit of our beverages, my mind drifted back to Kieran. Again. Images that I often tried to avoid flickered through my mind.

Kneeling before him. His hands around my throat. His mouth on my neck, my collarbone, my—

Gods. This was *truly* the last thing I needed to be thinking about. And yet my tipsy, errant mind kept imagining how he might react if I called him *Sir*. What that rasping voice of his might sound like, giving me commands. The thought alone had heat pooling between my legs. In the middle of a fucking tavern.

Just a friend. He's just a friend. You agreed to keep things platonic. You asked *to keep things platonic. So stop fantasizing about this shit every chance you get.*

"Here you go," Mason said cheerfully, proffering a fresh tumbler of whiskey and sitting back down beside me.

A little closer this time, I noted. Our thighs were almost touching now, though there had been plenty of space for us both. That would normally bother me, but I didn't really mind with all the alcohol swimming in my veins. Still, I silently thanked the damn Source—and Mason Park—for interrupting my train of thought yet again.

"You know, Ark," Mason murmured again after a while. "It sounds like you and I might have some compatible tastes."

"Do we now?" I mused, contemplating whether or not I wanted to encourage where this conversation was headed. Perhaps I did.

"And what gives you that idea?" I asked, turning to face him.

Between the ever-flowing drinks and our previous conversation, I was admittedly feeling touch-starved. Mason Park was handsome enough. He wasn't *Kieran* levels of alluring, but then again, who the fuck was?

I couldn't avoid the truth that my best friend was at least partially to blame for my lack of a sex life. I enjoyed sex. It was arguably one of my favorite pastimes, and it's not like I was saving myself for anyone or anything... I would just often prefer my dumb little adventures with Kieran—and his good company—over the risk of *bad* sex. Though, from what I could gather, it was starting to sound like Mason could offer an evening that actually aligned with my preferences.

"Call it an educated guess," Park offered.

He spoke with a slight accent, I realized. Vindyrst, if I had to guess. There was a subtle lilt, and a pleasant sort of musicality that most people from the mountainous region of Northern Atlas tended to have.

I smirked to myself as I took yet another sip of whiskey. I was well on my way to being drunk at this point, but I was also overdue for a bit of recklessness.

"Would you like to find out for certain?" Mason asked.

The confidence in his tone left me intrigued. That was the voice of a man who knew how to...

Fuck it.

"You know, I think I just might take you up on that," I purred.

A distant part of me recognized that I would not receive what I was *actually* craving tonight—but then again, that particular craving of mine was unlikely to ever be satiated. I mean, so what if when I spoke of submission earlier, I had only imagined offering mine to Kieran? There were a great many things that this mind of mine could conjure, and there were plenty of desires and daydreams that I could never, ever have. But I could have this.

"Lucky me," Mason replied, eyes darkening with desire.

I knocked back what remained of my whiskey, eager for the liquid courage to assuage my nerves and chase away what remained of those stupid, useless thoughts.

"Let's get out of here."

CHAPTER THIRTY-SIX

KIERAN

So far, this evening had been a total wash.

I had successfully resisted the urge to pester Arken immediately after I got off work. I had already dragged the poor woman out with me and my lieutenants almost every evening this week, traipsing about the town. And though she had given me no indication of her boredom, I couldn't bring myself to monopolize all of her free time. Only *most* of it.

I was a selfish bastard, after all—but she had her entry exams tomorrow. I could behave. But I couldn't help but smile to myself as I kicked my boots up, resting my legs on the desk.

For the past several weeks, at her request, I had been running Arken through daily strength training drills and exercises intended to improve her endurance for Physical Arcana. If she wanted to test into such a high-level course, the scholars were going to test both her arcane aptitude and her physical strength.

At first, the Little Conduit fucking hated me for holding her to it. The first time I had her run laps, I think she was about ready to strangle me. Every time I said *another one*, those golden-brown eyes had been brimming with adorable animosity. But Arken Asher was nothing if not stubborn as Hel. This morning, she could almost keep up with my pace as we ran around the Student's Quarter.

Almost.

I had used the last several hours to catch up on tedium—missives I needed to read, reports to file, notes to review from various sources across the city. Even cities as grand as Sophrosyne had their seedy underbellies, and I had informants lurking in every dark corner. I had been a little *too* efficient though, and didn't have much else to work on, leaving me restless.

It was right about now that I would be typically headed to a tavern, on the hunt for some pretty distraction. But, for whatever reason, that impulse felt less than savory.

For whatever reason.

I scoffed at my own thoughts. I knew damn well why those distractions weren't appealing lately.

The last time I had a stranger in my bed, I spent the entire godsdamned night thinking about *her* instead. I probably should have been ashamed of that, if not a bit embarrassed—but I had gotten away with it, and therefore I was not. Still, I wasn't exactly proud of the fact that I had taken some random, brown-haired woman to bed, just to treat her as a stand-in for the one I actually wanted to be balls deep inside.

Thank the gods that I had at least managed enough tact and self-control not to moan Arken's name out loud while I fucked the other woman, fast and hard and aggressive—the same way that I regularly fucked my own fist thinking about the same damn thing. Arken in my bed. Arken on her knees. Arken *screaming* my name.

Platonic. So very platonic.

As lovely as such images were in my mind, I was grateful when a tap at my window distracted me from my inappropriate, borderline pathetic obsession.

I could barely make out the figure of the mail sprite from across the room. From this far away, it just looked like a small, swirling vortex of air, but the sprite took shape as I approached the window. It was a stoat, standing up on its hind legs, presenting me with a small scroll sealed in emerald green wax.

A message from Tessa Kallys, the Viscountess of Amaranthe. Now *that* was unexpected.

I had reached out to Tess a few weeks prior, after the disturbance with the Mirkovics at the Western Gates had drawn my suspicions. Regrettably, I had no sources of significance in Freyston, and so I had settled for the next best thing: Someone with intimate visibility from the neighboring lands. I knew from experience that there was no love lost between the Kallys family and the Mirkovics, so I had entrusted Tessa to keep an eye on that group from Freyston.

As I unraveled the scroll, it appeared that the seeds I planted had potentially started to bear fruit.

"Town hall meeting" at the Dogwood Inn, S.E. Freyston. All expected to attend. 11 PM.
— TK

I glanced at the clock. It was just about ten. I could make it to southeast Freyston in less than half an hour, but I didn't want to go alone, so I summoned my sprite and scratched out two quick directives—a copy for each of my lieutenants.

Meet me at the stables. HQ. Immediately.

✧ ✧ ✧

"I swear to the Source, you better have a good reason for this," Hans groused as he strolled up to the stables.

I was preparing Muniin's saddles, but paid his qualms no mind. I would be more concerned if Hans Deering arrived for a last minute mission without complaint, honestly.

"Why's that, Deering?" Jeremiah inquired, rounding the corner from the other side of the stables. "Got something better to do?"

"*Someone,*" Hans muttered.

"My apologies, boys," I replied, adjusting Muniin's reins. "We've got a lead."

"Lose the uniform jacket," I directed, glancing over at Jeremiah. "I've got a few casual coats in my office, but be quick. We're leaving in ten minutes."

Efficient as ever, Jer was gone and back again within three minutes. As we mounted up and made our way towards the Western Gates, heading for Freyston, I briefed them on the situation.

"There was something off about that party of protesters a few weeks back," I began.

"The group who followed Mirkovic's caravan?" Jeremiah asked.

"The very same, yes. Like you mentioned, it was unusual for a group of Pyrhhan citizens to be *that* disgruntled with their leadership. I mean, sure—Gidgeon and Levi can be pricks. Bristol and Gwen are mostly fine, if not a bit up their own asses. But when it comes to policy? Lord de Laurent keeps them in check."

"We found no evidence of foul play or ulterior motives when we investigated, though," Hans pointed out. "It was mostly farmhands. A few artisans, traders. And they've apparently been on their best behavior ever since. Has something changed?"

"That's what we're going to find out. According to one of my sources, all twelve of those Pyrhhans are expected to be in attendance for some sort of town hall meeting that's taking place at the Dogwood Inn at the top of the hour."

"What sort of town hall meeting takes place at eleven o'clock at night?" Jeremiah scoffed.

"Nothing sanctioned by the House of Embers, that's for damn

sure," I replied.

The abrupt screech of a barn owl startled Muniin, interrupting her canter. I rubbed at her neck with soothing circles against her coarse coat, and we carried on.

"So what's our strategy?" Hans asked.

"We'll tie up the horses on the cusp of the woods," I instructed. "Dogwood is less than a kilometer out from the trail, and we'll draw less suspicion on foot. We'll disperse ourselves throughout the room. Jer—I want you monitoring exits. Take note of whoever might be coming and going, and look out for any Pyrhhan guards."

"Yes, sir."

"Hans, I want you focused on the speaker and the behavior of the crowd. Do what you do best."

Hans nodded. My second in command was a master at interpreting coded language. I had yet to encounter a cipher the man couldn't crack within a day, whether it was in Common, Aetheric, Irrosi—you name it.

"And you'll be the ghost," Jeremiah said, more a statement than a question.

"I'll be the ghost," I agreed.

This was where my Shadows offered a significant advantage in my line of work. For the most part, I could utilize my arcana to traverse through that tavern from the darkest corners, sight unseen. Observing those who think they're not being watched. People reveal far too much about themselves when they expect that everyone's attention is elsewhere.

Our horses were well-rested and fast, so we arrived at the edge of the forest with time to spare.

After dismounting, Jer and Hans made some subtle but meaningful adjustments to their clothing and hair. Jeremiah had even whipped out a small pot of concealer to cover up the slashing scar across his cheek and chin. Personally, I didn't bother. My Shadows would shroud me soon enough, but my lieutenants were clever. This crowd had seen the three of us before in an authoritative state, so obscuring noteworthy features was necessary if we wanted to successfully infiltrate whatever this "town hall meeting" truly was.

We made it to the Dogwood Inn on foot just as the clock tower in the town square struck eleven. Quiet murmurs began to disperse through a growing crowd of men and women as the bells rang out, and a throng of thirty-something Pyrhhans made their way into an otherwise empty first floor.

While folks situated themselves at various tables and benches, I fell into the Shadows and began collecting information.

"Things in Vindyrst have gotten worse," a decrepit looking farmhand whispered to the woman at his side. "There's been talk of banding together. Collectively."

Interesting.

"They call themselves the *Bloodborne*," another hushed whisperer confessed. This time it came from a young woman who was deeply tanned with hair like straw—messy and wild.

Her calloused hands and the dirt beneath her fingernails suggested that she, too, was a farm worker. All of that tracked, of course. Freyston and Amaranthe were largely agricultural lands. But what interest did Pyrhhan farmers have in the happenings of Vindyrst, of all places? And who the fuck were the Bloodborne?

I was hoping for answers when a man rose from his seat, his gait confident as he strode towards the center of the room. All eyes in the room followed him now, so he had to be a leader of sorts. As he made his way up to the front, I made a mental note of all of his features.

Approximately 6'3. Pale. Brown hair, mid-length, wavy. Brown eyes, thick brows. Barrel-chested. Casual attire, clothing well-worn, patches on the elbows of his long-sleeved flannel shirt. Strong posture. Mid thirties.

"My brothers and sisters!" the man called out, extending his arms out in welcome. "I thank you for your time. It has been too long since we last met."

The crowd murmured quietly, returning the greeting, and various heads bobbed with familiarity as their attention remained affixed to this speaker.

"Just as it has been *too long* since we have had appropriate representation within the House of Embers!"

Members of the crowd stomped their feet in clear approval of the message, several men raising flagons of ale towards the speaker in acknowledgement.

"We are *tired*, are we not? Of tilling soil we don't own? Of harvesting crops we don't eat? Of paying taxes to the godsdamned Mirkovics while our resources dwindle, our lacking infrastructure left in disrepair?"

I raised a brow while the room nodded out their affirmations. I spent plenty of time in Pyrhhas as of late. I had been all across Freyston in the last several months for various investigations. Their roads were well kept, their people were well fed...

So what was this *really* about?

"More importantly, we are *tired* of our lives and welfare being dictated by a privileged handful of these simpering servants of the gods. These filthy fucking *Conduits*."

The speaker spat out that last word as if it were a slur, and the energy in the room shifted. The people looked bitter, and angry. Worn-down. Exhausted. And there it was.

This was a room full of non-Resonants.

Certain things began to fall into place.

My thoughts immediately returned to the debrief with High General Demitrovic several weeks prior. We had yet to *firmly* identify the source of this growing movement of discontent, had no leads that had turned up direct evidence that linked these disappearance cases to any one group of disgruntled Atlassians. *Was this...?*

"The magick in their bastard blood is fading!" the speaker continued. "Fewer and fewer mortals are born with Resonance with every passing generation. I know it. They know it. We all know it! Certain elements are so rare now that they could very well cease to exist within our lifetime. And *maybe that's for the best.*"

The hair on the back of my neck stood on end. *Blood is thicker than Aether.*

The child found in Ithreac, mutilated and strung up in the trees. Our missing students. Fucking *Amir.* These things were connected, they *had* to be. But *how*? How were these networks communicating between the territories, fostering the same fear and loathing, without leaving *a single trace* for any of our respective forces to find?

"Hear, hear!" A voice called out from the back of the room.

"We all know damn well that the Atlassian elite serve themselves and their coffers, first and foremost. They send their spawn to Sophrosyne to study under those blasted Aetherborne, to continue this cycle of oppression built by *their* design, to preserve hierarchy based on one thing and one thing alone: *Arcana.*"

There was something off about the man as his energy intensified, growing red in the face as he continued his emphatic speech. It was hard to get a read on whether he was speaking genuinely, or putting on a show. His tells were in conflict, obscuring his intent. Did he even believe in the sharp words he was spewing off? Or was this a man acting in bad faith, pushing his own agenda?

"*We* are the mortal majority! What good does their paltry magick even serve the rest of us? Why should representatives of less than *five percent* of the population speak on our behalf? Why should access to the elements mean that these privileged pricks should own our land, dictate our laws? Why were they even chosen to lead us in the first place?"

He made fair points in that regard, I had to admit, but the more this man spoke, the less I trusted the authenticity of his intentions.

"It's not right!" An older woman seated close to the speaker cried out. "Damn these *aetherwhores*. Damn them to the Abyss!"

"Indeed," the speaker acknowledged. "Damn them all. And my friends, we could remain passive. We could wait for these bloodlines to die, for Resonance to fade out from history, making equals of us all. It's bound to happen. But only time will tell if that takes decades, or centuries. And so I ask this of you all: *Why wait?*"

Despite my growing discomfort, I continued to scan the room, moving about unseen to get a closer look at certain people's reactions. Expressions were grim as the man carried on, counting off various grievances against the Mirkovic family in particular. I could tell that at least half of the crowd was entirely on board with the message of this speaker, but others seemed more skeptical. They had yet to be radicalized.

That told me that whatever this movement was, it was relatively new.

But so were the disappearances.

My ears pricked up when the sighing croon of a mourning dove traveled through the air, setting me on high alert. That cadence was familiar—and little gray bird, it was not. There were no doves in the awnings of this building. That was a signal from Jeremiah. The Pyrhhan guards were coming.

At the signal, Hans made a quiet exit. Jeremiah followed suit shortly after, neither of my men drawing any attention to themselves as they crept out. I quickly followed, despite the urge to hang back and observe how this crowd might react to an interruption from local law enforcement. It was more important that my men and I weren't implicated here. We were technically outside of our jurisdiction, and the Lord of Embers would not stand for our interference... particularly not if I was involved.

Still, we had plenty of information to work with, troubling as it may be—with several leads to follow. This was a successful mission, and I made note to thank Tessa Kallys for the tip.

Once I was about half a kilometer out, I glanced back towards the Dogwood Inn and saw several of the Pyrhhan guardsmen ushering the crowd out. Their body language was stern, yet polite... Friendly, even. They were enforcing curfew, not stomping out the flickering embers of a resistance movement.

The Pyrhhan Guard had no idea what had been taking place in their own godsdamned backyard.

Useless bastards.

"So the speaker was definitely from Vindyrst," Hans began once the three of us met up, returning to our horses. "And he's clearly got some ulterior motives for riling up commoners in Pyrhhas."

"Wait. Vindyrstian? Are you certain?" I asked.

Not that I doubted my lieutenant's observations, but I was fairly skilled at picking up on regional accents... and the speaker had none to speak of.

"At least ninety percent sure. His belt buckle was Vindyrst steel—low grade leatherwork, I recognized it as part of a uniform set for the miners up in Squaller's Peak. And when he counted off those grievances, he started with his thumb. Pyrhhans start counting on their forefingers."

Two excellent observations. I felt a small swell of pride, the way I always did whenever the guards of my cadre reminded me why I had chosen them.

"That all tracks, then," I replied. "Some of the attendees were murmuring about tensions in Vindyrst, specifically. The speaker could have been the source."

"Bran Halsigg," Jeremiah added. "That's the name of the speaker, according to one of the guests. But he wasn't part of the group of protestors we spoke to. I didn't recognize his face."

Nor had I—and he was a fairly recognizable fellow, what with the strong brows and the broken nose, not to mention the commanding presence. We would have noticed him before.

"Me neither," Hans agreed. "He definitely wasn't in the throng that harassed the Mirkovics."

"We'll need eyes on him, then," I murmured, just loud enough to be heard over the stomps of our horses. "Run a background check through both our Archives, and the Pyrhhan Census. I want him followed, starting tomorrow."

"Do you think this could be related to the disappearances?" Jeremiah asked.

It seemed damn near undeniable at this point. The motive was clearly there—escalating resentment towards Resonance, specifically towards Conduits, and the politically elite, which were often one and the same in Atlas.

But only *one* Pyrhhan citizen had been abducted, as far as I was aware. Imogen Gillespie—a sixteen year old Fire Conduit, and an active attendee of the Studium—taken from her home during a break between academic quarters. And she came from a common family. The Gillespies were well off, if I remembered correctly, and their family was well-connected. But they weren't official members in the court of the House of Embers.

The Jerricks boy had been last *seen* in Pyrhhas, but he wasn't Pyrhhan. He was from Vindyrst.

If these people had a bone to pick with the House of Embers, there were other young Conduits that made more sense as potential targets.

"I think so, but certain things aren't adding up here. We're missing something, still. We'll need to debrief with Hanjae in the morning, regardless. Their vitriol towards the Aetherborne is concerning. And if this escalates, our student body could be at risk when they travel."

Jeremiah and Hans both nodded gravely.

After an exchange of the remaining details, the rest of the ride home was silent as we chewed on the implications of what we'd just witnessed.

By the time I made it back home for the night, it was well past two in the morning. That didn't do much to quell my hopes that a small, celestial fox might be waiting at my door, but alas. My front porch step was empty, and I was far too tired to be bothered to find a less satisfying distraction.

I found release by my own hand several times over at the thought of pale, freckled skin exposed, golden eyes gone wide and wild, of smudged kohl and tear tracks. Once I had spent myself to total exhaustion, silencing those racing thoughts, I let the oblivion of sleep take me for the night.

CHAPTER THIRTY-SEVEN

ARKEN

Gods above and below, my head was *throbbing*.

I groaned, silently cursing the Source for my idiotic reckless streak. I knew better than to stay out so late last night, and I certainly knew better than to down something like four or five glasses of honey whiskey. And I *most definitely* knew better than to have let a fourth-year Air Conduit with a mischievous smirk and certain proclivities take me back to his apartment last night.

And yet *here we were.*

I was exhausted, but truth be told, it was worth it. Despite my raging hangover and sore wrists, I had a good time last night... for the most part. Mason Park wasn't exactly long-term relationship material, but he hadn't held back in bed, which was refreshing. It had been awhile since anybody had tied me to a bedpost properly, and the man had some solid stamina. If only I didn't spend half the night thinking about someone else.

Still, when I left Mason's place this morning he thanked me for a good time, but made no indication that he wanted to pursue anything further—so the only real consequence I had to contend with over succumbing to my impulses was a bit of a headache, which I was attempting to resolve with a hearty breakfast.

As long as I could get rid of the dull ache between my temples before my exams this afternoon, we were golden. I would never confess it to Laurel, but the woman had a point—our little night out definitely helped take the edge off some nerves. *Some*, but not all.

"Late night?" Kieran asked, strolling up to my table at the café and snatching me from my various reveries and woes.

I hadn't even told him where I'd be this morning. Stealthy bastard. I nodded, rubbing at my wrists absentmindedly before returning to my tea. Thankfully the ropes hadn't left any marks behind.

"Color me shocked, Miss Asher," Kieran clucked. "You little rebel. Don't you have your entry exams today?"

That I did, though I was somewhat surprised that he remembered. Sure, he'd been helping me train—but in the grand scheme of things, my impulse to test into a course above my skill level was hardly important. Not compared to the things Kieran had on his plate.

Though the Arcane Studium didn't have many exams in the classical sense, in order to take upper level courses where more advanced arcana would be used, you had to test into them. It was mostly a safety measure, ensuring that ambitious minds weren't overextended... preventing accidental blood magick wherever possible.

Apparently, it was possible to try so hard to pull from your own Resonance, that you could inadvertently draw upon your own blood for power instead of your aether. It was exceptionally dangerous, and exceptionally illegal.

There were several other advanced courses I wanted to take next quarter that required testing besides Physical Arcana, so my afternoon would consist of putting my arcane abilities on display before a few of the High Scholars.

"Which is exactly why I was out and misbehaving last night. I had to take the edge off somehow," I shrugged.

He plucked a cluster of grapes off my plate, leaning back in his chair casually.

"I know the feeling," he said with a knowing smirk.

"I'm sure you do," I replied airily.

Again, I attempted to drown out certain memories of last night—namely the fact that it was *Kieran* who I had been thinking about when I finally got off.

I know the feeling.

I rolled my eyes. If the rumors were to be believed, the man was a sweet-talking sex god in the bedroom. I could confirm the sweet-talking to be true, intimately familiar with his silver tongue, but as far as his prowess in bed... I flicked the thought out of my mind. He had occupied far too much space there as of late.

Though Kieran and I were pretty damn comfortable around one another at this point, we both knew better than to cross that line. We were getting pretty godsdamned good at dancing on the edge of it, though. Always teasing and testing the boundaries between our firmly established *platonic* friendship. Constantly flirting with the sexual tension that I don't think either of us could deny still existed.

It was kind of fun, in a torturous sort of way. I was a masochist, after all.

"I'm sure you'll do well today, Ark. You've trained hard, you're already much stronger. Don't be nervous."

It wasn't really nerves, so much as a little bit of stage fright. There was a distinction between those two feelings, at least for me.

"I'm not nervous," I replied, brushing a few muffin crumbs off my sleeve.

Kieran rolled his eyes.

"Ah, right. Not nervous, you're just chomping at the bit to show off in front of the scholars. Can't get enough of that spotlight."

Sarcasm dripped off of every word, but his ability to get inside my head was still uncanny.

"What did I tell you about reading my mind, Kieran?"

"That it is an alarmingly attractive trait, and I should do it more often?"

I groaned at the sight of his winning smile, rubbing at my temples for dramatic effect. It was far too early in the morning for flirtatious Kieran. I wasn't even fully awake yet.

"What? I thought women were supposed to like not having to explain themselves," he teased, plucking another grape off my plate.

"Sexism? At this hour? Gods, you are so very irritating."

"I aim to be irritating regardless of gender, actually. I'm an equal opportunity prick."

"At least you're a self-aware prick," I grumbled. "And have you considered getting your own breakfast?"

"I could, yeah. But you don't like red grapes. Wouldn't want to be wasteful," he replied, popping said grape into his mouth with a wink.

Of course he would remember that.

"So what are your plans today, Captain?"

"Oh, you know, the usual," he started, as I yawned and began to pull my hair back in a ponytail.

He paused for a moment, another grape between his fingers as his eyes narrowed, zeroing in on my neck.

"Ah, so it was *that* sort of late night, huh?"

"Wait, what?" I started, before realizing that Mason must've left a mark or two. "Oh. *Gods*, I should probably wear my hair down to the exams, then, huh?"

"Probably," Kieran replied dryly.

I raised a brow at him, but said nothing. Was he... *jealous*? There was no fucking way.

The decision to keep the friendship platonic was a mutual one, and besides—that man had absolutely no room to talk. Though it seemed to hit him in waves and phases without any particular rhyme or reason, I knew damn well that there were weeks where he was taking a different stranger to bed every godsdamned night. And I'd seen plenty of similar marks on *his* neck in the past.

"Anyone of interest?" he asked casually.

"In what regard?"

"I mean, are you seeing them again? Do I need to look into him... or her?"

I scoffed. "Him, and no. I don't plan to see him again, I was just blowing off some steam."

"Considering you're still wound up like a top, I might be able to offer the poor guy some feedback on his form," Kieran laughed.

"Excuse you," I retorted. "His form was perfectly fine, I'm just a little anxious. You know as well as I do that this is going to be a tough course to test into."

"If he'd fucked you *properly*, that anxiety would be long gone," Kieran argued.

"Please. It does *not* work like that."

He looked at me incredulously for a moment before his smile turned mocking.

"Aww, have you never experienced a proper afterglow? That's terribly unfortunate. We're going to have to find you someone better in bed. Broaden your horizons." he paused, a wicked gleam in his eye. "I could call in some favors."

"Please shut up, Kier. It's too early for this," I groaned, head throbbing. I wasn't sure if that was the hangover, or this pain in the ass friend of mine who always seemed to show up from the Shadows.

"Just tell me who it was so that I know who to avoid in the future," he said with a smirk. "I do so loathe wasting my time on a bad lay."

"I'm not sure if Mason even swings both ways," I replied before immediately clapping my hand over my mouth.

"Mason, eh?" Kieran snickered. "And would that be his first name, or surname?"

Oh, godsdamnit. He could do way too much with that single scrap of information.

"Don't you dare," I hissed.

"What?" he asked, widening his eyes with feigned innocence.

"Leave that poor man alone," I warned. "I mean it, Kieran. It's one thing to stalk me, but leave my one-night stands alone."

"Sure, sure," he replied, still smirking. "So what are your plans after the exams?"

"Round two, of course. Laurel and I are going to hit The Clover again for some music and dancing," I explained.

"And booze, I'd presume," Kieran added.

"Naturally. Their honey whiskey is divine."

"Don't do anything I wouldn't do, Little Conduit," he said.

"You know, I'm not sure that really narrows anything down, Kieran."

His oddly sharp incisors gleamed as he gave me a wicked grin, popping another grape in his mouth before winking.

"Exactly."

CHAPTER THIRTY-EIGHT

KIERAN

I had no godsdamned right to be jealous, and I knew it.

That hadn't stopped the foul cloud of envy and resentment from following me all the way back to headquarters that morning. I had other important matters to focus on today, but those marks he'd left on her neck...

It was my turn to blow off some steam.

I made my way over to one of several training rooms, where we had rows of striking dummies, exercise equipment, and racks of practice weaponry, intentionally kept dull to avoid having our recruits maim each other. That said, I preferred to practice with my own weapons.

I felt more like myself with the Scáthic daggers in hand. Whether that was because of their origin—or despite it—I didn't know, and quite frankly, I didn't care to explore the matter. All I knew was that they were perfectly balanced blades, and I had carried them with me for so long that the weapons felt like an extension of my own arms when I wielded them. My blind eye put me at a disadvantage in battle, but my Shadows and my daggers tipped the scales back in my favor.

Strike.

Straw sprayed off the side of the striking dummy as I ran myself through drills in my head, trying to recalibrate my peace of mind.

Parry.

I wondered if she'd see him again tonight. Mason, whoever the fuck that was, was a lucky bastard. If she'd met him while out with Laurel last night, what were the odds he'd be joining them at The Clover tonight?

Strike.

The blow I had just landed would have been fatal to most, targeting the carotid artery on the dummy's neck. A well-placed laceration there could produce lethal results, as the target would bleed out from the jugular quite rapidly.

Dodge.

Not that we were typically trained to use lethal force in the Elder Guard these days.

Lunge.

No, I had learned much of that elsewhere.

Strike.

I really, really had no right to be jealous, I reminded myself, breathing hard. For every person Arken had taken home over the last several months, I had probably taken home tenfold. This simmering envy was both unhealthy for me and unfair to her.

I wasn't mad at her, though. I was mad at *him*. Not that that was any more rational, but for fucks sake. How are you going to take a woman like Arken to bed and not even fuck her *well*?

I set my daggers to the side and began to align the striking dummies in a pattern I could weave between for additional agility training. Stealth scenarios required more than just raw strength or even skill with a blade—you needed strategy and speed. I also liked to train myself in hand-to-hand combat, for situations where I might be disarmed.

These drills in particular would've been better with a sparring partner, but I wasn't about to subject anyone to the mood I was in. Instead, I was trying to sweat it out like a fever.

Arken had looked at me so incredulously when I'd suggested he didn't perform that I think she was being genuine. She really didn't think it was possible for sex to relieve her anxieties about the exams she'd be taking today.

If only it were possible for me to prove her wrong.

A bit presumptuous, don't you think? It's not like you even know what she likes in bed.

I didn't. And it didn't matter, I reminded myself. This was neither my problem, nor my concern. It wasn't like the man had mistreated her—she seemed perfectly content with her evening. If that hadn't been the case, I wasn't sure that this Mason would still be breathing.

What? It was perfectly normal to be protective of your friends, and Arken had quickly become the best friend I'd ever had.

✧ ✧ ✧

After training, I cleaned myself up, returning to my office to find a note from one of my informants—a woman who went by the pseudonym of "Holly." Even I didn't know her real name.

Meet me at Roshana's. Room 3. Preferably before sunset.
— H

I had spent the better part of my afternoon training, so I swung by the coffers to procure payment for Holly's information, whatever it may be, before I quickly made my way over to the Merchant's Quarter.

This time of day, Roshana's tavern was beginning to fill, so the flirty barmaid didn't have much attention to spare for me. She simply nodded off towards the kitchens, where a number of private rooms were hidden in plain sight for those who wanted to partake in pleasures beyond food and drink. I had never indulged in such pleasures with Holly the way I had with Ro on one occasion—though I wasn't entirely against the idea.

Hypocrite.

I nearly jolted at the invasive burst of self-loathing that had bubbled up, seemingly out of nowhere. I usually kept a better grip on such things, though the accusation wasn't wrong. I had spent the day pissy about my best friend having some harmless fun in the sack, but here I was considering fucking one of my own informants?

Gods, I was an asshole.

I found the third door and knocked twice.

"Come in," a sultry, throaty voice called out.

That certainly was Holly. I stepped inside, closing the door behind me, promptly sealing it with Shadow. One of the many practical applications of my arcane abilities.

"Prompt as ever, Captain."

"I figured I might as well come early. Wouldn't want to eat up the time of your other clientele."

"Hmm, you could always just join in so that I could charge them extra."

"I'm afraid even *your* clientele couldn't afford me, H."

She snorted.

"Fair enough, Vistarii. I do have a client coming around at sunset, so let's get down to business, shall we?"

"Indeed. What do you have for me?"

"My sources say that the Elder Guard has started making more... *official* alliances these days with the other territories, is that true?"

I nodded slowly, but didn't divulge details. Holly had her own ulterior motives, often trying to subtly squeeze me for information while giving up her own.

"How's the relationship with Vindyrst?" she purred.

"Why do you ask?"

"Curiosity. And it's relevant, I swear. You see... I heard there has been a certain degree of unrest in the mountains these days. That perhaps, Kole Zephirin is not keeping a tight enough leash on his various earls and viscounts, and his merchants run amuck with overtaxing the poorest regions in the territory. There may be talk of riots to come... and some that have already taken place."

Some that have already taken place?

That tracked with what we'd discovered at the town hall meeting in Pyrhhas, though—that tensions were rising in Vindyrst. But how could they have escalated so quickly without any warning? We'd heard nothing about this from the House of Gales.

If her information was good, and it almost always was, that could spell out some pretty major problems for the work we were trying to do with other territories.

"And where might these theoretical riots have taken place?" I asked her.

"The most noteworthy would be what took place in Squaller's Peak. It might do you and your men well to dig around a little, particularly there. See how the miners of that area and their families are being treated by Joseph Jerricks and his ilk."

I nodded.

Squaller's Peak wasn't a particularly large city in Vindyrst, but it was a noteworthy trade checkpoint between the House of Gales, the territories in Samhaven, and several trade routes between both Novos and Irros. If civil unrest was brewing there with such significance, it could cause all sorts of problems that would affect the rest of Atlas, too.

So *why the actual fuck* hadn't the Vindyrstian Guard informed us of this?

"Any idea on timings, here, H?"

"It's been at least a week," she replied, not looking at me. She sat down at a large vanity, focused on her own reflection as she applied kohl to her eyelids. "Maybe two."

That was more than enough time for those windy bastards to have sent word of revolt. What were they trying to hide? This was... troubling, but extremely useful information, as Holly often provided.

"Good to know," I murmured. "Anything else of note?"

"Depends on how heavy your pockets are feeling tonight, Captain."

I tossed her the pouch that I had in my pockets, one with quite a bit more Lyra than I usually paid my informants. She was my most expensive human resource, by far.

As she picked up the cloth pouch and weighed it casually in one palm, she grinned.

"You do like to spoil me, don't you?" Holly purred, unlocking the armoire beside her and placing the pouch surreptitiously underneath a pile of silks, where I could see a false bottom in the drawer.

I gave her a wink. I wasn't particularly in the mood to flirt tonight, but she would get pouty if I didn't play along. And Fates knew I was hardly in the mood to deal with *that*.

"It could be that much of this is happening right under the nose of the Lord of Gales, while he remains blissfully unaware... and that much of what's been covered up has been orchestrated by a certain *Lady* instead."

Fucking Cecelia.

Of course.

I pressed two fingers against the bridge of my nose, already irritated by the conversations to come, and who might have to get involved.

"Your company has been diverting as ever, Holly," I offered, pushing myself back upright from the wall where I'd been leaning.

"I would be more than happy to indulge further, should anything else come up."

Sunset was fast approaching, and I knew better than to waste her time.

"Always a pleasure, Captain Vistarii. You know where to find me if you're in need of any other manner of indulgence."

I saw myself out, and offered Roshana a quick, chaste kiss on the cheek before I departed—a thank-you for her continued hospitality and discretion. She just swatted me away.

"Oh, get out of here, will ya? You're going to scare off my tipping scoundrels."

"You have a good night, Ro."

CHAPTER THIRTY-NINE

Arken

My first entry exams were taking place in the Hall of the Seeing, the same building where I had presented myself before the Aetherborne all those months ago. How fitting that I would stand here yet again and have my measure taken, this time by the High Scholars of the Studium.

As Kieran had mentioned, Physical Arcana courses were typically reserved for upper level Conduits. The standard practice was to wait until you were in your third year of study here at the Arcane Studium, to have at least ten quarters under your belt before delving into defensive and combative spellwork.

I had... two quarters, stubborn determination, and a handful of letters of recommendation. Plus a few weeks' worth of training under the watchful eye of Kieran Vistarii.

Close enough.

Was I biting off more than I could chew? Possibly. Was I going to try anyway? Absolutely.

Because the more that I learned, and the more that I practiced, the stronger my Resonances became. I could feel them all these days, each element constantly buzzing beneath the surface of my skin.

And so it had practically become a ritual. Every night

when I returned home to my apartment, I pulled the curtains closed and immediately began to practice arcana. First, I would attempt to apply anything I had learned that day with Light to each element—though not every conjuring had a one-to-one application. Still, I took plenty of mental notes in class, constantly observing my peers and committing their gestures and incantations to memory so that I could practice behind closed doors. I did this every single night. And don't get me wrong, I loved it—absolutely adored the feeling of being connected to all six elements again, even if it had to be in secret. But that wasn't why I was doing it.

I did this because it was *necessary*.

Amaretta had not prepared me for the way that this aetheric energy would just build and build and *build* within me as my power grew. She apparently hadn't thought to mention that my Resonance would begin to *demand* release. She never once explained that if I didn't go through these motions every night before I went to bed, that I would be dancing on the edge of a blade come morning.

Maybe she didn't know.

The few times that I had failed to find that release, I had been riddled with anxiety for hours on end as the aether buzzed and thrummed beneath my skin. I'd been terrified that I was one emotional outburst away from exposing my secrets.

When I'd told Kieran that I worried my Light Resonance was too closely tied to my emotional state, he said that this was normal, especially for newer Conduits. He reassured me that, as per usual, I was holding myself to some unrealistically high standards, and that nobody would judge me if I lit up like the shimmering lights of a Yule tree from time to time. Obviously, that wasn't my exact concern here, but he didn't know that.

With damn near anything else around Kieran, I was an open book. He probably rivaled Amaretta at this point for who knew me best. Over the course of our adventures, I had told him all about my life in the Brindlewoods, about Graysen, about the rest of the village, and why I'd named my mail sprite Bluebell. And while he wasn't *quite* so open about his own past—particularly not his childhood—I'd still gotten to know present-day Kieran like the back of my hand.

Laurel often joked that the two of us were like long-lost twins. Not because of any visual similarities, but because whenever she saw us together, he and I had made an obnoxious habit of communicating without speaking out loud—or finishing one another's sentences when we *did* speak.

Kieran was easily the closest friend I'd ever had, and I was endlessly grateful to have him in my life, but I would still keep this one thing to myself. I had promised Amaretta that I would take the secrets of my true Resonance to my grave. I would keep that promise, if only in the name of self-preservation.

"Arken Asher?"

One of the High Scholars called out with a beckoning wave.

"Present!"

I made my way over to the podium where they stood.

"I see that you are looking to test into the introductory course of Physical Arcana, is this correct?"

I nodded with enthusiasm. "Yes, ma'am."

"This is only your second quarter with us," she noted, peering down at me from behind her thin-wired glasses.

"Yes, ma'am—though I do have several letters of recommendation from the scholars leading my current courses," I said, offering the woman several sheathes of parchment.

The High Scholar accepted them, reading through with pursed lips.

"It would appear you are quite advanced for your levels, Miss Asher. Tell me, have you considered reaching out to Lady Frey?"

"I have," I lied smoothly.

This wasn't the first time I had been pestered about this. Quite a few of my professors had made the same suggestion already, heavily encouraging me to reach out to the High Scholar of Light for mentorship to hone and elevate my skills, claiming that I was already displaying "incredible promise", that I was performing "well beyond the expectations of a first year."

While I had flushed at the praise, I wasn't sure that sort of encouragement would be enough to get me to swallow my nerves and approach the illustrious Lady Frey, because truth be told?

That woman scared the shit out of me.

Theia Frey—High Scholar of Light here at the Arcane Studium, and the current leader of the House of Light & Shadow—was arguably one of the most powerful Conduits of our lifetime.

According to the bits and pieces of gossip I'd heard around the city, her power was rivaled only by the Lord de Laurent of the House of Embers. Apparently, the two had never been at odds and actually maintained a strong alliance through the years, so it was hard to make a determination on who would win out if they were to go head to head.

I wouldn't really know, I hadn't ever met either of them. I also wasn't particularly motivated by the notion of doing *great things*.

It wasn't that I *didn't* want to contribute to Sophrosyne or make Atlas a better place... I loved my home. Of course I wanted to contribute to our growth, to the best of my ability. Of course I wanted to hone my skills. But it wasn't until that day I watched Kieran, Jeremiah, and Hans run through those training drills that I ever really found myself interested in the notion of *power*...

I had always craved skill. Expertise. Knowledge. But I'd never particularly coveted *power*... until I realized that it takes power to protect what you love.

"I don't believe I'm quite ready, though," I continued. "I wouldn't want to waste her time, which is why I would like to try out a higher level course before reaching out for mentorship."

The scholar nodded in clear approval.

"Excellent," she said. "Most excellent. In that case, let us proceed with your exam."

✧ ✧ ✧

One of the things that made arcana such a complex science was that it required quite a few different skills to be honed and utilized at once. You needed to implement power, concentration, and finesse—all in perfect balance.

Over time, my clumsy renderings of glowing Light became more refined, but I was still breaking a sweat trying to follow the High Scholar's instructions.

"There are many ways that arcana can be weaponized, should you ever need to protect yourself," she had explained. "The most basic of which would be creating and using an *aetherblade*. That is what you'll be starting off with in these courses—a basic blade and shield of Light. The first portion of the entry exam will be the formation of the blade."

Step by step, she ran me through the process of summoning and shaping a tangible, aetheric weapon. The first summoning felt almost like a pottery lesson. Like I was building a dagger out of clay.

She had placed a basic, steel dagger in front of me as an example.

"As you draw upon the Light, Arken, I want you to mold the weapon in your hand. Form the pommel first, followed by the grip."

I was able to follow her instructions with some concentrated effort, but the precision required was... intense.

"Yes, good," she encouraged. "Make sure the cross-guard is

well sized with your own hand. You don't need to mirror the example quite so exactly."

Okay, I understood the need for these entry exams now. This shit was *hard*.

My aether felt stretched thin as I focused on far more minute details than I had ever summoned before. I extended the fuller out a few inches, shaping the point before attempting to carve out a sharper edge on either side.

Why was a small blade so much harder than a fox?

I hadn't realized that I murmured that last part out loud until the scholar answered.

"It's because of the more corporeal nature of the blade, Miss Asher. You are summoning something that, once complete, will be able to pierce nearly anything with enough force. Also, the aether of a mail sprite will dissipate during travel and reform at the site of the aetheric signature you select. If you were to throw this blade, it would remain in existence until you consciously release the arcane energy back into the aether."

"Interesting," I murmured, wiping a small amount of sweat from my brow.

"Believe it or not, you're doing quite well. The first summon is the hardest, and it will come much easier each subsequent time. Your aether will remember the shape you are trying to create, unless you choose to alter it."

Well, that was encouraging at least.

"It also becomes much easier once you familiarize yourself with drawing from aetheric parallels on the fly. Though we would hope that you never find yourself in such a situation where you would need to summon a blade so quickly, that is one thing you will learn in future courses."

As the woman finished speaking, I finished the dagger.

"Well done, Miss Asher. Very well done. Now, please take some time to study the details of the blade in your hand."

I was impressed by the gleaming weapon. It looked as though it had been carved out of starlight. I ran a fingertip over the blade's edge with my non-dominant hand and gasped when I found it sharp enough to cut. I was nearly incandescent, beaming with both pride and a newfound surge of energy. This arcana, though difficult to wield, made me feel *powerful.*

"Please go ahead and release the blade back into the aether," the scholar instructed next. Begrudgingly, I allowed my hard work to fade back into the air around us, the Light winking out into nothing.

"Can you recall what it looked like? What it felt like in your hand?" she asked.

I nodded. "Yes ma'am."

"Good. Summon it again."

I took a deep breath, stilling my mind and attempting to clamp down on the vibrating, excited energy buzzing beneath the surface. This exam wasn't over yet. I focused on the Air and the Shadow aether I could feel around me in the room, drawing upon it as I inhaled and opened my left palm.

I converted the Air and Shadow into Light as I exhaled, and the blade immediately reappeared, hilt warming slightly in my hand.

"Holy Hel," I breathed.

Even the High Scholar seemed impressed.

CHAPTER FORTY

KIERAN

I told myself that I wasn't going to do this. I had better things to do, more important things to focus on right now.

Such as the fact that when my scouts returned this afternoon, they came back empty-handed. Bran Halsigg, or whatever the fuck his real name was, was nowhere to be found.

Jeremiah had sent them out at first light, only a handful of hours, *maybe*, after that gathering of non-Resonant rebels was broken up by the Pyrhhan Guard. By mid-afternoon, all three of the men came back with the same answer: He was gone without a trace.

But there was just *no godsdamned way*. So I sent Jeremiah and Hans back out to Freyston to search for themselves.

Meanwhile, I had been searching the Archives with a handful of others from my cadre. We had scoured our records of the Pyrhhan Census, the registries of Samhaven and Ithreac, and even managed to get our hands on the most recent citizenship records from Vindyrst.

We'd found nothing. Nobody by the name of Bran Halsigg was known to exist in all of fucking Atlas—at least not according to the extensive resources of Sophrosyne. After checking the damned files two, maybe even three times over, I sent the other guards back to their posts.

And yet here I was, still sleuthing around the Archives for another reason entirely while I waited for word back from Jeremiah and Hans.

Images of Arken's freshly bruised and bitten neck were still sharp in my mind, and I found myself on the opposite end of the building now, abusing my security clearance to poke through student records.

Was this a particularly healthy distraction? No. Was it right for me to do this? No. Did I particularly care at the moment? Also no.

I could lie to myself and say this was just a precaution—a safety measure in case Arken decided she wanted to see this guy again. A way to protect her. If the day ever came where Arken did want to settle down with someone she met here in Sophrosyne, I could see myself doing some background research... Though I found the thought of such things uncomfortably unpleasant.

As it were, I wasn't in the mood to lie to myself. Or maybe I just didn't have the energy. I was here because I didn't want to think about work, and my bitter, impulsive mind chose the next best thing to fixate on in a self-flagellatory manner.

It took me all of maybe fifteen minutes to find the most likely culprit.

Mason Park. Age: Twenty-four. Fourth-year Air Conduit, originally from Samhaven. A fitting focus of study on trade and economics, seeing as his family was in service to the House of Torrents. They were merchants, with direct ties to the Lord Gabriel Ymir.

I returned his folder into the large repository, striding into the next room to thumb through another stack of current course schedules. Arken would absolutely murder me if she knew what I was doing, but she would never need to know. I wasn't going to engage with the man, I was just morbidly curious.

Was he her type? Did she even have a type?

She and I could talk about damn near anything, but one of the few things we tended to avoid sharing stories about was our sexual conquests. I knew we both had casual sex, but I could probably count on one hand the number of times either of us had brought something up as it related to that particular subject matter. Even then, it was usually just when something particularly funny or awkward happened. Beyond that, it had just been something we naturally steered clear of, respecting one another's privacy. The only thing that I really knew about Arken and her sexual interests was that, like me, she was attracted to both men and women.

I shouldn't be this curious. It was none of my fucking business.

That didn't stop me from figuring out this guy's schedule, identifying his most likely location right about now, and stepping into the Shadows.

✧ ✧ ✧

I had to give Arken credit, Mason Park was attractive. Even as I watched the Conduit exit his lecture hall from a comfortable distance, I could see what she might've seen in him.

Lean, tall, carried himself with a casual sort of confidence, as much of the wealthy elite of Atlas so often did. He was pale, but he wore it well with striking, almond-shaped brown eyes, thick lashes, and thicker brows, understated clothing. The Conduit was laughing, arm in arm with another female, and I couldn't tell if that pleased me to see, or if it irritated me on Arken's behalf.

I wasn't about to follow him all night, but I also didn't have anything else better to do at the moment, so I continued on with my observations while the pair made their way from the Academic Quarter, passing through the eastern gardens.

The other woman was clearly into him, hanging off of every

word. I could only make out a few snippets of the conversation from the distance I kept, but it seemed quite bland to me. It made me wonder how many drinks it took to get Arken interested. She was way too smart for the likes of him, though the blonde on his arm now seemed vapid enough to make an even match.

She had just dropped one of her textbooks, a move so painfully obvious and intentional that I couldn't help but roll my eyes as Park bent down to retrieve it for her. As he leaned forward, the gray-blue scarf he was wearing slipped down to reveal a bloom of pinks and purples just between where his neck met his shoulders, and I felt my blood boil.

I had been irritated when I saw the bite marks on Arken's neck this morning, but realizing that she'd returned the favor with this prick somehow made things so much worse.

Was it the implication that I was wrong, and that he'd actually fucked her well? The idea that she enjoyed herself enough to leave her own mark on him? The potential of what that might mean, that maybe she had lied to me when she said it was just a one-night stand? Had it been her way of claiming Park as her own?

Not. Your. Concern.

My subconscious mind tried to chide me, but I didn't give a damn. He didn't deserve her attention, let alone her mouth on him.

And neither do you.

Yeah. I was well aware of that.

I took off in the opposite direction before I could say or do anything stupid.

✧ ✧ ✧

I didn't particularly want to go home, and I didn't particularly want to go out, and so I took to brooding alone in my office. I was attempting to review missives to distract myself and shake off the bitter mood, but it wasn't really working. Probably because these investigations continued to frustrate the shit out of me.

I *knew* I should have stuck around after the Pyrhhan Guard showed up last night. I should have stayed behind, should have tailed the man who was riling up the crowd with such vitriol. I *knew* something wasn't right.

Jeremiah and Hans had returned to HQ about an hour ago, confirming the worst. Our best fucking lead on this case had simply vanished, gone without a trace. And of fucking course, none of the Pyrhhans would talk. Even folks we *knew* had attended that meeting pretended they didn't recognize the name. Like they had no idea who we were asking about.

I should have trusted my instincts. I fucked up. *Again.*

I must've been radiating some particularly toxic energy, because even Jeremiah—who was just as frustrated with things as I was—seemed to hesitate after coming around to knock at my door.

"Yeah?"

"Oh. Apologies, Captain. Is this not a good time?"

I sighed.

"You're fine, Jer. What's up?"

"Can I ask you something sort of... personal?" my lieutenant inquired, scratching awkwardly at the back of his neck. "Not related to the case."

"Why do I get the distinct feeling that you're going to ask me anyway?"

"Because you know me well?" Jeremiah laughed.

"Go on, then," I muttered, rolling my eyes as I stacked the papers in front of me in a neat pile for later.

"Look, please don't kill me for this, but I have to ask. When you first started bringing Arken along for things, keeping her around... Hans and I just figured it was strategic. Because she's the

Light Conduit and all. We assumed that you wanted to keep tabs on her. Like the commander asked."

I said nothing, but motioned for him to continue with a slight gesture of my hand.

"I mean, it made sense. Befriending her would probably be the easiest way one could keep a close eye on a freshling."

"It certainly is a strategy one could take, yes," I mused, noncommittal.

"But... that's not the only reason you're doing it, is it? Not anymore, at least?"

It was never the reason, but I neither confirmed nor denied that particular inference. After a brief pause, studying Jeremiah's curious expression, I spoke again.

"Does it matter?"

"Yes," he replied, almost immediately.

"And why is that?" I asked, keeping my tone even and non-accusatory, even though Jer was approaching dangerous ground.

"Because we protect our own, Captain."

I raised a brow.

"You're sworn to protect every citizen in Sophrosyne, Lieutenant. You took an oath," I reminded him coolly.

"Yes, sir. But if the girl matters to you, that's different."

Again, I paused, deliberating on how difficult I wanted to be about my answer. Part of me wanted to challenge the man, make him explain exactly what made Arken different from anyone else in the city. But the other part of me knew exactly what he was implying, and I was sort of touched that he cared.

"Kieran, you know we'd watch over her either way. But... I've never seen you invest in anyone. Not a damn soul outside of the Guard. Not like this. Not like her. And with the way shit's been going lately, what with the threats and the kidnappings..."

I tilted my head, curious.

"Do you care about her, sir? Is she one of ours?"

I sighed, unable to deny what my lieutenant had clearly picked up on. The girl was important to me. More so than I had ever intended. More so than I really cared to admit.

"Yeah. I do. She is," I confessed.

"That's all I needed to know, Captain."

I nodded once, pretending to be particularly interested in one of the stray missives I picked up, avoiding Jeremiah's gaze.

"By the way," Jer added. "Hans and I, and a couple of the boys are going to hit The Clover tonight. There are a few traveling entertainers in town, most of us are off tomorrow, and today's been shit—seems like a damn good excuse to get plastered. You in?"

I opened my mouth to politely decline, and then closed it for a moment as I thought better of it. Wasn't that where Arken would be tonight, too?

If anything, that should have been even more of a reason to politely decline. If I were a more respectful man, I would be giving Arken her own space to let loose after her entry exams without my brooding, over-protective ass watching her prospective suitors like a hawk.

Too bad I wasn't a particularly respectful man.

"Eh. Sure, why not?" I said.

"Atta boy, Captain!" Jeremiah replied jovially. "C'mon then. We're leaving soon."

CHAPTER FORTY-ONE

ARKEN

It could have been the honey-whiskey or the wine talking, but *gods*, I felt alive.

I didn't drink that often, but I was starting to think that Laurel just might be onto something with her favored habit of drinks and dancing with strangers on the weekend. I was having a blast. I also needed to take the edge off of my disappointment. Even though I had passed *most* of my trials, I had failed the endurance test for Physical Arcana, which meant that I would have to wait another quarter before I could try and test again. It wasn't the end of the world, and it had been a long shot, but still. I really wanted to take those damn courses. I was already craving the weight of those aetherblades in my hands.

The buzz was helping, though. As the liquor coated my tongue, I was wrapped up in a more lazy, languid joy, and a sense of belonging. It was reminiscent of the first time Graysen and I had made love in the meadows back home—all slow and heated and heavy, a strange juxtaposition of weighted limbs and a racing heart. Strange, but enjoyable.

The academic quarter was wrapping up, and most of Laurel's little social club had completed their courses. We were all feeding off the same high of an upcoming month off, good company, and the fleeting freedoms of our youth.

Nestled in the corner of The Clover, to the left of the bar, was a decent sized stage. The floor had been cleared of most tables for tonight's event, where people from all over the city came to enjoy a few traveling bands that had come through. A string quartet was currently playing some plucky, upbeat tune that had Laurel and I strutting on the dance floor, laughing and whirling around with one another until we were out of breath.

"Gods, I've missed you," she said as we took a seat in the back of the tavern to cool off for a moment. "How have you been, Ark? I didn't get to see much of you last night, Park was hogging all your attention."

"I've been good," I replied. "Really good, actually."

Her smile was warm as she gave me a knowing look.

"I think Park is here tonight, by the way. You going in for another round?"

I laughed. That woman had such a one-track mind.

"Nah, I don't think so."

"Not good enough to hit it twice?"

"No. But gods, don't tell Kieran that. He gave me so much shit this morning," I groaned.

Laurel snorted.

"Of course he did."

Her voice was laced with implications, as if I was missing something obvious, but I didn't want to go there. Hastily, I changed the subject.

"What about you? Are you still with Cypress, or did you finally break things off last night after I left?"

Laurel winced as the music in the background slowed to a gentle ballad. We had picked a good time to take a break, it would seem, as couples began to take to the floor and sway together with lovestruck eyes and intimate embraces.

"I broke things off this morning, actually. She wasn't

particularly pleased. Claimed it was all a bit abrupt," Laurel explained airly, unbothered.

It was my turn to snort. I suppose it *would* seem abrupt, considering Laurel had spent a good portion of last night drunkenly draped over her now ex-girlfriend's lap. But, in my most humble of opinions, Cypress Glass was hardly worthy of a graceful exit. Good riddance.

"On the bright side, this means that I am free to go back to chasing the one that got away from me earlier this year," Laurel said, smirking over a sip of wine. "You know... a certain heiress."

But of course. How very *Laurel* of her. I wasn't sure she would ever stop chasing Hanna Cragg, the heiress to the House of Clay. I couldn't say I blamed her, either. The woman was gorgeous, intense, and powerful. Just her type.

"She here tonight?"

"I'm not sure yet," Laurel said with a pout. "I haven't seen her, but I saw one of her brothers when we were walking in, so it's possible."

"Which brother?"

"Anders."

We both made the same face of mild distaste at the same time, and then burst out laughing. I hadn't even officially met the man in person, but his reputation preceded him.

Gods, I'd really needed this night out. As the music began to pick up again, I knocked back what was left of my honey-laced whiskey, preparing to get my ass back out on the dance floor. I only had this sort of social energy in small bursts, and I wanted to take advantage of the moment. Make some memories.

As luck would have it, a memory seemed to appear out of thin air, ready to make *me* instead. One of the most gorgeous women I had ever seen in my godsdamned life was approaching us both with a confident strut, her eyes locked on mine.

She was so fucking beautiful.

"Sia!" Laurel squealed, clearly recognizing the tall, stunning female who had made her way over to our table with a feline smile. My friend turned to me excitedly, eager to make introductions.

"Arken, this is Sienna Makar. Gods, I've been dying to introduce you two. Sienna, this is Arken—the Light Conduit that I told you about!"

Makar. I recognized the name. This was the daughter of Lord Markus Makar, one of the few other Shadow Conduits here in Sophrosyne. Heiress to the House of Shadows.

"Call me Sia," she purred, extending a flawlessly manicured hand. As I reached out to accept, she let her soft grip linger for a moment longer than one usually might.

"Care to dance, Lightbearer?"

Her slight Irrosi accent was apparent as she said that last word, which I had learned was their term for Light Conduits across the Eastern Seas.

The warmth of the whiskey was already blooming beneath my cheeks, but the sultry look in Sienna Makar's eyes was absolutely intensifying the flush. I let her pull me up from my seat with grace, returning the intrigued little smile she'd flashed me first.

"I'd love to."

As I let Sienna lead me back towards the dance floor, I caught Laurel's eye and grinned. She tipped her glass at me with raised eyebrows, almost as if to mirror Kieran's words from earlier this morning.

Don't do anything I wouldn't do.

Intrigue, attraction, and whiskey were swirling around my veins, dancing with the blood and aether. What could I say? I had a bit of a thing for Shadow Conduits.

And this night was getting good.

CHAPTER FORTY-TWO

KIERAN

Once we'd made it to The Clover, I made myself sparse—occasionally lingering in the darker corners of the room to converse with my men, but more often slipping back into the Shadows. I'm sure they all assumed that I'd be off doing what I do best: Fishing for the attention of the most beautiful creature in the room.

In this case, said creature's attention was already occupied, so I fucked off to the second floor to observe from afar and nurse a single glass of red wine. I wanted to avoid bringing down the mood of my men, all of whom were here to get drunk and get laid.

I couldn't tell if I was envious, watching Arken slink around the dance floor with Sienna Makar on her arm, or if I was simply ensorcelled by the view. A bit of both, really.

Because the two of them were a sight to behold—the creamy porcelain of Arken's skin in contrast with the deep, dark brown of Sienna's glistening body, adorned with those silver Irrosi tattoos across her shoulder blades and collarbones. Arken's hair was free and flowing, fanning out like a halo around her every time she was whirled around under Sienna's lead. Makar's dress was skin tight and revealing, while Arken wore her more typical attire of a loose linen gown with a tight leather bodice that accentuated her perfect curves.

The pairing painted a divine feminine portrait of Light and Shadow, absolutely annihilating the rest of the room with their combined beauty. They had half of the dance floor utterly captivated, and I was fairly certain that they knew it. Makar certainly did.

Wicked, wicked women.

Honestly though, part of me was just genuinely pleased to see Arken move around so easily and lighthearted for once. She was laughing and blushing in the arms of the gorgeous Heiress of Shadows.

Sometimes I worried that our friendship had done Arken a disservice. I was greedy with both her time and her attention, eagerly taking whatever she was willing to give. It wasn't like I had consciously pulled her astray from her peers, though, and she had mentioned on multiple occasions that she preferred my company over that of the broods of Atlassian elite. I believed her, but in moments like this, where she was sparkling and carefree amidst a more appropriate peer group, I couldn't help but wonder...

As I watched Makar lean in to whisper something into Arken's ear, I realized what a terrifying powerhouse those two would make in the House of Light & Shadow one day, should this compatibility ever play itself out. I took another sip of wine, letting the taste of the bitter tannins mingle with my own bitter jealousies.

I really needed to get over myself.

From across the balcony that overlooked the floors below, I noticed another pair of eyes watching the same women as they danced, gazing greedily as Sienna wrapped her arms around Arken's neck. His dark brown eyes briefly flickered up to mine, and he tilted his glass in acknowledgment. He returned to his ogling before he could see the vicious scowl take over my face at the implication that he and I had even remotely the same interests at the moment.

Anders Cragg was a jackass, and a pervert.

The bastard should consider himself lucky that the only accusations I had heard whispers of were that of light misogyny, leering, and being generally unpleasant and demanding towards the women he wanted to sleep with. Anything beyond that would have landed him on my shit list, and I didn't give a damn how powerful his father was. There were a handful of things that I did from the shadows that were completely off the books with the Elder Guard, and I did not suffer abusers in my city. Never had, never would.

The music was beginning to slow again, and I turned my attention back to Arken, who was still smiling and laughing. Her dark brown mane had become a bit unkempt, her face flushed, and she hardly seemed able to walk in a straight line, leaning against Sienna as they made their way back to the table where a few of their other friends were seated. She wobbled around on Makari's arm, weaving through the sea of bodies like a baby deer.

I chuckled to myself.

Arken was drunk off her ass, and I found that oddly endearing. I don't think I'd ever seen her even tipsy before.

Park had been on the dance floor earlier as well, and she had paid him no mind, clearly focused on the superior prize in Sienna Makar. Though I envied Makar, too, the confirmation that the other male had been just some casual fling pleased the dark, unhealthy part of me that had been festering for most of the day. Because I would much rather watch Arken flit around from one casual hookup to the next than have to watch her legitimately fall for someone.

That's fucked up, and you know it.
Yeah.
What else was new?

CHAPTER FORTY-THREE

ARKEN

If I wasn't such a lightweight, I would've likely been making my way home with Sienna Makar right about now.

Unfortunately, the blend of whiskey, wine, and so much dancing had started to make the room spin and my stomach turn. I was zoning out, feeling somewhat dazed after the attractive woman had graciously offered to fetch me a glass of cold water. I wasn't sober enough to feel the normal burn of embarrassment that might've eaten me alive, and thank the gods for that.

As I nibbled at a stray piece of bread from the table, I let my eyes wander aimlessly. I could have sworn that out of the corner of my eye I had seen the back of a head full of raven black hair, pulled into that messy half-bun that was a telltale sign of a certain guardsman. Or was that just wishful thinking? I had completely lost my train of thought halfway through whatever casual conversation I had been having.

"Looking for someone?" Sienna asked lightly, and Laurel raised a curious brow. I shook my head vigorously, immediately regretting the way that the rapid motion left me feeling dizzy and nauseated.

"Oh, gods," I murmured, pressing a palm against my head.

From the other side of the room, I heard someone call out for

Sia's attention over the music. As she rose to go over and greet them, she lifted my chin gently with two slender fingers adorned in stacked silver rings.

"It was nice to meet you, Arken," she said, that natural flirtatiousness slipping back into her voice. I flushed. "Keep drinking that water, gorgeous. I'll see you around."

◇ ◇ ◇

As I started to sober up, my head throbbed ceaselessly, despite the several glasses of water I'd downed over the hour. It didn't help that the second band playing wasn't nearly as talented as the first, and every false chord plucked in an incorrect tune was starting to seriously grate against my nerves.

"Hey," I called over to Laurel, who had successfully found herself deep in conversation with Hanna Cragg. "I think I'm going to head out."

"Are you sure?" Laurel asked, biting her lip and looking conflicted. "Do you want me to walk you home?"

"Of course not, woman. I'm fine. You have a good night, though, alright? Don't misbehave too much," I laughed.

"No promises," she replied with a grin. "Send a note when you get home safe, alright?"

"Sure, sure."

For a short period of time when I'd first arrived in Sophrosyne, Laurel had been my only friend. Even though we didn't share the same depth of connection that I had these days with Kieran, I was still so thankful to have her in my life—even though our time together was few and far between. She had been a much-needed example for me, a reminder that the noblesse and the privileged offspring of the Atlassian elite could still be good people.

This world needed more good people.

I shivered in the chill evening air as I stepped outside, my body temperature shocked by the frosted winds of late winter. Between the blazing fires and the heat of the dance floor, it had been toasty warm inside The Clover, and I hadn't had the foresight to bring a sweater with me earlier.

I made my way over to the mouth of the alleyway behind the tavern, where an open bonfire was crackling, a handful of stray students smoking their rolled tobacco and wyldweed, talking amongst themselves. I warmed my hands by the fire, keeping to myself and letting my now-stiffening muscles rest for a few minutes before I made my way down the alley, heading back towards my apartment.

I was letting my mind wander aimlessly, only having made it a few yards in the direction of my apartment when I felt a prickle on the back of my neck. I got the distinct sensation that I was being followed, and the casual sound of strolling footsteps confirmed it.

Sighing, I turned to find a well-dressed, curly haired male with dark eyes smirking at me with a presumptuous grin. He looked *somewhat* familiar, but I couldn't quite place it. My head was still throbbing, and I was exhausted. Perhaps not entirely sober just yet.

"Arken, right?" he said, taking several steps closer to enter my personal space.

"Right," I said slowly. "Apologies, but have we met?"

"Mm, if only," he replied. "But I think you might know my sister, Hanna. I'm Anders. Anders Cragg."

A blend of arrogance and pride slid off his lips alongside his words, and I watched his eyes rove over me shamelessly, lingering here and there with obvious impropriety.

"Pleased to make your acquaintance," I said, dipping my head respectfully.

I was preparing to excuse myself when he took yet another step towards me, this time near enough that I could smell the booze on his breath and see the glassy look in his eyes. He was clearly still drunk.

"Oh, I'd like to make more than that with you," he said, voice thick and heavy, on the cusp of slurring. "You and that Makar girl tonight, my gods. Hotter than all Hel. You headed to her place?"

"Err, no," I replied, taking a measured step back to put some distance between us. "I'm actually headed home for the night, so if you don't mind..."

"Oh, c'mon. Don't be like that, beautiful," he said, stepping forward again, his eyes narrowing with visible irritation.

As the heir to the House of Clay—next in line after Hanna—I was sure this man often got his way, but I wasn't even remotely interested. I didn't exactly feel unsafe at the moment, but I was starting to get uncomfortable as Anders continued. I had a feeling that if I started walking away, he'd only follow.

"What's wrong? Do you only go for the women? Oho, I could change your mind," he said, his eyes darkening with desire. "Give me one round, pretty thing. Hel, Sienna can even join in."

I resisted the urge to gag. Abyss fucking take me, this man was a pig.

The arrogant prick took another step forward, all but cornering me against the wall. As he reached out his arm to snake it around my waist, I was about ready to pull a punch... And then I felt him. Felt his Shadows before he'd even rounded the corner behind us.

"If you'd like to keep that hand of yours, Anders, I suggest you keep it to yourself," a familiar voice purred in the darkness.

Cragg turned, and paled ever so slightly before straightening himself up again, chin held high.

"Ah. I didn't realize this was the piece you were screwing tonight, Captain. No matter. You'll be done with her soon enough, and I'll get my turn, eh?"

"Allow me to clarify, Anders," Kieran's voice was sharp now, a threatening growl as he took several strides towards us both. "There is no end date on that warning. Touch her again, uninvited, and find out what happens."

As I glanced over my shoulder, I could see Kieran had a firm grip on the hilt of one of his daggers, where his Shadows were beginning to coalesce.

Shit.

"Finally settling down then, Vistarii? Or are you just keeping this one around for seconds?" Anders hissed, before turning to me. "You really don't want to know how many cunts and cocks your man has drowned in, darling. Wouldn't you prefer something a tad... cleaner?"

His leering eyes were anything but clean.

"Besides, girlie—haven't you heard? Vistarii here is into some fucked up shit."

"She's my *friend*, you asshole," Kieran spat.

I could see his Shadows spread further, coiling around tight fists. He was trying to control himself. He didn't want to scare me, but I knew full well what he was capable of.

"You don't *have* any friends, Vistarii, you filthy fuckin—" Anders started, and Kieran took another menacing step forward, ready to lunge.

I stepped in front of him, inhaling sharply. I was acting on impulse now. *On instinct.* Instead of summoning my own arcana, I drew from *his* Shadows—and lo and behold, a blade of burning aether formed instantly in my palm, searing with unapologetic Light as I held it against Cragg's throat.

"He does, actually. If you're seeking out my favor, Anders, you sure as Hel won't get it by insulting *him*," I snarled before letting my face settle into the vapid, sweet smile he had probably hoped for earlier. "You can fuck off now. You absolute prick."

The sleazy heir to the House of Clay scowled, but took several steps back.

"Shoulda known you'd be a crazy bitch, hangin' round with the likes of him. Suit yourself, whore," he spat, turning on his heel and slinking back off towards the tavern, leaving Kieran and I alone in the darkening alley.

I exhaled slowly, allowing the blade to dissipate, releasing the aether that still felt hot in my hands. When I turned back to Kieran, the look in his eyes was... intense.

"You... Fuck, you shouldn't have done that, Arken," he said quietly, running one hand through his hair.

He was right. It was inappropriate of me to have drawn from his aether like that without consent. I had been pissed off and had acted on impulse, remembering how the High Scholar had mentioned it was easier to summon an aetherblade if you drew from a parallel source.

I hadn't even known if it was *possible* to draw upon someone else's manifested arcana in the way I could pull from the natural elements, but Kieran's Shadows had been easier to use in that moment.

"You're right. I'm sorry, Kier. I should have asked before I—"

He scoffed. "I didn't mean *that*. I meant you shouldn't have threatened Anders. Not for me. Are you alright?"

"I'm fine. And the Hel do you mean, "not for you"? He was being a dick!"

Kieran sighed.

"By all means, Arken, defend yourself as you see fit, but you don't need to defend me... Let me be the bad guy for both of us, okay? He won't be quick to forgive that insult."

"I don't give a damn."

"You should. He's an heir."

"He's a prick."

"Yes, that too. But still. You should probably be careful about who you threaten, especially with fuckin' aetherblades."

"Err, yeah. Again, I'm sorry about that," I said awkwardly,

wondering if he even knew what I had done in order to whip out that arcane blade so quickly.

"You can steal my aether any time, Little Conduit."

Well, that answered that question. I looked away, blushing a bit. Why did that phrasing feel so intimate?

"It was actually pretty impressive. Lemme guess, you literally just learned that earlier today in your entry exams."

I nodded shyly.

"Godsdamn, woman. Has anyone ever told you that you're like... irritatingly talented? Most of the Conduits here can't do that shit even half as fast. Not even the fourth and fifth year students."

I did not need this stroke to my ego while there was still alcohol in my system.

"Can *you*?" I asked, curiosity getting the better of me.

Kieran frowned. "Draw an aetherblade? Of course I can."

"I mean, obviously. But could you draw it from *my* arcana?"

"I'm not sure," he admitted. "I've never tried. I've never needed to."

I summoned a small orb of Light in an open palm, offering it to him—but he just laughed.

"Oh, I don't need to steal *your* aether to whip out a blade quickly, Little Conduit. I hate to break it to you, but I'm faster, too."

I tilted my head as he sheathed his actual daggers back at his sides, shifting his weight into what seemed like a stance intended for combat.

He took a quick breath, and then within a fraction of a second, two flawless daggers—shadowed mirrors of the ones he had just put away—appeared in his hands. He gave me a cocky grin as my eyes widened.

"See?"

"Damn," I breathed.

"That's not all," he said with a sly wink. I watched as he

released the aether and then pulled out his actual daggers again, assuming the same stance.

I stared in total fascination as the Shadows crept their way up his hands, wrapping around his wrists as if to strengthen his grip on the hilts. The Shadow aether spread, coating the blades themselves in total darkness, as if Kieran was wielding the sharp edges of the Abyss itself as weaponry.

He laughed again and shook the aether off as if it was simply smoke, sheathing his daggers and reaching out to ruffle my hair.

"As I said. You didn't need to do that, freshling. I can be plenty scary."

"I never doubted that. You have a very threatening aura."

He snorted.

"I am sorry, though, if me stepping in like that was obnoxious or offensive or anything," I offered with sincerity. "I just... got a little protective there for a minute. I didn't like how he was speaking to you."

It hadn't been the first time I'd heard someone speak poorly about Kieran, but it wasn't particularly common either. He was charming and well-liked among most everyone I had encountered thus far. If I had to guess, those around here who didn't like him were jilted ex-flings or guardsmen who were jealous of how quickly he'd climbed their ranks.

"Don't worry about me, Arken. I'm used to it. He wasn't exactly wrong, you know," Kieran said with a shrug. "Not about that first bit about you and I, obviously, but I do sleep around. I don't really have friends. Most people don't really notice that. Most people don't pay close enough attention to notice much of anything, really, but Anders is a nosy bastard."

I don't really have friends.

"I'm your friend," I said with a glare, a bit hurt.

I didn't care that he slept around. A tiny part of me was admittedly jealous, but I didn't resent him for his choice in stress relief.

"You're my best friend," he agreed. "Apologies, Asher. You know that you're the exception to most of my rules. And I'm lucky to have you around."

I rolled my eyes.

"Yeah, you never know when you need someone to pull a knife on the heir of the House of Clay to defend your honor," I joked.

His eyes darkened briefly before returning the smile.

"Yeah, do me a favor? Never do that again, woman."

"No promises."

He groaned, and I gave him a winning smile.

I mean really, what did he expect?

CHAPTER FORTY-FOUR

KIERAN

"I fucking hate you, Kieran," Arken groaned, those golden doe eyes brimming with murderous intent as I held out my standard-issue pocket watch.

I grinned as I glanced down, still counting the seconds.

"Might I remind you that you *asked* for this?"

The only reason that either of us were here right now, borrowing an empty training room at the Elder Guard's headquarters after my shift ended, was because *somebody* got it in her head that she had to test into a third-year course as a first-year Conduit.

"I asked for help with strength and endurance training," she grumbled. "Not cruel and unusual punishment."

"This is hardly *punishment*," I countered—though I could think of a number of ways that I *could* punish her, given the opportunity. I bit the inside of my cheek, attempting to cast out that particularly distracting, admittedly recurring train of thought. "I'm going easy on you, Asher. Thirty more seconds, you've got this."

"*You've got this,*" she mimicked in falsetto, rolling her eyes as she continued to hold the plank position, albeit a smidge shakily as the seconds ticked by.

We were focused on core work today—arguably the most vital element of prep training for something like Physical Arcana... and she absolutely hated it. Which, in all honesty, only made this more entertaining for me. I fucking loved that sharp and wicked tongue of hers. Especially when it was pointed in my direction.

"Keep that energy up, you little brat, and we'll go back to running circuits."

If there was one thing Arken hated more than core work these days, it was cardio. More specifically, running. But I think that had more to do with the fact that we had to run outside, which of course came alongside the risk of being both sweaty and perceived by the general public.

She swore under her breath, and then furrowed her brow, fixing her gaze to the floor with a shaky exhale.

"Ten. Nine. Eight... *Aht*—Lift those hips back up. There we go. Seven. Six. Five. Four. Three. Two. Aaaaaand one," I said, chuckling beneath my breath as she dropped unceremoniously to the training mat beneath her. "Nice work, Little Conduit."

"*Nice work, Little Conduit,*" she mimicked again, the high-pitched, snarky tone making my palm twitch. "Can we go back to sparring exercises now?"

"Maybe if you ask nicely," I purred, snapping the watch shut and shoving it back into the pocket of my trousers. Though I had shed my coat, I was technically still in uniform.

"You've already got me on my knees, Captain," Arken crooned back. "What more do you want?"

Fucking Hel, she was such a little menace. As time went on—the more comfortable Ark and I seemed to get with one another—the closer she and I seemed to drift towards slipping casual flirtation and innuendo in damn near every conversation. We had kept our promise, though—we'd kept things platonic. But Fates above, when she said shit like that...

Keep it in your pants, asshole.

Yeah, yeah. I knew the rules. I wrote the damn book.

"Is that typically how you show gratitude?" I smirked anyway.

"Depends," she replied with a grin.

"On?"

"Precisely how *grateful* I'm feeling."

I snorted.

"Get your ass up if you wanna spar, harlot."

Arken groaned as she pushed herself up, hopping to her feet. As much as she liked to whine and complain her way through these training sessions, there was an ever-present glimmer of ambition in her eyes, too. I knew she'd meant it when she said she wanted to be stronger. Truth be told, I don't think the woman even realized how strong she already was. The minute we got her body caught up with her arcane potential, the Little Conduit was going to be unstoppable. An absolute force to be reckoned with.

I nodded towards the striking bag hanging in the corner of the room, reaching into my other pocket and tossing her a pair of hand wraps.

"Let's start with positioning again. Go throw some punches at the bag, show me how much you remember from last week."

"And here I was hoping that you'd be my striking dummy today," she teased.

"You get mad at me when I'm your target, Ark."

"Only because you hold yourself back."

I snorted. "I have to, and you know it. I'm not gonna toss you around like a ragdoll."

Arken shrugged. "Maybe I'm in the mood to get thrown around a little."

"Will you shut up and get in position?" I groaned. Gods, she was such a tease—and truly in rare form today.

The devious creature simply giggled, traipsing over to the striking bag with a spring in her step that suggested she knew damn well what she was doing to me. I shook my head, taking a swig from my waterskin as I observed.

As Arken threw her first few punches, her stance was decent. A bit wide, maybe. When my gaze drifted over the lower half of her body, I was briefly lost to a moment's worth of self-indulgence. In my defense, it was a damn fine view. Gods, those thighs. Coated in the soft, supple leather of the training leggings I'd bought her, every last curve of Arken's generous hips, her ample thighs, and that frustratingly flawless ass of hers were on perfect display.

Sucking in a sharp breath, I forced my eyes to flick back up and— *oh, fucking Hel.*

Without really intending to, my eyes had zeroed in on her neck, the elegant and pale length of it exposed as she had tied her dark curls back in a high, perky ponytail. What I hadn't quite expected was the way a single droplet of sweat, trickling down from behind her ear, would send a pulsing wave of heat to my core. I typically had better self-control than to re-interpret her breathlessness, her pinkened cheeks, or any amount of sweat from these training sessions for my own deviant devices, but my mind was feeling rather... creative at the moment. Arken's tongue had been filthier than usual this afternoon.

I couldn't help but wonder if that had anything to do with the fact that she'd inadvertently caught me taking someone home for the night last week—when she and Laurel had decided to try out a new tavern, stumbling into one of *my* domains of distraction.

Ark had been a bit dry with me the next morning, but I'd honestly thought very little of it at the time. I hadn't really interpreted it as envy, considering it took me all of five seconds to get her laughing again, comfortably back in her good graces. Platonic agreements aside, today's attitude felt a bit less like envy, and more like *retribution.*

Two can play that game, Little Conduit.

A few short strides took me from where I'd been observing, to mere inches away from Arken's personal space. Gently, I kicked at her left angle with the side of my boot.

"A little too wide. You want your feet planted even with your hips, under your shoulders—to keep you balanced," I instructed.

Arken stuck her tongue out at me, but complied without any additional sass. Biting my own tongue, I attempted to actually focus on helping her now, as opposed to undressing her with my eyes, and so I continued to inspect her posture, her positioning, and the way she moved while beating up the striking bag.

I wasn't trying to teach her how to *fight,* per se—that would be the job of her Physical Arcana instructors. That said, a bit of boxing would help her build endurance and some muscle—and she would need both in order for her body to contend with arcane combat.

"*Aht—*" I said sharply, catching her left fist before it struck the bag. "What did I tell you about tucking your thumb in like that?"

I spread Arken's small hand out flat with my own, the size and color contrast between us a bit comical. I curled her fingers back, guiding her thumb *atop* her fisted fingers, not beneath them.

"Shit," she muttered under her breath, brow furrowing. "Sorry."

I rolled my eyes. "Don't apologize to me," I scoffed. "Apologize to your fuckin' wrist when you break it."

Arken sighed heavily, clearly frustrated with herself over such a simple, minor mistake... and I thought *my* perfectionist streak was vicious. I shook my head, more to myself than anything else.

"C'mon. Let's just walk through the basics again, alright?" I told her, taking on the instructional tone that I knew would distract her enough to listen. Like clockwork, the tension in her brow eased and her eyes flicked up to me with focus as she nodded.

"Non-dominant leg in front. Toes toward the bag. Yep, good," I said, walking slowly, circling her like a hawk. "Dominant leg back, toes towards me. Lean back more."

From behind, I stepped forward and slid one hand around her

waist, splaying my fingers firm against her stomach, guiding her... trying to disregard the sharp little intake of breath she'd pulled when my hand met the fabric of her sleeveless top. *Also* trying to disregard the way the scent of her sweat intermingled with that lemony sunshine of her hair, and those vague notes of earthiness I'd come to associate with her, like moss and rainwater and freshly tilled soil.

Focus.

"Always fall back to the dominant leg, shift your weight here when you need that center of gravity," I explained.

Her ponytail tickled my chin a bit as she nodded, and I took a step back, if only for my own sanity. I'd been far too close to her neck, my tongue too tempted to taste the salt of her exposed skin.

Fucking focus.

"Elbows up," I said, nudging one of her arms into a more appropriate angle. "Bend your knees a little more. There we go, atta girl."

The corners of her mouth crooked upwards, shy acceptance of my praise. I couldn't lie to myself, I was somewhat proud of my ability to get Arken out of her own head lately. Sometimes, it seemed like she just needed someone to help keep her in check—or just an alternate outlet for frustration, so she wouldn't beat herself up over stupid little things. I'd gotten pretty damn good at reading her signals, jumping in when she needed that redirection.

"Alright, you remember how to strike?"

Arken nodded again, biting her lip. I took another step back to observe as she followed through the range of motion for a straight punch, slowly at first, warming up.

"Almost," I murmured, briefly returning to my position behind her, placing one hand on either side of her waist, just above her hips.

"Remember, you've gotta shift your hips like this," I explained, applying gentle pressure to show her how to move.

Arken huffed a small but light-hearted sigh. "Who knew that such simple calisthenics had all these *rules*," she teased. "Isn't this just supposed to be alternative cardio?"

"Yeah, but it's best to form good habits now. When you *actually* start training for Physical Arcana, it will be harder—you'll have to control your muscles and your Resonance in tandem. Might as well make sure you get it right now, that way you don't have to retrain your brain and body later."

"Fair enough," Arken murmured, a fresh wave of determination passing through her expression.

I knew Arken was like me, in that anything worth doing—anything worth investing our time and effort into—was worth doing *correctly*. And she worked best when she understood the nuance behind every rule, the reasoning behind each step.

"As you pivot that foot back and turn your knee, twisting your hips the way I just showed you—that's where you create power. Momentum for the strike."

"Right."

With a steady breath, Arken applied everything we'd just reviewed, her fist meeting the striking bag with a heavy thump.

"Good. Just like that," I encouraged, earning me another shy smile. "Gimme another thirty of those, and then we'll move on to some alternative moves."

"Variety *is* the spice of life, Captain," Arken teased.

So they said. But as Arken continued her assault against the black leather bag, I couldn't help but agree to disagree.

I could watch her do this all damn day.

CHAPTER FORTY-FIVE

Arken

I was starting to think that asking Kieran to train me might have been a mistake.

As much as I wanted this, despite how *badly* I wanted to succeed next quarter where I had failed in the last round of entry exams, I hadn't necessarily considered the consequences of working in such close, continued physical proximity to Kieran *fucking* Vistarii, of all people.

Maybe I should have asked Hans. Or better yet, Jeremiah.

But either one of them would have been preferable at the moment, because I wouldn't be on the verge of panting if I'd felt *their* breath on my neck, *their* hands on my hips, my waist, my arms. And I most certainly wouldn't be tempted to grind my ass back into *their* groin every time one of these hypothetical lieutenants stood behind me.

Their captain? That was a different story.

He was behind me now, hands on my hips *yet again,* raising the hair on the back of my neck with his hot breath and low, rasping instructions as he walked me through the difference between a hook, a jab and an uppercut.

I was doing my godsdamned best to listen, to commit his words to memory the same way I might during a lecture—but that was arguably difficult to do while my brain was swimming, drunk off the cocktail of his voice, the spiced citrus of his scent, and the foreboding feel of his tall frame bent over mine.

I knew he wasn't *trying* to fuck with me. Kieran knew me well by now, and he understood the way my mind worked. He knew that I learned best through physical instruction, and that sometimes I struggled to pair the intellectualization happening in my mind with the actual motion of my body. This proximity was simply a tool, a teaching method that he knew worked best for me... or at least it did, when I could fucking pay attention.

"Gimme a sec," I wheezed, breathless not necessarily from the exercise, but the fact that I had been avoiding inhaling his scent.

Seriously though, why did this cocky bastard have to smell so *good*, even after a five-mile "warm up" run? There was nothing offensive about his natural musk—if anything, the residual salt on his skin seemed to amplify everything else, the cinnamon, the cloves, the orange peel.

The least he could have done was be even *remotely* repulsive to make this proximity more manageable, but *no*... the perfect, fit bastard had to remain a bronze god in my presence, the absolute epitome of temptation.

I scowled to myself before taking a long sip from my waterskin, rolling my neck and cracking my knuckles.

"Tired yet?" Kieran inquired, flashing me a lazy smile.

"Not really," I replied honestly. Tired of thirsting after him maybe, but physically? I felt fine. Energized, really.

"Good. You're getting stronger," Kieran observed. "Your endurance is miles ahead of where we were a few weeks ago. Keep this up, and there's no way you don't pass next quarter."

I knew my cheeks were already tinged red, but I felt additional heat flush beneath my freckles. This was another environmental hazard, a risk that I'd failed to calculate when I had agreed to let Kieran train me multiple times a week.

His praise.

I needed the validation like water, I had to admit. It was difficult for me to parse my own progress, so I had to rely on Kieran's sincerity to track when I was successful, when I was doing things right. That being said... he didn't bullshit me, so every commendation was genuine. There was legitimate pride in Kieran's voice any time he offered his encouragement, and that? That was dangerous.

But I'd be lying if I said I didn't pocket away the memories, every murmured *"Good," "Atta girl," "Just like that,"*—because I did. Greedily, I took them all, tucking the words away to be savored later.

It wasn't until we moved on to kicks that I realized that at least *some* of Kieran's behavior today might have been a counterattack. As the captain ran his hand under my thigh, I caught glimpse of a smirk in my periphery. My eyes narrowed.

"What's the matter, Ark?" he crooned, pausing his walkthrough of the left foot jab.

"The fuck are you smiling about over there?" I accused, and the cocky bastard simply chuckled.

"Forgive me if I'm *enjoying myself,*" he countered, his hand still underneath my leg, just above the crook of my knee. It wasn't lost on me, the way his forefinger was lazily stroking at the seam of my leggings as we spoke.

"I can't imagine why," I replied dryly. "Don't you do this all the damn time?"

"Three times a week," he purred—reiterating *our* schedule.

"I meant like, in general," I huffed. "For work?"

"Ah," Kieran replied. "Well, yeah, but that's... different."

I rolled my eyes, shifting my hips so I could drop my leg back to the floor for a second to regain my balance.

"Different how?"

"I can't say I get quite so hands on with my men. Nor do any of them look as good as you do in training leathers."

Godsdamnit.

The last thing I needed right now was Kieran complimenting me *like that*. Even if I knew damn well I had started it first this afternoon—this depraved little game of ours, constantly teasing at the edge of our platonic boundaries.

"Pig," I spat toothlessly.

"Am I supposed to pretend that I don't find you attractive, Arken?" Kieran laughed, cocking a brow as he stretched one arm behind his back. Bare and golden-brown muscles flexed beneath shimmering panes of late-afternoon sun as it streamed through the ceiling's skylights. "Or that I don't enjoy touching you? I'm a damn good liar by trade, but I'm not *that* good."

Oh, fuck off.

"Keep it in your pants," I muttered.

"I fully intend on it," Kieran purred. "You'd be far too distracted otherwise."

Abyss take me, we were on another level of our bullshit today. But with the endorphins and adrenaline swimming in my veins alongside the aether this afternoon, I was far too competitive to just let him win.

"You mean like how *you've* been distracted by my ass all day?"

"Among other things," he replied smoothly, unphased.

It was rare that he was so flippant, so open in admitting he was attracted to me. He was usually more subtle about it… Subtle enough that from time to time, I honestly forgot. It was easy to assume that this addictive allure was one-sided, but good fucking gods, did the confirmation otherwise do unspeakable things to my ego.

"Are you gonna teach me how to do this kick, or not, Captain?" I demanded, skirting around our flirtatious exchange for a moment so that I could catch my damn breath.

"Get back into position," he replied easily.

Tightening my ponytail, I bounced on the balls of my feet before running through the motions again. *Hands up. Elbows in. Lean back. Aim with the ball of your foot.*

"Lift your knee a little higher," Kieran instructed, keeping his hands to himself this time. He had taken a step or two back, giving a more comfortable berth. Something tight in my chest softened a bit, appreciative for how responsive Kieran was when it came to my boundaries.

He always seemed to respect my limits more than I ever could.

There was a particularly satisfying slap and thud against the striking bag this time when I kicked it—he wasn't wrong. The higher I lifted my knee, the more power I could put behind the jab.

"See?" Kieran said.

"Yeah, yeah," I groused. "You were right. What else is new? And what now?"

"Now do it again."

CHAPTER FORTY-SIX

KIERAN

Good. Fucking. Gods.

My walk home from Arken's apartment had felt so torturously slow that I'd been half tempted to bite down on my palm and cut-cast a rift just to make it safely behind my own door a little faster. I needed to lock myself in this townhouse and throw away the key in order to resist the overwhelming urge to run right back and shove my tongue down her throat.

Arken *fucking* Asher.

You're just friends, you're just friends, you're just friends. I chanted that shit like a mantra as I brewed myself some tea, stripping out of my sweaty clothes in the kitchen, tossing them to the corner of the room to be dealt with later.

Just friends.

And it was just an accident, I told myself as I recalled the way Arken's fingertips had brushed up against my groin right before we'd wrapped up her sparring training. There was nothing *intentional* when she'd tossed her hair back, either—nothing *calculated* about the way she shook out that dark brown mane while she'd arched her back to stretch right in front of me. There was certainly nothing *strategic* about that breathy little moan that had escaped her mouth while she did it.

Nope.

It's not like I had any room to deny it at this point. Hel, I'd never been able to deny how aggressively attracted I was to that woman. That was partially why this entire friendship had developed in the first place, I simply *could not* stay away. But godsdamn, we'd been playing with fire this afternoon.

And still, I burned.

I could handle the heat most of the time. I could handle that fire. I was damn good at compartmentalizing the parts of me that roared anytime another prospective partner deigned to even *glance* in her direction. I could manage the lust in my veins, I could keep my obsession in check without letting it infringe on our friendship. And when I got too close to the edge of slipping up around her, I had my ways of redirecting that energy with a handsome stranger or two.

Though tonight, the idea of any other was honestly repulsive.

You've already got me on my knees, Captain. What more do you want?

I wanted my fist in *her* hair. I wanted my cock down *her* throat. I wanted to hear *her* moan my name so many times that she forgot how to pronounce her *own*.

Too much. I wanted too much tonight. Too much for my own good, and far too much for hers. I needed to be way more careful, far more precise in this game she and I had been playing moving forward. Her companionship was far too important to lose in favor of my aching cock.

I wasn't sure exactly when that had happened. At what point had Arken become so... integral to my well-being? How was it that the tendrils of her Light seemed to permeate even my darkest of Shadows, illuminating pieces of myself that I'd once thought were lost?

The parts of me that laughed. The parts of me that *dreamed*. The parts of me that felt... worthy.

"Fuuuuck," I groaned, pressing my forehead against the wall as the tea kettle began to whistle and howl.

I didn't know how or when the girl had become so important to me, but at the end of the day, all that mattered was that she was. And though I literally did not have the capacity to avoid flirting with her altogether, I *would* be more careful in the future. I would be more realistic about my own limits. I had ruined a lot of good shit in my life, but I wasn't about to ruin this.

After a deep breath, several cups of tea, and a few chapters of a bone-dry military strategy book, I had managed to calm myself into a more rational state of mind. Feeling anchored now, I penned a quick note and summoned Hekate—Arken had *insisted* I give my mail sprite a name, lest Bluebell feel "isolated in his identity"—and sent off the reminder.

Don't forget to stretch, Little Conduit.

Even *my* muscles were aching after today's strenuous activities. Once Arken had gotten into the swing of things, I had dragged another striking dummy over, running through drills of my own. For a while there, the two of us had trained in quiet tandem, occasionally exchanging quick nods, having our silent conversations as we checked in with one another every now and again. I think we'd trained for nearly four hours today—over double the amount of time we typically spent.

But if there was one thing that I knew about Arken Asher: you do *not* stop that woman once she's on a roll. I would rather brush a wyvern's teeth than ever try to interrupt the momentum that she seemed to thrive on. Besides, her energy had been infectious. It always was.

My raven returned, carrying a curl of creamy white parchment and Arken's flowing cursive.

What exactly should I be stretching, Captain? Be specific.

I snorted. That right there was exactly why I'd waited to simmer down—I knew she wasn't done with me yet. Still, I felt my blood reheat... *because* she knew what she was doing. I tore a slightly larger scrap of parchment from the pile I kept stashed on the counter.

Stretch out your legs in particular. They worked pretty hard today. Looked pretty, too.

I resisted the urge to say anything more suggestive than that, though visions of Arken up against a wall, stretching one leg above her head were dancing around oh-so-prettily in my mind.

Are you asking me to spread my legs for you? How very untoward.

Very untoward, yes. But not nearly as untoward as I wanted to be. Still, I spun the pen between my fingers, ideating on just how far I wanted to push the envelope.

Asking? No, I'm not asking.

Smirking to myself, I took a sip of my tea, wondering if she'd pick up on the more subtle innuendo I was offering. It was only a few weeks ago now that she'd let slip *just enough* of a reaction in casual conversation that implied she and I might have... very compatible tastes in the bedroom. And considering it was taking her quite a bit to reply... I had a feeling my response might have met the mark.

Five or ten minutes later, Hekate returned to my shoulder.

Maybe next time we should incorporate the stretching as part of the cool down, if you're going to be so very demanding about it. I can only get so flexible on my own, perhaps you could assist with that?

I'd hate to pull a muscle.

Abyss take me.

If you want my hands on your thighs again, Asher, all you have to do is ask.

Or, you know. Beg for it. But I held my tongue in that regard, because if she escalated *that* kind of conversation, I would be out the door in about 3.5 seconds.

Like you could keep your hands off of them either way. Anyhow. I'm off to take a bath and spread — I mean, stretch my legs, as instructed.

Enjoy your evening, Captain.

Devious little thing.
But a bath did sound divine right about now.
I padded my way down the hall, smirking to myself as I snagged a fresh towel and a bar of spiced soap from the linen closet. Once I made it inside the large bathing suite adjoined to my bedroom, I followed Arken's lead and began filling my own tub. Feeling a tad more self-indulgent than usual, I slipped a few capfuls of an expensive bath oil into the water as it filled—scenting the air with my typical citrus and cloves.
Enshrouded in a warm mist, I could feel my body start to

release the tension even before I stepped into the tub, but a low hiss of pleasure still escaped my mouth as stiff muscles sank beneath the scalding surface of the water. I groaned softly as the heat of the bath went to work, serving doubly to slough off the sweat and grime of my day, while also attending to my sore flesh.

I'm off to take a bath and spread my—

Yeah, about that release of tension... Maybe it was more like *redirection*. Because that aching pressure and heat was simply coiling at my core now instead, that all-too-familiar tension building as I replayed certain memories, recalling certain images to mind.

When I thought about her pretty mouth and the filthy tongue that hid behind such perfect, freshly-bitten lips this afternoon, I felt my cock twitch and harden between my legs. It had been at least half-hard all godsdamned day, but at least now, I could allow my mind to wander.

I thought about those beads of sweat dripping down her neck. I thought about pink cheeks and panting little breaths as she worked hard for me, I thought about the way my praise seemed to make her flush a little deeper than usual today. I thought about how godsdamned *easy* it would have been to take her right on the floor of that training room, to toss her around that training mat as requested. I thought about how badly I'd wanted to.

"*Fuck*," I murmured, one hand slipping over my own thigh, reaching to grip myself hard at the base of my erection... and slowly beginning to stroke it.

Because she would start slow, I thought.

Yeah, she would ease into it, tease me until I was so fucking stiff that she could barely wrap her fingers around the length of me. Those golden eyes would go half-lidded and lustful, the tip of her tongue running over that plush lower lip of hers. She would start to whine and keen while I played with her pussy, achingly slow. She would beg me to let her taste it, to let her take me in her mouth.

Arken would fucking *plead* for permission to worship my cock. And she'd do it while riding my hand, my fingers knuckle-deep inside her.

I just had the strangest sense that my Little Conduit had a bit of an oral fixation. Or perhaps I was simply very, very observant—especially when it came to her.

I groaned aloud as I began to move my hips beneath the water, my thighs flexing as I fucked my own fist to these most infuriatingly tempting thoughts.

I could have her. I could have all of her, I knew I could. Arken would not deny me if I asked... I just knew better than to ask anywhere but here, in the confines of my own fantasies.

Here, though...

My eyelids fluttered closed as I summoned her image to the forefront of my mind. Her back against that training mat, breathing hard as I stood over her. The way I would have toyed with her as I stripped off her leggings, taking my sweet time as I unlaced them, exposing pale and perfect flesh. I thought about the way her thighs were probably decorated with those gorgeous silver slivers, evidence of the way her body carried every swell and curve. I thought about how I would run my tongue over each and every mark, every freckle I found on her skin. I thought about the way her tits would pool and flatten a bit against her chest, and the way they'd bounce once I finally had a hand between her legs, fucking her with my fingers first.

The water sloshed around the tub a bit dramatically now, as my cadence had already started to grow feverish, my grip against myself firm, my balls feeling tight and heavy.

Easy. No need to rush... We've got all night.

All night, and every night, if I were being truthful. I couldn't even remember the last time I'd made it a day without fucking to the thought of Arken Asher—whether that was via my hand, or a stranger in the guest room.

What would it feel like to actually fuck her, though? Gods, it would probably be heaven between those thighs. Hot and wet and wanting. I would never know what bliss could be found at Arken's center, I knew that much, but that never seemed to stop me from imagining it. Visualizing where I'd run my tongue for hours on end, given the chance.

You've already got me on my knees, Captain.
Maybe I'm in the mood to get thrown around a little.
Are you asking me to spread my legs for you?

She was so maddeningly sexy. It was the intentional, calculated nature of her torment that had truly done me in today, the way every quip spilled from her filthy mouth with ease, laced with just a hint of invitation.

More and more often lately, our game felt less like a tussle between our egos, and more like we were testing the waters. Dancing on edges. Wondering if certain rewards were worth certain risks. There was this hidden undercurrent between us now, one that whispered, *"It's just a game, for now. But is that all you want it to be?"*

Irritated by the inconvenience of all this water splashing around, I stepped out of the tub, steadying myself with one hand against the wall. My left hand remained firmly on my cock, still stroking, still emulating sensations I wished I was stealing from her body instead. Thieving straight from her hands, her mouth, her cunt.

My breath grew heavy, fast and hard as I reached for something very specific in my mind, unlocking a certain compartment that I kept close by, almost exclusively for this purpose. By day, I kept them locked up tight, but once nightfall came around... my more familiar Shadows eclipsing all that was good and kind and respectful in me...

I let the memories overtake me.

Every whine. Every moan that ever escaped her mouth when

she stretched or struggled. Every time I'd ever heard her breathless, the way she'd pant after sprints. Every time that she'd playfully called me *Sir*.

I loved every last visual that I could conjure of Arken in my mind, but it was the *sounds* she'd make that would truly be the death of me if these fantasies ever unfurled. Her voice was just so fucking pretty, already a siren song every time she spoke. But I wanted to play her body like the exquisite instrument it was—with the attention of a master composer—until Arken Asher sang for me, and me alone.

Focusing my fervor around the thickening crown of my cock, I imagined how she might whimper and wail for me if I ever thrust this length inside her. I bit my lip as I indulged in the notion of what it might take to get her to scream for me, to rip my name from her throat like a curse. And what it might take to hear her whisper my name like a prayer.

A more errant thought flickered through my mind for a moment, recalling the oddly intimate sensation, that strange little tug that I'd felt at my core a few weeks ago, when Arken had pulled from my Shadows to draw her aetherblade. There had been something sensual about that, too—watching her hold a knife to the throat of an heir in my name.

I thought about the poison that dripped off her lips as she'd snarled at Anders in my defense, and the way that in that moment, it almost felt like she was staking her claim. She hadn't said the words aloud, but I could have *sworn* I heard it in that scathing tone of voice.

He's mine.

With a sharp inhale and a low hiss sliding past my teeth, I found my first round of release over the mere thought of Arken Asher and her aetherblades.

CHAPTER FORTY-SEVEN

ARKEN

That man was ruining my fucking life.

As I soaked my aching muscles in a tub filled to the absolute brim with hot water and frothing, self-indulgent bubbles, that was all I could even hope to think about.

Him.

As one hand slid between my thighs, the tips of my fingers slipping past the slickness I found there and coaxing that liquid heat towards my swelling clit in a slow, rhythmic motion, all I even *wanted* to think about was him. And this was nothing new.

Night after night, for months now, I could only ever get myself off to the thought of Kieran godsdamned Vistarii.

Asking? I'm not asking.

I could hear his rasping croon against the shell of my ear as though the captain was right here in the room with me, watching me arch my back and tug on one of my nipples from the shadows. Gods, if only.

It was hard to describe the strange sense of helplessness, the jarring loss, the ache of absence that I'd felt once Kieran dropped me back off at my apartment. And it was even harder to explain, even to myself, why I felt so godsdamn desperate for him as of late.

It had taken every ounce of willpower I had not to ask him

to come inside. Still, he'd lingered—one arm hanging off my door frame as he gazed down at me, eyes a little hazy.

"You did very well today, Arken," he'd murmured gently. "I'm impressed."

"I bet you say that to all your trainees," I'd breathed back.

"Mm, not quite. It takes a lot to earn my praise."

Fuck me.

I groaned softly at the memory, my fingers moving faster, applying a bit more pressure as I thought of the myriad of ways I might capture myself more of Kieran's praise.

Gods, I wanted him—and simultaneously loathed him right about now. I hated the way Kieran kept hold on his willpower so steadily, while mine seemed to wriggle and writhe around in my hands like a venomous serpent. For just a fraction of a second, my favorite person in the world had become my bitter rival, if only because he'd managed to walk away.

You'll just have to try harder next time.

Through grit teeth, I clamped down hard on that thought. No. There would be no *trying harder,* I had already pushed the edge of our boundaries more than I should have today.

I knew that I was the instigator of my own torment this afternoon, what with every teasing quip I tossed his way. I just... couldn't help myself. I was admittedly still clinging to that tiny seed of jealousy he'd planted in my chest last week, the moment I saw him slip his hand around another woman's waist, murmuring something in her ear.

That isn't fair, and you know it.

I did. I knew that Kieran had no intention of running into Laurel and I that night—he would never purposefully bait me like that. He had just been doing what he did best, seeking out his temporary solace by seducing some poor soul who wouldn't know what to do with herself by the time she crawled out of his bed. Because I didn't have to fuck Kieran myself to know that the sex would be earth-shattering. Between the two of us? Realm-rending.

Everything about that man was life-altering, for better or for worse.

But no matter how heavily I yearned, no matter how deeply I ached, the longing I felt for Kieran and all these furtive fantasies were such a small price to pay for the pleasure of his company. I was content to pant after him from the comfort of my own sheets if it meant I could keep this friendship intact.

Am I supposed to pretend that I don't find you attractive, Arken? Or that I don't enjoy touching you?

I sucked in a sharp breath as the sound of his voice returned, a phantom echo in my mind.

I'm a damn good liar by trade, but I'm not that *good.*

"Gods," I groaned, becoming increasingly worked up by the memory of the way he looked at me today. The way he *kept* looking at me, all afternoon. It was like he knew, somehow, that I'd needed a reminder that I wasn't alone in wanting what I couldn't have.

I could deal with Kieran fucking other women, other men—but I wasn't sure I could deal with the notion that one day, he might find whatever he was looking for. It was callous and cruel of me to covet his desire like that, though. It was greedy and selfish and *wrong* to hope that my closest friend would spend the rest of his life alone.

But here, in the confines of my apartment, I could be cruel. Here, I could be vicious.

Behind these wards, as I fucked myself to the thought of him, I could admit—if only to myself—that every night, in the afterglow of my own release, I sent a silent, foolish prayer to the Fates, the Source, whatever powers that be.

If I can't have him... Let him remain wild, untamed. Let him sample, but never settle. Please. I couldn't bear it.

That probably made me a terrible person. An even worse

friend to the man who had given me so much, who had made my time in Sophrosyne perfect, beyond my wildest dreams. But I had never claimed to be a wholly good person. Yes, I was kind, I was compassionate...

But I had always known there was a dark and ravening thing that prowled beneath my skin.

And that darkness played so very nicely with Kieran and his Shadows.

Those godsdamned Shadows.

Eager for the distraction, I let go of that moment of self-flagellation, shuddering with distaste as I realized that the bath water had grown tepid. I had lost track of time, and though I could easily reheat the water using basic Fire arcana, I instead took this as a sign that my bathing ritual had concluded.

I wanted to carry out the rest of my efforts in bed, regardless.

Once I was warm and dry again, I slid my bare body in between the worn, soft sheets and let loose a contented sigh. The bath had worked wonders for my stiff muscles, as had the stretches I'd done by Kieran's command. My tongue glossed over my lips, a hint of a smile curving up one side of my mouth.

Are you asking me to spread my legs for you?
Asking? No, I'm not asking.

Fucking Hel.

As I sank into the plush comfort of my mattress, my mind began to wander again, and I let my fingers follow suit.

"Get on your knees."

He had never spoken those words before, not to me—and yet I could hear them, clear as day in my mind. It would fall from his lips with low and rumbling authority, leaving little room for argument.

"Good girl."

And I'd never seen Kieran's cock, but I could visualize it so very well—the sight of him standing over me, his presence towering as

I knelt before him, eyes wide and lips parted. I thought about the way he might suck in a breath hearing me beg for permission to touch him. I thought about the way he might groan and growl and curse beneath his breath once he gave me what I wanted, what I craved more often than was probably healthy. *Fucking Fates*, I wanted to choke on that man's cock.

I wanted to wreck him the way that he would most assuredly wreck me.

The way I wished he would.

The sight of Kieran sparring next to me earlier had me soaking through my panties as I practiced every kick. It had been borderline embarrassing, and whenever his back was turned, I'd glance down just to make sure there was no visible damp spot between my legs. Thankfully, the soft leather leggings had been thick enough to conceal my arousal, and I didn't have to expose that every inch of my instructor's hard, flexing muscle had me twitching... Craving.

But it wasn't just his body that kept me in a chokehold, however flawless that body was. It was the *violence*—his capacity for utter destruction.

However depraved these damningly dark thoughts made me, it was the sharp sound of every strike Kieran landed this afternoon that pulled me under. It was the way the edges of his blades gleamed in the light just before he coated them in wisps of smoke and Shadow. I would never admit it, not to anyone, but it was the evidence of how godsdamned deadly Kieran was—*that* was what left me dripping all afternoon.

His power called to me. My aether sang back, surging through my veins, even now. Little starbursts of Light pulsed beneath my sheets, the tips of my fingers flickering for a moment as I arched my back, hips bucking into my fingers, needing more. More friction, more pressure, more thoughts of him to tease and torment me into oblivion.

I thought about his hands, wrapping themselves around my

throat. I thought about the inherent supplication in allowing someone like Kieran to steal my breath, to control me to such an extent that the very air in my lungs followed his command. I thought about every limit, every edge that Kieran might lead me to if I let him.

For a moment, I paused ministrations against my clit just to run my hands up and down my body, imagining larger, rougher fingertips in their stead. I paused in every place that I'd imagined Kieran might, groping my own tits, sliding my palms appreciatively over my thighs, briefly allowing my forefinger to mimic the way Kieran's had stroked the back of my leg earlier today.

Lost in my own imagination, I writhed and tangled myself up in the sheets, beginning to thirst for things I couldn't emulate myself—like the way it might feel if Kieran pulled my hair, the way it might burn and sting if he slapped my ass, or if he took hold of my flesh so hard that his nails bit into my skin. *Biting...* Oh, that was a dangerous place to go if I wanted to draw this pleasure out slowly, and yet my mind took off in a sprint before I could contain it.

Those stupid fucking godling teeth of his, so unusually and absurdly sharp. The way those tipped canines gleamed and glistened, peeking out behind his lips whenever he spoke. It was just some trait that ran in his family, he'd explained to me once. Some odd, hereditary thing. But maybe my sick little urge to worship Kieran in more ways than one stemmed, at least partially, from the fact that his silver tongue danced behind the wicked, feral smile of the gods themselves.

I thrust my fingers deep between my legs now, curling and pressing against that most sensitive part of my core. My right hand was absolutely coated in the slickness that wept from my cunt, the same way it did for him every other night. Tonight, though, for whatever reason—he felt a little closer. I could practically feel his heated breath against my neck, could practically hear it hitch as I whined, grinding against my own hand.

And what I wouldn't *fucking* give for that hand to be replaced by what I knew was a perfect cock, what I wouldn't do just to have him shove me up against a wall, my mattress, any manner of surface so that he could fill me, fuck me better than I could ever possibly fuck myself. He would ruin me, that much I knew, and I would beg him to keep going. I would weep and grovel and plead for him to leave me in tatters by the end of the night, to cover my skin in pretty little bruises and bitemarks, to coat me in evidence of what he was capable of.

When I finally let myself imagine what it might feel like for those pretty white jaws to bite down against my throat, how blissful the ache of those fangs might feel if Kieran felt so inclined to grace my neck with such violent admiration, I was all too thankful that the wards of this apartment included sound-proofing spellwork.

Because it was Kieran's name that I screamed into the night as I detonated, gasping and trembling against my own fingertips when the tension snapped, waves of heat and pleasure overtaking my senses.

And it was Kieran's name that I whispered against my pillow once my body, now entirely spent, finally succumbed to the sweet allure of my darkening dreams.

CHAPTER FORTY-EIGHT

KIERAN

Gods help me, Arken was in one Hel of a mood tonight.

Earlier in the week, she mentioned some passing plan about how she intended to go foraging for herbs in the Wyldwoods. Apparently, she was hoping to find some herbs and other medicinal plants similar to what she might have gathered back home, seeming to be convinced that they grew in our woods as well.

"It's for tea," she had explained to me over breakfast, before her lectures began. "I haven't been able to find anything like what Amma used to make for sore muscles, and if I have to go through another godsdamned bleeding cycle without that blend, I'm going to commit crimes. *Crimes*, K."

"That would be awfully ill-advised, considering I would then have to arrest you," I had quipped back.

"You wouldn't dare."

Even though I had tried my best to keep my tone casual when I offered to come along, she saw straight through me that morning, too—immediately giving me shit and very vehemently reminding me that she was capable of taking care of *her damn self*. Nevermind the fact that she was still working on her physical training regimen, and hadn't even re-tested for Physical Arcana yet.

"I'm well aware, Little Conduit," I had replied, pinching the bridge of my nose. "But if you want darkmoss, that means foraging at night. If you're going at night, please just take me with you."

She'd rolled her eyes, but gave in without much fuss.

"Fine, suit yourself. Meet me at Mugwort's around dusk on Friday—but it'll be boring," she warned.

I could probably watch paint dry with Arken and not get bored, but I wouldn't dare tell her that. It'd go right to that pretty little head of hers.

But here we were now, standing in front of the old man's shop. I noticed her slight winces as she approached me, and before I could even open my mouth, the woman snarled out a warning.

"Don't you start with me, Vistarii. I'm fine. Can we go now?"

"Hello to you, too, Miss Asher. Lovely day we're having. Lovely weather," I replied, unphased.

I would keep an eye on those winces, though, and the way she nursed her side a bit as she walked. She had overdone it on strength training the other day—pulled a muscle. It was a minor injury, and she was tough, but if things got too bad, I would carry her ass out of the woods if need be. We'd see how much bravado that short, bratty little thing could muster while thrown over my shoulder.

"Do you have all the supplies you need?" I asked before we made our way to the Eastern Gates.

She wiggled her small muslin-lined basket and flapped a pair of worn but supple looking brown leather gloves in my direction.

"I think I'm covered. Foraging isn't a particularly complex task, Kier."

Fair enough.

As we walked silently through the Wyldwoods, I cast my Shadow out to scout the area nearby, vigilant but unseen. Arken began to gather all the little leaves, petals and mushrooms she needed to make this so-called miracle tea. I kept my focus on our surroundings.

When I had first learned how to use arcana like this, the spell effects were visible—a sheer but inky, black mist that sort of defeated any purposes I had for it. So I had altered the magick myself, tweaking the focus so that as I extended my Shadows, they crept around for me where Shadow aether already existed, slinking around corners and crevices, expanding my senses. It was essentially like having eyes and ears everywhere at once, and though it was a draining practice, it was incredibly useful. For situations like this, in particular.

Somewhere, about fifty feet behind us, my arcane sentinel detected a sharp crack, followed by an unnatural flood of Earth aether.

"Arken. Stop. Listen to me," I whispered urgently in her direction.

She turned to me sharply, hair whipping behind her in a wild halo like I'd somehow managed to irritate a lion... or a godsdamned manticore.

"No, *you* listen to *me*, Vistarii. I'm sure you get off on ordering people around but—"

She paused to scowl at the hint of a smirk that I had tried my best to contain. Due to the severity of the situation, I decided to put a pin in exactly what her phrasing was bringing to my mind.

"Might I remind you that I *literally* grew up in a forest?" she hissed.

"Asher, shut the fuck up for a second!" I hissed sharply under my breath, glaring as I put one finger over my lips.

I didn't have time to explain to her that the northern Brindlewoods of Samhaven, while dangerous enough in their own right, had nothing on what these Wyldwoods could conjure. The Brindlewoods didn't grow over top the singlemost point of leyline convergences in Atlas.

"Listen. Do you hear anything? Anything at all?"

Because I didn't. The entire forest had gone silent after that crack—that flood of aether. There were no chirping birds, no chittering rodents, not even a damn cricket. Arken froze, her eyes going wide with understanding. Something was wrong. Very wrong.

I took a deep breath then, closing my eyes and focusing hard on my extended senses, trying to detect the source.

I had immediately clocked the aetherflood as one of Earth, but there was something else I felt, too—a dark presence. An aberration.

My Shadows continued to spread further into the woods, acting as my eyes and ears until I found it. Just about fifty meters away now and headed in our direction, albeit slowly. This arcana didn't allow me to fully see things beyond my natural line of sight, but I could detect the shape of things for the most part, so long as the thing was living. If it had aether—which it did.

What was it, though?

The beast was crouched down in a thick brush, behind a pile of jagged rock and gnarled, rope-like branches that almost looked like bands of muscle, swaying in the wind. Except there was no wind blowing tonight. The air had been still and misty since morning.

Another sharp snap, and suddenly the creature was no longer crouching.

Those weren't branches. They were *arms.*

Oh Hel no.

"Don't. Move," I whispered, casting a frantic, pleading glance in Arken's direction.

Anger flashed in her eyes and she opened her mouth again, most assuredly to argue. With a fast flick of my wrist, I summoned a wispy, semi-corporeal raven—a Shadowspeaker. I sent the specter towards her, silently flapping its wings and landing gently on her shoulder. As I spoke the words into the temporary arcane bond, no sound came from my mouth, but she would hear them within her mind so long as the raven was touching her.

Listen to me for once in your life, Arken. Do. Not. Move. Do. Not. Speak. I understand that you're in a mood, but there is something extremely dangerous in these woods right now. Something that shouldn't be here. If you focus on the raven, you can speak back to me with your thoughts. And I'll hear you. But please, woman, I am begging you right now. Don't make a sound. It hasn't scented us yet.

A flash of panic crossed her face, but she remained silent and still and I almost exhaled a heavy sigh of relief when I saw her nod.

I didn't know Shadow Conduits could do this, she sent through our invisible tether.

Most can't, I replied. She raised an eyebrow.

I'll explain later.

I wouldn't, but hopefully by the time we escaped this ordeal she would forget about it... Or I'd manage to come up with a decent lie.

Where is it, Kieran... And *what* **is it?**

It was... a problem.

The Leshen were not native to Aemos, but rather creatures that had crawled through the cracks within these woods and several others during the Cataclysm. Dark beasts that fed on aether, particularly Earth aether. Tall, faceless monsters of bark and bone, existing only to feed. To harvest. Born of the Abyss, and not the false one that the people of Aemos believed to be the horrifying afterlife of the damned. The true Abyss. The void.

Leshen were harbingers of death where I came from, and for good reason. They were incredibly dangerous, and incredibly hard to kill. They were also incredibly *fast*. Too fast for us to flee. I silently sheathed my sword at my hip, drawing my daggers in each palm instead.

Scáthic blades for Scáthic monsters.

About forty meters now, northeast. Time for a Bios quiz, Little Conduit. Have you ever heard of the Leshen?

Oh, fuck.
Yeah. Fuck.
What do we do?
You stay put. If I can take it by surprise, I'll have a better chance at taking it down before it scents us both.
You're asking me to stay behind while you go try to take down a deadly daemon single-handedly?!
I glared at her.
That is exactly what I am telling you to do.
Screw that. I'm coming with you.
Source be damned. Of all the times for Arken to choose to be stubborn. I suppressed a groan of frustration.
Also, they're not technically daemons. Not exactly. They came here from the Shadow Plane, but they originated on the Plane of Earth. All of the Leshen used to be dryads.

Thus their insatiable hunger. A single Leshy could drink Aemos dry of all the Earth aether that the realm contained and still want for more. Nothing could ever compare to the near endless font of Earth to be found in their homelands. How it is that the dryads came to find themselves on the Shadow Plane and become such twisted, corrupted versions of their once-peaceful selves was beyond me. It had apparently happened thousands of years ago. All I knew is that whatever had been done to the dryads produced something... evil. Wrong. Like they were agony and vengeance incarnate.

This wasn't my first encounter with one, but every time, I begged the Source to let it be the last.

Thank you for the Bios lesson, Kieran. But seriously, what the fuck do we do?

If Arken refused to stay put, I was left with no choice. I wouldn't—couldn't—force her to stay behind. But if she came with me to take this thing down, I needed her to be an asset and not a liability, lest we get ourselves killed.

Do you remember how to summon those aetherblades, Little Conduit?

Yep.

Okay. Bring 'em out. And look at me for a sec, I instructed silently, waiting to catch her glance and confirm she was paying attention. Her eyes had been darting all over the forest, searching for the threat.

They're faceless, but humanoid in shape. Aim here, I explained through the raven, pointing at the space between my neck and collarbone. *Or here*, I pointed at my midsection, just below the ribcage.

How comfortable are you with wielding the Light daggers so far?

We hadn't even touched aetherblades in our training sessions thus far, but she had summoned one quick enough in the alley with Anders. You know, the same exact day she had even learned how.

Comfortable enough, Arken replied.

Good. I'm going to keep you shielded to the best of my ability, but stay away from the talons. Their poison works fast. If you make a clean hit in either of those two places, though—light it the fuck up. Give it all you've got, Ark. Pull from me if you have to. Light will probably do some serious damage against it, given that they're Shadow-aligned.

She gave me a quick nod of understanding, her brow furrowing with focus.

Follow my lead, okay? I'm going to cloak us and silence our footsteps as much as I can, but as soon as we're within 15 feet or so, the Leshy will scent us and it's going to be time to fuck shit up.

Let's go fuck shit up, then, Captain.

Despite the danger and the intensity of the situation, I couldn't help but return her wry smile.

CHAPTER FORTY-NINE

ARKEN

I was admittedly putting on a brave face for Kieran, but the second he'd put the word *Leshy* in my mind, my mouth went dry and it was an effort not to shiver. Even though I had successfully played it off, the hair on the back of my neck still stood on end.

I wasn't a fighter. Regardless of the strength of my Resonance, a Leshy was so far beyond my skill set that I was half-tempted to listen to Kier when he told me to stay put, but I couldn't let him go alone.

It was sentimental stupidity and I knew it. The same stupid urge that had me drawing my blade on Cragg a few weeks back when he'd been talking shit. It didn't matter that Kieran was one of the youngest captains the Elder Guard had ever seen, or that his martial prowess went so far beyond what I could ever hope to attain that it was almost laughable.

In the short time that I'd known the man, he'd made it clear that he always had my back. I would have his, for whatever that was worth.

And so I followed him silently through the woods, attempting to mimic his stealthy prowl, leaning forward in the same way he did as he dodged his way through gnarled branches and bushes. I did my best to match his graceful, silent strides.

Before I was truly ready for it, we had gotten within range, and a discomforting noise shot through the forest. It sounded like an unnatural cross between a wolf's snarl and the harsh creak of snapping branches. We hadn't reached a clearing, and the woods were thick enough here that I couldn't see the Leshy yet either, but the sound was quickly growing closer. *Shit.*

Kieran's voice rang through my head again.

Breathe, Arken.

I ran through his instructions. Avoid the talons. Aim for the base of the throat, or under the ribs. Light it up if I can get a clean hit. I could do this. He hadn't fought me when I demanded to come along.

I'm good, I sent back through the raven, the strange psychic mail sprite he seemed to have summoned from thin air.

His reply was almost immediate.

I know.

My chest tightened a bit at the vote of confidence. If Kieran truly believed I could handle being his backup for this fight, then I could handle it.

It's almost here. Let me step into the clearing first and get its attention, okay? When I drop the cloak, it'll probably go into a frenzy for the aether. Once it's fully focused on attacking me, slip into the fray with your Light blades when you see openings, but don't take any unnecessary risks. You're clever, Little Conduit. Put that big brain of yours to use. Dodge first, strike second.

Aye, Captain.

I couldn't see it from behind him, but I could practically feel him roll his eyes in response.

We reached the clearing just moments before the Leshy did, and as Kieran dropped his cloak of Shadows, the dark creature charged.

✧ ✧ ✧

I had seen what Kieran could do with a sword before, hanging around the guardsmen as he ran them through training exercises in the past, but I had never seen him in true combat with his weapons of choice. Not even when he'd been showing off with Hans and Jeremiah last quarter. Not like this.

As the Leshy howled and tore across the clearing towards him, Kieran transformed into something both beautiful and terrifying. His jagged daggers in hand, his Shadows rippling off of him like a second skin...

I realized this man could easily rival the monster he fought for the crown of darkness incarnate.

He moved faster than I could really fathom when the horrid daemon attempted to swipe at his ribcage, Kieran catching its clawed arm with one of his daggers. As the dark metal blade cut into the Leshy's mottled flesh, it drew blood—a black, oily ichor—that hissed and sizzled as it hit the forest floor. I made a quick mental note to try and avoid the substance as it slashed out at him again, forcing him to throw up arcane shields around himself, too.

I was briefly distracted by how stunning they were—the shields glimmering like he'd pulled the darkness straight from the night sky—but then a loud and ugly snarl of frustration escaped the creature's maw, and my focus returned.

Terrifying, muscular looking tendrils shot out from below ground, aiming for Kieran's ankles, and for a moment I thought he was screwed. Somehow, the guardsman remained two steps ahead, slashing each rope of muscle and vine before they could reach him.

By now, the raven on my shoulder had dissipated into smoke—there was only so much aether you could wield at once, and Kieran was hitting capacity. He had to be. He was shielding himself, shielding me, *and* channeling his Shadow into every strike and blow.

The crunch of the Leshy's gnarled fist against Kieran's shields caught my attention, and I watched with horror as the Shadows appeared to splinter and crack. When the monster found its way through and landed a hit, Kieran stumbled back—just an inch or two, but it was enough to send anger and adrenaline surging through me.

Fear gave way to fight, and I found my opening. Aetherblades in hand, I sprung forward, flanking the beast. As it raised an arm overhead, preparing to strike at Kieran again, the beast paid me no mind. It was clearly focused on the larger threat.

That was its first mistake.

With a snarl of my own, I shoved one of my blades precisely where Kieran had instructed—just below what looked like it once might've been a ribcage. The Leshy let out a blood-curdling screech of pain, attempting to twist its torso away from me—but with grit teeth, I shoved the blade in further.

"Atta girl!" Kieran shouted.

Half of my forearm was inside the creature's strangely hollow body now, and I could feel those freakish vines constrict around my wrist.

"Don't look at her, you ugly fuck. Look at me," Kieran continued with a taunting grin. "I'm the one that's going to kill you."

Like Hel he was. This thing had ruined a perfectly calm evening, and I wanted my pound of flesh... or bark, or whatever the fuck this thing was made of. *Light it up*, he'd told me. While it was still distracted, I shoved my other blade into the space between its gnarled shoulder and neck, and the dark creature continued to scream into the night.

Gods, the screaming. How could it even scream so loud without a damned mouth?

My ears were ringing, but I tugged at Kieran's Shadows, preparing to unleash a world of hurt when it whipped a thick vine straight into his chest, knocking him to the ground before he could dodge.

Heart pounding with fear and rage, I lit the damned thing up like kindling. Instinct and emotion took over, and the aether I unleashed within the Leshy's body wasn't Light... It was Fire.

Fuck.

I could already smell the smoke, and my mind was racing as I watched Kieran quickly scramble to his feet, vague confusion flickering in his eyes before it was immediately replaced by panic.

Before I could even process whether he was panicking about the monster, or catching me flame-handed, the Leshy's claws ripped into my ribcage, and suddenly I was the one screaming.

I fell to my knees on the forest floor, keeling over in agony. The gashes were significant, yes—but that wasn't the source of the pain. It *burned.* This burning was unlike anything I'd ever known, and when I pulled my hand away from my body, it was slick with blood.

I had to get up, I had to fight back, but—my ribs, my lungs. It felt like my chest had been doused in acid, like the wound was immediately festering, the ichor eating its way into my flesh. I tried to draw on my Light, just to craft a shield, a temporary bandage to stop the bleeding, anything... but I couldn't. I couldn't feel any of my Resonances. What the Hel?

I could vaguely hear Kieran shouting as my vision began to blur.

Why did he sound like he was underwater? And was I seeing double, or had a second fiend joined the fray? My tongue felt thick, my senses dull and delayed, and my body... Heavy. Much too heavy. I could barely keep my head up.

Stay away from the talons, he'd told me. *The poison works fast.*

Shit.

CHAPTER FIFTY

KIERAN

A brief moment of distraction was all it took for me to fuck up.

I had paused just a second too long, my attention diverted by the scent of smoke. I dropped my shields on her for a fraction of an instant, my reckless attempt to redirect my arcana and catch the Leshy's gnarled arm as it flew towards Arken—but my daggers just barely missed their target.

Too slow. Too godsdamned slow, trying to strike from my blind side.

But where had the smoke come from?

My heart was pounding with adrenaline and Shadow as they surged through my veins in tandem, mind racing—desperately trying to make sense of everything that was happening all at once. Words could not describe the depth of the fear, or the *fury* that rose up like bile in my throat the moment I heard her scream. My hair stood on end, something primordial and fiercely protective stirring at the sound of that desperate, blood-curdling cry.

"Kieran!"

Immediately, without even thinking, I released the damper I typically kept on my Shadow. Consequences be damned, now was not the fucking time to hold myself back. I didn't have much time. Ten minutes at most. Shit. *Shit.*

We were too deep in the Wyldwoods to get her to an infirmary in time, and I didn't even know if the clerics carried what she would need to heal. I had to get her out of here, and fast, but first I needed to restrain this son of a bitch.

"Arken? Hang on! Breathe— breathe slowly!" I shouted, praying to the Source that she was still lucid. If she could slow her own heart rate down, the poison would take longer to disperse.

All I heard in response was a weak whimper, and I bit down hard on my lip, willing myself not to panic. She was still conscious. I still had time to save her, but I had to fucking focus. This was not the first daemon I had encountered alone, but I wasn't about to gamble on my strength versus Arken's constitution.

Restrain it. Save her first.

With a sharp inhale, I drew from every single element I could find in my vicinity. The Air, the moisture in the soil, the Earth itself, pulling it into my chest. With a flick of my wrist, thick bands of Shadow shot out and encircled the corrupted creature's arms and legs, binding it in place. The dark tethers wouldn't hold for long, not for a monster of this size, but they'd hold long enough for me to get her out of here.

I sprinted over to where Arken was now lying on her side, moaning in pain. The sound threatened to pierce my heart and tear me to shreds. *You should've focused on the shields, you dumb bastard.* But I could ruminate later—we needed to get back to the city, and fast. As I picked Arken up, cradling her as delicately in my arms as I could, I realized with horror how deep the Leshy had struck.

There was no way I could run her back into Sophrosyne without making those wounds much, much worse. If the poison didn't kill her, the blood loss very well could. Her eyes had already fluttered closed, and she could barely speak—though that didn't stop her from trying.

"Kee-reh? Eh hurts..." she whimpered, her tongue thickened

by the ichor.

"I know, sweetheart. I'm gonna get you home and all fixed up, I just need you to hold on to me, okay?"

"Kay," she mumbled, resting her head against my shoulder. The weak grip she had on my coat was the best I was going to get from her in this state.

Fuck.

I had no other choice.

Briefly propping Arken's body up with my thigh, I lifted one hand to my mouth and bit down on the flesh of my palm, drawing blood to the surface with a single sharp incisor. Prioritizing speed over perfect accuracy, I smeared two fingertips in the blood, and with a quick gesture, tore a dark, shimmering cut into the very fabric of reality.

"Hang on tight," I reminded her, locking my arms around her body before stepping through the rift.

The nausea hit immediately, followed by the immense, head-splitting pressure that came alongside traversing the space between the planes. I hated putting her through this, but I could handle her pain if it meant saving her life.

Even so, this was reckless, stupid of me to do—and I knew I would pay for it, one way or another. It didn't matter. I had to save her. With a deep breath, I located the other side of the rift and pushed us both through.

Oh thank fuck. We were just outside the gates, and nobody was within a close enough radius to have seen that ripple in reality before it dissipated.

"Rorick! Hans!" I bellowed, moving as quickly as I could without jostling Arken in my arms.

The latter came running immediately, and I was flooded with relief to see my second-in-command had arrived early to his shift tonight.

"Leshy. Northwest. It's wounded, but not down. I just barely got her out—but she, the claws—the poison, I have to get her healed. Grab Jeremiah, Hanjae—whoever you can spare. I'll meet you as soon as I—"

"Understood, Captain," he cut me off before I could promise to join them. "We've got it covered, get the girl to a cleric."

I nodded once, and then took off. Not to the infirmary, but to Mugworts—the closest apothecary, where I'd met with Arken earlier.

The old man behind the counter was having a quiet conversation with a customer as I burst through his doors with my bloodied companion in tow.

"Willowsbane," I demanded, panting and out of breath. "I need a poultice with willowsbane and whatever else you have on hand for fresh wounds, now." I could apologize for being a jackass later, but Arken was running out of time. "I also need red ivy extract in water—hot."

"Er, yes, right—one moment," the shopkeep stammered awkwardly, but quickly sprung into action, gathering the ingredients and heating his kettle. The other customer took one look at Arken's gruesome wounds and quickly left the shop.

"What on Aemos happened to her?" he asked as he poured a splash of hot water over the ingredients, grinding them into a paste. He poured what remained of the water into a mug and pushed it towards me with a dropper bottle of the extract. "Use whatever you need," he added.

"Leshy. In the Wyldwoods."

"Good gods! But they—they're extinct!" the old man exclaimed.

"Not extinct. Just rare. But please, don't be alarmed. The Guard is dispatched, and the damned thing is likely already dead. I can assure you, we're safe here. Can you apply that poultice to some strips of cloth for a dressing?"

"Yes, sir—one moment."

While he worked, I hastily added the necessary extract to the mug of water, hoisting Arken up against me so that she was more upright in my arms. She groaned in protest, but was thankfully still conscious—barely, but conscious.

"Arken, honey, I need you to drink this, okay?"

She nodded slowly and reached for the mug. I let her grasp the handle, but held on to the base. By now, the toxins had left her significantly weakened. The extract would stop it from spreading, and the poultice would help draw them out while the clerics did what they do best. This particular antidote was uncommon, nearly forgotten with time as it had been decades since we'd last seen a Leshy anywhere near this part of the continent. I only knew how to make it because I was taught... a long time ago.

I couldn't help but wince at the grimace on her face as she drank. The taste was not pleasant, I remembered that much. Still, she followed instructions and finished the makeshift tincture.

"Good girl," I said under my breath, pushing her hair out of her face. Her skin felt clammy and feverish, but I could already see some color returning to her cheeks. Thank the gods.

The shopkeeper wrapped the wound dressings in some waxed cloth, and I promised to return with payment the next day—double whatever the cost of labor and ingredients. He tried to assure me that it wasn't necessary, that he was happy to be of service to the Guard, but I would return with the Lyra later regardless.

I ignored the few meandering townsfolk who stopped to stare as I carried this woman a few blocks east, to the nearest infirmary. I'm sure we were a ghastly sight to behold—clothing torn up and covered in blood, dirt, and ichor from the fight. Arken's breathing had steadied a bit, but she was still in rough shape. My own body had started to ache as the effects of my arcana faded, but those pains were easy to ignore.

Finally, we made it to the infirmary where the clerics—Water

Conduits who specialized in healing arcana—immediately flocked to attend to her. I gave them a brief, terse explanation of what had happened and how to apply the poultices, directing them to change the dressing every half-hour.

I meant no disrespect to their staff, but this remedy was not from Pyrhhas or Sophrosyne—it wasn't even native to Atlas. Leshen were so rare that I had to make certain they would not attempt to close the wound before the ichor was out of her system.

I was relieved to find that High Scholar Helvig, arguably one of the best healers Sophrosyne could offer, was on duty tonight.

"Well, well, Captain Vistarii," she murmured after getting Arken situated in an empty bed. "It's usually your men that I'm fixing up. Who is this one?"

"A friend," I said. "Her name is Arken."

A noticeable flicker of surprise passed through her expression, and I could see the ghost of a smile forming on her lips, though she simply nodded and said nothing. Was it really that surprising that I had a friend outside of work?

"We're going to give her a sleeping draught now so that her body can focus on removing the poisons," she said softly. "We can't draw these out manually, I'm afraid."

"I know," I said. Another flicker of surprise. Yeah, that one was fair.

"Once we confirm her blood is clean again, we'll help get those wounds closed and she'll be significantly recovered by morning."

"Good. You and your team have my thanks, Fen," I said with sincerity, preparing to head out. "I need to debrief with my men and make sure the Leshy was taken care of, but I'll be back soon."

"Oh. There's really no need, we can send for an escort when she's ready to go home, Captain."

I tossed a glance back over my shoulder at the familiar cleric.

"I'll be back soon," I repeated.

Fen raised her eyebrows, but nodded, barely holding back the smile now. *Ridiculous.*

I rolled my eyes and offered her a lazy wave as I left, making my way back towards the East Gate to find my men and ensure the daemon had been taken care of.

✧ ✧ ✧

It was only after my debrief with the Guard that I felt the adrenaline begin to fade, leaving my system in shambles.

What the fuck just happened?

As I'd told Hanjae, I had absolutely zero explanation for the arrival of the Leshy.

One of the reasons that the Elder Guard kept active, daily patrols throughout the Wyldwoods was to search for residual weaknesses. Pockets of space where the veil between realms still ran too thin after the Cataclysm. Any time we found one, it was immediately reported to the Convocation, and one of the Aetherborne would come out to repair it.

Our guards were well-trained, they knew how to catch those weak spots in the veil well before any creature could feasibly pass through. And I, more than anyone else, should have been able to detect if something was amiss.

It didn't make any fucking sense.

That flood of dark, tenebrous aether as it snapped through the void had come out of nowhere. It was *immediate*, almost as if...

But no. It was too early for that. And even if it wasn't, they would never be so reckless as to leave a rift wide open and let a daemon follow.

And then there was the smoke.

The only explanation my mind could parse was that Arken's Light was so intense, so searingly white-hot that the carapace of the Leshy had caught fire from the inside. These beasts were borne from rotting wood and ichor, so it was reasonable enough to presume that it had caught fire from the inside out once Arken had shoved her aetherblade into its chest… Right?

Except everything I knew about arcana suggested there was no way that a first-year Conduit could be that powerful, that precise. Sure, Arken was exceptionally advanced—she had passed tests for courses two years beyond expectations—but for her Light to *burn*?

I sighed heavily, running one hand over my face.

Stranger things had happened in life or death situations. It wasn't exactly well-studied, but there had been reports of similar phenomena in the past.

What mattered was that she survived, and she was safe now.

Logically, I knew that I could do very little for Arken except wait for the clerics to get her system stable. As I left headquarters, I knew that the reasonable thing to do would be to go home, and visit her in the morning.

But I had almost lost her, and we were past the point of reason. If I wanted to get any semblance of sleep tonight, it would have to be in a shitty armchair in the infirmary, by her side as she slept.

◆ ◆ ◆

I woke up the next morning to a glaring scowl from Scholar Helvig.

"*Shoo*, Vistarii. We need to work on her injuries before she wakes up. Go make yourself useful somewhere else. You're in my way."

Begrudgingly, I left the room, casting a pained glance over my shoulder. I knew she was recovering, but Arken's skin was still so pallid, slick with sweat as her body fought off the foul toxins of the Leshy's claw.

I wasn't expected back at work for at least the next few days. Hanjae had made himself clear that he'd much prefer I make sure the only Light Conduit in Sophrosyne made a full recovery—and so instead, I made my way back over to Mugwort's with a pouch full of funds and an apology for being such a blunt, demanding prick last night.

He tried to refuse me, at first, but I was persistent. The old man was as stubborn as a mule, but so was I—and I wasn't leaving that shop until he accepted what I owed him.

"Seriously, Maxwell, just take the Lyra."

"No, no. I couldn't possibly accept this. It was my honor to assist, Captain. I trust your wife is recovering well?"

My fucking what now?

The slack-jawed expression on my face must've given me away, because the herbalist immediately stammered out an awkward apology.

"Oh! I. Well, I apologize, sir, I had just assumed. I, erm... Oh dear. I meant no offense," Max stressed.

"It's fine. She's just a friend," I explained calmly, though I was still flabbergasted. "But yes, Arken is recovering well. I cannot thank you enough for your assistance in that."

"Yes, yes, of course," he replied, though he wouldn't meet my eyes.

Seriously though? What a strange assumption to make about two strangers. He didn't even say *girlfriend*, or partner, just went straight to *wife*? A bit old-fashioned, though I guess the shoe fit the old man.

Me. Married. I snorted to myself, disguising it as a cough when the man raised an eyebrow.

But because I was apparently a fucking masochist, the image of Arken in a wedding gown was briefly conjured in my mind—and I shut it down, groaning internally.

Yeah, can we not?

I really could've done without that image. That was the last thing I needed to be thinking about when my next stop was to check on her in the infirmary.

Your wife.

For fucks sake.

I was usually much better at compartmentalizing, but as I made my way towards the infirmary, I was still reeling at the old man's assumption. Every time I thought I'd shoved the thought out of my mind, I found myself revisiting the night prior, trying to overanalyze my actions and determine what Maxwell could have possibly interpreted between us that suggested matrimony, of all things.

Was it my clear panic? She could've died, of course I was panicked. Sure, I had rushed into his shop with the woman cradled in my arms, but again—she was fucking dying.

Between Maxwell and Fen's cheeky little smirks... *Gods.*

We were just friends. Close friends. Why was everyone else assuming there was more to it than that?

I mean shit, even Hanjae had questioned if Arken and I were dating last night. I was accustomed to quips from my lieutenants, but from *my commander*? Godsdamn.

"No. I was just following protocol, sir," I had answered. "We know her safety is of the utmost importance to the Studium."

Commander Ka had seemed skeptical at best over that excuse. Most of the guardsmen who worked in close quarters with me saw past the charismatic front to an extent, and Hanjae in particular knew that I was more solitary in nature. Not to mention my reputation for being spectacularly brutal against any threat to our city.

I supposed I could see where they were coming from, though. To prioritize one woman's life over dispatching a larger threat was... unlike me. Me, the man without commitments beyond his oath. Me, the man with no *interest* in commitments beyond my oath. Or at least, I used to be.

It didn't matter, I reminded myself. It was human nature to

gossip, and half of the people in Sophrosyne just liked to hear themselves talk.

That's what I kept telling myself, at least. But as I entered the infirmary to find Arken sitting up in her bed, with color in her cheeks again, I was so flooded with relief that I nearly staggered.

And when she saw me approaching and immediately broke into a smile, practically beaming at the sight of me? Something in my chest tightened. I felt my own cheeks heat under her gaze.

Gods. That fucking smile.

Fen walked past me and said nothing, just gave me a knowing smirk as she carried a stack of linens into the next room.

Ah, Hel.

CHAPTER FIFTY-ONE

ARKEN

"I'm fine, Kieran," I swore, rolling my eyes at the arm he'd extended. "I really don't need an escort, I can make it home just fine on my own."

My words were immediately contradicted by the sharp intake of breath and the wince I couldn't mask as I pushed myself up on the infirmary bed.

Kieran's eyes flashed.

"I'm *fine*," I repeated. "Seriously, the clerics did incredible work, I'm just a little bit tender, is all."

"Will you just take my arm, you stubborn little brat?" he snapped.

I shook my head. I couldn't keep imposing on him like this, he was busy as Hel these days.

"You've done enough, Kier. You've probably missed enough work already as is," I groaned. "Did you even get any sleep last night?"

The guardsman stared at me incredulously.

"Are you seriously asking about my well-being right now, Asher? You just got sliced up by a deadly daemon less than twelve hours ago, and you're stressing out over my beauty sleep?"

"Yes." I said stubbornly. He didn't sleep enough.

He sighed heavily again, looking at me as if I were the bane of his existence.

"Jeremiah and Hans are perfectly capable of holding down the fort for me, Arken. And I stepped out for a few hours while you slept. They're both worried sick over you, by the way."

I frowned. Worried sick? Over me?

"And yes, I got a few hours of sleep while they were treating your wounds. Ask Fen if you don't believe me. Now will you please stop being so stubborn, and let me take you home?"

Right on cue, High Scholar Helvig made her way into the room with a few small vials and a fresh change of clothes in hand. As she handed off the soft chemise, sweater and tights, I realized that Kieran must've sent for them himself, because they were perfectly sized.

"I'm afraid I can't let you leave without an escort, Ms. Asher," Fen said brusquely, backing Kieran up. "But if you'd like me to kick this one out and send for another, just say the word."

I grinned, half tempted to have her do it just to fuck with Kieran—who was still hovering like a mother hen. He scowled.

"Don't you dare," he warned.

Fen just smiled, and shook her head.

"I want you to take this first vial in about half an hour, and then take the other two at twelve-hour intervals," she instructed.

I glanced over at Kieran, and could see him making a mental note on those timings so he could get on my ass about them. I was secretly grateful for that, knowing my own short-term memory would be lacking in my exhaustion.

"The tinctures will help expedite healing, and should also eliminate any pain or tenderness entirely. And then this," Fen said, holding up a small tin of some sort of salve, "should lessen the scarring over time. I must apologize for that again. We couldn't seal your wounds early enough to avoid scarring altogether because of the toxins."

"It's fine," I said softly, trying not to peek over at Kieran again. "I sort of like scars."

Fen glanced back at Kieran, giving him a strange look, one that he steadfastly ignored.

"Are you feeling well enough to walk a bit, Arken? Do you want to head home now, or do you need more rest?" he asked.

I resisted the urge to roll my eyes.

"How many more times do I have to tell you that I'm fine, Kieran?"

"At least seven more," he quipped back.

"Oh, I am going to murder you," I warned.

"You can hardly even stand up straight. You really think you can start swinging on me?" he challenged.

"Please do not," Fen added, and I cracked a smile.

"Only because she asked," I told Kieran.

"It's not the first time she's saved my ass, and I'm sure it won't be the last," he muttered.

✧ ✧ ✧

Our walk back to my apartment started off quiet, the two of us processing the chaos of the last twenty-four hours.

"Before I drop you off, remind me to send a sprite off to my commander, will you? I promised to keep him posted on your recovery after the attack."

"Of course," I said, disregarding my vague curiosity on why his commander would care about my well-being.

Though...

"Speaking of mail sprites. How did you do that, Kieran?"

"Do what, exactly?" Kieran asked, keeping his gaze fixed on the road ahead.

"That thing, with the raven. At first I thought it was just your mail sprite... but it looked different. And then it felt as though you were speaking inside my mind. I didn't know anyone could do that. I don't think I've ever even heard of such a thing," I explained.

I tried my best to keep my tone even, feigning disinterest even though I was burning with curiosity. There were several things about that night that I couldn't comprehend, and this was probably one of the tamest of the questions I had.

Kieran sighed.

"Yeah, about that. Do me a favor, Ark. Can you avoid... *sharing that with the class*, so to speak? I hate to ask this of you, but if you could avoid bringing that up, even with your friends..."

Every now and again, a request like this would crop up. Kieran never looked particularly happy to ask me to keep secrets, but I figured it just sort of came with the territory when your best friend was essentially a spymaster.

"Oh. Of course, yeah. I wouldn't dream of it. Can I ask why?"

For a moment he was silent, continuing to stare off into the crowd ahead.

"It's... Well. It's not a common practice, basically. It's an extremely complex form of arcana that takes a great deal of energy and focus. As far as I'm aware, they actually don't teach it here. It's considered to be too dangerous."

"You seemed to handle it perfectly fine," I replied.

"Training, Little Conduit. A great deal of training."

"But not from the scholars."

"No, not from them."

The change in his posture was so subtle that I doubt anyone else would have noticed, but I knew him well enough to notice how he'd stiffened. It was as if he knew what I would ask next. Perhaps I should have held my tongue in that case, but I couldn't help but ask the obvious question.

"And not from the guard."

"No."

"If not from them, or the scholars, Kier... then who taught you?"

All of the light and life behind his eyes seemed to flicker briefly like a flame in the wind. Like it was on the verge of being snuffed out as he opened his mouth to speak, and my stomach churned with regret. I shouldn't have asked.

"My birth father."

I blinked, taken aback.

"Oh. You don't often speak about your family," I breathed. I had not been expecting this, not at all.

"There's not much to speak on, Arken. Most of my family is dead."

CHAPTER FIFTY-TWO

KIERAN

This conversation was inevitable, and I had known it was coming.

Anticipated it for months now, really, and so I had already prepared myself, mapping out the artful disclosures and side-steps where I would reveal just enough to sate her curiosity without dropping the mask... without putting her at risk.

"I'm so sorry, Kieran..." she whispered, her fingertips brushing against my arm in gentle reassurance. She still had no idea how those slight touches set me on fire, every time.

"Don't be."

We were both silent for several minutes, not a sound between us besides the soft crunch of gravel beneath our feet as we continued our walk, passing through the local gardens. I took several deep breaths, attempting to still my mind before giving her the bare minimum. Hoping it would be enough.

"My mother died when I was very young. I barely knew her. I had a rough childhood, but things got better when my adoptive father took me in. I had been alone for a long time, fending for myself for the most part... And then he came along, bringing in my older brother as well. For a long time after that, things were good. We were all very close, for many years."

I could feel her eyes fixed on me, but couldn't dare meet that gaze. I knew the minute I glanced back at her, I would be tempted to bare my soul in front of those honest, golden eyes. There was something about her trust—the steadfast loyalty she had shown me as a friend...

I always wanted to give Arken so much more than what I was actually capable of offering.

"My father died a little over five years ago, and the circumstances of his death... they caused a rift between my brother and I. In a way, he blames me for what happened. We haven't spoken since. Though he is the last of what I'd call my family, I don't think he'll ever see me as such again. So that's why you don't hear me talk about them much."

Arken leaned against me for just a moment, resting her temple against my arm, and I resisted the mounting urge to wrap my arms around her and pull her in closer.

The weight of last night was really starting to settle in.

She had almost died.

Died.

What the actual fuck would I have done if I lost her? The thought alone made me sick to my stomach.

"Thank you again," she murmured, as if she could read my mind.

"For what?"

"Saving my life."

I wondered if she had any idea that I'd really just been returning a favor. Saving the life of someone who had made mine worth savoring. My dearest friend. The closest friend I'd ever have.

"You don't need to thank me for that, Arken."

"I do," she murmured sleepily. "And I will..."

She leaned against me a little harder now, and for a second, I was relishing the weight of her body against mine and the comfort it seemed to summon. Just for a moment, before I realized that her steps had turned into slower shuffles, and she began to slump forward where she stood. Right in the middle of the cobblestones where we'd been walking.

"Shit," I swore, scrambling to try and catch her by the arm. My fingers gripped at her sweater, but it only stretched and slid off her shoulder as Arken collapsed in the street. *Shit.*

"Oh, ow," she groaned as I rushed over to slide an arm beneath her head, which had struck the ground with a nauseating crack. Thank fuck she was still conscious.

"Fucking Hel, Arken. Are you okay?"

"I'm alright," she said, holding a hand against her head. I could see a small trickle of blood form between her fingertips.

"You are most certainly not alright. For fuck's sake," I replied. "Did you take that first vial that Fen gave you?"

"Oh," she said meekly. "I might have forgotten about that."

"If you weren't already bleeding, Asher, I would kick your ass. Drink that godsdamned tincture. Right now," I growled.

This woman needed to take better care of herself. Did she have a death wish?

"I'm taking you back to the infirmary," I muttered.

"Oh, gods—*please* don't," she begged.

"You're bleeding."

"It's fine, it's just a scrape. I can clean it up at home."

Absolutely not. Her apartment was still something close to twenty minutes away, and that was walking at our usual pace. It would take twice as long with her walking around on baby deer legs, partially concussed.

"I'll give you two options, Little Conduit. You're either going back to the infirmary, or I'm taking you to my townhouse to take a look at that scrape myself. Your choice."

"You live nearby?"

I realized now that in the year or so we'd known one another, she had never seen where I lived. We always met up at her place, HQ, or other various locations on campus. *I really was a closed-off son of a bitch, wasn't I?*

"Yeah, just a few blocks from here, actually."

She winced as she straightened herself up, pulled one of the vials from her pocket, uncorked it and knocked it back like a shot.

Good girl.

"Pick your poison, Asher. I'm not letting you out of my sight until you're stable and healthy."

"Ugh, fine. Take me to the townhouse," she groaned. "I am not going back to tell the clerics that I fainted in the middle of the road."

"As you wish," I replied, proffering an arm to steady her as she lifted herself up off the ground.

"Sorry," she said quietly as I steered us both in the direction of home.

"Tell that to your head," I muttered, still irritated by her lack of good sense.

In the ten minutes it took us to get to my place, the tincture had already started to take effect. Arken's eyes were brighter, with color returning to her cheeks. She didn't need to lean on me or the railing as I'd led her up the stairs to my front door.

"This is where you live?" she asked, eyes widening as she took in the casual grandeur of the neighborhood.

"I make good money as a captain, thank you very much," I replied, unlocking the door and leading her inside.

◇ ◇ ◇

"Tea?" I offered after getting her settled in on my couch with a damp rag for her head.

"I'll take some cold water, if you have it."

I pulled a small carafe from the icebox and poured her a glass. I also quickly grabbed a scone, slathered it with some orange blossom jam and clotted cream, and tossed that on a plate as well.

"Eat," I said, returning to the kettle to prepare my own tea. Fates knew my frayed nerves could use it—this girl was going to put me in an early grave.

"Don't start with me, Asher," I warned as she opened her mouth, most assuredly to argue.

"You are so demanding," she said, clearly suppressing a grin.

She had no idea.

"Eat, and then I'll take a look at your head, and then maybe let you go home."

"Fine," she sighed, glaring at me as she took a bite. Her expression quickly melted into one of deep contentment.

"Holy Hel, this is good jam. Where did you get it?"

"I made it."

"Really? How domestic of you."

"My family's kitchen maid taught me how to make it myself because I used to eat it out of a jar with a spoon and finish it off within days of her making a batch," I confessed.

"That's adorable, actually. And you still have a thing for citrus, don't you?" she mused.

I thought of that first day she'd caught my eye, the lemon-and-sunshine scent of her skin that immediately captured my attention. I hadn't managed to look away since.

"Yeah, maybe."

CHAPTER FIFTY-THREE

ARKEN

As Kieran got up to finish brewing his tea, I let my curious eyes wander. This was the first time I'd ever actually had an opportunity to see his place.

The townhouse was surprisingly sophisticated and expensive looking, between the matching furniture sets and the built-in floor-to-ceiling bookshelves—filled to the brim with books. Some of them looked like first-edition novels, others were thick tomes on art, history, arcana, and so much more.

There were a few gold and bronze accent pieces, sculptures and abstract art on canvas placed elegantly throughout the room, which contrasted flawlessly with the deep blue filigree wallpaper and the plush carpets against the dark wood flooring. And gods, were those real plants on the windowsill? The man managed to keep plants alive on his work schedule? In all its elevated elegance, this looked like the type of townhouse one might inherit—not something Kieran would have purchased for himself. Curious.

There were bits and pieces of the Kieran I knew scattered throughout, though—you just had to look a little closer to catch them: the uniform coat strewn across the tufted leather chaise, and several cups of tea in various states of completion placed in odd locations, along with some half-eaten oranges. There was one heavy-looking ceramic mug acting as a very precarious bookend on the shelf to my left, and I couldn't help but laugh. It even had a teaspoon in it still.

His voice startled me as he re-entered the room, supplies in hand.

"What are you even giggling about in here?"

"How many teacups would you say that you own?" I teased. I was sort of surprised, he didn't often order tea when we were out. Though I usually did.

He shrugged.

"Tea helps me sleep."

Yet another thing we had in common. Would we ever run out of similarities to stumble across? I wasn't sure.

As he sat back down next to me, he began to prepare a cloth strip with some antiseptic solution. I reached for it, extending my hand towards his lap.

"Here, I can do that," I offered. "You've done more than enough for me today."

Kieran rolled his eyes and batted my hand away before I could take the medicine kit from him.

"Hush. Let me see your head," he said in a brusque tone that almost reminded me of... Amaretta, of all people.

I sighed.

"I mean it, Kier... I can clean these scrapes up myself and get out of your hair, just point me to your—"

I trailed off, my train of thought interrupted immediately when he took two callused fingers and pushed my jaw to the side, ignoring my words. He was inspecting my forehead with the surgical attention of a cleric, and continued to steadfastly ignore my protests as he began dabbing at the scrape on my scalp, just above my forehead.

"I'm not sure if you realize this, Arken, but it's perfectly alright to let yourself be taken care of from time to time." Though his tone was serious, there was a glimmer in his eye that told me he was mostly teasing. "And you don't even need to be on death's doorstep to deserve it."

Kieran gave me a pointed glance before returning to his work. I grumbled some incoherent noise to express my disagreement with his general sentiment. Was it such a crime to be accustomed to self-sufficiency?

"Sorry, sweetheart," he murmured with an apologetic grimace when I bit down on my lip, trying not to yelp at the sting as he dabbed the laceration on my head with antiseptic solution. It began to fizzle audibly, making its way through the dirt in the wound. It was easy enough to distract myself from the subsequent burning sensation with some shameless self-indulgence.

Even when we trained together, it was rare that Kieran and I were ever *this* close, his face mere inches from my own. I let myself take advantage of the view, studying the sharp angles of his jawline, his slightly crooked nose, and the brutal, pale scars that were slightly raised, slashing through the blind eye. I would never admit to him how much I actually loved the imperfection, and how much more attractive it made him to me... that scar, and those stupidly soft looking lips.

Continuing to feel emboldened by the fact that his focus was elsewhere, I studied his eyes. The cloudy whites of the left, blind eye had struck me when we first met—it was part of what made him so alluring, what with the scars cutting through his brow, making it clear the man was dangerous. Anyone who could survive a blow like that...

I'd been intrigued, of course, but then I had nearly cursed the godsdamned Fates when I saw the other eye, which was even more stunning, somehow. I had studied those hues over the last however many months it had been with every stolen glance, but up close? Gods. Under the frame of Kieran's thick, dark lashes, I could see that glacial blue iris was speckled with shades of lilac and even a bit of yellow. The iris was ringed with a deeper shade of blue, which only served to contrast and intensify the beauty of the paler colors.

This close to his face, I could see that he had dark circles under his eyes, too. It was hard to tell from a distance, given how warm the tones of his skin were naturally, but here was the evidence of the last several nights being sleepless, like subtle little bruises beneath his—

"What are you thinking about?"

Kieran caught my eye as he began to unscrew a small tin of ointment.

"Mm, apologies. That's classified information, Captain."

"I'm fairly certain that I've earned my clearances in that regard," he countered as he gingerly applied a dab of the salve from High Scholar Helvig to my head. The relief was almost immediate.

"Just because you're playing nurse tonight doesn't mean you get access to my innermost secrets, Kieran," I replied.

A slight smirk began to curl on his lips.

"Do you often find yourself pondering over your innermost secrets while staring at me, Little Conduit? That's rather... intimate."

I flushed.

"It's not really staring when you are quite literally right in front of my face. What else is there for me to look at?"

"Whatever you say," he replied, the smirk spreading.

He had to know that, even for me, his smile was a deadly weapon. He *had* to know. He certainly wielded it like one.

"Okay, fine. You're also, admittedly, the nicest thing to look at in here. I will give you that," I reasoned.

"I'm not sure if that's a compliment to my face, or an insult towards my taste in interior design."

"Mm. A little bit of column a, little bit of column b," I teased.

He ran one hand through his hair, rolling his eyes.

"Do you ever give straight answers, woman?"

"Only under duress."

After such an intense twenty-four hours, my spirits were already lifting. This was one of my favorite elements of our friendship—the banter, the way Kieran could so effortlessly go toe-to-toe with me in snark. We could quite literally go back and forth for hours, volleying quips like it was a sporting event, just to pass the time. Sometimes, he even beat me at my own game.

There was a wicked gleam in his eyes now that suggested he was ready to play.

"Perhaps I should put you under duress, then," he mused. "I am ever so curious about what secrets might be locked inside this pretty little banged-up head of yours."

My pulse quickened. Surely, I was just imagining the genuine sensuality that had just slipped into his tone? That smirk remained as he began to put items from the medicine kit away with tidy precision.

"Hah," I replied, voice calm. "Good luck with that, Vistarii."

"It's cute how you think I'd need luck to accomplish such things, Asher," Kieran said, mocking my tone as he set aside the small pouch and soiled strips of cotton, turning his attention back to me. Those godsdamned eyes could pierce my soul, I swear.

Summoning as much false confidence as I could muster, I snorted and tossed my hair.

"Oh, you would need so much more than luck, my friend."

He didn't take the bait.

Instead, Kieran leaned in towards me again, this time leaving mere centimeters between our faces. My breath caught in my throat.

"You seem like the type who might enjoy being under duress, though, Arken," he murmured. His voice was low, velvet over gravel, so soft and husky and gods, I hated what the sound of it was doing to me.

What are you doing to me?

He had always been better than me at this gods-forsaken game of ours. Just the other day, I had been giving him shit over it, too—the way he used his silver tongue and sex appeal to get what he wanted out of damn near anyone. I'd caught him laying it on the barmaid that afternoon, thick as honey.

"Oh, please," he had argued. "It's just another tool, one that makes for much easier investigations. Why resort to fear or violence if seduction works just as well?"

When I had suggested that perhaps it was unethical to toy with people's heartstrings like that, he'd doubled over laughing.

"Trust me, Arken. Nobody in this city is walking around with a broken heart over the likes of me."

But I had my doubts. I was also sincerely struggling to come up with a witty response as the influence of his sheer proximity was starting to overtake my wit.

Or maybe it was the way he looked like he was currently undressing me with his eyes.

Just a game. Get over yourself, Arken.

I was just about ready to shake it off and think up something clever when the bastard went for my damn throat.

"Oh," Kieran crooned softly, slipping a hand back under my jaw—this time with entirely different intent. He cocked his head gently, maintaining that searing eye contact before allowing his gaze to drift just a little bit lower. "I'm actually right, aren't I? You do..."

My heart beat scattered, frantic and erratic. *Perceptive motherfucker.* He knew godsdamned well...

But why was he staring at my mouth like that?

The sun had already started to set outside, and the orange glow of dusk wasn't doing me any favors. The warm panes of light poured through as the room began to darken, leaving his skin looking positively golden.

"Don't go silent on me now, sweetheart."

That was the second time he'd called me sweetheart tonight.

"Err. I... Um. Sorry. What was the question again?" I stammered.

Source be damned, I sounded pathetic. He chuckled softly, and the way it rumbled in his chest left my eyelids feeling heavy.

Why did he have to be so good at this?

Kieran gently stroked my cheek with the pad of his thumb, his dominant left hand still cradling my jaw. The other hand moved to brush a stray lock of hair behind my ear, and he let his fingertips brush skin ever so slightly, raising gooseflesh on my arms. I really hoped that wasn't obvious.

He drew his response out slowly, voice dripping with sensuality.

"The question was... Do you *enjoy* being put under duress, Arken?"

Gods above and below, I was being put under duress right here and now. *Just a game*, I reminded myself. There was no need to fixate on the way he'd just said my name like a prayer.

"That exists within the realm of possibilities, *Kieran*," I breathed, letting my arousal slip into his name in the same indecent way he'd uttered mine.

There we go, Arken. Two can play this game.

What I hadn't anticipated was the genuine flicker of surprise that would pass behind the lazy, bemused bedroom eyes he was giving me, or the way that for a moment, he seemed to struggle to return to form. It was only a moment, though, quickly replaced with a seductive and calculating half-smile.

I felt the lightest of pressure beneath my jaw as he began to tilt my face upward. We were close enough now that I could feel his breath against my lips, and it seemed like he was about to say something—another round of heavily weighted innuendo, if I had to guess.

I wasn't about to give him the chance. No, the gloves were off now, and before he could speak another stupid, sexy word, I leaned into his caress and...

I kissed him.

Though I'd closed my eyes out of habit, I could feel his mouth freeze under my lips—the briefest hesitation, followed by a small gasp that came and went so quickly I might have imagined it. But no, I felt that pull of air between us, just before he leaned into the kiss... and he leaned in hard.

Oh.

One hand slid around the nape of my neck as he pulled me even closer, his tongue brushing against my lower lip in gentle request. I let my mouth part for him, temporarily forgetting that this was supposed to be a game.

As Kieran's tongue began to explore my mouth, I could taste him. I found myself pleasantly surprised at the heady mix of black tea, a hint of citrus, and... clove, maybe? *Fuck*, he was good at this—I could feel every slow, deft stroke of his tongue all the way to my very core. Hesitant, I let my own tongue wander into his mouth, and was startled again by the sharpness of his canines.

I was running out of breath, and I pulled back just barely for a moment's pause, only for him to tighten his grip on my neck. Without warning, he planted a soft but demanding bite on my lower lip, tugging at it, pulling me back in. I felt heat pool at my core almost immediately, and in that moment—against my godsdamned will, *Fates above and leylines below be damned*—a small whimper of pleasure escaped my mouth.

Oh, fuck.

CHAPTER FIFTY-FOUR

KIERAN

Holy Hel, that sound.

That fucking sound.

Arken almost immediately leapt up off of my couch after the whimper left her lips, her cheeks flaming with embarrassment. I had to take a few seconds to blink, trying to process what had her so clearly horrified with herself.

Oh. She thought I had just been teasing her.

"That was so inappropriate, gods, I am so sorry," she said quickly, one hand still covering her mouth. She couldn't look me in the eye.

Inappropriate? Oh no, sweetheart.

This was probably the most appropriate thing that had ever fucking transpired between us, no matter how long we'd both been running from it. As she started to try and take a step back, perhaps to put some distance between us, I caught her by the wrist.

"Arken," I said, trying to keep my voice calm, though my heart was pounding. "Don't... Come back here, please."

Please don't run away from me, Arken. Not now.

I would beg, if she asked me to. I needed her to stay. I needed her, period.

She was staring at the carpet now, looking somewhat pained,

conflicted and still clearly mortified. When she finally peered back at me through those thick, dark lashes, I could see hints of shame lingering in those golden eyes.

I let my own smolder in her direction, finally letting her see just how fucking badly I wanted her. I licked at my lower lip absentmindedly, reveling in how it had swollen after she'd kissed me.

She kissed me.

"Stay," I requested softly.

"I—We... We really shouldn't do this, Kieran," she whispered back.

I knew that, I did. I just didn't care, not anymore. I had carried her weak, lifeless body out of the woods last night and almost lost myself inside the terror that I had been too late. What I was about to do would surely complicate things between us, but I didn't fucking care anymore.

"I know," I said, tilting my head. Studying her. Searching for what she really wanted. "I know we shouldn't. But since when do we always do what we're supposed to, Ark? Please, just come back here and kiss me again."

My voice had dropped so low that it nearly matched her hesitant whisper, and my mask crumbled. Because this had never really been a game. Not to me. There was no hiding the pleading behind my words, no way to disguise how much I wanted her or the fact that I would kill just to hear that she wanted me back.

I knew she did, but this was her decision to make.

"Would it help if I begged, sweetheart?" I asked with sincerity. I would much prefer to hear *her* beg—and hear that fucking whine again, for that matter—but I would beg for this.

"Maybe?" she said the word with indecision, as if it were a question as she pinched at the bridge of her nose with her free hand.

I still held her other wrist, and started to rub gentle circles against the inner skin there with the pad of my thumb. The small shiver it earned me was all it took for me to take my chances. I rose up from the couch, and started to gently tug her towards the hall.

Please.

I kept my pace slow and deliberate, giving her time to think. Her breathing was erratic, her chest flushed, the telltale signs of arousal there, but I also knew it could be anxiety. As utterly feral as the taste of her mouth had left me, hardly able to think about much else—I did distantly recall that there was a reason we had kept things platonic for so long.

In the grand scheme of things, though, all of those reasons felt like paper-thin excuses to avoid this, the most explosive chemistry I had ever experienced in my life.

My heart was beginning to pound as we passed by the doors of each of my spare rooms. I had probably fucked somebody in every last room in this townhouse, save one.

My own.

I had never let anyone else in that far, into the room where I slept every night. It felt too personal. Too intimate to sully with someone who meant little to me outside of flesh and release. It could only ever be her.

I swallowed hard, leaning gently against the open doorway and suddenly terrified as I met her golden gaze.

"Consider this me begging, Ark. I want this. I want *you*. Gods, you have no idea how long I've wanted this, how many times I've..."

I exhaled slowly as I trailed off, reaching out to trace her jawline with a fingertip, bringing her gaze back to mine. There was so much I wanted to say, but I didn't want to pressure her, either.

Her chest was starting to rise and fall faster, and she was biting her lip. Fuck. Was it anxiety, or arousal? For once, it was hard for me to tell—my head spinning, my keener senses still clouded by the taste of her lips.

She *kissed* me.

I cleared my throat. "Please also let me be transparent: I only want this if you do, Ark. You can say no, and I will drop it. Immediately. I can walk you home, and we can pretend this never happened. I promise you, I will."

But please say yes.

"So before I kiss you again and lose my ability to be the gentleman you deserve, Arken, I need to know. Would you rather go home?"

Please say no.

"No," she breathed, and elation shot through my veins for a moment before she stammered. "I mean, wait... Yes?"

My heart sank, but I gathered up as much self-control as possible to keep my expression indifferent.

"Okay," I replied, voice neutral. This was her choice.

She groaned, suddenly exasperated. "Fucking Hel, Kieran. I can't even think straight when you're looking at me like that."

I felt my heart skip a beat.

"No, I don't want to go home," Arken confessed. "Yes, I want this. I want you."

"Thank the gods," I swore, wrapping an arm around her waist to close the distance between us that had grown unbearable.

Thank the fucking gods.

CHAPTER FIFTY-FIVE

ARKEN

"Thank the gods," Kieran swore, closing the distance between us by wrapping one arm around my waist. His other hand found its way under my jaw again, tugging my face towards his.

He pulled my body closer while still walking backwards, as if he couldn't bear to keep his hands off me any longer. I couldn't bear it, either.

As we tumbled into bed together, the lingering scent of orange zest and cloves clung to the sheets, confirming my suspicions. These were his sheets. This was *his* bed. We weren't in some spare guest suite—this was his own private space. The realization sent a thrilling wave of pleasure through me.

Again, that man interrupted my entire train of thought—this time by rolling me over to my back in one fell swoop and straddling me so that my lap was in between his legs.

"Is this okay? Am I hurting you at all?" Kieran asked, his fingertips gently brushing over my torso where the Leshy had struck, where scar tissue had already started forming thanks to the dedicated efforts of the clerics.

I shook my head. "I'm good. The tincture is still working wonders," I breathed. "I can't feel a damn thing."

"Not a damn thing?" he teased, rolling his hips against mine.

A self-satisfied smirk curled across his mouth as I moaned softly, feeling exactly what he wanted me to feel.

Godsdamn.

My eyes roved over the sight of him on top of me with both awe and greed as he shrugged off his jacket, his hips still pressing into mine. Deft fingers made their way from his collar to his navel, swiftly unbuttoning his shirt. I marveled at the hard expanse of muscle revealed, the gleaming golden-brown skin made all that more beautiful by a collection of scars, and those strange, dark tattoos. Hungry and aching, my eyes followed that thin trail of black hair from his belly to below the waist of his well-tailored trousers. Now in a state of partial undress, Kieran threw both articles of clothing off the bed so aggressively that he overshot—the buttons of his coat making a sharp little *thwack* as they hit the wall.

"So violent," I giggled.

He grinned, his fingers already beginning to toy with the hem of my sweater. "You have no idea. May I?"

"By all means," I offered, lifting my arms above my head.

Slowly, Kieran began to push the fabric up. Too slowly. Desperate, I started to writhe beneath him before reaching down, attempting to speed up the process. He caught both of my wrists in one hand without even trying.

"Oh no you don't," he growled, shoving them both up against his headboard. "Do you have any idea how long I've been waiting to do this? I'm gonna be taking my sweet ass time with you, Little Conduit. Let me savor this."

I shivered, absolutely fixated on the commanding look in his eyes as he released my wrists and shifted himself, leaning down to press a kiss just below my navel. One of his arms snaked underneath me as he did so, gently lifting up my torso. With the other, he tugged my sweater up and over my head, the static cling taking the chemise I'd been wearing below right along with it.

That left us both naked from the waist up, and there was an

unholy degree of reverence in his gaze as he looked down at me, eyes coasting over every inch of exposed skin.

"Fucking Hel. You're so beautiful," he whispered hoarsely.

"Get back down here and say that to my face, Vistarii," I demanded, drunk off his praise.

He smirked. "Oh, with pleasure, Asher."

In one fluid motion, Kieran shifted himself again, this time so that we were nearly chest to chest. As he shoved one of his knees in between my thighs, I couldn't help but wonder if he could feel how wet I already was for him. These tights were far too thin to conceal my arousal for long. He kept his torso hovering just above mine, his body forming a cage of muscle and skin and heat around me as he leaned most of his body weight against his forearms. His eyes gleamed with adoration and something a bit darker as he spoke.

"You are," he whispered. "You're so fucking beautiful, Arken. It devastates me. You know that, don't you?"

Abyss take me. I couldn't handle what his affection did to me, it was driving me insane. I slid my hands around his waist, digging my nails into his lower back and begging him to come closer. I wanted to feel the weight of his body against mine, I needed to know what it felt like, I had imagined it so many times...

As my nails bit into flesh, Kieran gasped, his eyes going wild as whatever grip he'd had on his self-control seemed to be severed. He didn't want to hurt me, I knew—but I hadn't been lying when I said I couldn't feel the ache of my wounds. Even if I could, I'd never tell. Everything about this moment would be worth the pain, should it return. So I dug my nails in harder, and my reward was instant: His body crashing into mine, his mouth claiming me again with unapologetic fervor as we picked up where we'd left off in his living room.

I groaned as I felt the warmth of his bare skin against my own, and the hard length of him pressing up against my inner thigh. As I slid my tongue back in his mouth, fingers tangling themselves in his soft hair, I could feel him twitch and throb.

For one gasping moment, our mouths broke apart. He ran his crooked nose against my jawline as I tried to catch my breath, tilting my head back against the pillows in pleasure. It was then that I noticed his windows. The curtains were still open, leaving us in clear view of any occasional passers by in the alley. *Whoops.*

"Kieran—" I started, struggling for coherency as he was nipping at my earlobe.

"Hmm?"

"I'm going to hate myself for asking this because I'm fairly certain I'll actually die if you leave this bed, but... could you close those curtains? I'm afraid I'm not much of an exhibitionist."

Kieran chuckled, the low vibrations of his rumble running straight between my legs.

"Anything for you, Little Conduit," he purred. "But I do think I've had enough of your little near death experiences." Lazily, he flicked his fingers in the direction of the curtains in question. "Good thing I don't *have* to leave this bed to keep you all to myself."

I felt a ripple of his power pulse through the air as pitch-black Shadow began to creep across each pane of glass like hoarfrost. The umbral effect coated his windows until they were fully opaque, darkening the room.

"Better?"

I nodded, biting my lip.

"It's okay, Ark, you can admit you find my arcana sexy," he teased.

I did, and he knew it. He didn't use it particularly often around me, though I suppose I wouldn't even know if he had. Such was the nature of Shadow, but I had always been equal parts attracted to and fascinated by Kieran's darkness.

His mouth returned to my neck, the clever bastard having already caught on to the fact that I was... *excessively* sensitive there.

I ran my hands over his thighs and felt them flex beneath my touch as I replied.

"Would you laugh at me if I confessed that I actually do find it sexy?"

I felt his mouth curl into a smile against my skin. He didn't laugh, but he was most definitely going to remember I said that. No chance in Hel would he let me live that down, but I didn't even care. His touch felt like heaven as he ran his fingers through my hair, continuing to press kisses up the column of my neck, straying towards my jaw.

More.

I needed more, and wrapped one leg around his waist just so that I could grind myself against the warmth of him, aching for his entry. Kieran groaned in response, throaty and low and I swear my eyelids fluttered involuntarily. Gods, that sound was fucking hot. I wanted to hear it again, and so I stretched my arms out above my head before allowing them to wander—but it was like he could read my mind. Again, he caught both of my wrists in one hand and pinned them against the headboard.

"I told you, Arken..." he growled.

"Hmm?"

"I am taking my sweet. ass. time. with you."

"Gods," I groaned as he pressed the pad of his thumb against my lower lip. I licked it, in protest. "Are you trying to torture me?"

He snorted. "If I was trying to torture you, sweetheart... You would know. And you'd thank me for it."

Oh, fuck.

"So I *was* right," he chuckled, gaze darkening as he read my expression. Perceptive son of a bitch.

"I can neither confirm nor deny that statement," I breathed.

"Uh huh."

As his mouth returned to my neck, biting down as if to prove a point, I gasped. Not just because of the way he ran his tongue over the bitten flesh, but rather... something else entirely. As Kieran continued to kiss me, running his hands anywhere and everywhere they could find purchase, I could detect what felt like... curling wisps of smoke. A cool, weightless darkness licking its way across my skin, too, creating delicious contrast with the pressure of his touch and the warmth of his breath. Heated, heavy breath that was growing more and more ragged by the minute.

But Fates, what even was that? His Resonance? I opened my eyes, but there were no tendrils of Shadow to be found. Whatever he was doing, it didn't seem to be intentional, and it didn't exactly *feel* like the buzzing arcana that I'd drawn from before. This felt different, somehow. More like an extension of his touch. Did he even know he was doing it?

But by the time Kieran's mouth had made its way from my collarbone down to one of my breasts, I lost any ability to theorize... or even *think* for that matter. I didn't care what it was, I just didn't want him to stop.

"Gods, Kier," I moaned, tossing my head back against his pillows as his tongue drew slow, intentional circles around my nipple, leaving it swollen and sensitive.

He hummed appreciatively as he read me like an open book, taking the other nipple between two fingers and kneading softly. He tugged at the former with his teeth.

This man was going to be my undoing.

We both knew this was a bad idea. Despite our explosive chemistry, despite how perfect every inch of him felt beneath my hands... I knew there was a reason we'd both kept one another at arm's length, I just couldn't exactly recall what it— *Oh, sweet Hel.* How the fuck was I supposed to think straight when his fingers were stroking up against the center of me now, with only my tights serving as a barrier between us?

"You like that, sweetheart?" he murmured.

"Yesss," I hissed. I very much liked that, and I needed more. I rocked my hips desperately against his hand, forcing his knuckles to graze against my clit beneath the clothing—the existence of which was growing more and more maddening with every passing second.

"Good," he growled, pressing those fingers against me harder, tongue returning to my nipple as he grabbed the surrounding flesh, hard.

That strange, dark sensation returned, this time with tendrils weaving their way around my throat as Kieran trailed a series of love bites across my chest. The feeling only intensified, tightening when he slipped several fingers beneath the waistband of my tights, teasing at the skin just above my panties.

Gods above and below.

He hadn't been lying when he said he'd be taking his sweet ass time. My eyelids fluttered closed again as I focused on the feeling of his every ministration. Finally, when I felt like I couldn't take it anymore, I tugged at his hair. Releasing my poor, swollen nipples, Kieran kissed me hard on the mouth before pushing himself off me, abruptly climbing out of bed.

"Excuse me, sir," I objected, and something in his eyes seemed to flash. "Where do you think you're going?"

"Oh, I'm not going anywhere," he replied, grabbing me by the hips and pulling me towards the edge of the mattress so that he was standing in between my legs. "But uhh, quick question."

"Hmm?"

"Do you always glow for people in bed, or...?"

Did I always *what now*? I glanced down at my fingertips. *Oh.* They were, indeed, glowing. Godsdamn it. I really needed to work on controlling that. I was well-established as a Light Conduit by now, but gods forbid any of the other elements come out and play the next time I felt a strong wave of emotion... or pleasure.

Kieran cleared his throat a little, still looking down at me with bemused curiosity.

"I can't say that's ever happened before," I confessed.

He looked a smidge too pleased with that answer, the cocky bastard. And I expected him to tease me, but instead, Kieran laced our fingers together and allowed his aether to manifest, Shadows creeping up slowly until they coated his hand like some sort of arcane paint.

The tenebrous tendrils crawled from his fingertips, up his wrist and forearm. Again, I felt connected to his arcana in a way that felt far more intimate and personal than it should. I didn't dare ask him if that was intentional. Instead, I turned my focus to mirroring his little trick, centering my mind. I allowed the Light aether to extend beyond the tips of my fingers, the sensation tickling a bit as it grew and stretched, until I wore my arcana like a matching pair of gloves.

I wasn't sure what would happen at first, half expecting that one of our elements would cancel out the presence of the other. We were elemental parallels, after all, with our specializations lying at the very opposite ends of the aetheric spectrum. But no... there was nothing negated—the dark, smoky tendrils wrapping around his fingers just served to amplify the glow emanating from my own. In turn, the wisps of darkness encircling his hands were illuminated in a haunting, ethereal sort of way.

For a moment, we just lingered like that in silence, mutually entranced by the view. It reminded me of summer nights in the forest, like flickering fireflies in the dark.

"Well, that's rather pretty," Kieran murmured.

"*You're* rather pretty," I teased.

"Mmm, and here I was thinking you'd never notice," he quipped back, paired with a smile so genuine that it almost *hurt*.

I laid back in bed, leaving myself just about eye level with his waist, and stole a hungry glance at the way his pants were beginning to slide from his hips. Kieran caught my gaze and held it, leaning his tall frame over me as he released his hold on one of our interlaced hands, drawing the other one up to his lips to kiss my palm. Without breaking eye contact, he guided one of my fingers into his mouth, sucking at the tip of it softly. The look in his eyes was so godsdamned indecent while he did so that I was already on the cusp of release. Over a godsdamned *glance.*

Growing impatient again, I took it upon myself to scoot forward and wrap my legs around his waist where he stood, pulling him in towards me. Kieran hissed, but leaned into it, pushing his trapped erection up against me for just a moment before pulling himself back.

"Easy, Arken," he warned, tugging at my tights. "I still have to get these off."

"The tights? Or me?" I smirked.

"Both," he replied simply, canines gleaming as he returned my wicked grin. "In quick succession."

"Aw, what ever happened to taking your sweet time, Kier?" I teased.

"The road to Hel is paved with good intentions."

I laughed. He was so godsdamed clever. Even in my depraved state of mind, about to be entirely naked in his bed, I had to appreciate the quickness of his wit. But it wasn't Kieran's wit that I was appreciating when he knelt down after peeling the fabric from my legs, spreading my thighs apart with a firm grip.

It was his fucking mouth.

CHAPTER FIFTY-SIX

KIERAN

The road to Hel is paved with good intentions.

If that wasn't the story of my entire godsdamned life—but truth be told? I couldn't care less at the moment. Every single gasp that came out of her mouth was glorious validation that I hadn't been alone in my longing. Miraculously, it seemed that Arken wanted this just as badly as I did.

It somehow made up for all of that suffering in silence, if only because I knew now that I hadn't been suffering alone. But *gods*, I didn't want her to suffer any longer. I never wanted her to suffer again.

I would give this woman anything she ever wanted, so long as she asked for it with that same breathy moan. I'd set the world ablaze. Fates, I'd set *myself* on fire just to see another flicker of the desperate, needy hunger in her eyes as I stripped her of what remained of her clothing.

As I pulled off Arken's tights, I drank in the sight of her—entirely exposed now, and writhing with anticipation. I marveled at the way my touch seemed to affect her, raising gooseflesh anywhere I wanted with the slightest brush of my knuckles against her sensitive skin.

"*Kieran*," she groaned softly as I dropped to my knees before her.

"Yes, sweetheart?"

The only response I received was a subtle whimper as she let her legs part for me, and heat pooled in my lower abdomen, my cock twitching in response to the stunning sight. As I dipped my head between those lovely, soft thighs to meet what was waiting, I was certain.

All of the torture. All of the waiting. All of the risks be damned.

To see her glistening cunt drip for me like this? The fucking *sounds* she made as I lowered my mouth to taste her?

Oh, this had been worth it all along.

And perhaps I could have brought myself to regret my impulsivity later, had I not felt her quiver against my tongue—had I not tasted the sweetness of her impending release as she called my name out again into the darkness, those glowing little fingertips pulsating with Light as they tangled themselves gently in my hair. So eager. So encouraging.

"*Fuck*, Kier," she moaned. "That feels so... You feel so godsdamned good."

"Yeah?" I whispered, teasing at her swollen clit with a single fingertip before replacing it with my tongue again, savoring the taste.

"Yeah," she panted, tossing her head back against the pillows. "Please don't stop."

"Who said anything about stopping, Asher?" I growled, taking hold of her hips and tugging her ass closer to the edge of the bed.

I had only just gotten started. I had no self-restraint left, I needed to *devour* her. Evidence of her arousal was already slick against my chin and throat, and it was somehow not enough. It wasn't until I felt her buck and shudder, her body teetering on the edge of orgasm, that I finally pulled back, planting a quick bite down on the tender flesh of her inner thigh. Her whimpers returned, and my eyes nearly rolled into the back of my head with pleasure as she fisted both hands in my hair and tugged me up hard so that my chin was now resting on her belly.

"I need you," she whined, her golden eyes wide and wild as they gazed back down at me. The kohl around her eyelids was smudged, and her lower lip swollen as if she'd been biting down this entire time. "*Please*, Kieran, I can't—"

If I wasn't already ravenous and rock hard, the sound of her begging would have been my undoing. But she didn't need to beg for me... Not yet.

"*Shhh*, sweetheart," I whispered hoarsely, rising to my feet and crawling back into bed with her. "I know." As soon as I slipped in beside her and pulled the blankets over us both, her hands were on me, small keening noises escaping her lips.

"I need you," she repeated, tugging me closer.

"I'm here, Ark," I murmured, burying my face against her neck. "I'm right here."

It had been damn near an entire year of self-restraint, and after all this time, we had finally given in.

And when I finally slid inside her, shuddering at the sensation of her flawlessly perfect fit, I cursed myself for ever having held back in the first place.

This was rapture. It was ruination. It was everything I had ever fucking wanted, but never once dared to dream of experiencing. Made for me. She was fucking *made for me.*

And she was so. fucking. tight.

"Oh. Oh my gods," she whispered, tiny tears welling up in her eyes as I sank myself deeper, inch by inch.

"*Fuck*," I groaned, feeling her clench around my cock as she took me to the hilt. I slid my hands up her waist, still trying to be delicate where the fresh, pink scar tissue had formed across one side of her ribcage.

"You don't have to do that," Arken half-murmured, half-moaned.

"Don't have to do what, exactly?" I asked. I hadn't even started moving yet, I was far too content with the feeling of her hot, wet warmth coating my cock. Obsessing over the way she was already twitching, spasming beneath me after one slow, measured thrust.

Those star-flecked eyes of hers seemed to darken and heat beneath her lashes, precious metal going absolutely molten as she held my gaze with confidence.

"You don't have to be so gentle, Kier. You're not going to break me."

"No," I breathed, extending a hand to caress her cheek. "I won't break you, Little Conduit. Not tonight."

She sucked in a sharp breath at the implication, and I smirked.

"But if you want it rough, pretty girl, I will so very happily oblige. Is that what you want from me right now?"

"Please," she whispered.

Gods. I fucking knew it. Oh, I was going to have so much fun with that little masochistic streak of hers. Another night, though. No matter how well that tincture was working, this woman had been on her deathbed not twenty-four hours prior. She needed time to recover... and regain some stamina, for the things I had in mind. But I could give her this.

"Lay on your stomach," I instructed, immediately missing the slick heat of her cunt as I withdrew, shoving the blankets aside. "Wait, actually—"

On second thought, I leaned in and kissed her hard, needing the taste of her mouth paired with the taste of her arousal that still lingered on my tongue. She moaned as I invaded her mouth relentlessly, my fingers teasing at her clit just to get her all worked up before I flipped her over.

"*Now* you can lay on your stomach," I murmured.

Arken tossed her hair as she shifted, and I let myself admire every inch of her flawless flesh, from her pretty little shoulder blades to the dip of her spine, right down to the freckles beneath those dimples just above the ample expanse of her ass and thighs. Fuck me, this woman was an actual goddess. Under any other circumstance, I could study this view for hours just to memorize every curve and crevice, but I had run out of patience for that slow admiration. Another time. Another night. I just needed to be inside her again.

And so I took hold of my throbbing cock with one rough stroke, notching myself against that exposed sliver of pink flesh that was still so wet and wanting. Arken whimpered as I placed one hand against the small of her back, pressing her hips down hard into the mattress, holding her in place.

"Tell me what you want again, Little Conduit."

"I *need* you to fuck me, Kieran," she panted. "*Hard.*"

Music to my godsdamned ears.

If I thought the sounds that Arken Asher had made as I ate her out were heavenly, they were downright *tame* compared to what escaped her throat as I drove the entirety of my length back into her weeping cunt without hesitation. Gasps became moans became an agonized, garbled mess of whimpers and whines as my hips found a brutal rhythm, pistoning in and out of her with as much force as I could muster.

Groaning, I ran one hand over my face in utter disbelief as I kept going, keeping a relentless pace. How did she feel this fucking good?

"Don't stop," she begged again. "Fates, please don't stop. Gods *fucking* damnit, I can't—"

"You can take it," I groaned, grabbing hold of her ass cheek with my free hand. "I know you can."

And oh, she took it. She took it so godsdamned well from this position, rocking her hips and pushing her ass back to meet my every thrust and take me even harder, deeper. I couldn't even begin to describe how good it felt to feel Arken slam and tighten against my cock, over and over again. I was quickly losing myself to delirium, to this fever dream of perfect pleasure, a riot of heat and friction.

I had sampled my way through half of Sophrosyne at this point, having lost count of the notches in my bedpost years ago. I *thought* I had enjoyed plenty of great sex in the past—but that was *nothing*. All of it had been pitiful compared to... whatever the Hel *this* was.

This was everything. It was ecstasy. She was so—

"Gods!" Arken screamed, the sound slightly muffled as she pushed her face into the mattress. Gooseflesh raised on my arms in response to her piercing cry. At the soul-deep sense of fulfillment that I felt, knowing I was giving her just as much as I was taking—*stealing*—from the satin in between her thighs.

I was close. I was so godsdamned close already. I had *never* been this quick off the mark but she just felt so incredibly divine that I could feel my muscles start to tense, my balls beginning to tighten. But there was no chance in Hel that I was getting off before she did. I bit down on my lip, pouring everything I had into penetrating her faster, harder, coaxing her right to the edge with me.

As she started to tense, I leaned forward and slid both hands underneath her to clutch at her breasts, kneading those sensitive little peaks and drawing her back flush against my chest. I could taste the salt of her sweat as I ran my tongue against her neck, and her entire body went taut like a bowstring in my arms.

"Kier, I'm gonna—"

"Come for me," I demanded, with more authority than I'd earned. But it worked, and with one more rough thrust, we found simultaneous release, Arken's tight cunt pulsating as I spent myself inside her.

Godsdamn.

"Fates," Arken panted as she recovered, flipping herself back over and tossing her head back against the haphazard pile of pillows. The smile that spread across her face was borderline delirious as her eyelids fluttered closed. "That was so... *Godsdamn.* Is this even real? Are *you* even real? Am I dreaming? Good *gods.*"

I chuckled, smirking with dark pride and a deep sense of self-satisfaction.

"Oh, my sweet Little Conduit," I murmured, leaning in close to the shell of her ear. "I'm very, very real. And I'm not done with you yet."

✧ ✧ ✧

Even hours later, I couldn't bring myself to regret it.

As Arken slept soundly in my arms, entirely spent for the night, I couldn't bring myself to regret a single godsdamned thing.

All the self-control in the world couldn't have stopped me from giving her anything she wanted the moment I heard that beg beneath her whine. I had needed her, she had needed me, and maybe we both knew better, but fuck.

There was just something about having her here, in my own private space, for the first time. It felt so natural and easy. We had been so close as I tended to her scraped up little head that I could feel her breath against my cheek and that alone had been intoxicating enough.

Only under duress...

Fucking Hel.

No, I couldn't bring myself to regret any of this, though flickers of guilt passed through me every now and again as I stroked her hair.

Had I manipulated her into this?

Consent was paramount to me, and I knew I had given her adequate space to make her own decisions, but I knew damn well what I was doing, teasing her like that after tending to her head. I could tell that she thought we were just playing that same old game, toeing the line to see who would chicken out first, but she hadn't realized I was playing to win this time around. Or that she was my prize.

The moment she'd kissed me, I had gotten exactly what I wanted out of that little exchange. I hadn't even dreamed that I would actually get her to kiss me—would have never guessed that I would get *any* of this—but I'd needed to try. I felt like I would've died on the spot if I ignored those impulses again.

Still, perhaps it had been wrong of me to push her like that. To even tempt her in the first place. But fuck if the taste of her mouth wasn't worth it. And I would go to the literal ends of this realm and back to taste the rest of her again.

Just before Arken fell asleep, I felt her lips move as she murmured against my skin.

"I would hardly call that duress, Vistarii."

I chuckled softly.

"All in due time, Little Conduit."

CHAPTER FIFTY-SEVEN

ARKEN

The days that followed were an inexplicable blur of heated flesh, tangled limbs, and gasping pleasure—all sought out with reckless abandon. The moment Kieran had touched me behind closed doors, the very second his mouth had met mine, it was as though I had never been touched before. Not in this lifetime, nor any other. I was a ravenous, starving thing, losing hours upon days of my life to the throes of desire—my most carnal impulses. Greedily, I took, and graciously, he gave.

Kieran and I had already been inseparable before—but now? *Gods above and below*, we were practically living together. As soon as I got out of a lecture, or within minutes of Kieran finishing his shifts, we both ended up in the same place, day after day: At the other's doorstep.

We hadn't spent a single night alone after falling into bed together that first night. That first kiss had been over a week ago now… and yet every spare second, *every waking moment* was being invaded by this desperate need to be near him, this driving force that I couldn't quite comprehend.

Strangely, I found that I did not mind the intrusion. I was typically a creature who craved her personal space, needing time alone from the world to reset after each day. I was too easily overwhelmed, so often overstimulated... but Kieran had become my reset, my respite.

This wasn't just lust, it was *lunacy*—and I was blissfully lost in this mutual madness of ours.

We had even tried to stay away from one another last night. It had been an experiment of sorts, an attempt to convince ourselves that we could preserve some semblance of rationality in whatever the Hel was going on between us. But then Kieran kept sending me dirty little notes all godsdamned night until I had outright *demanded* he come over and make good on certain promises—and he showed up with that stupid smirk plastered to his face like that had been his plan all along.

Cocky bastard.

At least today was his day off. We'd actually managed to leave the bedroom for once in favor of visiting one of his favorite galleries in the arts district, where a local painter had some new works on display. Kieran had failed to mention the subject matter of this particular exhibit, though.

A stunning study of oil paintings and the feminine form... with most of said feminine forms being bound by ropes in a variety of intricate patterns and positions. It was all rather tasteful, but the man knew damn well what he was doing.

"Trying to imply something here, Captain?" I murmured quietly as we browsed through the gallery, which was largely empty this time of day.

"I have no idea what you're talking about," he replied, his tall figure leaning over mine from behind, one hand resting against the small of my back.

It hadn't taken him very long at all to start touching me in public, in subtle ways like this that made my heartbeat erratic for multiple reasons.

The two of us were particularly physical people, and it's not like we had really shied away from touching one another before all of this played out—we'd often nudge and shove the other around, even as friends.

As friends.

My mind lingered on the word for just a moment before it became deeply uncomfortable, and so I simply brushed it off. I could unpack that later, at another time where his breath wasn't hot against my neck.

"Ah, right, of course not," I parried, already bracing myself for how he was going to react to my snark. "Because that whole *duress* thing was just a joke, right?"

I felt him stiffen behind me, and could practically feel the heat radiate off his body as he dipped his head, his mouth beside my ear again. His voice dropped dangerously low.

"Is this really the game you wanna play right now, Little Conduit?"

"I have no idea what you're talking about," I mimicked.

"Hmm," was all he said at first as we moved on to the next image.

"Would you like to be tied up like this, beautiful? I wouldn't even need the rope," he whispered.

I swallowed hard and tried not to show how flustered the thought left me. We were playing a different sort of game these days, though the win condition was similar: *Who would break first?*

"Hmm," I replied, mimicking him yet again.

"Oh, I am going to fucking ruin you when we get home," he hissed beneath his breath.

When we get home. It must've been a slip of the tongue, really. It was easier to say than *my townhouse,* or *your apartment,* or *the studio.* That was all.

"Don't tempt me with a good time," I said.

"Why not? I'm so very good at it…" Kieran trailed off, running his fingers softly against my exposed shoulders.

In response to his touch, I leaned back against where he still stood behind me. After taking a careful glance to confirm we were still alone, I very intentionally ground my ass up against his groin. I heard his sharp inhale at the same time I realized that he was already hard.

Insatiable.

"Who's under duress now?" I teased, pressing my palm up against his cock and rubbing slowly. My pulse quickened, though I kept a straight face on the off chance that somebody walked in on us.

Kieran groaned softly under his breath.

"*Godsdamnit, Arken...*"

That only encouraged me to attempt to subtly dip my hand beneath the waistband of his pants and feel him up further. I felt his rough, calloused fingers encircle my wrist gently before clamping down like a human shackle.

"Your place or mine?" he asked roughly.

"Whichever one is closer."

◇ ◇ ◇

"*Gods,*" Kieran gasped as I traced the pulsing vein beneath his jawline with the tip of my tongue.

He had all but dragged me back to his townhouse after I had touched him in the gallery, his pace so brisk that it had been an effort to keep up as he kept hold of my wrist. Technically speaking, I think it had been my apartment that was closer, and he had just enjoyed watching me squirm with anticipation.

"Have I mentioned that I've wanted that smart mouth of yours on me since the first godsdamned moment I set eyes on you?"

My ego purred at the confession, and I smiled, lips still pressed against the warmth of his skin, where I could practically feel his pulse racing beneath the surface. He was so reactive to my touch, and I could hardly contain what euphoria that was awakening within me.

"What, in the Wyldwoods?" I asked, running my fingers through his hair.

These raven-dark strands were much silkier than I'd ever imagined.

"Before," he confessed, his breathing growing more and more ragged with every touch. "I was in the Wyldwoods that day, looking for you."

My heart fluttered for a moment and I paused, curiosity piqued.

"I beg your pardon?"

"Don't you dare stop," he demanded, both hands squeezing at my hips as I had him straddled on the couch—where all of *this* had started in the first place.

"Explain yourself, then, Vistarii," I murmured, leaning back down to trail more kisses up the side of his neck.

"I had seen you a few days prior," he began, lips brushing up against the shell of my ear. I shivered.

"You had your head buried in a book, on your way to the Biblyos or something. I was intrigued," he explained. "And devastatingly attracted to you."

I rolled my hips at that, grinding into where I could feel him hard and ready underneath me.

"Mm, couldn't tell," I teased again, remembering the way he'd made his point last week.

At that, Kieran grabbed a fistful of my hair at the nape of my neck and tugged down, hard enough so that my head was tipped back, my throat exposed to his eager mouth. I gasped at the pain for the briefest of moments, and then felt myself melt against him as it faded into a warm, tantalizing ache.

"You sure about that, Little Conduit?"

That was one of his favorite questions as of late. I had no coherent thoughts in this position, all I could really do was whimper as he bit down—just once, and gently, before continuing his explanation.

"I signed up for that guard shift in hopes that I'd see you again."

"Lucky you," I whispered.

"Lucky me," he whispered back, his voice a blend of rasp and gravel. My eyelids began to flutter at the sound alone, and then he bit down again. *Hard.*

"Fuck me," I hissed.

"I'm about to," he growled back.

It was then, Fates be *damned*, that we both heard a sharp knock at his door.

"I swear to the fucking Source, if that is either Hans or Jeremiah, I am going to—" I started.

"*Shit*," Kieran interrupted, glancing at the clock. "Oh, I am so screwed."

It was both Hans *and* Jeremiah, looking gravely concerned at the fact that Kieran hadn't shown up to an important strategy meeting this morning. All it had taken was one look at me, standing off to the side with tousled hair, disheveled clothes, and a furious blush, for the two men to burst out laughing.

"My gods," Hans said, jaw practically on the floor. "There's a first time for everything, ain't there, Jer?"

"Don't start," Kieran warned.

"Ooof, you got him good, Ark," Jeremiah noted, tilting his head to get a look at the bruise that was blooming on one side of his neck.

I covered my face with my hands, mildly mortified.

"Oh, don't be shy, Arken," Hans laughed. "It's not like we didn't see it coming. Kier gets 'em all eventually."

"*Hans,*" Kieran snapped.

His lieutenant winced slightly, before straightening. The other, more level-headed officer stepped in, offering an apologetic glance in my direction.

"We covered for you at the meeting, said that you'd sent a sprite this morning suggesting you weren't feeling well, Captain. Commander Ka would like to see you as soon as you're... uhh, recovered," Jeremiah explained.

"You uhh, might want to recover quick, by the way," Hans added. "There are some... *things* you need to know."

Kieran's lieutenants knew that I wouldn't pry, that I respected the secrecy in their line of work, but they still didn't quite know how to deal with my presence when it came to discussing confidential subjects.

"Go," I told him. "Leave a key or something, I'll lock up before I head home."

"You could always stay here," Kieran offered gently. The two men behind him exchanged a look, but tried to be subtle about it.

"I have a lecture," I replied apologetically. "But here, let me just clean up real quick—"

"No, don't rush," Kieran said, pulling his ring of keys from his pocket and deftly removing the one to the front door of his townhouse. I recognized the old-fashioned looking handle, oddly ornate compared to what I assumed were other keys related to work.

"I'll come pick this up from you tonight, okay?"

"Alright," I replied, not meeting his eyes. I was feeling more tender than I cared to admit as I mentally braced myself for his absence. Truthfully, I would have much preferred to spend another day or three—*or another nine*—in bed with him, but I was a selfish, greedy creature.

Kieran paused for a moment, studying my face, before he turned around and slammed the door on his lieutenants' faces without warning.

I heard a muffled noise of confusion from the other side, but didn't even have time to laugh before Kieran had me up against the wall in the foyer, his mouth on mine and hands cradling my face.

"Later," he swore as he pulled away from the kiss. "We'll pick right back up where we started, I promise."

My heart skipped a beat or two as he pressed his thumb against my lower lip. I could see the conflict in his eyes, how he didn't want to leave, but his sense of duty was the one thing that could claw him away from sex.

"Don't miss me too much," I murmured, attempting to be demure.

"Ah, I don't make promises I can't keep," he replied. "I'll see you later, beautiful."

CHAPTER FIFTY-EIGHT

KIERAN

To no surprise, Hans and Jeremiah were waiting for me outside.

"I appreciate the two of you stepping in to cover for me this morning," I sighed, running my hand over my face. In all my years serving the Elder Guard, I had never missed a meeting. I had never even been *late*.

"Of course," Jeremiah said casually, though he kept his face fixed on the road ahead, the corner of his mouth slightly upturned.

"I really don't know how it slipped my mind that there was a briefing."

"You sure about that one, Cap?" Hans snickered, and Jeremiah promptly smacked his fellow lieutenant upside the head.

"I told you to drop it," Jer hissed under his breath.

I rolled my eyes.

"Nah, it's fair of him to give me shit for once. It's not like me to get *that* distracted by sex. I've admittedly been out of focus lately."

"Can't imagine why," Hans said airily, still smirking to himself.

"You got something more specific to say, Deering?" I challenged.

Hans shrugged.

"Just never thought I'd see the day."

Jeremiah groaned, as if this was precisely what he'd been

instructing his fellow officer to avoid talking about. Why, though?

"And what day is that, dare I ask?" I challenged again with a raised brow. They were acting strange, and I was exhausted.

"Oh, come on now, K. Don't play dumb when it's this obvious. We're not the ones with a blind eye."

"Will you just spit it out, asshole?" I grumbled, growing irritated as the pair of them glanced back at me like I was missing something.

"Just never thought I'd see the day you caught feelings, sir," Hans laughed. "But hey, I'm happy for you. So is Jer, even if the bastard won't admit it."

"I never said I wasn't happy for him," Jeremiah countered. "Just that you should keep your damn mouth shut about it."

"It should hardly be news to either of you that I care about Arken," I reasoned.

"I think it's a little more than—" Hans found himself interrupted as Jeremiah shoved him harshly off the road, causing him to stumble.

"No, we knew," Jeremiah said. "But... If I may, sir. Are you sure this is a good idea? You and Ark? Thought you two were keeping things, uhh, platonic."

I bristled under the implication. The unspoken concern that I would toss Arken aside eventually. I exhaled slowly through my nose, not wanting to get overly defensive when I knew Jeremiah meant well.

"I don't mean—I just. We like the girl, Captain. We like having her around, too, you know."

"It's not like that," I replied. "Arken's not going anywhere."

"Right," Hans added. "Because you *care about her*."

"Is that such a crime?" I snapped.

"'Course not. I just think it's hilarious that you think that's all—"

"Hans." Jeremiah warned, his tone dropping deadly low, more

serious this time.

Though I understood where both of these men were coming from, I wasn't in the mood to think about it. I knew that I had a certain pattern of behavior, yes. And Arken and I had yet to define exactly what had been transpiring between us as of late.

In our defense, we hadn't exactly had the *time*. We'd been fucking like rabbits for over nine days straight, utterly ravenous. Nine days, and it was still all that I could think about when I was at work, or when she was in lectures. This twinned sense of addiction was starting to feel like it was more than just a consequence of a year's worth of pining and sexual tension. If that were the case, surely we would have simmered down by now. We hadn't, and I had neither the time nor the attention span to explore whatever else it could be. I was too busy burying myself in her. Losing myself in her as often as fucking possible.

All that I knew was that I had no interest in pushing her away. Not when I was constantly desperate to pull her closer. I mean, shit—I had just missed a meeting for the first time in my career because I'd been all too happy to let myself be distracted by her all morning.

Truthfully, I didn't know if any of this was a good idea, but I wasn't going to stop myself any time soon.

✧ ✧ ✧

I did my best to shake off the petty irritation towards my lieutenants as I reported in to my commander.

"How's the girl? Still recovering alright?" Hanjae asked.

"Yes, sir."

I didn't elaborate, and he gave me a long look before speaking again.

"It's not my business, and to be blunt, I don't want to know.

But for the sake of our work—and given her rarity—I must ask that you try to preserve a respectful relationship with the Light Conduit, whatever else transpires."

I nodded.

"Understood, sir."

"As for what you missed this morning... Well, we're not quite sure what to make of it, and I was hoping to get your take."

"What's going on?"

"After the Leshy attack, we sent some of Rorick's rangers to scan through the Wyldwoods, to make sure that the creature had been traveling alone. Though they didn't find any more traces of daemon activity, they did pick up on something... odd."

"Odd in what way?"

"That's the thing. We're not even sure. According to the rangers, it was some residual arcane energy that felt off somehow. Foreign. They couldn't really describe it, but reported that it felt distinctly different from a Conduit or even an Aetherborne's magick, and it was scattered around in pockets of the wood, but it faded too fast to track."

Foreign aether? Scattered around in pockets? That was... unsettling.

What Hanjae was describing was simple aetheric reverberation. There were certain types of magick—arcane methods that weren't taught here—that drew so much energy at once that they would leave behind an echo of power before the aether could be reabsorbed by the surrounding flora and fauna. The rangers had found these echoes throughout the forest, but I had only drawn from my blood magick *once*. And it sure as Hel shouldn't have taken over a week to dissipate.

"That's strange," I said. "I didn't sense anything other than the Leshy that night. And you said they found no other trace of daemonic activity? How far into the Wyldwoods did they go?"

"They've been at it all week, so they covered the whole damn forest. Nothing."

"I'll send my cadre in as well. See if there's anything they can find that the rangers might have missed."

My commander nodded.

"We'll also be setting up regular patrol shifts in the area. Make sure your men align with Rorick's, at least on coverage and strategy."

"Of course, sir."

I tried my best to stifle a yawn, not wanting to appear bored or disrespectful. I was just really fucking tired.

"You alright over there? That's like the third time that you've referred to me with proper honorifics, and we're not even in public. Still feeling sick?"

"I'm fine, Hanjae. The past several weeks have just been... a lot."

In the best of ways, lately. That said, without Arken by my side, the weight of everything else she seemed to keep at bay was quickly catching up with me.

"I know I normally give you shit for this, Kieran, but why don't you go rest in your office for a while? You look exhausted."

And I really must've been, because the idea of a quick nap at my desk sounded as appealing as the softest feather bed in the world.

"I'm going to remind you of this later," I warned. "This is clearly enabling my bad habits."

"Yeah, yeah. Get your ass out of here. I expect a report from your men about the Wyldwoods within a week."

"Yes, sir."

I debriefed quickly with Jeremiah after leaving Commander Ka's offices, instructing him on which men I wanted on the Wyldwoods patrols, before the exhaustion truly started to get the better of me.

Once I made it back to my own office, I flicked the lock closed, sank into my desk chair, and fell asleep within minutes.

◇ ◇ ◇

Mist enshrouded the Wyldwoods that night, providing the cover I needed as I fled from the estate, clutching at my face in blind agony.

When I was far enough away, I leaned against the gnarled oak to catch my breath, chest heaving, hands bloodied, heart shredded. I didn't bother to check behind me. I knew that once I left, my brother would not follow—the distance was only a precaution born of what little self-preservation I had left.

A dark, sick chuckle came from across the clearing.

"Fuck you," I rasped.

As my sire stepped into the light, his face was as cold and indifferent as ever.

"Let this be the last lesson I have to teach you, my unfortunate heir," he sneered. "There is a price for fighting against fate—and you won't always be the one who pays that cost, Kieran. Who else has to die? When will you accept your duties?"

One day, I would end his pathetic existence and let that be the last lesson between us. For now, all I could really do with what remained of my stamina was spit in his direction with bared teeth.

"Never," I hissed.

Without another word, the man turned away from me with clear disgust, took a single step forward, and then evaporated into Shadow.

I wanted to chase him down and make him pay for what he had done. A life for a life. But I could barely even keep myself upright. Instead, I stumbled back towards Sophrosyne, praying that I wouldn't pass out from the blood loss before I could find a cleric...

My surroundings warped and twisted, and suddenly I was no

longer in the Wyldwoods.

Now, I stood before a familiar obsidian table, inlaid with dark and ancient runes. Nausea surfaced at the memories I had here, but this time, it wasn't a younger version of me being strapped down to that table.

It was Arken.

I lunged forward, trying to run to her—trying to call out her name—but my mouth and legs were bound. I couldn't move, I couldn't breathe, I could only thrash in place and watch in agony as the Crones began to carve into the flesh of her back with ink, the same way they had done to me all those years ago. I remembered the pain all too well, the way the ink had *burned.*

I was thrashing internally, drawing on every ounce of aether I had within to break whatever bound me. I would gladly strike down those withered bitches where they stood, but even at full strength, I could not escape.

Arken's face crumpled with desperation as she cried out in fear and agony, but they held her down and continued their wicked work. Her blood mixed with ink as it spilled against her pale skin, a morbid canvas for their sadistic purpose.

"Kieran, please!"

I fought, and fought, and fought, but I still couldn't move. I was silently screaming myself hoarse, I could feel my throat burn, but she still couldn't hear me as tears slid down her cheeks. And then...

My sire returned, appearing just behind Arken atop the stone table.

As Dagon drew his jagged blade, wicked fangs gleaming in the dark, he smiled at me. Just before he slit the throat of the woman I loved.

◇ ◇ ◇

I woke up in a cold sweat, gasping, daggers already in hand.

Fuck. *Fuck.*

I hadn't had one of those nightmares in years. I tried to steady my shaking hands as they returned the blades to their proper holsters, breathing hard through my nose. Dagon had not haunted my dreams in ages. Why now?

Because you're in love with her. You're in love with her, and now you have something you're not willing to lose.

No, it went beyond unwilling. Such a thing had become an unfathomable horror. Something beyond comprehension. No, I couldn't stand the thought of losing her—and I had known that since the night with the Leshy—but could I ever really *have* her, either? The burden of my secrets might have been agonizing to bear alone, but it was the lesser of two evils. I had decided that a long time ago.

Nausea curled in my gut. I couldn't deal with that train of thought—not now, not here, where the walls of my office felt as though they were closing in on me. This room was far too small, too contained. I needed to get out of here.

Hans attempted to approach me as I strode through the halls at a brisk pace.

"Hey, Cap, I just wanted to apologize about earlier—"

"Don't," I cut him off. "If anyone asks, I'm out for the rest of the day. Make sure Jeremiah has what he needs to start patrols tonight."

"Yes, sir," Lieutenant Deering said, clear concern in his eyes. "Do you need anything else?"

"No," I said bluntly, taking a hard left towards the stables, leaving the man standing alone and confused in the hall.

I found Muniin, my favored cavalry mare, quickly prepared her saddle, and took off towards the Pyrhhan Coast before anyone could even realize we were gone.

✧ ✧ ✧

Something about the scent of saltwater and the gentle repetition of crashing waves had always soothed me.

I had spent a great deal of time on these beaches over the years, particularly as an angst-ridden, brooding teen, and I still found myself coming back to the sea whenever I got overwhelmed. It had been awhile, though. I hadn't been back here since I met Arken last year.

Arken.

My throat began to constrict as I dismounted, that sense of overwhelm and dread beginning to take over again.

Breathe.

I just needed to breathe.

I left Muniin tethered to the rickety old driftwood fence that marked this particular subset of the beach as private property, knowing that she would stay put. Also knowing that the owner of said private property never came down here, anyway. Not anymore.

It wasn't until I made it to the shoreline that I allowed myself to think. To feel. And as the seafoam and saltwater began to break down my defenses, the first thing I felt was *fear*.

Complete and utter terror.

Because I loved her.

I was in love with her.

Fuck.

I didn't even know what to do with that information. I had never even considered it as a possibility—never intended to get close enough to anyone for such a thing to ever happen. I had successfully kept everyone and everything at a comfortable, safe distance for years. *Years.*

And then Arken fucking Asher came along.

Confusion and guilt joined the fray alongside the terror, rippling through me in waves as I realized that in breaking my rules for her—in allowing myself this one, single exception... I had left myself vulnerable. I had carved out a perfect hole in my armor. I had something to lose, now—and if I ever lost her, I wasn't sure that I could bear it.

I thought about the way she looked at me lately, like I had personally hung every star in the night sky. Like I had crafted the constellations she so adored with my bare hands. I thought about the purity of her trust, the vulnerability that those gorgeous, golden doe eyes held, the way that she said my name. The way every kiss tasted like a promise on her tongue.

I thought about how immediately Arken had developed the habit of curling her body against mine after we exhausted ourselves, how quick she was to fall asleep, so long as her head was on my chest.

It was one thing for me to be in love with her. But if there was even a fraction of a chance that Arken felt similarly...

I was done for.

And yet the mere thought of it sent frissons of pleasure up and down my spine, awakening the most desperate desire of my life, as I realized there was one thing in this world that I wanted more than Arken's body.

I wanted her heart.

I would die for it. I would kill for it. I didn't deserve it—I could live a thousand lifetimes and still never possibly deserve it, but that wasn't enough to stop me. Though perhaps it should have been.

I wasn't born for love. The prophecy that had been forcefully etched into my skin with needles and ink was not one that had a happy ending—or so I thought. I had always told myself that there was no Light for me at the end of this tunnel, only the briefest moments of it, flashing too fast for me to hold on to, always leaving me blind by the time the Shadows fell again.

Because in the face of so much pain and unavoidable despair, you learn to wear apathy like armor. A child weaned with blood on the tongue has no room to develop a taste for things like milk and honey.

There was just something about her, though, that left me desperate for an alternate fate. I didn't want to be apathetic around her—I didn't have the capacity to be apathetic around her. Arken Asher had torn through all my darkest nights, shimmering across the skies like a violent meteor—brilliant, awe-inspiring, and dangerous. Something worth wishing on. Someone worth living for.

For Arken, I would go to war with my own demons. I would fight the Fates, the gods, and the very Source itself—if that's what it took for me to hold onto her.

As I trudged past the shoreline, making my way back to Muniin, I took pause at a small glint of iridescence in the sand. As I bent over to pick it up, I realized that it was a small chunk of astral quartz, fitting neatly in my palm and tumbled smooth, like seaglass. I immediately pocketed the stone, knowing that Arken would adore it. As I so adored her.

Though this newfound vulnerability—this *terrifying* uncertainty still crashed around my mind as violently as the tides behind me, I also felt something else. A flicker of something so foreign, so unfamiliar that it took me a moment to give it a name.

Hope.

This was uncharted territory. Hallowed ground. These were emotions I never expected to have to navigate. For the first time in a very long time, I felt entirely out of my element.

No matter how she felt about me, whether this feeling was mutual or not...

She and I would figure it out.

I knew we would.

CHAPTER FIFTY-NINE

ARKEN

Of all the days for lectures to be canceled, I sighed to myself.

Shortly after Kieran left, I made my way home and promptly received a notice that all classes in or around the Wyldwoods this afternoon would be postponed—something about routine maintenance on the wards. Conduits were instructed to either stay home, or meet for independent study groups at the Biblyos.

I had no interest in the group study option, though part of me wished that I had the foresight to linger just a little bit longer at Kieran's townhouse. Something about this studio—once my private safe haven and soft place to land—now felt isolating and empty. The space felt several degrees colder without the warmth of his presence, the heat of his gaze. Gods, that was a terrifying thought.

Oh, don't be shy, Arken, Hans had said. *Kier gets 'em all eventually.*

I shook the thought from my mind, in dire need of a distraction. Stupid routine maintenance—we'd never had classes canceled for ward work before. And hadn't Kieran said that the Elders refreshed the wardpoints pretty regularly? Odd that the Studium grounds would need something specific, right around the same time that Kier got dragged back to headquarters for what sounded like an urgent request from his commander...

I knew better than to snoop around the business of the gods or the Elder Guard, but I hoped everything was okay... and that everyone was safe.

Unsure of what to do with the irrational and arguably misplaced anxiety growing in my chest, I decided to go for a run. Not my *preferred* source of exercise these days, but if I wanted to pass my endurance test for Physical Arcana next quarter, I needed to keep up with the routine. Training clothes on and hair tied back, I began my standard circuit from my studio to the Eastern Gates.

Every time an invasive thought tried to wriggle its way into my consciousness, I upped my pace and focused on that challenge instead—so needless to say, I made it to the edge of the city in minutes. I hadn't even realized that I *could* run that fast. It was sort of exhilarating. The gentle breeze felt more like a powerful tailwind, pushing me forward, lightening every stride. By the time I reached the gates, my lungs were burning and I was breathing hard, stretching out my sore abdominal muscles with every heaving gasp of air.

I leaned against the limestone city walls to catch my breath, grateful for the shadows they cast against the midday sun. The white stonework was deliciously cool against my back as I drank deeply from my waterskin. Wistfully, I stared out towards the entry trail to the Wyldwoods and sighed. I had promised Kieran that I wouldn't wander them alone anymore. Not after the Leshy.

It was a silly promise to make, really. I was born in the Brindlewoods, I grew up crawling through blankets of moss and pine needles. My younger years were practically defined by how often I would find myself lost in the woods... but then again, I was a bolder, more fearless creature back then.

Absently, I brushed my fingers over my ribcage, where the scars would remain—memories of the Leshy's claws still so visceral and violent. The pain was the last thing I really remembered from that night, before it all began to warp and fade. I shuddered a bit, remembering the way the toxins *burned,* the way I had to cling to Kieran for dear life as my body had started to weaken and shut down after the daemon's blow...

I was truly lucky to be alive. So even though I craved that quiet calmness, that stillness of mind that the resinous scent of pine always produced for me when I took my little walks through the forest alone... I kept my promise to the man who saved my life.

After a few more sips of water, I turned around and ran the rest of my circuit around the Student's Quarter instead. I could always drag Kieran into the woods with me later, and replace those bad memories with something better.

Fucking Hel, I missed him already. It had been, what—an hour? Two at most, and already his absence felt like some phantom limb, an extension of myself that had been severed.

That's sort of pathetic, Arken, I groaned internally.

And it was, wasn't it? I mean, I knew that part of this was just me being pouty at this point, but Kieran's lieutenants had rudely interrupted an artful game of seduction that he and I had been playing all morning, a game that I had been winning. I had been right on the cusp of receiving my prize, with his fist in my hair—the man still had promises of duress to make good on.

I am going to fucking ruin you, he'd sworn—and godsdamn, I hoped that promise extended to whenever he wrapped up with work today. Nevermind the fact that we had been having nearly non-stop sex for over a week, the man still left me both sated and insatiable. I had been half-tempted to beg him to stay home, to lie to his commander again, just to remain in that decadent moment on his lap—but I had nipped that thought in the bud before I could make an absolute ass out of myself. Because there was more to all of this than just lust, now wasn't there?

Kieran's work, for as little as I truly knew about it, was important to this city. It was important to *him.* I hadn't forgotten his confession at the wardpoint—that becoming a captain on the Elder Guard was one of the few things in life that he was proud of. I refused to be so needy as to pull him away from what actually fulfilled him in life. And yet I felt so *godsdamned* needy in his absence, even after the run.

I wasn't used to this. It had never been like that with Graysen, and no other relationship had ever come close to this inexplicable magnetism, these tangled ties between Kieran and I.

He gets 'em all eventually.

Fucking Hans. I loved Kieran's lieutenants like they were my own brothers, but *gods*, that was the last thing I needed to hear this morning. I scowled at the memory of the lieutenant's little slip up, and the way Kieran's eyes had flashed in warning. Was that for the sake of my feelings? Or was it because Hans was right?

This was the exact sort of introspection that I had hoped academia would help me avoid. I had been dancing around it for something close to nine days now, side stepping every reminder that Kieran and I had kept things platonic for a *reason*. I really didn't want to think about what came next, whenever the afterglow of all the flawless sex began to fade. Whenever Kieran got bored, or came to his senses. It was bound to happen, right?

I could hardly offer a fair substitution for his freedom to sample every gorgeous creature that Sophrosyne had to offer, unfettered by the burdens of regret, or expectations.

Except what killed me was that Kieran was breaking all of his rules with me, as of late. In the quiet moments in between our desperate hunt for pleasure and release, he was letting me in. Exposing tiny slivers of vulnerability. Gaps in his armor. In between tangled sheets and tangled limbs, Kieran had started letting down his walls.

And I could never return the favor.

It was for this exact reason that I was currently alone, too. Kieran's dedication to the Guard would always be a secret point of contention, something that prevented me from giving myself over to him in full. Even if I really, really wanted to give him everything.

So maybe it was for the best if Hans was right in suggesting that, at the end of the day, I was just another notch in Kieran's bedpost. There was no denying the fact that I was falling for him. And perhaps I had been falling for a long time.

But could I really risk it?

I had no reason to doubt the ferocity of Amaretta's warnings—her sharp insistence that if I were to expose my secrets in Sophrosyne, it would be one of the most dangerous things I could ever do. I believed my mentor when she told me that the truth of my Resonances could very well put my life at risk. She had told me explicitly to avoid two things in this city when I could help it: The Elders, and the Elder Guard. I still didn't fully understand *why*, having fallen behind on much of my research on the matter, but that didn't mean I was prepared to flirt with my own demise.

It wasn't as if I thought that Kieran couldn't keep my secrets, either. The man was essentially an expert in that regard. If Kier had any feelings for me at all, and he somehow found out that I could wield more than just Light, there was no doubt in my mind that he would keep that to himself. But I could never ask that of him.

It would essentially be asking Kieran to put his loyalty to me above that of the Elder Guard—and exactly what had I done to earn the right to make such a demand? How could I possibly expect him to betray that sense of pride and loyalty and *honor* that clearly meant so much to him? His father was dead, his brother estranged—the Guard and his men were the closest thing he had to a family.

At the same time, the burden of this secret would always be an integral part of who I was. It was why, prior to Kieran, I kept everything so close to my chest. The Resonances had altered my childhood, sown seeds of doubt into my very identity. Doubts that I had yet to dispel. These secrets were the only reason I was even *here*, in Sophrosyne—or at least, they used to be.

If I let myself love him, I would be lying to him for the rest of my life.

Could I live with that?

◆ ◆ ◆

Hours passed by for the remainder of the afternoon, sluggish and slow.

In between reading and occasionally dozing off, catching up on lost sleep, I continued to oscillate between missing Kieran, *wanting* Kieran, and ruminating over the inevitable serious conversations to come.

Just before the sun began to set, his raven appeared.

So sorry this is taking so long, sweetheart. I'll be back in the city within an hour or so. Can I bring dinner?

The immediate swell of relief and the sheer, unbridled happiness that bloomed in my chest just seeing his *handwriting* was absurd.

Yes, please. I'm starving.

It only took him a moment to reply.

I mean, so am I. But that would be for your cunt, not necessarily a meal, Little Conduit...

There was a brief pause before the next scrap of parchment showed up, as if Kieran needed to take a moment to laugh at his own depraved commentary. I couldn't help but grin at the thought.

Okay, sorry. I'm on my way. For both.

My shoulders shook with the laughter I tried to suppress, while simultaneously pressing my thighs together in an attempt to disregard the pooling heat. Horny bastard.

Despite all of my fears, and the doubts that still lingered in the back of my mind, the promise of his presence left me feeling lighter already.

CHAPTER SIXTY

KIERAN

The ride home from the Pyrhhan Coast was swift thanks to Muniin and her steady gallop. While most men in the Elder Guard rode standard-issue horses from our stables, I had brought Muniin with me when I moved from Pyrhhas to Sophrosyne.

She had been a gift from my father on my sixteenth birthday, and the mare was easily one of the fastest and most reliable steeds one could ask for. My commander had raised an eyebrow at the request to keep her back then, but allowed me to stable her along with the other cavalry horses so long as I remained responsible for her care.

I was thankful for her haste tonight, guilt beginning to gnaw at me for keeping Arken waiting over my lazy office nap and the silly little urge to get introspective on the beach. The woman was hungry, and I was eager to provide in more ways than one.

I made it back to the city just as the skies began to darken from sunset to dusk. After returning Muniin to the stables and setting her up with an indulgent trough of oats and apples, I walked briskly towards the Merchant's Quarter—hopefully Roshana's specials tonight could travel well. As I wove through throngs of people, I thumbed the smooth stone in my pocket, pathetically excited to give her the crystal I had found, just to show her that I had been thinking of her all day.

It was bizarre how *immediate* my mood had shifted from somber hope to something more akin to incandescence, just by being within ten minutes of her studio. Or... perhaps it wasn't strange at all. Not anymore.

The pleasant, brassy clang of the city's central clock tower rang out seven times as I left Roshana's tavern with a dinner worthy of my apology—the scent of roasted duck and freshly baked bread reminding me that I hadn't really eaten much today.

Within a single knock, Arken opened the door.

"Hello there, Little Conduit," I said, unable to resist smiling at the very sight of her face. "I do believe you have my house key."

"I do believe you have my *dinner*, Captain," Arken replied with a smirk, scooping the bags from my hands as I stepped inside.

As she attempted to turn and bring the food over to her kitchen table, I wrapped my hands around her waist.

"Oh no you don't, woman," I murmured. "Come here."

Arken's sigh was soft and melodic as her body melted against mine. She let the paper bags in her hands sag towards the floor, releasing her grip once she knew they wouldn't topple over—and then her hands were in my hair, fingernails against my scalp, eagerly returning the kiss I had needed to claim.

"You smell like the ocean," she said after we eventually managed to part.

"I had to make a stop on the Pyrhhan Coast," I explained, still feeling guilty. "And I *may* have ridden Muniin by the ocean just for fun on the way home."

The lie left my mouth a little less easily than it once might have, the misdirection feeling heavier on the tongue. This wasn't the first time I had to offer Arken half-truths to side step something too dark or too dangerous to share, but this time, I was just being a coward.

Still, she didn't need to know about my nightmares—I never

seemed to have them when she slept by my side.

"Chasing your own cheap thrills on the clock? How unbecoming of a captain," she teased. "Your secret is safe with me, if only because whatever you've brought for dinner smells like heaven."

In her proximity, food was the *last* thing on my mind, but if I knew Arken half as well as I thought that I did, she hadn't eaten today either. For her sake, I kept it in my pants. For now. And Arken was right, the food did smell divine.

As we settled in to eat, making casual conversation here and there, I studied her like an artist might study their muse, eyes wandering from her collarbones, up the length of her neck where I could still see evidence of my affection blooming against her skin in the form of bruises and bitemarks. I was thankful to be seated at the table with her today, instead of our usual spot on the couch, lest she think I was getting hard over the discussion of her studies. It was only when my gaze drifted to her mouth that I noticed something was a little off.

In between bites of food and tidbits about her day, Arken was chewing on her bottom lip with surprising fervor. She didn't even seem aware of it, either. My eyes flickered to her arm—though her left hand was on her lap beneath the table, subtle movements at her elbow told me she was picking at her fingernails, or perhaps at the hem of her sweater. That wasn't entirely abnormal for her, but as time went on, her lip was looking a little raw. She was clearly anxious about something.

"You alright over there, Ark?" I asked before taking a sip of the white wine she'd poured for us to accompany the meal.

"What? Oh, yeah. I'm fine!" she chirped, her face brightening with clear intent to mask whatever it was she'd been thinking about just then.

If you say so, sweetheart.

I had no right to push her on the matter, I just hoped that

whatever it was that was eating at her wasn't my fault.

By the time we wrapped up with our meal and Arken began to clear the table, I was losing my grip on my self-restraint. Despite everything else that had transpired in between, I hadn't forgotten how brazen she'd been at the art gallery—reaching for my cock in public like that.

And I could read between the lines when it came to our little exchange, just before I dragged her home to act upon it. We had enjoyed a *lot* of sex as of late, and plenty of it rough—but she was demanding something specific from me. Tempting me to take something that I had only really teased her with so far. But that threat to ruin her when we got home hadn't been an empty promise. Not by a long shot. She had no idea how badly I had been craving this.

I wanted my hands around her throat, I wanted her choking on my cock, I wanted her perfect body strung up and suspended by ropes of Shadow, my own pretty little painting to admire and devour.

Only under duress.

Did she even know how those three simple words had condemned me for life?

It was all terribly ironic, considering the woman was the perfect picture of innocence right now, humming softly to herself as she cleared our plates and silverware, flitting from the table to the sink like a sparrow. And I was clearly the tomcat, ready to eat her alive.

"I can take care of that," I said, not wanting to be rude... Well. Not wanting to be *impolite*. "Here, let me help."

"No, no—I've got it," she replied airily. "It'll only take a minute."

When I got up to follow and help her with the dishes anyway, she gave me her best attempt at a threatening glare, though it turned out more like the petulant pout of a child. Fates, I adored her.

"Amma would *kill* me if she knew I was letting a guest clean up after themselves," she whined. "It's poor hostess behavior."

"Well, Amma isn't here right now," I replied. "And thank the gods for that, because I've got plans for you tonight."

Arken's eyes widened before they began to glimmer.

Oh yes, Little Conduit, I mused to myself. *I didn't forget.*

CHAPTER SIXTY-ONE

ARKEN

My breath hitched in my throat as the weight of Kieran's stare kept me pinned in place.

"And what do those plans entail, Vistarii?" I asked as he took several strides forward, meeting me in the kitchen.

"You'll find out soon enough, Asher."

And then his mouth was on mine, moving faster than I could parse as the distance between us evaporated, Kieran cornering me between the countertops and his tall, muscled frame. One hand held me at the nape of my neck, the other tightened around my wrist. This kiss was hungry, maddening, *demanding*—and I gasped as I felt my lower lip split beneath the force.

"But first things first," he murmured, releasing my wrist to press his thumb against my lower lip. He inspected the blood drawn for a moment before licking the pad of said finger. He watched me intently as he did so, sending heat straight between my legs.

"Tell me what you were so anxious about earlier that you felt the need to tear up this perfect mouth of yours, hmm?" he crooned. "I do believe that's *my* job."

I glanced away, my face flushing under his careful observation, among other things. I had hoped that when he dropped the subject earlier, that would have been the end of it. I wasn't sure I was ready to expose myself like this, and yet…

"Don't tell me you were worried about me," Kieran teased, smiling as he tipped my chin up with two steady fingers.

"N-no," I stammered. "Not exactly…"

At that slight admission, he raised a single dark eyebrow. "Not exactly?"

"It was nothing, Kieran," I tried to claim, painting my face with false confidence. "Really. It's nothing important."

That was a lie. The thoughts that had plagued me over dinner felt like some of the most important things I had ever worried about in my life. The weight of certain decisions that were still hanging in the balance between Kieran and I. Whether I wanted this to be a temporary fling, or a permanent alteration to our friendship. Whether or not we could ever be *more*.

"I don't believe you," Kieran said softly, fingers drifting from my chin to my jawline.

"I'd much rather talk about these plans of yours," I replied, attempting to flirt my way out of this conversation.

"Oh, I'm sure you would," he murmured, tucking a stray lock of hair behind my ear. "As would I. But I'm not going to tell you a damn thing until you let me know what's bothering you."

Gods, that was just unfair.

"It's not that I was worried about you, per se., I mean, gods know you can take care of yourself…" I said, trailing off. "I was more worried that maybe, you wouldn't be coming back?"

My voice was small, and I felt exposed.

"What, did you think I *died*?!" Kieran exclaimed, incredulous as he misinterpreted what I meant.

It was my fault for being unclear, but the words were sticking to the roof of my mouth, heavy and viscous, too uncomfortable to admit.

"Tell me this isn't about what Hans said earlier, Arken. I swear to the fuckin' Source, I will beat his ass if that's what got under your skin," Kieran said, eyes darkening. "Actually, scratch that. I'll hold him down so that *you* can beat his ass."

"I mean, you have to admit that he had a point," I countered. "We've broken so many rules this week, Kieran. Don't act like you don't know what I'm talking about."

A muscle in his jaw ticked as he paused, tilting his head to one side and allowing his hands to fall loosely at his sides. He seemed to be holding his breath, his eyes searching mine in silence. Finally, he exhaled.

"No, I know what you're talking about, sweetheart. I just… don't have a good explanation," he said quietly.

A pang of regret sank through me as I heard his voice crack, just a little, towards the end of that sentence. *Fuck*. I really shouldn't have said anything. Why did I have to be so godsdamned transparent around him?

"I wasn't asking for one," I said softly, and with sincerity. "You don't owe me an explanation."

"I'm at least glad that you didn't think I was *dead* after a few hours of errands," he muttered. "I'm not sure my ego would ever recover."

I groaned, pinching the bridge of my nose. Of course he was making jokes. This was the exact conversation that both of us had been trying to avoid.

"I'm sorry," I sighed. "I really shouldn't have said anything."

"Hey," Kieran said, taking hold of my wrist, pulling it away from my face. His voice was slow and gentle. Reassuring, just as it had been the night this all started. "Arken, I—. You *know* that those rules don't apply to you. They never have, not really. We've been over this."

You're almost always the exception to my rules, Arken.

There seemed to be more that he wanted to say, but he was holding himself back. It was as if my nerves had rubbed off on him, a sympathetic illness.

"Listen, I didn't mean to bring this up tonight," I sighed. "And I didn't admit that I was anxious about it in an attempt to corner you into some sort of *answer* or explanation. I'm not trying to manipulate you, I promise. Your presence just has this... unnerving way of loosening my lips. I kinda hate that about you sometimes."

Kieran's lips twitched, a poor attempt to hold back a smirk.

"No, you don't," he crooned.

"No," I admitted. "I don't."

I loved it about him. All too often, I found that my true thoughts died on my tongue in common conversation—unable to find a place amongst the idle chatter. Over the years, I had learned how to mask, to present an inauthentic version of myself more suitable for public display, with words that were prettier and less direct. It was such a habit to self-edit that sometimes I lost sense of who I was entirely, dissolving into the expectations of others.

I had never needed to do that with Kieran. Not once.

We were treading dangerous ground, now. Dancing on the cusp of confessions that could change everything. My heart was racing, pounding, throbbing like the erratic thing it was, caged behind my ribs.

When I glanced back up at Kieran, his expression was a devastating cocktail of patience, affection, and desire. I had hardly touched the wine over dinner, and still found myself drunk.

CHAPTER SIXTY-TWO

KIERAN

As each troubled word tumbled from her mouth, my heart sank.

I had a feeling this was what had been on her mind. From the moment Hans made that dumbass remark, I worried about how Arken might interpret or internalize it. I had almost started feeling guilty for the way I had snapped at my second-in-command earlier, *but not anymore, fucker.* He and I were going to have *words* later.

I ached with the realization that she thought I was even capable of such a thing. Did this woman not realize how much I adored her? What lengths I might go to just to protect her, even from my own bad habits?

"Arken, you don't need to apologize," I began.

"No, I do—I didn't—I don't—*Gods*, I'm not trying to—"

She scrambled to find the right words, to explain herself in full, not realizing just how *deeply* I understood her headspace. But maybe I should have left this alone. I hadn't intended to exacerbate this anxiety she'd been dealing with, though it was clearly unresolved. Still, as she struggled for words, I could only think of one decent way to shut her up for a minute.

I kissed her.

Gently, this time, mindful of the raw skin of her lower lip and the split that I had accidentally worsened earlier. I could still taste her blood on the tip of my tongue, and though that alone had done things to my libido, I wanted to make *certain* that she was okay before dragging her off to bed again.

Her mouth followed mine as I began to pull away, attempting to linger... It was an effort not to groan at that, not to pull her back in and taste her mouth on mine again. We'd both had our fill of supper, and yet I was still ravenous. Even so, we needed a moment to breathe. Emotions needed to be settled, calmer, for the things I wanted to do with her tonight.

"Arken," I repeated softly. "I understand why you were nervous, and I'm terribly sorry if I gave you any particular indication that's... what was happening here, but it wasn't. It's not. I'm not going anywhere. Not tonight. Not in general. I fear you may be stuck with me."

"It's fine," she murmured, still not meeting my gaze. "I've got no right to—"

I didn't let her finish the sentence, leaning in to kiss her again. Partially to interrupt whatever silly little train of thought *that* might have been, and partially because I couldn't resist. I still had her cornered against her pantry door and the kitchen countertops, and the proximity to her mouth was just too tempting for my own good.

"Do shut up, woman," I replied while my mouth was still against hers.

You've got every right.

She sighed, but did so with a smile. And she was smiling still when I finally pulled away.

"Can you do me a favor, though, Kier?"

"Hmm?"

"At least give a girl a warning. If you ever change your mind. If it ever comes to that."

If I were ever to abandon her, she meant. If I were to toss her aside like one of my fleeting distractions. If she ever became the rule, not the exception. I growled in irritation, not even wanting to dignify that request with a response.

Just tell her, you idiot, I chastised myself. *Tell her, and alleviate all these stupid fears.*

But it was my own fear that kept the words locked behind my teeth. Not yet. *Not yet.*

Arken rolled her eyes before dipping her head beneath my arm, wriggling herself free to resume what remained of the dishes. I resisted the urge to pull her back and entrap her in my arms again. For now, I was content to lean against her from behind, resting my chin on her shoulder and letting my hands wander.

"That's very distracting," she murmured as one of them cupped her ass cheek, the other toying with the band of her leggings, fingers tracing the dip in her hip bones that led towards my final destination for the evening. Her skin was so warm, and so, so sensitive.

"I think you'll live," I whispered against her ear, savoring that lemon-and-sunshine scent of her hair.

"I should hope so," she replied. "You still haven't told me about your *plans*."

"Are you certain that you're even ready for them?" I teased.

She snorted under her breath, but didn't reply.

"I'm going to need an answer to that question, sweetheart," I said, pulling my hand away from her tights.

Her whine as I withdrew was quiet, but I sure as Hel heard it, and the sound sent my pupils to the back of my skull. Gods above and below, that fucking *sound*.

"What was that?" I crooned.

"Yes," she breathed. "I'm ready."

When I bit down on her neck in response, she slammed a soapy palm against her countertop and whimpered again. I let my fingers splay against her lower abdomen, applying light pressure as they traversed lower, and lower—and then the whimper turned into a low groan.

"Are you sure?" I murmured, savoring the way she had started to writhe up against me.

"Kieran, I swear to the godsdamned Source, if you don't fuck me soon I—"

I caught her by the throat, interrupting her train of thought with a fierce grip. Oh, how perfectly my hand fit here, where it belonged. How lovely it was to feel her pulse beneath my fingertips. It felt like coming home.

"Watch your tongue," I hissed in her ear. "Before I put it to better use, Little Conduit."

In one fluid motion, I released her neck and turned her around to face me. My eyes flickered to her arms, where gooseflesh had set those little sun-bleached hairs on end.

"I do believe you're overdue for a bit of duress, Arken. Wouldn't you agree?"

For once, I seemed to render her speechless as her own fingers drifted up to her throat, resting where mine had been. I might have worried about being too aggressive, had it not been for the haze of lust that slipped into her expression, and the way her breath seemed to quicken. I took a single pace backwards, allowing for some distance between us in this moment. I cocked my head to the side, studying every element of her body language. Already, the tips of her fingers had started to flicker with tiny little starbursts of Light.

I knew it.

"I asked you a question, love."

"I would agree," she said slowly, eyes raising to meet my own. "*Sir.*"

Oh.

If I wasn't already in love with the woman, I might have fallen right then and there. *Holy fuck.*

"Good girl," I breathed, not even remotely ashamed that my

breath had grown ragged. "Very good girl. You remembered."

✧ ✧ ✧

It had been months ago now since she'd teased me about it in a passing conversation. I had made some errant implication about being dominant in bed, and I could hardly remember now how that had even come up, but I *did* recall her response.

"So do you keep your uniform on when you take them to bed? Do you make them call you *Captain*? Gods, you would—I bet you do," she'd laughed.

"I prefer Sir, actually, if we're going for honorifics," I'd replied, slipping some honesty into my returning quip.

Who knew she'd been paying such close attention, even then?

"I pay attention, Sir," Arken said now, as if she could read my godsdamned mind. Her tone was subdued, but her eyes were lit up like a Yule tree, sparkling and borderline feverish with anticipation.

Could it even be possible that she had wanted to give this to me for just as long as I had wanted to take it from her? I could hardly stomach the thought of having waited this long, if that were the case, but as her tongue ran over her lower lip again... *Fuck me.*

"Bedroom. Now."

It took her all of two seconds to follow my command, darting straight out of the kitchen and towards her bedroom. I watched her from behind, taking notice of the way her fingers seemed to stretch and splay out at her sides, as if they were impatient. Eager to touch. It made my cock twitch.

Already, it felt as though all the godsdamned blood that I had in me had rushed to that part of my body. I was borderline lightheaded, in a euphoric sort of way, just from hearing her speak to me with such lascivious deference.

This woman was going to be the fucking death of me, and

what a divine way to die.

Arken stood by the foot of her own bed now, facing me as I leaned against the doorway.

"Take off your clothes," I commanded quietly, watching as she began to slip off her sweater without so much as a moment's worth of hesitation.

Her camisole came next, and the lacy little underthing that had cupped her breasts so flawlessly. It was almost a shame to see it go, were it not for the fact that shedding the garment left her soft, rosy nipples exposed to the chill of the night air, and I got to watch as they pebbled over. Naked from the waist up, she began to peel off her socks, her tights, and, finally—her panties.

Fuck.

Every inch of Arken's flesh was exposed now as she stood before me in shy silence. It wasn't as though I hadn't seen her naked, I'd probably seen Arken without her clothes more often than seeing her fully dressed as of late—but I understood the way it felt to be put on private display. The way that it could thrill and simultaneously terrify.

"You are the most gorgeous creature I have ever seen, Arken," I purred, slinking away from the door frame but not quite close enough to touch. "The most stunning little thing I have ever had the pleasure to touch."

Her mouth parted slightly.

"Thank you, Sir," she whispered.

She was already so well behaved, so *immediately* prepared to submit. It was clear that she was no stranger to this sort of dynamic in the bedroom, and had probably had a taste for other dominants. Whether that was here in Sophrosyne, or back home, I wasn't sure. Not that it mattered.

I would sate every craving, slake every thirst she had ever had in her life. I would erase any memory of past lovers, past pleasures, past orgasms... and replace them with my own.

I would ruin her for anyone else.
She was fucking *mine*.

CHAPTER SIXTY-THREE

ARKEN

My mind was a blank slate.

The energy that Kieran radiated as he walked a lazy half-circle around me felt dark, alluring and otherworldly. Our physical chemistry had always been incredible, but this was something well beyond sexual attraction.

This felt like a godsdamn drug.

I had never offered anyone else the amount of submission I was willing to give to Kieran tonight—what I had already offered up, the moment the honorific left my lips. The unspoken exchange of power was rippling through the air now as if it were another form of aether. As if the tension between us was an entirely new element.

"Get on the bed, laying on your back. Facing me," Kieran commanded after the weighted moment passed. "Just like that, *good girl.*"

My feet were dangling off the side of the mattress, but just barely. Kieran stood in between them, slowly starting to shrug off his jacket.

"Tell me, Arken," he said softly. "Do you touch yourself often, lying in this bed?"

"Yes, Sir," I admitted freely.

Of fucking course I did.

"How often? Before all of this, of course."

"Every night," I replied. "Sir."

"And how often did you think of me when you did it?"

My pulse quickened.

"Every time," I whispered. "Every night."

Kieran inhaled sharply.

"Show me."

I knew what he meant, but couldn't resist the urge to be at least a *little* bit difficult—especially after he had drawn that confession from me with such arrogant ease.

"Can you be a little more specific, Sir?" I asked innocently.

His eyes darkened.

"Show me. How you touch yourself," he replied evenly. "Show me how you get yourself off to the thought of me, Arken. I'm right here now, you won't even have to close your eyes."

Cocky bastard.

I let my thighs part for him regardless, slipping two fingers between my legs where I was already slick with arousal. Together, they circled my clit with a familiar pattern, starting slow and with gentle pressure. My other hand cupped at a breast, teasing at my hardening nipple with the pad of my forefinger.

"*Fuck*," Kieran breathed, the susurration sounding more like a prayer than a curse.

His arousal only served to feed my own, and I let my fingers find a faster rhythm against that swelling bud, occasionally slipping them inside as well. Kieran watched me with the gaze of a scholar, studying every motion with dark admiration.

"Tell me, sweetheart," he murmured. "When I fucked you in your dreams, was it good?"

"Yes, Sir," I panted.

His eyes glittered.

"Was I gentle?"

"No, Sir," I confessed, kneading at my breast, starved for *his* touch, not my own.

"Did it hurt?"

"Maybe," I huffed, and he smirked.

"And did you like that?"

Yes. And part of me hated him for asking these things, but the other part of me adored him for it. He was stealing words from my lips that he knew I would never offer on my own, forcing me to tell him exactly how I liked it.

"Yes, Sir."

A low chuckle, like thunder rolling in the distance.

"Oh, you really were made for me, weren't you, sweet thing?"

"I'd like to think so," I whimpered, half out of my mind with need.

Logic and reason were long gone, replaced by my most carnal desires laid bare before the man I had been desperate for, the only man who had ever fucked me like I wanted. The only person who had ever treated my submission like the gift that it was. I would have happily wrapped myself up in ribbons just so he could watch me come undone.

"Come for me, Little Conduit."

It took all of thirty seconds for me to find the perfect pattern and cadence needed to follow his instructions, gasping for breath as the tremor of my orgasm shot through me. It was rare that I ever felt so spent by my own hand, but relief washed over me like the comfort of a blanket as my muscles relaxed. For a moment, I just stared at the ceiling, dazed.

"You're such a good girl," Kieran praised. "I think you've earned a reward."

Was that not a reward?

Apparently, in my dizzied state of mind, intoxicated by endorphins and the most attractive man I had ever met watching me get myself off, I accidentally spoke those words aloud.

"Oh, Arken," he said. "That wasn't even *close*."

All that I could do was sigh with pleasure, holding his gaze.

"Can my reward be you taking that godsdamned shirt off, then?" I requested. "*Sir?*"

He smirked.

"I was getting around to that," he replied. "Forgive me if I found myself *distracted*."

"By feeding your own ego?" I laughed.

"Something like that. And this is *not* what I consider your reward, for the record," he replied, pulling the soft black undershirt over his head.

My eyes traveled ravenously across the tanned flesh he had just exposed—admiring every nick and scar. The hard muscle, the haunting ink that crawled up his neck, all of it was captivating.

"Though, allow me to offer you a confession or two in return, you insatiable creature." He leaned forward and let the tips of his fingers trail across my thighs. "Sit up. And give me your hand."

I extended my left palm, and he swatted it away.

"The other one," he demanded.

I offered him my right hand, fingers still slick from my self-induced release. Kieran took it by the wrist, raising it to his mouth before murmuring the first of his confessions.

"I have fucked my own fist to the thought of you every godsdamned day since I met you, Arken Asher," he breathed, before proceeding to lick the arousal from my fingers. "And you *still* taste sweeter than I could have ever imagined."

Gods.

If that was my reward, it might have been the best exchange of currencies that I had ever participated in. Idly, I wondered what the probability was that we had often been touching ourselves at the same time, getting off to the same exact thoughts. Probably high, all things considered. It had probably happened often.

"And no, that wasn't your reward either," he said finally,

releasing my hand. "Good girls who can come on command get to choose their own rewards."

Had I not just gotten him shirtless? Besides, the only reason I had been able to orgasm so quickly was *because* he had been watching.

"Tell me what you actually want," he demanded.

A slight wave of anxiety shot through me as I grappled with my own indecision. I wanted so many things. Too many things. I was greedy. Insatiable. Starving.

"I'll have the answer to that question *now*, Arken."

"I want you in my mouth, Sir," I confessed.

His eyes darkened, glimmering with intrigue.

"Is that so? Get on your knees, then," he crooned.

I swallowed hard, eyes drifting to where his erection was pressing hard against his slacks, the length of him on perfect display. As I sank to my knees, I nearly sighed with contentment as he took a step closer, finally close enough to touch.

"*Good girl,*" he murmured, slipping off his belt and tossing it aside.

"May I touch you?" I breathed.

"Only if you ask me properly, Little Conduit," he replied.

His gentle reminder left me feeling emboldened to be a little more specific with my language, what little shyness I had left starting to fade.

"May I take out your cock so that I might give it the attention it deserves, Sir?"

"*Gods*, yes," Kieran groaned. "Yes, you most certainly can."

Thank the godsdamned Source. I needed this more than words could truly explain. Every time I had attempted to get on my knees for this man in the last week or so, he'd managed to interrupt—or counterattack, really—distracting me entirely.

But I wanted him in my *fucking* mouth.

CHAPTER SIXTY-FOUR

KIERAN

As Arken licked her lips in anticipation, I couldn't resist the urge to reach out and stroke her cheek. This wasn't *precisely* what I had in mind for tonight, but it was almost... better, somehow. There was a certain softness present between us, an affection that I had never experienced before, at least not while indulging in this specific taste.

Yes, I was still holding myself back a bit, but after our conversation in the kitchen, that felt right. It felt appropriate, given that our nerves were frayed. We had all the time in the world to explore the depths of her depravity—because Fates only knew that *mine* was a nigh-endless pit.

She was eye level with my waist now, an adorable expression of focus affixed to her face as she began fumbling with the buttons on my trousers. I resisted the urge to help her, instead weaving my fingers through the hair at the back of her head with gentle encouragement. Watching her fingers tremble as she continued her quest to slip my erection free was a dark pleasure in and of itself.

I smiled to myself as she finally managed to claim her prize, looking up at me with hesitant pride.

"Thank you, Sir," she whispered huskily before taking me in her mouth—suddenly, and with no further hesitation to be found.

For a moment, I lost the ability to think straight.

As her lips wrapped themselves firmly around the sensitive head, pushing me into her mouth against the wet warmth of her tongue, it was all I could manage not to immediately thrust the rest of my length down her throat.

No amount of fantasy or schoolboy acts of self-pleasure could have ever prepared me for the way it felt when Arken took that tongue of hers and swirled it over the crown of my cock, where a bead of pre-cum had already started to leak. She lapped it without so much as a flinch, and then began to use her hand to stroke my shaft while simultaneously taking me in and out of her mouth.

Every time, she took it deeper, until finally, I could feel that I was starting to hit the back of her throat. The hand of mine that had been playing gently with her hair had now gathered those silken locks in a tight grip at the nape of her neck.

Easy... Don't lose yourself to this just yet. Let her lead... For now.

Still, I allowed myself to apply a small amount of pressure to the back of her head, and she moaned while keeping me deep in her throat. I could *feel* the gentle vibrations as she took me in even deeper, and it was at that moment that I realized she wasn't even pausing to take a breath. She'd just started breathing through her nose, determined to keep as much of me in her mouth as possible.

"*Fuck*, Arken," I groaned. "You are absolutely incredible."

Her eyes sparkled with pleasure at the compliment, stroking her tongue even harder against my shaft with impressive enthusiasm.

I was a selfish bastard in so many ways, but not tonight. Despite my most carnal desires to fuck her throat raw and watch her swallow my release, I wanted one thing more than anything else tonight. Holding that fistful of hair tight, I tugged upward.

"I could watch you do this literally all night, but there are only so many hours until morning," I murmured.

Arken made a small noise of discontent.

"What about my *reward*?"

"I promise you, Little Conduit, I'll make it worth your while. Now up, please. Turn around. *Good girl*," I crooned.

As she turned to face the bed, exposing her back to me, I took a moment to admire her glorious ass. First with my eyes, quickly followed by my hands.

"Can you spread your legs just a little for me?" I nudged at her foot, showing her the stance I was looking for.

"Yes, Sir."

Good gods, I loved the sound of those words coming out of her mouth.

This was hardly the first time I had dabbled in power dynamics in the bedroom—one of the few benefits of a lack of serious relationships meant that I had little to fear in my sexual exploration. You can't really ruin what was never meant to last.

But this was different. Arken made me feel like a damn *god* as she gave me her submission. And though I was unworthy, I was also a greedy motherfucker—and so I took it. I'd take anything, *everything* she had to give.

"Do you have any idea what the sight of you like this is doing to me, Arken?"

My voice came out heavy and thick under the weight of this, the most decadent indulgence of my life.

"You know, I think I may have *some* idea..."

Slowly, and with obvious intention, she pushed herself back a little and bent over to grind her ass into my cock, still wet from that talented mouth of hers.

"Oh, you have no idea," I warned, grabbing her ass with both hands. "But you will, soon enough."

At that, I pushed on the small of her back with enough force that she fell forward, torso pressing into the mattress, hips still high. Thanks to the way her legs were spread just wide enough, her ass was in perfect view—as was the slightest sliver of her pink cunt. As my hands ran down her back, I let my nails dig in, just a little.

Another soft whine escaped her mouth.

So pathetic, I mused to myself. *So fucking perfect.*

When I slipped one finger between her thighs to tease lightly between those wet, delicate folds of skin, she buried her head in the mattress to moan. My hand shot out, instinctively grabbing her by the hair and pulling back her head so she instead had one cheek resting against her sheets.

"None of that," I ordered. "I want to hear you."

I grabbed her ass again with both hands, harder this time, in emphasis.

"*Kieran, please!*"

The desperation, the begging, the *want* within that wail was like a siren's song to me. I was drunk on the confirmation that I had been right all along. Arken didn't just like being under duress. She fucking *loved* it.

So sweet. So compatible with this dark heart of mine.

The errant, dangerous thought flickered through my mind like an echo. I was too consumed by the sounds she was making to bother mitigating the risk.

"You like that, sweetheart?" I growled in approval, gripping her even harder, nails beginning to bite into the ample flesh below my palms.

"Fuck—*Yes*," she panted.

I bent over, leaning my frame above hers. With my cock still out, it slid naturally between her slick thighs, absolutely coated with her arousal. I truly couldn't wait to be inside her again, but there was something to be established, first and foremost.

"Do you want it to hurt?" I whispered in her ear softly.

I kept my tone neutral and even. It was a struggle not to expose myself as I offered a desperate prayer to the Fates that she would say yes. Regardless of how much I wanted this, regardless of what we had already so clearly implied, I needed an honest answer from her.

She stiffened, and for a moment my heart sunk.

Too much, you dumb bastard, I scolded myself. *Too much, too fast.*

I could feel the oily knot of self-loathing make its way into the pit of my stomach before immediately vanishing at the sound of the two sweetest words I'd ever heard.

"Yes, please."

The words slipped from her mouth like her most furtive confession, and it was music to my ears. I felt her body relax beneath me, melting as she offered herself in deep, intimate submission. Flawless. She couldn't see the shit-eating grin that crept across my face at her angle from where I stood, but even I could hear it make its way into my voice as I replied.

"Thank the *fucking* gods."

I slid one hand around her throat again, a light caress with just the slightest hint of pressure. More a prelude than a threat.

"Do you trust me, sweetheart?" I asked.

"Yes," Arken sighed.

"Hmm, I'm sorry? I didn't quite catch that," I murmured, slowly letting my fingers tighten around her neck. I felt her throat bob as she swallowed hard.

"Yes, I trust you, Kieran," she said with sincerity.

"Mhm. From *Sir*, back to *Kieran* already?" I admonished. "That won't do."

I applied just a bit more pressure on her throat, forcing her to focus on her breathing and center herself.

"Let's get one thing straight, Little Conduit. I don't want to hear you say my name again tonight unless you are *screaming* it while I fuck you. Understood?" I growled.

"Y-yes, *Sir*," she corrected. There was just the hint of beautiful strain in her voice. "I trust you."

"Good. Now put both arms behind your back," I ordered, focusing my arcana as she followed her instructions with haste.

Cool, smoky coils of Shadow aether began to manifest in the form of ropes—smooth like silk, but stronger than any cord or textile one could purchase in the Market District. As I began to weave the arcane material around her arms in artful loops and knots, Arken craned her neck, trying to glance back at what I was doing. I caught her eye and smirked, pulling the ropes of Shadow taut, fashioning a restraint that left her in a rather compromised position. She inhaled sharply as the rigging enforced some improved posture, bringing her shoulders back and binding her wrists and forearms in place.

"Well now," I murmured. "I can't say I don't adore the sight of you like this. But before we continue, we're going to make one thing perfectly clear, alright?"

I released my grip on her neck.

"Yes, Sir?"

"Good girl," I reminded her, because she was. She was so fucking good.

Gods, I loved her.

"Everyone's definition of pain is a little different, Arken, and so I need you to make me a promise. If I push you too hard, if I start approaching a line that you're not ready to cross—all you need to do is tell me to stop. You just say *stop*, and we stop. I'm not going to ask you for a safe word because that's not my goal here, not tonight. But I do need you to *promise* me that you'll stop me before I hurt you in a way you don't enjoy. Can you do that for me, sweetheart?"

"Yes, Sir."

Perfection.

CHAPTER SIXTY-FIVE

ARKEN

There was a glimmer of pride in Kieran's gaze that I caught as I glanced back at him, and it was doing unspeakable things to my ego. I was desperate for more of his praise, reveling in his approval and appreciation as if it were the very moonlight that poured through my window.

Even though I had been naked all night, had even stripped down to my skin under his watchful gaze, for some reason it was *now* that I felt most exposed. Perhaps it was the lack of mobility, now that he had me bound by his Shadows. The artful manner in which he'd tied me up was almost a relief on my aching muscles, not at all uncomfortable. It was...

Perfect. He was perfect at this.

I continued to allow myself to unravel in the safety of his control and supervision. The only thing keeping me tethered to this plane was the sound of his voice, and *gods*, I felt drunk on that low rumble. His dark command. My eyelids felt so... so very heavy.

At the very edge of my consciousness, I remembered that just before this moment, I'd been feeling a little hesitant about the honorifics that pleased him so much—unable to ease the embarrassment, the fear that he wouldn't be able to take me seriously. Was I using them too often? Not often enough? All of that insecurity was gone now, released into the aether without a care in the world.

Gone, gone, gone.

There was nothing weighing on my heart or mind at that moment, and that was a very, very unfamiliar sensation. In the absence of all the other noise, there was barely a thought in my mind. It was only him, and the sensation of his fingertips as they teased at my skin with a feather-light touch.

"Ready?" Kieran asked, his voice husky and low.

"Yes, Sir," I said.

The flesh of his palm swiftly met my ass, and I cried out—startled by the sting. I had been spanked before, but never quite that hard. Adrenaline surged through my veins. I wanted more.

The second strike came without warning, harder this time, as though he could read my mind. My toes curled, tears beginning to prickle in my eyes, though they did not fall.

There was awe and admiration present in his voice when he spoke next.

"You really do enjoy this, don't you, Little Conduit?"

I did. I always had, and I couldn't quite explain where it came from. It hadn't been Graysen, not really. Our tastes had just simply seemed to align at the time, and over the years I continued to find that the rougher the sex, the better it felt. There was an exquisite edge to the pain, something that wasn't just psychological—it actually felt physically pleasant to me. Like scratching an itch in *just* the right spot.

"More," I begged.

"Address me appropriately, you demanding creature," Kieran growled. "Or I won't touch you at all."

"Harder, please, Sir," I whispered in apology, and he so graciously obliged.

Even as the pleasure gave way to pain, I was enthralled. Kieran was giving me everything my more casual encounters had been too afraid to try, because he *trusted* me. He believed that I knew what I could take. *Gods*, I adored him for that. It felt as though I was finally waking up from a dream, the winds of a tempest clearing all the fog from my mind, and suddenly I was more alert—more *alive*—than ever.

After several more delicious strikes, Kieran took a step back, withdrawing his touch. I was prepared to complain until he came into view in my periphery, crawling into my bed.

"I'm getting awfully tired of not being inside of you," he explained, as if it were obvious.

For a moment, I just stood there, marveling at the sight. Kieran was fully naked now—one arm casually strewn behind his head. My eyes drifted down from his chest to his lean, chiseled torso, to his thick, muscular thighs and the twitching erection between them.

"Like what you see, Little Conduit?"

I nodded aggressively, biting my lip.

"Come ride it, then."

Following his instructions was somewhat of a challenge. Lifting my legs up to get onto the mattress without my hands required some extra concentration as I tried to remain steady. Something about the sated, amused expression he wore told me he knew damn well what he was doing, too.

That smirk of his melted into something far more reverent once I managed to straddle him, slowly sinking onto his cock.

"*Gods*," he groaned, and I sighed in unison, tipping my head back as I took him in full.

Slowly, I began to rock my hips. Kieran let me lead like that for some time, allowing me to find my own pleasure as I bucked and writhed against him. Eventually though, he grabbed at my hips, a wicked gleam in his eyes.

"Don't worry, sweetheart. I've got you," he swore.

And then he began to move.

CHAPTER SIXTY-SIX

KIERAN

"*Oh. My. Fucking. Gods. Kier—*"

"*Shhh*, Arken. I know. I know," I said, gently pushing her hair back from her brow, slick with sweat.

My other hand remained relentless, quickening my ministrations around her clit as she rode me into oblivion. She was following her instructions quite well, only using my name—or parts of it, I supposed—while she screamed out with pleasure.

"You're doing so well," I crooned before the sharp bite of my palm met her ass once more.

"*Ffffuck*," she hissed as her body tensed beneath the blow.

I felt her tighten around my cock again and knew she was getting closer to release. I gave the area where I'd struck her another soft caress, loving the feel of her flesh as it raised and warmed beneath my hands.

Her body relaxed again, and I was sure the sting had started to fade into the sweeter ache that she'd been craving. It was too dark in here to tell, but I secretly hoped that I was leaving a mark or two. I wanted her to remember this tomorrow.

We continued on like that for some time, her hips finding their eager rhythm on top of me, occasionally tipping her head back to moan, or—when I was luckiest—cry out my name as I thrust into her, *hard*.

A few of her screams had been intense when I'd hit her. Every time, I would pause to check in on her, just to find an unholy smile plastered across her face. It was a gorgeous addition to the sweat and the absolute mess I'd made of her hair.

Such a carnal little creature.

"Getting close, *kenna*?" I asked as her cadence slowed, noticing how she began to still beneath my touch.

The Scáthic had just slipped out. Not that she could possibly speak the language, and even if she had noticed the term in her current state, she wouldn't have realized that I'd just called her *my lover* in my mother tongue.

Careful.

"Yessss— Yes, *Sir*."

Gods, she had to be exhausted by now, and yet she still corrected herself, following her instructions. That shy embarrassment had faded, and now the honorific simply spilled from her lips like a prayer.

Flawless.

In one fluid motion, I shifted my hips and used the strength of my legs—what little remained at this point—to pull myself out from underneath her. With a flick of my wrist, the shadowy knots I'd crafted to keep her bound dissipated. I tugged on her arm to guide her off the bed, pushing her back into our original position. Her core had to be burning, riding me with such intensity. And without the help of her hands to keep herself steady…

It was honestly incredible how well she'd done. She never ceased to amaze me.

"Ready, sweetheart?"

She whined, a little incoherently, but it sounded like approval—or maybe it was more of a beg. Either way, her aggressive nod was the confirmation I needed.

I made quick work of her pleasure in that position, thrusting into her hard and fast, losing myself in her—getting close myself. With a certain finality, I pulled Arken up by the throat—so violent and abrupt that she gasped, her back arching to meet my chest—and bit down on her neck. Almost hard enough to break skin. *Almost.*

As she tensed and tightened, trembling around my cock again, we found our final release together—so raw and perfect that it left us both shivering in the afterglow as we breathlessly collapsed back into bed.

So. Fucking. Flawless.

✧ ✧ ✧

Arken was already on the verge of sleep, nestling herself in my arms, head cradled against my chest. I could feel her chest rise and fall, her breathing slowing into the calm, steady cadence of comfort. I couldn't say I was surprised, either. I had counted *at least* four times where she had found release, calling out my name. I was blissfully sated, myself—still intoxicated by the honor of her submission. Of her pleasure. Her pain.

"Sometimes I think we really were," she murmured dreamily, clearly still adrift in her own submissive headspace.

"What's that, sweetheart?" I asked quietly, stroking her hair.

"Made for each other," she sighed.

If my heart could swell any further, I was afraid it might burst. Instead, it thrummed rapidly in my chest, my pulse racing at her words.

Do you feel it too, then? Have you felt this tether between us? That inescapable pull? All this time? I wanted to ask.

Realistically, though, I knew that Arken was just drunk. High on the endorphins of submission, basking in the afterglow of our perfect chemistry. And so was I. But that didn't alter how I felt.

Not in the *slightest*. Quite the opposite, really.

There were so many things that I wanted to ask her. So many things that I wanted to say. But I had done my job well, pushing Arken's pleasure to the absolute edge of exhaustion. Already, her breath had steadied, her chest beginning to rise and fall against mine at a gentle, familiar cadence.

Arken was fast asleep, and did not stir when I leaned in to press a soft kiss against her forehead. Even as I lingered, savoring the warmth of her skin, her eyelids didn't so much as flutter.

"Táieach kyn chroí, myon-Caindélach," I whispered.

I love you, Little Conduit.

CHAPTER SIXTY-SEVEN

KIERAN

Arken already knew that I had to leave early this morning, but that didn't make it any easier to walk away. I woke up before sunrise, feeling both elated and forlorn as I held her in my arms. Delicately, quietly, I managed to detangle myself from her without waking her from whatever pleasant dreams had left a soft smile on her face, even now.

Before I left, I stole a strip of parchment from her desk and scrawled out a quick note:

I forgot to give this to you. I found it on the beach yesterday. Pretty sure it's astral quartz. Either way, it made me think of you. Thank you for everything last night, Little Conduit. That was a gift I didn't deserve—as are you.

There was so much more that I wanted to say, but certain conversations and confessions would have to wait. I left the note and the smooth, shiny stone on the pillow where I had been sleeping beside her, leaning down to press a soft kiss against her forehead. Leaving Arken's bed was my own private Hel, but there was work to be done.

In truth, I had been slacking a bit over the last week or so.

While this woman's affections were clearly the most delicious, distracting substance known to mankind, I couldn't justify any further distance from the growing threat of the Bloodborne—I needed to focus. By the time dawn began to crest over Sophrosyne, I was already halfway to headquarters.

For the first several hours, HQ was relatively quiet outside of the shuffling steps of a scant few who had worked overnight shifts. I took advantage of the calm silence, using that time to review missives and correspondence from my various sources, cross-referencing the latest information with existing intel. We had several briefings scheduled this morning, though, so the majority of the upper ranks began to trickle in by 9 AM. As I made my way over to my commander's offices to check in, I overheard the tail end of a conversation between several of Rorick's rangers.

"*You found another one? A disturbance in the Wyldwoods?*"

"*Aye. It's already startin' to fade, I reckon. But I swear on the Source, I felt at least three pockets of that eerie shit out there during rotation this morning.*"

"*Gods. D'you think it's another Leshy?*"

"*Who the fuck knows, Brennans? Do I look like a scholar of daemons to you?*"

Their voices began to fade as we were headed in opposite directions, but my brow furrowed. New aetheric reverberations in the woods? That didn't make sense at all. It had been over ten days now since the incident. When I sent my own cadre in to investigate after Rorick's, they hadn't found anything new. And there hadn't been any further reports on daemonic activity. *One* Leshy was a rare enough thing, but multiple? Practically unheard of.

"Come in, Captain," Commander Ka called as I knocked at his door.

"Morning, Commander," I said as I entered, concern still gnawing at the back of my mind.

"You're in early," Ka noted.

"Just catching up on anything I may have missed while under the weather," I lied smoothly.

Hanjae Ka raised a thick brow over his stack of missives, but said nothing. Whether that was because he saw straight through my bullshit, or because he was giving me the benefit of the doubt—I could never seem to tell.

"How long do you think it'll be before you summon us for briefings, Commander?" I asked.

Most of our internal meetings were on specific, set schedules—but as of late, we had started to play certain things by ear. Leadership knew to expect summons at random these days when it came to updates on this rising domestic threat.

"About two hours. I'm waiting until I hear back from Demitrovic. Why do you ask?" Commander Ka inquired.

"I overheard some of Rorick's men chattering about another disturbance in the Wyldwoods. I may head out for a bit and make sure nothing is amiss."

"Could just be a touch of paranoia," my commander reminded me. "Some of those rangers are still young and got real spooked by the attack. That Leshy was the first daemon some of 'em had ever seen. But yes, at the very least, you should debrief with whoever's on patrol right now."

"Yes, sir," I replied. "Will do."

✧ ✧ ✧

The rangers on patrol had nothing of interest to report. They were light on coverage, though, and only running circuits within the first fifteen kilometers or so from the Eastern Gate, considering there were no scheduled lectures in the woods today. It made sense, not to spread themselves too thin. That said, Arken and I had been much further into the forest that night when we encountered the

Leshy, and I had this morbid, gnawing feeling in the back of my mind...

Despite the fact that protocols *clearly stated* that any venture into dangerous territory required us to move in groups unless otherwise authorized, I decided to take a stroll towards the heart of the Wyldwoods. Alone.

And I didn't have to go very far to realize that something was very, *very* wrong.

I could sense it within minutes—a low, pulsating wave of dark aether, a tear between worlds that hadn't been properly closed. The tenebrous energy of the void, leaching out into the atmosphere. The hair on the back of my neck rose.

Shit.

Hackles immediately raised, I whipped my head around furiously looking for the source, seeing nothing among the trees that could possibly explain that ripple of power that I felt, both foreign and familiar. That wasn't a daemonic disturbance. That was *blood magick...* And not of the native variety.

Where are you? My subconscious hissed as I continued to scan the surrounding area, walking further and further into the woods. Following that pulse. *Who are you, and why the fuck are you here?*

It didn't make any sense. The emissary wasn't due for at least another several months. They had no reason to be here. Why the fuck could I sense Scáthic magick being used in *Aemos*? And here, of all places? And why in the name of the godsdamned Source weren't they closing their rifts?

Finally, I saw something—a hooded figure in the distance, stepping into a small clearing. I recognized the cloak and immediately knew I had found my target, fury seething in my veins. They hadn't noticed me yet, so I continued to slink closer and closer—and that was a mistake. They scented me first.

Their head whipped around so quickly that the hood dropped, exposing a mane of silver-white hair pulled back in braids—and pale, familiar eyes filled with a hatred so searing, it almost reminded me of my sire.

That wasn't just a member of the Scáthic royal guard. That was a *Ravenhound*. One of Prince Caen's personal guards. Extremely well-trained, extremely sadistic, and *extremely* far from home.

Berith Apollyon and I locked eyes, the Ravenhound baring his fangs with a low hiss before disappearing into Shadow.

Shit.

Though I immediately gave chase, there were too many routes of escape through these woods, and there was only one way I was going to be able to find the Ravenhound at this rate. Dodging branches and brambles, I sprinted towards the clearing and bit down on my palm hard enough to draw blood.

Still moving, I drew the sigil on the other palm, pulling as much aether towards me as possible, allowing it to fill my lungs like smoke. The power I normally kept buried deep within exploded in my veins, heightening my senses to an extreme degree. I could hear every heartbeat, scent every person wandering within a fifty kilometer radius, blood thrumming in my ears. But there was only one heartbeat, one scent that I was looking for... and I would fucking find it.

Northeast.

My body knew where to go before my mind did, but I quickly caught up. The Ravenhound had fled towards the darkest parts of the wood—the most dangerous. *Of course.* Shoving my sleeve up my forearm, I drew another sigil with the blood that was still trickling from my palm, took a deep breath, and cut my own rift between worlds.

Following Berith's scent, it took a total of three excruciating strides through the void to pass through from one point in the Wyldwoods to another. As I exited the rift, I managed to appear right behind the bastard, who froze in place as soon as he sensed my presence.

Gotcha.

"Well, hello there, Berith. What the fuck are you doing here?"

"*Kieran,*" he replied evenly.

I snorted at the intentional informality. The disrespect that would've been a crime worthy of death where he was from. Where he *belonged*. I cast out my Shadows in thick ropes of binding aether, and within an instant they were crawling up his legs, keeping him in place. Binding him the same way I had kept that damned daemon bound.

The man remained silent, his own Shadows rippling off the dark silver, chitinous looking armor he wore beneath his cloaks. He was attempting to wrest free from mine, but I was stronger.

"Why are you *here*, Berith?" I repeated. "An emissary isn't due for several months, and you sure as Hel aren't who they'd send to *me*."

"That's none of your business, traitorous filth," the Ravenhound replied, malice glittering in his eyes.

"It sure the fuck is my business. What bullshit is Caen up to now? And did Dagon sanction it, or is he acting on his own accord?"

"Wouldn't you like to know?" Berith taunted.

"I would, actually. That's why I asked you so nicely."

The guard spat at my feet, and I sighed heavily. He was really going to make me do this, wasn't he?

So be it.

I took a deep breath and tunneled into my own aether, digging out what was buried at the very core. Pulling upon something that I had worked so *godsdamned* hard to suppress after all this time. Just to dredge it back up for the likes of this motherfucker.

My blood began to sing in recognition of the power I reclaimed. I took a step forward, and the Ravenhound's knees buckled under the weight of that dark, foreign magick.

"That's no way to treat a Vistarii, now is it, Berith?" I snarled.

The pressure I was exerting on the guard was already starting to make my head throb. I hadn't touched this power in years, save that one night with the Leshy. And with it, came darkness. Venom. Cruelty. *Fury.*

I drew my daggers.

"No," Berith gasped as one blade kissed his throat. "It is not. But you are hardly worthy of the name you bear."

"I take that as a compliment," I replied through grit teeth, beads of sweat beginning to form at my brow as I grappled with this power I had unleashed. "Now *tell me,* Berith Apollyon, servant of Caen. *What is your purpose here?*"

Berith groaned, grasping at his throat as if he could silence himself. Whatever magick Caen might have used to swear his hounds into servitude and secrecy, my own superseded it. But I had to respect the man for trying. My compulsion was stronger, and Berith was beginning to break.

"My *purpose,*" Berith spat angrily, "Is to spy on you, on behalf of the prince. And report back on anything of interest."

My lip curled with disdain as I crafted my expression as one of cruel disinterest, not the panic that was flooding my senses.

"And have you found anything of interest, *mutt?*" I demanded.

Despite the agonizing pain that the Ravenhound had to be in as he was clearly attempting to resist a certain arcane chain of command, the man laughed.

"Hardly," he barked out. "You lead an awfully pathetic life among these miserable creatures."

My eyes narrowed.

"Are you speaking the truth in full, Berith Apollyon?"

What little entertainment he'd found in attempting to insult me faded from his eyes, and yet again, the Ravenhound spat in my face.

How dare he?! My blood seemed to howl, my abandoned

birthright developing a mind of its own. *Make him pay for his insolence!*

No. I was not Dagon.

"Tell me what Caen knows," I commanded as Berith continued to struggle against his bindings, panting and panicked.

"He knows that you continue to serve the enemy. He knows where to locate you, should he ever deign to do so. He knows that you've grown *soft* and *weak* and even more *pathetic* than you ever were before—"

I could sense that Berith was using the insults to stall, attempting to mask something else. Something else that Caen knew. I continued to dig deep into the wellspring of power at my core, scraping the edge of my sanity to do it.

"What. Else. Does. He. Know. Berith?" I snapped, interrupting.

Berith Apollyon gave me a morbid grin, full of sickening mirth.

"He knows how to *hurt you,* Kieran," he hissed. "I made sure of it."

I was running out of time, energy, and godsdamned patience for these games. I applied heavy pressure on the dagger that was still at his throat, allowing it to sink in, piercing the skin.

"You're going to be very specific, now, Apollyon," I warned. "Or you're going to die very slowly. So how do you want to go about this?"

I was giving him a chance. It would be highly advantageous for me to have a turncoat in Caen's inner cadre—an informant. I could easily bind the Scáthic guard to an oath of fealty if he chose to participate. Caen would never know. The Ravenhound knew what I was asking, and stiffened.

"I would rather die than kneel before you, traitorous bastard."

"Then die," I snarled.

The Hound made one last attempt for his life, viciously

shoving an elbow into my gut and slicing at my side with the sharpened, jagged edge of his gauntlet. Taking advantage of my brief distraction, Berith managed to wrest himself free from my binds and took off in a sprint, deeper into the darkness of the forest. It had been too long, and so he had forgotten. He must've.

A Ravenhound was fast, but I was faster.

My Shadows melded effortlessly with that inherent power surging through my blood, whispering sweet nothings in my ear, begging to take over. I let them. The Ravenhound hardly made it a mile before I had overtaken him, catching him by the throat. By the time he even realized that I had caught up, my dagger was already in his back. The man staggered against me, laughing incredulously as he realized that I'd struck vital organs from behind.

"How *fucking* fitting," he wheezed.

"What have you told your prince, Berith? What else does he know?" I demanded, tugging at the dregs of what magick I had left to spend.

In his weakened state, it was even easier to impose my will on the man. I could hear the struggle, the hatred in his voice as he tried desperately to remain silent, coughing up blood as a consequence of his resistance. But the answer inevitably came, the Ravenhound forced to answer to the power of my bloodline.

"Prince Caen knows that you've developed a pretty little weakness, *your Grace*," Berith replied, his tone taking a turn for the mocking. "He knows that you've found some mortal *plaything*, and you seem attached to this one. He finds that to be rather interesting, indeed. So send me to the fucking Abyss, because I regret nothing. I hope she dies screaming."

I saw red. Nothing remained in me but the fury and the beast.

I tore out the Ravenhound's jugular with my teeth, letting his corpse drop to the ground without any semblance of respect.

CHAPTER SIXTY-EIGHT

ARKEN

I woke up alone, and found myself surprisingly comfortable with the silence. Perhaps it was because the scent of him still lingered on my sheets—orange peels and cloves melding with the sweat and the sex in a surprisingly pleasant fashion. I smirked to myself as I stretched out in bed, the various aches and soreness providing some very obvious reminders of what had transpired the night before.

Kieran also had the foresight to let me know over dinner last night that he had to leave before dawn, a seemingly simple gesture that actually meant the world to me. It eased my mind when I knew what to expect, and he knew that last minute changes in routine had a tendency to stress me out.

I ran my thumb over the astral quartz he had left behind on my pillow. The stone was smooth, flat and rounded—and it fit perfectly in my palm.

It made me think of you.

The quartz captured the morning sun flawlessly in irisated, opalescent little fractals. In a way, it reminded me of the way my Light often manifested, too. If Kieran could see me in the beauty of this tiny treasure... I felt my chest tighten.

Gods.

I was starting to think that Kieran and I had been kidding ourselves—and that the sex was all it had taken to wipe away that thin veneer claiming that what we had together was *platonic*. Had it ever been? Had we ever really been *just friends?*

I felt my cheeks heat as I remembered some of my lust-addled confessions last night. If it weren't for his sweet, hand-written note, and the quartz, I may have been afraid that I had scared him off.

Sometimes I really think we were made for each other.

It had sounded like the mallow-soft, saccharine confessions of a pre-teen crush, and I *had* admittedly been drunk on submission and satisfaction as I had said it, but sometimes, I did legitimately get the sense that there was something... *more* to the bond between Kieran and I. Something meant to be.

If Kieran had said anything in response, I hadn't heard it. While it used to take me quite literally *hours* on end to fall asleep, it took mere minutes when I slept with him in my bed. The warmth of his chest and the way he liked to draw lazy, loving circles on my back with his fingertips as I drifted off...

Good gods.

If I didn't get my ass out of bed and enforce some productivity upon myself now, I ran the risk of spending my entire day in bed—fantasizing about a man who had only left 3 hours ago. I needed to get my shit together. I summoned a small orb of Water from the washroom, icy cool, and let it splash against my face. I jolted and shivered as I jumped out of bed, but hey—it did the trick.

I padded into the kitchen to prepare myself some tea, only to find a small rabbit perched on my windowsill, sparkling in the sun. No ordinary rabbit, naturally. This one looked as though it had been carved out of amethyst and labradorite while also being semi-corporeal—it was Laurel's mail sprite.

Oh, right, I thought to myself as I opened the window latch and retrieved Laurel's note. *We've got brunch plans.*

I swear to the Source, Asher - if you cancel on us because you're too busy getting laid, I will break into your apartment and tear Kieran off of you with my bare hands.

See you at eleven!

I burst out laughing before I peeked out my window, towards the clock tower in the center of the city.

Shit. I had to start getting ready.

✧ ✧ ✧

I slathered my toast with butter and jam as Sienna Makar ranted and rambled about the expectations of her father.

"And like... Tell me why *Theia* had to be the one to tell him that was unrealistic. He thinks that I should come home on *every break* between quarters so that I can shadow him at Court, as if it's not a week's worth of travel both ways. Sure, Theia does it all the godsdamned time, but she doesn't even *teach* right now. She barely needs to be in Sophrosyne!"

"Wait, so Markus thinks you should travel for a week, spend a week back home in Luxtos & Stygos, and then journey *back* to Sophrosyne. Just to then take the week-long journey home *again* in between every academic quarter? To train for a role that you've, uhhh, literally grown up training to inherit?" I asked, incredulous. "That would eat up your whole break."

"Right? *Gods*, the man is exhausting. Thank the gods for Theia. She's the only one who can keep my father in line, I swear."

"At least she *can* keep him in line," Laurel laughed, though the smile didn't quite meet her eyes. "Mama Ansari couldn't keep my dad in check if she *tried*. And she does try, to be fair. He's just as stubborn as an ass."

I chewed on my toast, a little bit lost in thought. Sometimes when Laurel or Sia talked about their family lives, I felt strange pangs of wistfulness—a certain morbid curiosity overtaking me. *What were my parents like? What would our relationships look like, if they hadn't... If they were...*

"You alright over there, Arken?" Sia asked, nudging me with an arm.

"I mean, just take a look at her fucking *neck*," Laurel crowed. "That rude bastard kept her up all night, I'd put every Lyra I have on that bet."

"We fell asleep *eventually*," I murmured, cheeks heating.

Sia cackled.

"Good for you, girl," she said with a smirk, clinking her glass of juice against my tea cup.

"Am I allowed to say *I told you so* yet?" Laurel inquired, reaching across the table to swipe the grapes that I had pushed aside on my plate.

I rolled my eyes.

"If you need to get it out of your system, go right ahead, Ansari. By all means."

She didn't even hesitate.

"I *fuuuucking* told you so! 'Just friends' my ass," Laurel snorted. "What did I tell her, Sia?"

"That they just needed to bone and get it over with?" Sienna replied, smirking over her juice.

"You keep that shit in mind the next time I offer you my advice, Asher," Laurel cackled.

"I dunno, Laur—I'm not sure they've *gotten over* anything. It's what, day ten? Eleven? And they're still going at it like horny teenagers," Sienna said, pushing my hair back to get another glance at my neck.

Kieran had bit me hard enough last night that those strange godling teeth of his had nearly punctured my skin. I couldn't help but laugh when I'd caught a glance in the mirror. I looked like I'd fallen prey to yet another daemon attack—a vampyric one, this time.

Close enough.

Laurel let loose a low whistle, craning her neck to see just how shamelessly the man had claimed his territory.

"We've gotta get you some concealing powder or something, godsdamn. Or we could hit up Elise. She's getting pretty good at her cleric shit. Fixed my sprained wrist last month without any issues. I'm sure she wouldn't charge ya to clean that up."

My blush deepened as I realized that the dark little creature stirring in my chest didn't *want* to cover it up. Or conceal it. Or heal the wound with arcana. Not when the bite had made me come harder than I think I ever had before.

"Oh, you've got it so *cataclysmically* bad, Arken," Sia said with a wicked grin.

"So is he your boyfriend now, or what?" Laurel tacked on.

I shrugged.

"We haven't really had the conversation yet," I admitted, though saying that out loud didn't bother me as much as I thought it might. Things were surprisingly comfortable between Kieran and I after last night's... explorations.

"Ah, right," Sia replied dryly. "Of course. It's only been eleven days, Laur. Wherever would they find the time to talk about their feelings?"

"Alright, these are some bold jabs coming from you two. You know, the ones who rotate through the women of Sophrosyne like it's a professional *sport*," I groused. "What's the overlap in your body count at this point? Has anyone done a Venn diagram?"

The conversation devolved into further jabs, cackles, and screeches for the majority of our meal—so much so that I was grateful that it seemed to be a slow day for Corinne. We made sure to tip generously all the same, just in case we had scared off any of her other customers.

"Gods, I missed you two," Laurel said. "It's good to be back."

"How are things going back home, Laur?" I asked gently.

She had taken about a month off her coursework recently to go home to Samhaven, checking in on her parents after the disappearance of Amir.

My friend sighed. "I don't know. It's hard to gauge how they're *actually* doing right now. Mama's been putting on a brave face, my dad is just burying himself in work. I don't have the heart to tell them that I think these private investigators that they've hired are total frauds. It all just feels so fucking pointless. I don't know what they think those hacks could find that Lord Ymir's men couldn't. Or the Elder Guard, for that matter?"

"In a way, they might just be paying for their own peace of mind," Sienna pointed out. "So they can at least know they're doing absolutely everything they can for him right now."

"I suppose," Laurel sighed. "Regardless, I'm glad to be back, I'm not sure how much longer I could've dealt with how quiet that house is without him. And I felt like such an asshole, but every time another body would show up and they would confirm that it's not Amir..."

"You're not an asshole," Sia said softly. "There's still hope."

Laurel nodded, her gaze going distant and wistful.

The three of us sat in silence for a while, soaking up some much needed sunbeams until the bells of the clock tower sang out to interrupt.

"Gods, it's already two? I've gotta get going," Laurel said.

"I should probably go reply to my father's missives," Sienna groaned, getting up from the bench.

Personally, my day was looking to be uneventful at best. I had one lecture left, but that wasn't until early this evening, so I was half-tempted just to go home and take a nap. I had admittedly been operating at something of a... *sleep deficit* lately.

"Oh, and don't forget, Ark. We're meeting up for drinks at The Clover next week. Bring Kieran if you want. It'll be fun," Laurel called over her shoulder, just before she left.

"Friday, right?"

"Yes ma'am. I think the band that Hanna was talking about starts some time after eight."

"I'll be there," I promised.

"Pfft. You don't have a choice," Sienna said with a wink, heading off in the opposite direction.

Walking home, I caught myself smiling, feeling sentimental.

Before I came to Sophrosyne, I had never had friends like this. I loved the village, and I missed them all dearly—Hattie, Willem, *gods,* I even missed Thistle sometimes—that old daemonic chicken. But save one single soul in the Brindlewoods, nobody else had ever seen the real me. Not truly. And I owed everything to Amaretta, but even my mentor hadn't quite seen past certain facades I had built in an effort to please her.

Here, in the City of the Gods, I finally felt like I could be myself. I had nothing to prove, nobody who knew the awkward little girl from the forest. I had a handful of dear friends, maybe not much to anyone else in this sea of a thousand souls—but they were everything to me, because they saw me. They loved me. And I loved them so.

I had already been laying down roots. Slowly, but surely, I felt the leaves of my heart unfurl.

This whole thing had been a shot in the dark, my journey to the Arcane Studium—a blind leap of faith into the unknown. All I had hoped for was to survive it. It had been almost a year now.

We did it, Ark.

I hadn't just survived. I was *thriving* here.

Sophrosyne had become my home.

CHAPTER SIXTY-NINE

Arken

I wasn't too concerned when Kieran's raven showed up at my window later that night, in lieu of the guardsman himself.

I'm so sorry, sweetheart - I can't come over tonight. There's some shit I have to deal with for work... I could be pretty busy over the next few days. Be good. I'll come find you as soon as I can.

Yawning, I scribbled back.

Miss you already.
Be safe, Sir.

His reply was instantaneous, and I felt my heart flutter over three simple words.

Only for you.

I ran my fingertips over the words, memorizing the indentations of his quill strokes against the parchment, relishing in what was left unspoken behind them.

Despite a glaring lack of warmth beside me that night, I fell easily into a dreamless sleep.

◇ ◇ ◇

The second day was fine.

The third day was harder.

By the fourth day, I was starting to lose my mind. Kieran's responses to my messages were growing shorter, more clipped—when they even came at all.

I told myself to trust him. I fought against every insecure urge to go out *looking* for him around headquarters, just to check in and make sure he was okay. Because if he wasn't, he would tell me. If he couldn't, somehow—Hans or Jeremiah surely would. Kieran was *fine*, I kept reminding myself. He was the fucking Scouting & Reconnaissance Captain of the godsdamned Elder Guard. He could fend for himself. He was just busy.

That deep ache that I felt in his absence was haunting, but that was just... to be expected, right? Kieran and I had spent nearly two weeks straight together, only having parted for a few hours at a time. Prior to that, we had been through a near-death experience together. It was fair that I felt so attached... It was normal to miss him so badly that it *hurt*.

It was fine.

Until it wasn't.

I slept like shit by the fifth day of Kieran's absence, tossing and turning fitfully. He hadn't said goodnight the night prior, and there were no messages waiting for me at my window. My confidence was beginning to unravel as I replayed our last night together, picking myself apart. Over-analyzing everything I said. Everything we did. I had a sinking feeling in my gut that this was somehow my fault.

I had *tried* to hide my feelings for him, I really had—but I had also lapped up every ounce of affection he ever gave me, and fuck, it must have been so obvious.

Did I scare him away? Did I disappoint him somehow? Was this all in my head?

Determined to get a grip, I swallowed my pride and summoned my sprite.

Are you avoiding me, Kieran?

I waited for over an hour. No response.

I'm sorry if I sound pathetic right now, K, but it feels like something is wrong. If you're getting these, can you at least let me know that you're okay?
That we're okay?

I tried to disregard the way my hands trembled once his sprite appeared, thirty minutes later. I unfurled a scrap bit of parchment and a response that left me gutted.

I'm fine.

Logically, I knew that I was reading into this.

Kieran was a fucking upper-ranking leader, in an elite military force, that defended the largest godsdamned city in Atlas. While I had been spoiled with his uninterrupted attention for quite some time now, it was *statistically impossible* for him to be so constantly, readily available. He had more important things to do than keep me entertained, well-fucked, and emotionally comfortable. And he had every right to the space that he was currently taking.

I just wished that it hadn't been so abrupt.

Because in chasing the high that Kieran provided, I had been exploring the summits of my own bliss. My capacity for happiness, comfort, and confidence had been soaring to new heights, leaving certain doubts and wounds of mine behind in the valleys below. Because I had felt so *safe*. I had been climbing so recklessly, so fearlessly, that I hadn't stopped to think about what happened once I reached the pinnacle of it all.

And here I was, teetering dangerously on the edge of the world. Ready to fall.

Breathe, Arken.

I did my best. I managed to lose myself in my studies for a few hours, channeling all of my irrationalities into practicing my arcana in the privacy of my apartment. I always felt some semblance of relief whenever I let myself channel the Resonances that I normally kept hidden. Light was still my most comfortable, the most familiar—but playing with the others was like releasing a pressure valve in my chest.

And so I had resorted to the basics, summoning each element in their most base forms—little orbs of Light, Shadow, Fire, Air, Water and Earth, and I sent them drifting through the air above me as I laid in bed. I let myself indulge in delusions of grandeur like I used to as a child, pretending to be the master of the universe, graced with such powers of creation.

That had always been my favorite flavor of escapism—the fantasy that my hidden Resonances weren't a *problem*, but rather, a gift. That I wasn't broken or dangerous, I was *special*. The older I got, the harder it became to untether from the truths of reality. But as I crafted my own little constellations of aether in my room, I could *almost* remember what it had felt like, all those years ago.

That had been sorely needed.

✧ ✧ ✧

I really didn't think I was up for the idea of going out tonight.

I hadn't slept for longer than an hour or two, I was dehydrated, and couldn't recall the last time I had eaten a full meal. Mixing my misery with the company of strangers, alcohol, and a hit or miss lineup of evening entertainment sounded like a slog—whether or not I had promised my friends I would be there. I knew that they would fight me on it, but that didn't stop me from attempting to send off a weak excuse to stay home. I should have known they wouldn't even bother to reply via mail sprite. Less than an hour later, Sienna Makar was about ready to kick my door down.

Fuck.

When I finally gave in and opened the door, both of their faces fell.

"Oh, honey. What happened?" Laurel asked.

Sia was a bit more blunt, speaking over her. "I'm going to kill him."

A morbid burst of laughter escaped me despite myself, and, begrudgingly, I let my friends inside. It wasn't even seven yet, so I wandered towards the kitchen to put the tea kettle on, releasing a heavy sigh and waving for them to follow.

"I just don't get it," I repeated for what had to have been the tenth time in the conversation, pacing back and forth like a woman possessed.

I had spent the last half hour, *at least,* trying to verbally sort through this strange silence that had fallen between Kieran and I. Laurel and Sienna exchanged a look, the pair sitting cross-legged on my bed.

"I mean, am I crazy? Is this on me? Am I expecting too much here?"

Sia looked like she was about ready to smack me upside the head.

"You spent what, like nine? *Ten* days riding him non-stop, and then the man disappears into thin air? For five days straight?

You're not crazy. I'm surprised you haven't burned down their damn headquarters by now. I would've."

I slumped into the corner of my bedroom, staring at the wall and starting to feel like shit for subjecting my friends to this pity party.

"Not to be the irritating voice of reason here or anything, Ark," Laurel said softly, treading carefully. "But have you considered that there's a chance he isn't lying? He's a pretty high-ranking officer of the Elder Guard..."

As she trailed off, I heard what she left unsaid. What I hadn't really considered, having been stuck in my own selfishness, stuck in my own feelings.

People in Atlas were *disappearing*.

Even Sia seemed to blink a few times with unexpected clarity, neither of us expecting Laurel to be the more level-headed one between the three of us... but I mean, of course she would be in this circumstance.

"Nah, that's a good point, Laur," I said, exhaling heavily. "Maybe I just need to give him some space."

"Clearly, there is only one solution here," Sia said, standing up and dusting off her thighs with a determined look on her face. "We are going to go out, and we are going to get your mind off this shit. We are going to have fun. And we are going to look hot."

Sia's smile took a turn for the devious.

"And we are going to get you *very* drunk tonight, lightweight."

CHAPTER SEVENTY

KIERAN

Caen Vistarii was a sadist.

He should have been the firstborn. He should have been the one the Crones chose. He was everything that my people had expected me to become: vicious, cruel, and ruthless. A flawless reflection of our sire, the Shadow King of Scáth Saoirái.

Caen was only ten years old when I left the Shadow Plane, and he had already been corrupted by the legacy of our bloodline—all too happy to blindly follow in Dagon's footsteps and every other sick fuck who had Ascended the throne of Hel over the aeons. Caen had been a child, yes—my younger brother had been born not a year after me. And yet, by the time I came to Aemos, he had already cut his teeth on torture, killing and brutality. For his ninth birthday, Dagon gave him the Ravenhounds—and carte blanche to play judge, jury and executioner over what little remained of our homeland. I don't believe that Caen ever even had the chance to be a child. He was born a weapon.

I don't know why I was born any different, and yet I was.

Everything I had heard from the emissaries over the years suggested that the Prince of Shadows had only gotten worse with time. They said that he had grown into a man who delighted in psychological warfare, with a taste for the blood of the innocent.

And in truth? I had paid that very little mind. I had no intention of ever coming home. The day that Dagon and the Crones decided to cast me out—abandoning me alone in the woods, as a *child*, left to fend for myself in *another realm entirely*—was the same day I turned my back on the fate of Scáth Saoirái.

I had taken naive comfort in the fact that I was supposedly protected by the very same prophecy that I had chosen to defy. That Dagon would not—*could not*—act against Aemos on his own accord. If they wanted their vengeance, it would have to be through me. And after the Blight began all those centuries ago, the laws of the Shadow Plane were also *very* clear: Crossing between worlds was forbidden. A crime punishable not only by execution, but a slow, brutalized death in the Pits of the Undying.

So why the *fuck* was Caen in Aemos? Even princelings weren't above the laws of that land.

Because he was most assuredly here. Somewhere.

After dragging Berith Apollyon's corpse over to rot in the depths of the Pyrhhan Strait, I slowly regained clarity and control over myself. I had calmed the beast, buried the dark power I had reclaimed in the Wyldwoods, tightened every damper, lock and seal on it.

And then, once my heart rate had slowed and I had washed the blood from my face and hands in that cold river water, I allowed myself to *think*.

In order for Caen's hounds to have successfully gotten past the wards of Sophrosyne, they would have needed his blood magick. Spellwork could not survive the traversal between planes, because the void space in between each plane of existence was the very *absence* of aether—it stripped you of any arcane effects. So the *only* way that Berith could have successfully spied on me for however long was if his liege was in Aemos, too. The Hounds couldn't cast it themselves.

And since I had drawn that conclusion, I hadn't eaten.

I hadn't *slept*.

I would not know peace until I knew that my home was safe from the errant impulses of this dark intruder.

Until I knew she was safe.

It had been nearly five days since I last saw Arken, and I felt the ache of her absence with every godsdamned breath. The further away I got from Sophrosyne as I chased every stray trail of foreign arcana, the more it felt like there was legitimately some sort of tangible bond—a tether between the two of us. A resistance in her magnetic field.

Too far, that unspoken force seemed to say. *You're straying too far from her.*

But I had no other choice.

If there was even the slightest possibility that the prince and heir presumptive of the Shadow Plane had eyes on me right now, I couldn't dare go to her. I couldn't dare expose her as my most obvious weakness. *Especially* if he was already aware of her existence.

But if I had to guess, the Scáthic forces had only just recently arrived. It was probably their rift that allowed the Leshy to appear in the Wyldwoods in the first place, which meant that Caen and his hounds had been here for about two weeks, give or take. I had scoured through the forest and most of Southern Pyrhhas at this point—every trail leading to a dead end. It seemed highly likely to me that Caen was keeping his distance, and for good reason. The coward was probably sending his personal spies out, one by one, for the sake of whatever sick game he was playing from afar.

On one hand, that was a relief, because whatever details Berith may have managed to glean, they were surface level at best. The Ravenhound would have had to have kept a *significant* distance from me and mine in order to successfully stalk me. And to be frank, Arken and I had spent a majority of the last two weeks behind closed doors.

From such a distance, Arken's features were fairly nondescript—average height, dark brown hair, female. There were *thousands* of humans in Sophrosyne that met that profile. Unless Berith had somehow determined that she was a Light Conduit, which seemed unlikely. And *if* the Ravenhound had discovered such a damning detail, he would have delighted in tormenting me with that before he died. The bastard would have wanted me to know that *he* had sealed her fate.

So statistically speaking, so long as I kept my distance for now, Arken would be relatively safe. It was only a minor relief, but I would take whatever the fuck I could get as crippling terror and protective fury went to war in my bloodstream with every moment I still drew breath.

Terror and fury and *guilt*.

Because ultimately, this was my fault. My friendship with Arken had already been a risk. Now? I might as well offer her up to all of my enemies on a silver platter. Here she is, you heartless bastards! My weakness. My heart. *My whole fucking heart.*

I should have known better. I *had* known better.

Whether I'd acknowledged it or not, I *knew* I was in love with her. From the moment her life hung in the balance. When the Leshy attacked her, and I carried her broken body to safety like my own life depended on it. I had known, even then, that I couldn't live without her. And now, I would have to—at least for a little while.

There was a bitter irony here that I could hardly stomach.

Whether taking her to bed had been a mistake or not, last week had easily been the best thing that had ever happened to me. After a lifetime of self-imposed isolation, I finally had a taste of true intimacy—and it was sweeter than I could have possibly imagined.

Blinded by both lust and adoration, I had let my guard down, lowering the mask and letting her sink beneath my skin like a salve. Like salvation. And in granting myself this one selfish exception to the rules I had made for myself so long ago, I had inadvertently risked it all.

In allowing myself to fall in love with Arken Asher, I had damned her to a life of danger. I was painting a target on her back every time I had the audacity to touch what I had never deserved.

And the Fates were fickle, cruel bastards. As if this new threat was not enough to contend with alone, I also had to watch as, day by day, Arken's faith in me collapsed. Every scrap of parchment she sent over the last few days was a dagger in my gut, knowing that I had all but abandoned her on the precipice of a very, *very* important conversation. The cusp of a confession that might have changed everything for us.

When I left her bed that morning, I knew that I was leaving her vulnerable. I had *every godsdamned intention* of coming back that night and assuaging any fear that might have remained. I wanted to kiss every bruise and bite, and remind her that for each and every mark I had left on her flawless skin, she had left her own permanent mark on my entire fucking existence.

What made this all so viscerally terrifying was the distinct possibility that everything I felt for her was mutual. Because my Little Conduit was a stubborn, reckless, willful creature, and if she felt this, too? Fucking Hel, we were screwed.

So was it worth it, you dumb bastard? Was one week of perfect sex worth the risk of losing her forever?

If it had been anyone else, maybe. Maybe such glorious pleasure after all of the pain would have made the memory worth savoring, regardless of the cost. Not her, though. No.

She would never be collateral damage against my sins.

I knew what I had to do.

CHAPTER SEVENTY-ONE

ARKEN

Three shots of honey-whiskey on an empty stomach and a wounded ego had certainly been... a choice.

Even so, the liquor felt less like a buzz and more like a sedative as I went through the motions, trying my best to be present for my friends. This band was *gods-awful*, though. Even Sia, in all her effortless elegance, had a hard time finding the beat as we danced together amidst throngs of our peers.

"Oh, look, Ark! Mason's here tonight," Laurel chirped, dancing with Hanna several feet away. I resisted the urge to cringe.

"She means well," Sia murmured, wrapping a protective arm around my waist as Mason glanced our way. "But girl, please. We could find you something so *much better* than Mason Park."

My memories of that particular one-night stand had been effectively obliterated, so I had no real argument there. Though, to be fair to Mason, that was less about how forgettable he was in bed, and more about how infuriatingly memorable somebody else had been.

For the next few songs, Sienna attempted to distract me by pointing out other attractive strangers, offering tidbits of information on those she knew, and making scathing assumptions about those she didn't. Her colorful commentary kept me *just* distracted enough to enjoy myself, legitimately laughing a few times as she exposed some of her own personal exploits.

That said, even when I tried to see through Sia's playful lens of "alternate possibilities," all I could really see was Kieran. He remained in the back of my mind, a presence that was somehow both haunting and welcome.

"Oh, gods no. *Never* sleep with an Archeron," Sia was hissing in my ear now as a tall, curly-haired gentleman passed by. "Nathaniel is a skeevy prick, and his brother Emil simply does not bathe. I had to sit next to them both at a dinner party last month and spent the entire evening trying to devise a spell that would plug my ears and nose at the same time. Shadow can be so *useless*."

At some point or another, halfway through the night, one of Laurel's other friends had weaved her way through the crowd with bubbly enthusiasm. In truth, I didn't bother to catch her name, though she had invited us all to join up with another group of friends at a different tavern, a few blocks over. I guess we weren't the only ones who had been feeling less than enthusiastic about the band and their warbles.

We ended up taking her up on it. I downed the last of my whiskey, savoring the smooth burn in my throat and the warmth in my chest as we stepped back out into the night air, a throng of us just openly meandering through the industrial district. I was less familiar with this part of the city, so I linked arms with Sienna and attempted to tune back into their conversation. They were talking shit, from the sounds of it. Something about Percy Zephirin making an ass out of himself yet again, as we rounded the corner and made our way to the entrance of the smaller venue.

I had just about caught up on the story when suddenly, Laurel froze in her tracks.

"Oh, *fuck*," Sia said, after craning her neck to follow Laurel's gaze.

I couldn't quite see what they were reacting to, the view

obscured as the rest of the group was making their way inside. But all of the color seemed to drain from Sienna's face when she glanced back at me, and her eyes were frantic.

The Hel? I was so confused—until the small crowd cleared the doors. Then, I felt my heart stop dead in my chest.

No.

There was no fucking way—but I wasn't drunk enough to be delusional, and I was certainly not drunk enough to be imagining this scene of public indecency. There was a fever dream, a nightmare taking place right there on the opposite end of the dimly-lit room as various strangers milled about, blissfully unaware of my rising fury as my fingers curled and tightened into fists.

That fucking bastard.

"We should go," Laurel said quietly. "Come on, Ark. Let's just leave."

But I wasn't going anywhere. Because there he was, just a few feet away, after six godsdamned days of silence.

Kieran fucking Vistarii.

The prick was a perfect picture of unbothered self-indulgence. He was lounging on a red velvet chaise with one hand resting lazily behind his head, the other nursing a glass of some clear liquor. And how very *odd* for him to be in civilian clothes right now, all things considered—his black shirt in a state of partial undress, the buttons undone nearly all the way to his godsdamned navel.

The man who had apparently been so busy with work that he'd been ignoring me for days on end seemed perfectly content and care-free in his current situation: legs splayed wide as a lithe feminine form slowly writhed in between. Another feminine looking hand was already slipping against his neck, joining from behind. Of course.

Of fucking course.

I probably should have just listened to Laurel. Maybe I could have left with my dignity intact, if it weren't for the fact that in that exact moment, Kieran glanced over in our direction, catching my eye and holding my furious gaze with his own languid, self-satisfied smirk.

He didn't break that eye contact once as he dipped his head down to press his lips against the stranger's fingers, now resting on his collarbone. And I was just drunk enough to be brave.

As I started to stride forward, Laurel tried to catch my arm.

"Ark, *honey*, don't bother—"

Sienna cut in, her voice nearly as stone-cold and deadly as I was feeling at the moment.

"Laur. Let her go."

I was going to fucking strangle him.

I made it across the room in just a few strides, and I couldn't tell if it was because the room was small, or because I was just that angry.

"Busy with work, eh, *Captain*?" I asked, my voice low and sickly saccharine.

I disregarded the irritated glances I was getting from his choice in companionship this evening. My eyes narrowed in on him, and him alone. He just gave me a lazy smile, taking a long sip from what smelled like gin in his tumbler.

"I got off early."

My temper flared to cataclysmic levels, nails biting hard into the tender flesh of my palms.

"You've got to be fucking kidding me right now, Kieran."

"Am I?" he mused.

Oh, for fucks sake.

"Why are you doing this?" I demanded.

"Doing what, exactly?"

I stayed silent for a moment. Was this supposed to be a challenge? A trap? Some way to get me to humiliate myself in public by admitting my feelings for him? Was I supposed to act like this was anything other than a complete and utter betrayal?

"Aww," he said slowly, cocking his head. "Did you really think you could change me so easily, Little Conduit? That's almost... sweet."

"Don't fucking patronize me right now, Kieran."

"Later, then?"

Between the whiskey and the heat of my anger, masking a much deeper undercurrent of pain, my aether was absolutely roiling beneath my skin. I needed to be careful. I knew what could happen in the heat of a moment.

"I mean, I'd offer to let you join us, but there's only so much room left on the chair, you see. Hans and Jer are here, though. Perhaps you could show one of them a good time instead," Kieran suggested, nodding towards the other corner of the room.

I glanced over, tears prickling in my eyes. Hans blanched, meanwhile Jeremiah looked quietly furious.

You and me both, I thought bitterly—though I had no idea what Kieran's lieutenant was so angry about.

Something about the glimmer in Kieran's eye, his quiet challenge towards me, and the half-lidded, lusty glance of appreciation towards the woman in his lap had me on the verge of breaking something. I could practically taste the smoke in my mouth, the way I wanted to burn this entire place down.

"Go fuck yourself," I spat.

"I won't need to," he smirked. "Oh, and Arken?"

"What?" I snapped.

"Consider this your warning."

My mouth ran dry. For a moment, that motherfucker had actually rendered me speechless—and he didn't seem to care, turning his attention back to the blonde between his legs. Before I could do something that I'd regret, I turned on my heel and stormed off, walking straight past Laurel, Sienna, and the rest of them.

"Ark," Sia called, trying to follow.

"Don't," I snarled, tasting blood on my freshly bitten tongue. "I need to be alone."

I didn't bother to slow down or apologize. I just took off into the night with blood in my mouth, tears in my eyes, and crescent-shaped cuts on my palms, desperately trying to hold myself together. I needed to make it home.

Consider this your warning.

I just needed to make it home.

And then I could fall apart.

CHAPTER SEVENTY-TWO

KIERAN

"Are you fucking kidding me right now, Kieran?"

Sienna Makar had some very choice words for me at the moment, and I deserved them all. If only she knew that there wasn't a damned soul on this plane who hated me more than I hated myself.

I let the other Shadow Conduit tear into me, though, waiting for her to get it out of her system so that I could fucking leave and wash my hands of this place. It would probably take a hundred baths before I'd feel clean again.

And maybe even then, this damning act would linger on my skin.

You're a fucking monster.

Yeah. A monster that did what needed to be done. I still needed to make sure it worked, though. The woman I loved, who I had just disrespected to a disturbing degree, was a *very* stubborn creature.

"Are you done?" I asked Sienna, standing up.

She looked like she was almost ready to hit me. I almost wished she would.

"You're unbelievable," she sputtered. "You don't deserve her. You will never fucking deserve her."

Yeah. I knew that, too.

Makar continued her tirade, but I had stopped listening when I saw Jeremiah approach us from the corner of my eye. His voice dropped deadly low, quiet fury brewing in his eyes.

"Can I speak with you?"

I turned to Sienna, who was clearly still seething as well, and offered her the simpering smirk she expected of me.

"If you'll excuse me, Miss Makar," I said with a false bow. "Duty calls."

"Eat shit, Vistarii."

Hopefully, Fairchilde would make this short and sweet. I followed my lieutenant out towards the back exit of the tavern, into a quieter alley. Hans slunk out behind us both, keeping his head down.

"What the *fuck* was that about?" Jeremiah demanded.

"You're going to have to be more specific, Jer. But also, do you think you can be quick about it? I have somewhere to be."

"Don't play dumb, jackass. You set Arken up to find you like that, didn't you?"

I raised a brow at the clearly protective tone of voice my direct report was taking. Did he really think he needed to step in and protect Arken's feelings? He barely even knew the woman. Not like I did.

"You should know by now that I always have a reason for the things I do, Lieutenant," I said quietly, staring him down.

"Yeah. I do know that," Jeremiah spat. "And I also know you well enough to know that whatever reason you *think* you had to do that to her, *it wasn't good enough.*"

He didn't know anything. Not a godsdamned thing. I had to clamp down hard on the rising fury in my veins, remembering that this was exactly what I had set out to accomplish. I needed it to be believable... even if it meant a little bit of faith lost between myself and the two men I trusted most.

"Are you questioning your superior officer, Fairchilde?" I

asked, allowing haughty disdain to color my tone.

The forced attitude wasn't playing nice with the gin in my system. It was making me nauseous, truth be told, but I couldn't let on that this was all smoke and mirrors. Not yet. Not until she was safe.

"No, Kieran," Jeremiah said, shaking his head. "I'm questioning my *friend*, who is acting like a sick bastard right now."

"I don't owe you an explanation," I bit out, and I heard Hans heave a sigh behind us.

Jeremiah just stared me down for a moment, his smoke-gray eyes still subdued but furious, and incredulous. Just a few days ago, he and Hans were so quick to assume I'd cast Arken aside soon enough. Why were they acting so surprised now?

"No, I suppose you don't, Captain," Jeremiah said slowly. "But you sure as shit owe *her* one. Find her. Apologize."

A bark of laughter escaped my lips before I could really help myself.

"I don't owe her shit, either. And you? *You* don't give *me* orders," I snapped.

I heard a sharp intake of breath and turned towards Hans for just a second—morbidly curious as to how he, of all people, would be looking at me right about now. He, who had been so convinced that this was who I was in the first place. I barely had any time to parse the wide-eyed expression as my second-in-command opened his mouth to warn the other man.

"Jer! Don't—"

I got my wish. Jeremiah Fairchilde's fist met the left side of my face with a sickening *crack*—and oh, how I deserved that blow. He'd taken advantage of my blind side. *Clever.*

Part of me wanted nothing more than to swing back, just to tempt my lieutenant into beating me into a bloody pulp. I savored that pain as it shot through my skull—relished in the excuse to focus on anything other than the raw turmoil in my chest. But he didn't even give me a chance to act on those baser impulses, which was probably for the best.

Without a second glance, Jeremiah walked away, muttering to himself beneath his breath. Hans shot me a slight, apologetic wince before following suit, leaving me alone in the alley.

With an aching jaw, I stepped back into the Shadows.

◇ ◇ ◇

I had spent days trying to find another solution. Trying to find a way to avoid this. Trying to track Caen down. In the end, this was the only way to keep her safe until that motherfucker was dead and buried.

All of my best intentions aside, there had to be a special sort of torment planned for my soul in the Abyss, considering I was about to go stalk the woman I had just emotionally maimed. On purpose.

It was surprisingly difficult to catch up to her without rifting, though. She was faster these days, having stayed consistent with her strength training in preparation for the Physical Arcana test.

Impressive as ever, Little Conduit.

By the time I managed to catch up to Arken, I almost wished that I hadn't.

She was sobbing.

It was then that I realized that even though I'd just seen her through a terrifying, near-fatal experience, I'd actually never seen Arken cry. Misty eyed, yeah. Full blown tears? Not until this very moment.

It was devastating. The way that the kohl from her eyelids left tear tracks running down those golden doe eyes, now rimmed in red, as she struggled to sniff through swollen sinuses, occasionally choking on a shaky inhale...

I wanted to flay myself alive for this.

I was desperate for a way out, regret coating my mouth and throat. I had to find another way. There had to be another way to keep her safe.

But *how?*

Never let the woman out of my sight? Pick off my most dangerous enemies one by one, praying to the fucking Fates that I never slipped up? There was no decent option for risk mitigation when *I* was the godsdamned risk.

And if there was another way, you would've found it by now—implemented it before you had to hurt her like this. Better to see her miserable than dead, you selfish prick.

The truth tasted bitter on my tongue. As she stepped into her apartment—slamming the door—I slunk in behind her, entirely unseen. It took a great deal of arcane energy to pull total invisibility off in close quarters like this, even for me. But in a way, this was my penance. A tiny, microscopic fraction of penance.

I had to be absolutely certain that I'd done enough damage to keep her away from me for the time being.

Yes, I had set the entire scene up at the tavern with intention from the start. Even as I was hunting through Pyrhhas, searching for Caen—I had eyes on Arken all week. Thanks to Jeremiah and Hans, I knew exactly when her friends had managed to get her out of the house, and I set my fucked up little plan in motion. It was all too familiar, playing this role again—straight down to the flirtatious manipulation that convinced Laurel's friend to bait them to the tavern where I had been lying in wait.

I had let Arken think she stumbled into something I hadn't intended for her to see—and then I dug the blade in deeper by pretending I didn't even care. I was playing with her insecurities like some daemonic marionette, and *gods,* it had worked all too well.

I suffered in silence, watching from a darkened corner as Arken collapsed to the floor, pushing her knees up against her chest and burying her head in her arms, crying harder than before.

I am so, so sorry, sweetheart.

"Why?" I heard her whisper to herself quietly.

I wish I could tell you. I just need you safe.

And that's when I smelled smoke. Arken hadn't moved though, hadn't lit any candles or...

Wait. *What?*

Tiny, flickering flames had formed around her fists, and my heart began to pound.

When Arken realized her tights were getting scorched, her misery gave way to anger. We were indoors, but I could've sworn I felt a strong gust of wind swirl around the room in emphasis of that. A few crumpled strips of parchment blew off her coffee table, confirming my suspicions. All I could do was simply stare in horror as those small flames around her hands gave way to smoke—*no*. Not smoke. Arken's flames had given way to *Shadow*.

She noticed that, too, and it made her furious.

"For fucks sake!" Arken shouted down at her own hands, as if they were sentient. Like they had a mind of their own, but also... *like this had happened before.* Light arcana immediately flashed from her palms, an act of rebellion to dispel the darkness.

The scent of smoke stirred a recent memory in my mind: that moment of confusion in the Wyldwoods that had distracted me—the way the daemon had seemed to crackle and *burn* under Arken's blow. I had just chalked it up to the potential that Light could burn too, if it was bright enough.

But that wasn't Light aether. Those were *flames.*

I knew what Fire arcana looked like. I was intimately familiar.

There was no fucking way.

As Arken continued to pace with visible distress, her thigh bumped up against the kitchen table, knocking some small object to the floor. I watched with growing horror as instead of bending over to pick it up, the woman simply summoned the stone back into her palm. Her lip curled with disdain as she glanced down at it, and then I realized that it was the astral quartz that I had found on the beach. The gift I had left behind.

I flinched as she hurled the stone at the wall with alarming force—force beyond what muscle alone should have reasonably been able to accomplish—and the crystal shattered on impact, dropping to the floor in tiny shards.

Fire. Air. Shadow. Earth. Light.

I knew if I watched from the Shadows long enough, I could probably see her control Water, too. I felt an eerie prickle against my neck and back.

In the realm where few can wield one, He must find the one who wields all.

She was…

No.

I begged the Source in silent desperation. *Please.* Let this be a figment of my imagination, another fucking nightmare.

Not her.

Anyone but her.

A brand-new form of terror shot through me, a voice that did not belong to me ringing in my ears.

You can only run from Fate for so long, little prince. Did you really think you could escape the prophecy so easily?

I could practically hear the cackles of the Crones, reminding me of what had been written on my skin, carved out in ink and blood—a foretelling that I had been trying to flee from my entire life.

That tether. That *pull*. That inexplicable way that I'd been drawn to her like a moth to the flame, unable to stay away from her this whole damn time.

The Catalyst and the Conduit. Bound by a fate of inevitable destruction.

Arken was the second Harbinger.

CHAPTER SEVENTY-THREE

ARKEN

When I finally fell asleep last night, I had been on an emotional warpath—bloodthirsty and feral and *furious*. I had been ready to fight, wanting to carve my pound of flesh from Kieran's godsdamned chest if I had to.

When I woke up this morning, I was just... tired.

Tired, bitter, sore, and hungover.

As I sat in silence at my kitchen table, brooding over black coffee, I felt a certain sort of resigned acceptance, a miserable moment of subdued clarity.

I got fucking *played*.

I had known who Kieran was from the very beginning: a silver-tongued, sweet-talking *liar*—someone who had mastered the art of manipulation and had no shame about those skills, putting them on public display. I mean, shit—it was part of his godsdamned *job*.

Somewhere in between the friendship and the sex, I must have just misread signals. Maybe I had been presumptuous. Or maybe I had just been looking for signs that I'd *wanted* to see—imagining emotional ties, imagining a true bond where it didn't exist.

I always did have an overactive imagination.

After a long bath and a pathetic excuse for breakfast, nibbling on a few crackers and gulping down several glasses of water just to ease the splitting headache—I sent Bluebell off to Sienna and Laurel with notes, thanking them both and letting them know that I was okay.

It took another hour's worth of deliberation for me to finally send one off to Kieran.

We need to talk.

It didn't take long to get a response this time.

Fine.

I wasn't having this conversation through sprites, though. He would face me, whether he wanted to or not. I desperately tried to bury whatever hope that I had left as I tugged on my boots and swallowed my pride.

I walked slowly down the cobblestone path to Kieran's townhouse, my cadence a slow shuffle, as if my feet were trying to prolong the inevitable. I tugged at the loose strings on my sleeve, begging myself to let go of that tiny sliver of longing, the prayer that *somehow,* this was all some sort of exceptionally fucked-up misunderstanding. I had ignored one too many warning signs already.

My heart was a stubborn thing, refusing to submit. It clung to that fleeting sweetness, those soft kisses and the warmth of his body when I'd slept in his arms.

Gods. All of that perfection, all of that bliss—it had only been a week ago. How had we strayed so far off course?

It felt like defeat when I knocked on Kieran's door. When he opened it, I could find nothing familiar in the expression he wore... It was cold. It was hard.

It was bitter.

Angry.

I stepped past him in the doorway, letting myself in.

"Hey."

Kieran remained silent and stoic as he followed me into his living room.

What the fuck did he have to be angry about?

I realized, then, glancing at that couch, that this was probably a conversation more suited for neutral ground. But at this point... there weren't any particularly *neutral* places for Kieran and I, now were there?

Everything between the two of us was personal.

The anger in his eyes had dulled slightly as he followed my gaze, his visage growing somewhat listless instead. He was certainly carrying himself like a godsdamned corpse—no Light or life to be found as I searched his face, looking for answers. Trying to figure out what the Hel I wanted to say to him.

Silence fell between us. It was probably only a minute at most, maybe two—but it felt like hours.

My palms prickled with sweat.

Just say something, Arken. Anything.

"You know, that wasn't exactly what I meant when I asked for a fucking warning," I finally said, surprised by how bitter my voice sounded.

He raised a single brow, but said nothing in response.

"But I suppose you never actually agreed to that, huh?" I continued. "Listen, Kier..."

I trailed off for a moment, sighing heavily as I ran one hand through my hair.

"I'm sorry. I'm sorry if I let things get weird between us. I'm sorry if I pushed your boundaries, or if I took things too far when it came to my feelings for you. I *know* that we both had our reasons for keeping things platonic, and we fucked up. I'm guessing this is your way of putting me back in my place."

He kept staring back at me, impassive. Not a single emotion passing through his face, no confirmation or denial.

"So... go ahead," I said quietly, resigned to this as our only way forward. "Put me back into whatever box you're most comfortable with, Kieran. I can handle it. Keep your secrets, keep your space. You didn't have to *lie*. You could have just said something. And please, don't try to lie now. Don't act like I don't know you better than that."

He had been so stoic and silent that it was almost a surprise when he spoke.

"No, Arken. You really, really don't."

His voice was dull, but unyielding. My temper flared, bristling against the *finality* of it all, and the audacity that he had to try and put up a front.

"Oh, spare me the bullshit, Kieran," I snapped. "You're my best friend. I know you."

He snorted.

"*Friends*. Is that what we are?"

There was clarity in his eyes now as he took several steps towards me, carrying himself with that familiar feline grace—only this time, it actually felt predatory.

"Of course," I said.

"No," he said slowly. "I don't think so."

My brows knit together as I tried to parse whatever he was trying to imply here. Even if Kieran was trying to push me away, push us back behind our own respective walls of platonic safe-keeping, how could he suggest that we weren't even *friends*?

"None of this was real, Arken." Kieran said, looking at me as if that should have been obvious.

It was honestly a little bit terrifying, the way he could make such a lie sound genuine as it slid off his tongue. But I would face it down. For him.

"And what, pray tell, would you call the last year or so of your free time?" I challenged.

"I was just doing my job."

What?

"What are you even talking about?"

"Come on now, Ark—you're clever enough. A rare Conduit shows up in Sophrosyne as political tensions are rising. I got *assigned* to keep an eye on you—forgive me if I found ways to pass the time and ease the boredom of following some first-year freshling around."

"I don't believe you. There's something else going on here, there's something that you've been hiding from me," I accused.

"I mean, I thought that much was obvious," Kieran purred.

"Shut up. That's not what I meant, and you know it. You *know* I'm not talking about the sex."

"Not much else to talk about, is there? I mean, I got what I wanted out of this little game, didn't I?"

"Fuck you, Kieran! You didn't spend an entire *year* following me for work, and you didn't use that time to befriend me just to get your cock wet. Not when you could take your eager pick from half of this godsdamned city. You're a pretty liar, Captain—but I don't believe you."

"What can I say?" Kieran shrugged. "I like a challenge, on occasion. The game gets terribly dull when you always win."

I resisted the rising urge to punch him in the face.

"This isn't fucking funny."

His lip curled into a cruel sneer.

"No, you're right. It's not very entertaining for me anymore either, Arken. It's just desperate. And, honestly, it's a little bit sad having to stand here and watch you scramble like this. I gave you your warning. But if it makes you feel any better, at least the sex was halfway decent. You were *almost* worth my time."

"Please don't do this," I whispered. "*Please.* Fuck your secrets. Fuck whatever it is you're hiding from me. Fuck this stupid game you're playing."

My voice cracked, and it was as if something visibly snapped in him at that same exact moment. Suddenly, Kieran was completely up in my face—his anger resurfacing. He was *livid*, but also so close that I could lean in and kiss him if I wanted. If I wasn't so afraid.

"Oh, you want to talk about *secrets*? Are you fucking *sure* about that one, Asher?" he hissed in my face.

Yet again, I was thrown for a loop.

"I'm— What? What are you trying to say?" I stammered.

A muscle in Kieran's jaw feathered as his gaze darkened, like Hel freezing over.

"A bit bold of you, don't you think? To act as if we were *so close*. To waltz your demanding little ass in here and accuse me of hiding shit from you, as if you haven't been doing the exact same thing this whole time. Do you *really* want to go there?"

This was the first time he'd ever raised his voice with me, and he was breathing hard, as if he was trying to keep his own temper in check. What the fuck was he *talking* about? And why was he so *mad* about it?

I swallowed hard, struggling to reconcile what it felt like to be afraid of the one person I had always felt safe with.

"I... I have nothing to hide from you, Kieran."

"Ah. Well, then. Look who's the liar now," he replied bitterly.

"Kieran... what are you talking about?"

"I want you to stay away from me, Arken."

"What?! *Why?* Gods, Kieran, I can let it go, I'm sorry. I'm so sorry. We can just be friends, it's fine—"

"I have no interest in being your fucking *friend*," Kieran growled.

Most of his words had rang empty so far—bitter, but disingenuous. But there was a certain degree of sincerity present now, and my heart dropped to the pit of my stomach as I realized... He was serious.

Gods, Arken. What have you done?

My voice was small when I finally found words to reply.

"What... What are you saying, Kier?"

"We're not friends. We're not anything. We never were. And you? You need to stay the fuck away from me from now on. Don't ever come back here. Is that clear enough?"

For a moment, all I could do was stare at him. Hopelessly confused, lost in the animosity that was simmering behind his eyes.

"I don't understand," I breathed, the sharp bite of tears prickling behind my eyelids as I swallowed the words that I actually wanted to say.

Please stop. Please don't do this. I don't want to lose you.

"Gods, you're really going to make me spell it out for you? Only clever when it's convenient? Fucking fine, Arken. If that's how you want to play, then how about this? You need to stay away from me, because *I know what you are.*"

I sucked in a sharp breath.

No. There was no way. He couldn't.

"I don't know what you're talking about."

My voice cracked as I lied straight to his face.

"I don't have time for this shit," he snarled. "Keep playing dumb with me, and I'll drag you to the Nineteen right here and now."

"Why would you—"

"Because I think the Elders would be *very* interested in you, now wouldn't they, Arken?" Kieran interrupted. "Because you're not *just* a Light Conduit... Are you?"

No.

"You..."

"Yeah," he replied bitterly. "I know."

"You wouldn't," I whispered.

He had to know that it was dangerous. He had to know that taking me to the Nineteen was the equivalent of a death sentence, if they knew what I was capable of. He *did* know... I could see it in his eyes. He knew. *He knew.*

My heart began to splinter and crack.

"Please," I begged. "*Please*, Kieran, you can't—"

"You have no *godsdamned* idea what I can and cannot do, Little Conduit."

This time, the nickname fell from his lips like venom. Like an insult. Like a fucking dagger, held against my throat. Kieran almost seemed pleased with himself as the poisoned, pointed words finally met their mark.

"Never speak of this again. Never speak to *me* again. Are we clear?"

I was going to be sick. I broke into a cold sweat, taking shallow breaths, nausea churning in my gut as I stood there, dumbfounded, like an idiot. Like a godsdamned *fool.*

The man who stood before me was a stranger. Kieran had finally taken off the mask for me, and what remained was darker, colder, and more cruel than I ever could have guessed.

"Are. We. Clear. Arken?" Kieran snapped, demanding an answer.

"Crystal," I whispered, eyes dropping to the floor.

I couldn't look at him. I knew I would regret it later, but if I glanced back up at that glacial gaze, if I looked into his eyes, I would have kept fighting. I wanted so badly to keep fighting...

But this was a battle that I could never win.

A fight I couldn't afford to lose.

And so instead, I did the impossible. The unfathomable.

I betrayed my own heart, and I turned my back on Kieran Vistarii.

Heart pounding, hands trembling, utterly *terrified* of the man I loved... I walked away from the best thing I ever had.

And each step forward was agony.

EPILOGUE

Every year, when the Blood Moon rose, Scáth Saoirái sent an emissary to their crown prince in the dead of night.

It didn't matter where he was in Atlas. Whether he was on a mission halfway across the continent, safe behind the aetheric wards of Sophrosyne, or lurking somewhere in the Shadows in avoidance—on the eve of his birth, they always found him.

Though the identity of the emissary had changed from time to time over the years, the intent was always the same: To pass along messages from the Crones. To remind the prince of his duties, his destiny. To ensure that he never forgot about the prophecy, even if he had long since decided to leave it behind, letting those weighted words gather dust in the back of his mind.

This was his fate, they would remind him, year after year. Written in dark stars, before he had taken a single breath. There was no escaping what had been foretold, they would claim. No matter how long the prince chose to delay it.

They would try to convince him that the ruin of Aemos was inevitable, and that the survival of his people depended on the destruction of theirs.

His people. It had been a long, long time since the crown prince of the Shadow Plane had held on to any illusion that the people of Scáth Saoirái were his to serve, or even to rely upon.

Tonight, he did not bother to hide from the emissary. He would be waiting for them, whoever they were. He had questions of his own.

On the cusp of midnight, the envoy arrived as expected.

"Greetings, my prince."

The man who stood at the threshold of his townhouse door shared just enough of the prince's own bloodline for his features to read as a dismal mirror. Just looking at the brother of his sire was a reminder of his place amongst a family fueled by bloodshed and cruelty.

"Abraxas."

As much as the heir to the throne of Hel had tried to pretend that he could escape the consequences of his birth, the curse of his own blood—he had already proven otherwise, just a few weeks ago. Cruelty would always be in his nature. He was a bitter, cold-hearted bastard, just like the rest of them.

At least now, she saw him for what he truly was.

"I come bearing messages from the King and the Crones," Abraxas said, handing over the sealed scrolls.

The emissary flinched as his prince accepted the missives, and then promptly tossed them in the fireplace.

"Fuck the King. Fuck the Crones," he replied, letting them all burn.

"So this is still the role that you choose to play, Kieran?"

"Did I fucking stutter, Abraxas?"

"You did not, Your Grace."

"Don't call me that."

"As you wish. Still, it would be remiss of me not to make the observation that something appears to have changed in you. Your aura is... different."

Abraxas Vistarii had what they called the Sight—the ability to detect reflections of the soul, the waves of energy that surrounded any living creature that apparently gave insight into their base natures and motivations. It was a rare gift, and Kieran didn't particularly like that his uncle was reading his right now, but it was no exact science. Hardly a concern.

And he was not surprised to hear that his aura had changed, now that he had crossed paths with the second Harbinger.

Arken.

Her name had a sharp edge in his mind these days. It all seemed so obvious in hindsight.

The immediate familiarity he'd felt around her. The ease with which she'd entered his life. The inexplicable, unrelenting magnetism between them both.

Arken was his other half, in the worst possible way. A mirrored reflection of his crooked soul, and damning evidence of a fate he had fought so desperately to escape.

It had been so stupid of him, so incredibly naive, to presume that he had been successful. That he could have found something beautiful and holy that belonged to him—not that godsdamned prophecy. Several weeks had passed now, and the question still haunted him.

Had any of it been real?

"Your aura has not changed in all the years I've known you, Kieran," Abraxas said slowly, eyes narrowing.

Kieran shrugged, donning the mask of the lax, arrogant princeling that his uncle expected him to be. It was a comfortable facade.

"My hair is also longer than it's been in the last twenty-six years, if you're collecting dull observations to bring back to the Crones," he replied, sounding bored.

"The length suits you, my prince," Abraxas replied, still eyeing him with suspicion.

He rolled his eyes. Of all the emissaries his father sent, Abraxas was the one who treated Kieran with the most undue reverence—the only one who seemed to respect his primogeniture. Abraxas was older than the others, and always spoke as if he had deluded himself into thinking that eventually, one day, Kieran would return home. He still seemed to believe that his nephew had some semblance of love left for the world he left behind. Abraxas still saw him as the promised prince. The Catalyst.

The others simply saw him as a traitor.

They stood there in silence for some time before Abraxas spoke again.

"I feel compelled to inform you that your father has fallen ill, considering you have reduced his missive to ash. The king is... quite unwell, I fear."

Good, Kieran thought to himself.

"I suppose that would explain why Caen and his Ravenhounds have been sniffing around here as of late. Can none of Dagon's advisors keep that little shit on a leash?" he asked sharply.

Abraxas Vistarii was one of said advisors on his father's council.

"The other advisors see Caen as the most likely heir in your absence," Abraxas replied, frowning. "Few would deign to condemn the actions of their future king, no matter how reckless they may be."

"Even if he and his cadre are leaving traces of themselves everywhere? In Sophrosyne—within spitting distance of the Aetherborne? Even if they're leaving half-open rifts between the realms, the very risk that damned Scáth Saoirái in the first place?" Kieran challenged.

"Krysx," Abraxas swore, slipping back into their mother tongue.

Clearly, even the Council didn't know what their presumptive heir had been up to as of late.

"I don't know what any of you expected," he replied. "Caen has always been foolish. A slave to his own impulses."

"All the more reason for you to come home, Kieran."

That was not an option.

"Or I could just kill him," he replied, malice coating the dark prince's tongue.

"Why are you so opposed to claiming your birthright?"

"Is it really so strange that I might be adverse to slaughtering millions of innocent people to save my abusers?"

He had never understood how men like Abraxas, who carried themselves with some manner of honor and empathy, could accept such a thing. All because three demented, accursed creatures claimed it to be the will of the Source.

"And what of the innocent lives in Scáth?"

"Last I heard, there were not many of those left, uncle. That blood is on Dagon's hands, not mine. I am not the king who let Scáth fall to ruin through neglect."

"No, you are not. But you could be the king that saves us. You could salvage our legacy."

"No chance in Hel, Abraxas."

"I understand that you are attached to this realm, Your Grace," Abraxas said slowly. "But have you considered that you could save it yourself, if you just come home now? Return to Hel, and when Dagon dies, you can Ascend as king and even Caen would have to bend the knee. If you have yet to encounter the second Harbinger, the prophecy wouldn't..."

He trailed off, and then his pale eyes widened.

"Oh, but you have, haven't you?" Abraxas breathed, and Kieran's hands instinctively met with the daggers at his side. "Your aura..."

"Not. Another. Word. Abraxas," Kieran hissed, staring him down.

With the emissary's gaze locked on his, a visage of sheer shock and disbelief, his prince nicked a single fingertip against the edge of his dagger, drawing blood. It wasn't as difficult, this time, to draw upon that same dark force that he had used to subdue the Ravenhound. He dragged that bleeding forefinger against his wrist before Abraxas could even try to stop him, and the raw umbral power shot through his veins.

"That is none of your godsdamned business, Abraxas. You will not breathe a word of this. Not to my father, not to my brothers, and certainly not to those godsdamned Crones," he said through grit teeth, focusing all of his energy into pouring the arcane exertion of his will.

"Your aura..." Abraxas repeated, shuddering under the weight of the compulsion. "The solys... the Light entwined... Who are they? What have you found, Kieran?"

The aether in his veins turned to ice.

"If you bring that information back to Hel, Abraxas, I will follow you. I will return to the Plane of Shadows just to flay you alive, and cast your body into the Pits of the Undying. Before I hunt Caen down and do the very same to him."

The dark imperial magick was thrumming throughout his body now, emanating from his skin. Again, his Shadows began to whisper their sweet nothings, their promises of indomitable might like chains, attempting to wrap around his throat and pull him under. This power had a mind of its own—an insatiable desire to devour him whole, to force his hand towards the most base, carnal instincts of his ancestors. There was a reason he had kept it buried deep.

Sweat dripped from Abraxas' brow as his knees buckled, his attempts to resist his prince thwarted. This was the Vistarii legacy—subjugation. Oppression. An unbroken bloodline of conquerors who held more power than they deserved to wield. The throne of Hel was beyond redemption.

"Understood, Your Grace."

It was not enough.

"Swear yourself to me, Abraxas. I want a blood oath."

Kieran could not trust that his influence would extend once the emissary returned back to their home realm, but he didn't want to kill the man if he didn't have to. A pathetic weakness, perhaps, but in the scant few pleasant memories that Kieran had of his childhood, Abraxas had been there. Abraxas, and his mother.

"If that is your will, it shall be done, my prince."

He tossed one of his daggers to Abraxas, who caught the blade with a trembling hand. He expected to see resentment in his uncle's eyes, *anger* as he forced him to carve the sigil of binding on his own wrist, to repeat the incantation. Kieran was forcing him to betray the crown, to withhold vital information that could have led to the salvation of the Shadow Plane, of his people, *their* people. For that, Kieran had expected nothing less than hatred.

Instead, he saw softness. As the rune sealed and bound the emissary to secrecy, Kieran saw gentle understanding.

"No matter how this unfolds, I am... I am happy for you, Your Grace."

"I beg your pardon?" he asked, incredulous.

"I am comforted to know that you have finally found something you'll fight to protect," Abraxas explained. "Your solys."

Your guiding light.

"I never said I was protecting anyone. Or anything," Kieran bit out, hoping his tone could shroud the relief that he felt, knowing he already had Abraxas bound by a blood oath.

His uncle knew too much.

"You didn't have to, Kieran. It is woven into your aura. That Light... It is inextricable from you, now. You found the Conduit. The other Harbinger... Gods. Their presence is exquisite. They have imprinted on your soul."

The Harbinger of Hel swallowed any acknowledgement of those words in silence as Abraxas spoke, blood oath or not.

They could not have her. He would die first.

Still, Abraxas managed to stare straight through his soul, those pale blue eyes alight with awe as he spoke.

"And so it begins."

TO BE CONTINUED...

END of HARBINGERS, Book One.

AUTHOR'S NOTE

Thank you so much for reading Of Blood & Aether. I hope you enjoyed your first foray into the Aetherverse—because we've got at least five books (and a novella) to go. Harbingers, Book Two will introduce our third and final protagonist of the series... And I can't wait for you to meet him.

If you enjoyed this book, it would mean the world to me if you'd consider leaving a review on Amazon or GoodReads. As an indie author, your support is immediately felt and endlessly appreciated.

To keep in touch and stay tuned for future releases, bonus content, chaotic ramblings and so much more, please feel free to check out my website at harperhawthorne.com, subscribe to my newsletter, or follow me on social media. I'm most active on places like Twitter, TikTok and Instagram, but I'm essentially *@harperhawthorne* anywhere else I might wander.

GLOSSARY OF TERMS

Abyss - A colloquial term for the void space in between planes of existence, where it is believed that there is a total absence of aether. Some Atlassian religions purport that damned souls do not return to the Source when they die, and are instead left to suffer in this sea of nothingness. It is also referred to as "The Void".

Aemos - Aemos is the seventh elemental plane of existence in the Harbingers universe. It is also known as the Plane of Life.

Aether - The lifeblood of the universe, a substance present in all living things to some extent. Pure aether is the source of all magick and can also be broken down into specific elements: Light aether, Fire aether, etc.

Aetherborne - Also referred to as "the gods" or "the Elders," the Aetherborne are the immortal predecessors of the human race on Aemos, the elder species and first known intelligent life forms to develop in Aemos after the plane was created.

Aetheric - An ancient language, once spoken by the Aetherborne.

Aetheric Signature - A unique method of identification that is tied to the blood and aether of an individual, which can be used to identify or even locate them.

Aetherstorm - A storm that is caused by an upheaval or upset balance of aether on an elemental plane, typically stronger and more dangerous than a regular weather event.

Arcana - A complex form of magick developed by the Aetherborne, which typically utilizes incantations, somatic gestures, and other components to amplify one's elemental Resonance as they channel aether.

Arcane Brand - An arcane tattoo which serves to identify one as a citizen of Sophrosyne, allows one to pass through the protective wards surrounding the city, and also prevents Conduits from speaking on knowledge that is considered exclusive to the Studium.

Arcane Studium - The most prestigious college of arcane arts and sciences in the realm of Aemos, nestled in the center of Sophrosyne. The Studium was built by the Aetherborne for the sake of teaching Resonant humans how to use their innate elemental magick.

Atlas - The largest continent in Aemos, comprised of seven independent territories: Samhaven, Vindyrst, Ithreac, Pyrhhas, Luxtos & Stygos, and Sophrosyne.

Conduit - The official title of those who have been accepted as students at the Arcane Studium, wielders of arcana.

Exxem - Also known as "The Deadlands," Exxem is the southernmost continent in Aemos. The people of Exxem are nomadic in nature and do not maintain active political alliances with Atlas.

Hel - To most denizens of Aemos, the term "Hel" is synonymous with the Abyss or the Void. Hel is also the capital city-state of the Shadow Plane.

Irros - A largely tropical continent to the east of Atlas, best known for the highly valuable export of Irrosi silk.

Ithreac - A large valley territory nestled in the very center of Atlas, ruled by the House of Clay.

Luxtos & Stygos - Also known as the Astral & Umbral Isles, these islands are considered a united territory, ruled by the House of Light & Shadow.

Lyra - The universal currency of Atlas.

Mail Sprite - A complex conjuration, usually in the form of some manner of elemental animal, able to deliver correspondence between Conduits.

Novos - The northernmost continent in the realm of Aemos.

Pyrhhas - The largest and southernmost territory in Atlas, ruled by the House of Embers.

Resonance - The term used for a mortal's capacity to wield an element of aether, and which type.

Resonant - A mortal born with the increasingly rare ability to summon a single element of aether: Fire, Water, Earth, Air, Light or Shadow.

Samhaven - The northwestern territory of Atlas, ruled by the House of Torrents.

Scáth Saoirái - The native term for the Shadow Plane.

Scholar - A specialized professor of the arcane or arcane-adjacent arts at the Studium. Highly specialized scholars that are considered experts in their field are often referred to as "High Scholars".

Sophrosyne - The City of the Gods, a city-state and independent enclave nestled in the heart of Pyrhhas. Home to the Arcane Studium, Sophrosyne is the largest city in Atlas, and falls under the jurisdiction of the Aetherborne.

The Biblyos - A massive collection of interconnected libraries and archival buildings located in the Academic Quarter of Sophrosyne.

The Brindlewoods - A large forest in Southern Samhaven, home to a number of small villages, including the one where Arken grew up.

The Cataclysm - A large-scale, violent event that took place in Aemos as a result of a great upheaval in the balance of aether across the plane, which threatened to end all mortal life, were it not for the intervention of the Nineteen.

The Fates - According to most creation mythos in Aemos, the Fates are omnipresent arbiters of destiny that watch over the realm.

The House of Clay - The ruling house of Ithreac, led by the Cragg family.

The House of Embers - The ruling house of Pyrhhas, led by the de Laurent family.

The House of Gales - The ruling house of Vindyrst, led by the Zephirin family.

The House of Light & Shadow - The united ruling houses of Luxtos & Stygos, led by the Makar & Frey family.

The House of Torrents - The ruling house of Samhaven, led by the Ymir family.

The Nineteen - Also known as "The Convocation of Nineteen," or just "The Convocation," this is a collective of the last known Aetherborne to exist in the realm of Aemos. Together, they oversee the Arcane Studium and preside over the city-state of Sophrosyne.

The Source - Also known as the Divine Source of All Life, the Source is considered the center of the universe, the wellspring from which all life is born and where all living things return after death. Often deified as a divine feminine presence and master of the Fates.

Vindyrst - The mountainous, northeastern territory of Atlas, ruled by the House of Gales.

Wardpoint - Large chunks of astral quartz that have been reinforced with umbral ore, enchanted to preserve intense warding arcana to protect the city of Sophrosyne.

Wards - A form of protective arcana that can create barriers or preserve protections of some kind.

Yvestra - The capital city of Samhaven.

ACKNOWLEDGEMENTS

They say it takes a village to raise a child, and for the last several years, this series has been my baby — the story of my heart. Harbingers, Book One would still just be a silly little story concept, a mere thought floating around in the aether of my mind, were it not for my support system — my village.

I owe them all a thousand thanks.

To Matt — don't say I didn't warn you about your place here. Thank you, so godsdamn much, for believing in me and in this story long before I ever did. You understood the vision from day one, and helped me lay the groundwork for this universe with all the world-building questions, the song recommendations, and the unending hype for even my most half-baked, messy attempts at drafting. Thank you for always letting me flood your DMs with my hyper-fixated tangents, and for helping me keep this dream alive when it was just a flickering ember. I've said it before, and I'll say it again: without that early support, this book might have never seen the light of day.

To my earliest alpha readers — Eva, Sophie, Leanne, and the girlies of *Headcanon Hell*. Like Matt, y'all believed in me before I even knew what I was capable of. Thank you for reading the earliest iterations and snippets of this book and asking for more.

It's because of you guys that I came to believe I had a story worth telling. And thank you, Soph, for convincing me to make Kieran pull his hair back all sexy-like in the Wyldwoods. It was *very* important to the lore.

To all my beta readers — Nico, JD, Russell, Bree, Ros, Morgan, Cat, Mawce, Taylor, Hayden, Shane, Marley, Breanna, Tiff, Tina, Alx, Aimee, Rari, Sophie, Leanne. I was absolutely floored by the way you all showed up for this book. The amount of love, support, hype and thoughtful feedback y'all offered was absolutely invaluable. The dramatic memes, the threats of violence and bodily harm over the ending also sustained me for months on end, as I am an evil, evil author who loves her dramatic cliffhangers. It was the beta reading phase that finally convinced me that I could *actually* do this. That I could actually publish this thing one day.

To *The Congregation*, the first online writing space that I found that ever felt like home. All the sprint sessions, writing prompts, QOTDs, late nights in voice, unhinged memes, rants and spirals kept me going as this series transitioned from a possibility to a plan.

To Mawce, who drew the very first piece of Harbingers fan art, and then continued to annihilate me (affectionately) by bringing my babies to life again and again. I can never fully put into words how special your support in particular has been. The way you talk about Harbingers and how much it means to you is everything I've ever wanted as an author.

To Morgan, my mortal enemy, favorite gemini and chaos ravioli — who started off as a stranger in my DMs, offering to beta read, and then quickly became one of my best friends. Thank you for the unhinged, absolutely feral levels of support, and for the honor of allowing me to be a part of your creative processes, too. You're a godsdamn treasure and I am so glad to have you in my life. And thank you for letting me borrow Ezra. *Majestic mycelium.*

To my editor, Cat — you were the very first person that I ever let touch my work. Ever. As a beta reader, you understood this book, its themes, and my characters on such a visceral and intimate level that it made it so much easier to trust through a vulnerable process. Thank you for the amount of love, care and attention to detail that you put into helping me polish this manuscript. Thank you for the feedback write-ups, the video recordings, the death threats, and all the unhinged comments left all over the Google Doc (until we literally *broke* said Google Doc). And thank you for letting me keep most of my beloved em dashes.

To my tree twin, Roslyn. Gods, where do I even begin with you, bitch? The essays you wrote about my book and my characters that cut me to my core? The way you have firmly planted your flag as the number one Kieran stan and apologist in existence? The constant threats of violence and aggressive compliments to force me to acknowledge my own accomplishments every step of the way? The way your prose and masterful storytelling inspires me constantly? Your insights and ideas made Harbies so much better... and also so much worse. We came from the same tree and share one too many roots, but that just means that my growth is your growth, too. Thank you for being my ride or die.

To Nico, my beloved. As my very first critique partner, you were closer to this manuscript than any other. You read almost every single iteration of this book that developed since we met, and understand the universe and its characters almost as intimately as I do. In *seeing* my characters so clearly, you also saw me, at my core, and never once shied away from the good, the bad and the ugly it revealed. Thank you for being my sounding board, my gut-check, and an endless source of encouragement and inspiration. Thank you for arguing with my brain lizards at all hours and threatening my imposter syndrome in a myriad of clever (and increasingly violent) ways. Thank you for expanding my vocabulary and improving my prose just by allowing me to exist in your creative orbit. Thank you for the innumerable ways you helped make this manuscript the best that it could be, and in turn, all the ways you've made me a better writer, and a better version of myself.

To my grandfather, who, gods-willing, will never read this book. But it still needs to be said: Papa, I will never forget the day you pulled me aside and told me that I could really make something of my writing one day. That the talent I had was special. It took me years to finally follow my heart and embrace that, but you saw me. You knew.

And last but never the least, to my husband and the love of my life, Jason. Thank you for keeping me fed and hydrated through hours, days, and weeks of hyper-fixated fervor. Thank you for loving me through the madness, for never taking the late nights and long hours spent at my keyboard personally, and for dragging me out of my office to touch grass on occasion. Thank you for reading for me, and contributing to my delusions of grandeur by regularly reminding me that my prose could contend with some of my favorite authors. Thank you for the endless inspiration, and for reigniting my love of telling stories from the very beginning of ours. Our love story lit up a spark in me, one that stoked a flame and later became a wildfire, and I am so deeply appreciative of how you've stood steadfast beside me through some of the hardest, most transformative moments of my life. It's because of you that I actually believe in soulmates. And of course, thank you for never,

ever letting me give up on this dream. Thank you for knowing that I needed this. I love you endlessly, from here to Mars.

About the Author

Harper Hawthorne is an adult fantasy, romance & speculative fiction author in love with telling dark, emotionally evocative, and character-driven tales. Her stories feature neurodivergent experiences, honest explorations of mental health, and queer-normative worlds in her favored realms of fantasy.

Though she was born and raised on the beaches of Los Angeles, CA, she currently resides in the forests of the East Coast with her husband, her collie, and a demonic entity disguised in the form of a very large tuxedo cat.

When not lost in the throes of drafting one to three novels simultaneously, she can be found wandering the woods, hunting for mushrooms, befriending local frogs, practicing witchcraft and screaming into the void.

HARPER HAWTHORNE

Printed in Great Britain
by Amazon